8-27-2011

TO Mark & Linda,

Best of everything!

Jack & Scott

Madstone McPhail

Story of the Civil War as seen through the eyes of a Confederate Medic

By
Jack E. Scott

As crazy as it sounds this is based on a true story!

Printed in Hong Kong by

Regal Printing Limited

ISBN: 1-4243-1469-0

"This book is dedicated to Loys, my wife, who has put up with this crazy Scotsman for 49 years."
-Author

A word from the author

The story of Madstone McPhail brings very special memories for me when I was a young man. The first place I stepped off the train when returning from combat as a sailor during the Korean War was Crockett, Texas. Crockett was the home of my ancestor, John McPhail, who's story this book is about.

When the Korean War ended so had my tour of duty. I was given my honorable discharge at the Brooklyn Naval yards and wasted no time in catching the train in New York City to head for my hometown of Houston.

About halfway I decided to stop off in Crockett to see my grandparents and my aunts and uncles before returning home. For some reason that small train station that had been there for so long, seemed to hold a magic feeling for me. Somehow it held a feeling that there was a story, a very special story, about my ancestors.

I did not know then that it would be a story about the civil war and a Scotsman by the name of John McPhail and his wife Elizabeth along with the unusual stone called a Madstone.

Understand that Crockett, Texas is a small farming town about 114 miles north of Houston but it is a special place. First of all Davy Crockett stopped off in his travels and drank water at a spring close to the train station giving the settlement its name and second a very special gentleman by the name of George Lawson Keene (Sept. 21,1898—Oct. 20, 1956) was born there.

Of course you recognize Davy Crocket's name, but probably do not know who George Keene was. He was a man who had his medals placed in the hall of fame. He was a man who was modest about his accomplishments. He was a man that was still alive when I stepped off that train in December, 1953. He was of southern heritage who loved stories of history and heroes, especially as told by his grandfather, an ex-member of the Confederate Army. He was a man whose mother was great-niece of General Stonewall Jackson.

Sadly she died when he was only three years old, but most of all he was said to be the most decorated American soldier in World War One. He won the Medal of Honor, the Distinguished Service Cross, Silver Star with oak leaf cluster, purple heart and many other American awards. On top of this, he won the cross of honor and the French Croix De Guerre with palm, Knights of Verdun, Tadac St Mihiel and the French Commemorative Medal. He became a member of the legion of

Valor, a service organization founded by Civil War veterans in 1890. Membership requirements are: the possession of either the Medal of Honor or the Distinguished Service Cross. Colonel George Keene's picture and newpaper stories and even one of his uniforms are on display at the old train station turned museum in Crockett. I acquired an old picture of the train station and someone many years ago had written the words... (The Wonderful Station!) at the bottom of the snapshot.

Evidently the old station held very fine memories for others as it did for me. The station is now a small museum and holds some loving memories for a lot of people.

When you read the story of John and Elizabeth McPhail it will give you some idea of the type of men and women that have come from Houston, (Crockett) County, Texas. The stories surrounding the history of the East Texas area are rich with brave men and women that settled here from all over the world.

If you ever travel to the Crockett area you'll understand why the Houston County area is called the heart of the piney woods...

Crockett Train Station about 1940.

Preface

Although a great deal of this story comes solely from my imagination, the Madstone is based on fact. Some of the information written here was compiled by Charles Wesley McPhail and countless others over years of research. It is contained in the family book "John and Elizabeth McPhail and their descendents." Published for these proud Highlanders from Scotland. An articled printed in the Houston Chronicle on April 6, 1959 by David Wills on the "McPhail Madstone stated: Old writings indicate that the McPhail madstone is one of a long line of "Mad or Magic stones." Pliny the Elder (23-79) wrote about a Sicilian agate that "Availeth much against the venomous spider and scorpions."

From accounts of older members of the family the McPhail madstone was applied to and saved the lives of a number of people; how many we do not know, but it could have been several hundred over a fifty year period. The McPhail Madstone has no monetary value now, yet it is a McPhail treasure that has been in the family for almost one hundred and fifty years. Upon Jesse McPhails' death on January 18, 1922, the Madstone was placed in a safe deposit box in the bank at Trinity, Texas by his brother Lee, as there was no longer any need for its' use.

Just before Lees' death in 1959 he placed the Madstone with Mrs. Wessie Bowers and it is unclear which of the descendants had tucked it away in some trunk for years until it was placed in the Sam Houston Museum around 1972.

This priceless stone was used to combat rabies and poisons from snakes, scorpions and infections as late as the 1930's. It was a proven means of determining if the bite was poisonous. If the stone stuck to the wound, poison was in the blood stream and it would help remove the foreign body.

Madstones were looked upon as a rare gem and demanded a high price, which was often paid. After researching the Madstones, I wonder if modern medicine shouldn't pay a little more heed to mother nature and her way of countering infectious diseases. During the Civil War, when treatment was almost nonexistent for lack of disinfectants, it was discovered that maggots ate the diseased flesh while leaving the healthy alone. This knowledge had been known for centuries, but was again forgotten after the Civil War only to be relearned during World War One.

The Houston Post article of December 15, 1988, tells of an outbreak of rabies in the valley of the lower Rio Grande in which forth-five people had been treated for the potentially fatal virus, started by wild coyotes. Even to this day the threat is real if humans exposed to the disease are not given a series of injections over a period of a month. For the people of the eighteenth and nineteenth centuries it was a slow and painful death sentence. Only one treatment was known to remove the poison; not only for rabies, but snake bites and other poisonous animals. The Madstone was to become more valuable than gold itself for those in need. The stone was matter of life and death for hundreds of people contacting the poison. There are cases on file of people killing for the Madstone because of the torment from a venomous bite.

Although I'm unable to thank everyone who has been of help to me in the research of this book, I do wish to acknowledge the help of Katy Wilma (McPhail) Sebastian for her help in finding the Madstone in time for the picture to be shown in the contents. Also thanks to Mr. Mac Woodward curator of collections at the Sam Houston Museum, Huntsville, Texas for permitting us to examine and photograph the Madstone where it is on display for the public.

In my quest for information of the great battles of the Civil War, the folks of the National Park Service were very helpful when I toured the battle site of Manassas, where the stone bridge was still intact and the muddy creek pretty much the same as it was over a hundred and fifty years ago. I walked the hills where the battle was fought and was overcome with a feeling of awe knowing that so many men had died here on American soil. The heavily wooded area opens into the fields where Stonewall Jacksons' statue overlooks the rows of cannons that had been returned to their original positions by the Park Service.

The grave sites about a mile away had little or no names on the headstones, simply the state they were from; mostly known by the clothing and banners they wore when they were buried. The old stone house still stands that was used as a field hospital and the unfinished railroad the scene of heavy fighting during the battle of second Manassas (Bull Run) which was more violent than the first. During my walking tour, the bitter cold wind was almost unbearable in the opening days of December. How in the world these fighting men survived the harsh weather and wild terrain with little food and scant clothing was wonder to me. As I crossed Bull Creek I couldn't possibly imagine that they really drank the water or made coffee out of it. The pain that was suffered here must have taken generations to undo. Located only twenty-six miles southwest of Washington, it became the final resting place for thousands of soldiers from the North and South. No one should forget the bitterness and total waste of life that was the Civil War, for it cost more American lives than any other war before or since.

Hopefully this story about a Scotsman that most likely became one of the first full time medics in U.S. history will tell the tale of one warrior of the Civil War. Of course, there were many, many more…

Synopsis of Madstone McPhail

"Story of Civil War as seen through eyes of a Confederate Medic"

By Jack E. Scott   March, 2005

In this fictional history where fact and fancy meet (as in E.L. Doctorow's best-seller, Ragtime) my great, great, grandfather, John McPhail found a magic stone in the stomach of a white deer in 1844. He carried the Madstone in a leather pouch around his neck for fifty years and saved almost 200 lives with it. One of the lives he saved was Abraham Lincoln's son, Thomas "Tad" Lincoln **while** he was fighting for the south **during** the Civil War.

McPhail carried the stone with him when he marched off to fight the intrusive union soldiers that he believed was invading his southern homeland. Along with Benjamin Davis Brown, another volunteer for the southern cause, **the two Texans rode north to Virginia to battle the Yankees not realizing that they would go down in history not as warriors, but as compassionate medics treating the wounded and sick soldiers. Through a quirk of fate their destiny was suddenly changed during their very first fight with the Union Army.**

At the heat of the battle of Bull Run McPhail and Brown would be captured when they run through some bushes trying to flank the Yankees. The two Texas farmers quietly make their way through the heavy underbrush until they thought they were in place to attack but are shocked to find that they have not come out on the side of the Yankees but instead are now standing in an open field facing the whole Union Army. Of course they are captured with ease.

After being forced to march to a prisoner of war camp outside Washington, they would soon find that their lives were destined to cross paths with none other then the president of the United States.

About the same time the two Texans were taken to the P.O.W. camp, Abraham Lincoln's son was bitten by a dog suspected of having rabies. General McDowell of the Union Army was standing nearby with the president when the boy was attacked. The General promptly pulled his revolver and shot the animal while the horrified Lincoln looked on. He then told the president about a rebel in the prisoner of war camp that had a Madstone; the only known treatment for a rabies bite.

The chief executive ordered that the prisoner be brought to the Provost Marshall's office immediately where he would have his son waiting to be treated. In this way the president would keep Mary Lincoln from knowing that her son was being treated by an **enemy soldier** with a **magic stone** that smacked of being somewhat close to **vodoo**.

McPhail and Brown were totally shocked at seeing Lincoln's son lying on a table with the president standing nearby when they entered the Provost Marshall's office. Still, John wasted no time in treating the president's boy when he realized why he had been brought there. The stone was soaked in hot milk and placed on the bite and soon the agate had turned green indicating it had done it's job. After placing it back in the hot milk the Madstone returned to it's natural color which meant it was ready to be used again.

McPhail stepped back and made a gesture showing that he had finished treating the boy. Lincoln made it be known that he wanted to show his gratitude but admitted to John that he could not give two rebels a medal.

How on earth would it look to the northern fighting men if it got out that their president was running around decorating rebels? However, the president stated that he did have the power to release them and he would do so...**provided they gave their word never to fight against the Union again from that day forward.**

John quickly accepted the terms but Brown refused to give his word not to fight. When the president realized McPhail would not go without his buddy, he released both the southern soldiers without hesitation. The powerful leader ordered the Captain of the Guard to escort them to the southern lines and return their weapons.

Not happy with the idea of returning their rifles, the union officer still obeyed his order but not before he poured the power and shots on the ground so the rifles could not be readily used.

As the union soldiers rode behind McPhail and Brown towards the southern lines the small group came upon a large number of Yankee wagons overflowing with foodstuffs, blankets and other supplies heading north from the battles. McPhail's brain came alive with thoughts of retrieving the full wagons so that he might hand them over to the southern army. Shortly after, they watched intently as a second row of wagons passed by carrying many dead union soldiers being brought back for burial.

The sight of so many wagons caused McPhail and Brown to devise a plan to steal supplies even before they had reached the southern lines. After being released by their Union escorts they secretly crossed back over into union territory and followed the wagons until it was dark. When the opportunity presented itself they quietly stole uniforms off several corpses so that they might pass themselves off as being sent by a Union

General to bring several wagon loads of supplies to the field hospital area.

In reality, the pair rode all night to reach the Army of Northern Virginia so that the supplies could be turned over to the south. John laughed when he made the statement to Brown. "I told Lincoln I wouldn't fight...but nothing was said about stealing.

The pair knew that they couldn't continue stealing because eventually they would get into a fire fight and John did not want to break his word to the President. They then decided that they could go from battle to battle to help the sick and wounded. **Thus that was the moment the pair of southern boys probably became the first full time medics in United States history.**

As they rode the stolen wagons south, McPhail suddenly had yet another brilliant idea. He had remembered something an Englishman had told him about finding a different kind of Madstone.

"These Madstones were only found in the heads of certain frogs. Lots of frogs have them," the man from Britain had said. "It had something to do with their chemistry...or some such thing."

McPhail and Brown wasted no time in heading for a large pond full of frogs that they had passed earlier. Here they would investigate frog heads in search of Madstones. Their thinking was simple. The more of the healing stones they had, the more sick and wounded they could treat.

A hundred dead frogs later the pair sat beside a tree stump reeking to **HIGH HEAVEN OF THE AWFUL SMELL OF THE AMPHIBIANS**. What the Englishman had forgot to tell him was that the stones where only found in certain frogs in England, not the U.S.

The pair had just given up their quest for more stones when a large group of Confederate soldiers marched by. Knowing that the rebels were probably on their way to join up with Stonewall Jackson's regiment, the two frog hunters mounted their wagons and joined onto the tail end of the marching army.

When they arrive at the encampment of Jackson's rebel army, **THEY ARE NOTICED BECAUSE OF THEIR SMELL! None of the troops could possibly miss the two southern medics because their bodies reeked of the awful smell of frog.**

Stonewall Jackson himself walks out of his tent to see what all the commotion was about and gets more than his share of the smell of the two frog killers setting on the wagons.

Stonewall Jackson

My God men what is that smell?

McPhail

Frogs sir…

Jackson

What's that?

McPhail

Frogs sir, we've been cutting the heads open to find some Madstones but we…we…

(McPhail sees that the general doesn't understand what they had been doing and is looking at him like he is a crazy man. He tries to clear his throat without much success.)

McPhail

Well…anyway we do have a lot of supplies for you, sir. We kind of took a couple of wagon loads from the Yankees…

Jackson

(Looking at all the supplies pilled high in the wagons.)

We really appreciate the supplies soldier but I'll pass on learning about your encounter with some frogs.   Put the wagons over there by the mess tent and get something to eat.

(He turns to the captain next to him trying to disguise the fact that he is holding his nose with his gloved hand.)

Jackson

Give them a medal for getting the much needed supplies and a hot meal and wash them in the river…

My God, I've never smelled anything so bad!…**Then take them out and SHOOT them for the smell!**

Captain

General, surely you don't really mean…

Jackson

of course not, just put them to bed

Brown and McPhail eat and take a bath in the river close by. They quietly ride out of camp to keep from being forced into fighting again. They have no problem passing the same guard because he assumes they are going after more food and supplies. Now they are free to begin looking for more battles in progress to start their new medical duties.

It was not long before they find their first conflict to begin their new calling of treating the wounded.

Little did McPhail know that the battle of Balls Bluff near the Potomac would be the place where he would first meet a Spunky nurse by the name of Elizabeth Malloy and fall madly in love. Elizabeth turned out to be the daughter of Doctor Malloy; the surgeon treating the fallen southern soldiers at the battle site.

Unknown to Brown and McPhail, they were soon to find that their horses would have to be replaced. Without realizing it, they had tied the animals to bushes that were right between the two opposing armies and a second fire fight was about to begin. **Both men watched in horror as the beautiful mounts that was given to them by Lincoln were totally shot to pieces.**

After the second battle, the two medics decided to leave the field hospital in an effort to replace their dead animals. They headed off on foot into the direction of the hills where many horses had been seen running to. Because of the terrific fighting, the animals were still wearing saddles but had no riders. The two southern medics convinced themselves that they would surely be able to capture a couple of fine mounts within hours and return to their duties. Turned out, the animals were so spooked it was several days before the men were able to find and catch replacement horses and head back to the hospital area.

When they reached the top of the hill overlooking the hospital campsite, they were shocked to found that the wounded, along with the doctors and nurses, had begun traveling south because of imminent fear of new battles.

The Scotsman had fallen hard for the beautiful nurse and he wasted little time before following the wagon tracks south. He had no intention of letting such a lovely creature get away. All else in his life was now put on hold until he could find the beautiful nurse. All he knew was that her name was Elizabeth. He didn't even know what state she was from.

He would catch up with Elizabeth 375 miles later in Lumberbridge Township, North Carolina and marry her in a snowstorm with her father looking on with approval. However a short time later, a stupid accident would almost kill McPhail while he and his new bride were trying to treat the incoming wounded.

Ben Brown joined his lovesick friend making the decision to eventually head west away from the fighting as soon as the opportunity presented itself. However he couldn't help himself, he felt compelled to return to the battles and shortly thereafter found himself deeply involved in the battle of Antietam where he would have his left arm removed after being badly shot.

Elizabeth would join the old witch, Fannie Mae in saving John McPhail's life with outrageous medicines that she had concocted but the old woman of mercy would lose her life in an accidental shooting a short time later.

John would stay at Doctor Malloys farm while recovering from his injury sustained at the armory turned hospital.

After his healing period, he and Elizabeth traveled through the snow towards town in an attempt to secure more food but met up with a giant of a man named McGee on a one way bridge. The huge Scotsman was a mountain man that was very rough around the edges but would turn out to be one of their finest life long friends.

Shortly after, McPhail received the news that Lincoln had been assassinated and Lee had surrendered, causing him to make the decision to move back to Texas with the giant joining the family. The huge man had killed Yankee soldiers with his bare hands for stealing a farmers' land under the disguise of legal taxes and he thought it best to leave the area as quickly as possible.

McPhail would return to his home in Crockett, Texas and continue using the Madstone to treat sick and injured people of his county for the rest of his life, but had difficulties settling into a farmers routine after all that had happened to him. He would start a new business, only to have it fail because of progress and the times. He saw their lives changing with the growth of his son and would live to see southerners marching off to World War One.

Elizabeth would live to wave goodbye to young men leaving to fight Hitler during World War Two and leave behind a history of bravery for the coming generations of women. She often talked about the crazy Scotsman she married in a snowstorm and the four leaf clover given to McPhail by a Yankee Captain who befriended her husband after the battle of Bull Run.

McGee would become a Texas Ranger, only to find that he missed Tiny and the children too much to travel such a large state after murderers. The giant of a man would however go down in history as killing the Baker Brothers, some of the worst murderers and thieves in history.

John McPhail Jr. would grow up to marry a red head that fell from the roof of her house into the snow at his feet and continue the McPhail blood line to this day.

Benjamin Davis Brown would survive to marry Mary Margaret McPhail, a distant relative of John McPhail. The two settled in Mississippi and not Texas. His grandson became a doctor and his great grandson was killed on a battlefield in Korea while serving as an Army Medic.

Thomas (Tad) Lincoln was born on April 4, 1853 with an unusually large head which Lincoln thought made the tiny baby boy look like a tadpole. The soon to be president gave his son the nickname of "Tad" which stuck with him for the rest of his life. In 1861 the eight year old boy moved into the White House with his family and quickly began playing pranks on the servants and anyone else that would be in the Mansion at the time. When the Civil War broke out he was permitted to be outfitted with a Union uniform of an army officer. He played the role well marching around the mansion having a good time upsetting the presidents servants and staff.

Mary Lincoln took the boy to Europe for two years after the death of his father and upon their return the boy fell ill and died on July 15, 1871. He was buried with the remains of President Lincoln and his two brothers Eddie and Willie. The photo of the boy in uniform is from Chicago Historical Society. Photo of child and young man is from Lloyd Ostendorf Collection.

The Madstone would be handed down from generation to generation finally ending up in the Sam Houston Museum in Huntsville, Texas where it remains today and the McPhail coat of arms is still passed on to the descendants.

Jack E. Scott

"Memor Esto"

McPhail

"McPhail Coat of Arms"

Chapter 1

"Leave me alone" was the motto of the Highlanders of Scotland, against the powerful English nation. Yet the scotch people struggled with England for hundreds of years, never to break free. To rid themselves of many of these arduous Scots, the English forced them to take passage to the colonies of America.

Most did not want to leave their beautiful homeland, but death was the only other choice, for the whole of their land was but a northern extension of the powerful English Empire. Forced to pay heavy taxes to the king and treated as though they didn't exist, the Scots lived in fear for centuries.

It was a dreadful time to live in the beautiful rolling hills and mountains of the highlands; for no Scotsman was safe from the ever-present danger of the English army crossing into the Scottish countryside. They came and went as conquerors, forcing their will onto the men, women and children of the northern province of the highlands.

Because it was a long and tedious journey through the Grampian Mountains, the English army traveled to Fort Augustus only under special orders and then rarely went into the highlands without a major force behind them. Sometimes years would pass before the English again flexed their muscles of their immense army. Such was the case in the mid 1700's when there came an onslaught of the brutal English force passing through Fort Augustus and around the Loch Ness climbing ever higher into the mountains of the highlands.

It was the year 1764 and Augus McPhail was using his craftsmanship as a brick mason to help build an addition to the Macintosh's farmhouse. In exchange for his labor, he would be given three head of cattle to better his own small herd. This would enable him to have additional food on the table for the long cold winter and still raise the same amount of beef come spring.

A brisk wind blew against Augus as he moved slowly across the top of the house carrying bricks that were used to repair his neighbors roof. These bricks were made from mud and lighter then the type used for walls and brick fences. They were curved and worked well for the hard winters of Scotland.

The bitter cold wind had a bite to it and it was certainly blowing harder than usual against his body each time he crossed the roof to add another layer to the new edge that would control the coming heavy rains.

McPhail was making sure he kept his coat rapped tightly around his body to keep out the cold. He had his collar pulled up high on either side of his neck causing him to totally miss seeing the English army appear on a hill overlooking the Macintosh Farm.

From that distance, the mounted army looked like a group of small ants moving towards them, but they were anything but small harmless insects.

Had these highlanders been able to see the awesome looking leader setting upright on his fine mount, fear would have certainly raced through the village.

The leader was the Duke of Cumberland; affectionately known as the Butcher of Cumberland. He was the one Englishman that would use the soldiers of the king to lay waste to the countryside for the sheer pleasure…of killing.

Now Cumberland's vast army began driving and slaughtering the cattle, but that was just the start of the madman's pleasures. He would soon begin burning the Scotsmen's homes and killing any clansmen in sight and of course capture any maiden to warm his cold bed at night.

Winifred Macintosh was no match for the horseback riders and their fine weapons and armor. He was cut down first, as were all seven of the Macintoshes this day. It made no difference that there were women and children. There was no discrimination as to who was killed next, only who was close at hand.

Chilling screams caught Augus McPhail totally by surprise as he worked on the roof of the Macintosh home. Silently he made his way to the very top of the straw covered roof where he could peer over the side in the direction that the screams were coming from. What he saw made his blood run cold with fear as it raced down his spine. Even the freezing wind of the Scottish Isles couldn't possibly hurt him as bad as the sight he was watching.

Tears ran down his cheeks as he watched the brutal English soldiers hack their way through the farmers and their families like a man harvesting wheat. Everyone fell before the onslaught of the horseback riders. No one was being left alive, not even the animals.

McPhail slid his body a little further down the roof trying to keep from being seen by the evil men. He heard one of the horses moving closer to the side of the house and he peered over the edge just in time to see an officer turn his horse towards the back side of the building. Now his hate over took his reason and it reached a point of no return. He simply was unable to hold it back any longer. The soldier was about to give him the opportunity that would not come again.

Quietly the Scotsman rolled his body over and slid down the side of the house that the man was approaching. He grabbed a stone from the mason pile that was stacked near the edge of the roof and wrapped it in a red cloth from around his neck. He began swinging it over his head around and around preparing to let the killer know of his presents. The fast riding

3

English warrior was about to learn that someone was near; just as soon as his horse cleared the corner of the building.

Unfortunately for the Englishman it would be the last thing in this world that he would ever learn. Augus delivered only one crushing blow to the man's head, but it was more than enough. The soldier's head armor flew off, and with it, almost the man's entire head. McPhail jumped from the roof and quickly drug the body out of sight before the others could follow suit. Wasting no time, he mounted the officer's horse and rode into the tall grass to avoid being discovered; then urged the horse into a full all out run using the grass as cover.

Now he was heading for his own small farm, which was in the same direction that these killers were heading. His farm was the next property in the path of the oncoming English soldiers and he was only moments ahead of them. Marionette and the two boys would have to be hidden until the danger passed. It could possibly be months before the army of North Hampton would tire of Scotland and retreat as they had done before. In his youth, he had seen such carnage when the English came through and knew of the outcome if they stayed. Wasting no time the family took what food and supplies could be carried and fled to the hills. Women were trying to hide their children in thick underbrush while their men carried swords and joined together preparing to fight a useless battle. The huge English Army was just too powerful for the small bands to resist, but never the less, they had every intention of slowing the evil soldiers down so that others would get away.

Augus led his family through the forest, climbing ever higher into the mountains leaving the smoke columns behind. Time and again he looked back at the burning houses down below. Smoke was curling high into the sky and his heart sank when he suddenly realized his home too was going up in flames. To make matters worse, rain began falling making the ground slick and muddy but even this would be of little help. It was a soft drizzle that in no way would be enough to put out the burning farms stretching across one hill and then another.

McPhail stood looking down at the valley full of farmhouses that were now burning totally out of control. He turned his face toward the sky to let the water run down his forehead. Perhaps he was trying not to let the awful sight tear him apart or his anger get the better of him. Still he couldn't help but have his stomach tied in knocks with extreme pains grabbing his gut deep inside. He would be the only one to hear his scream, yet he still had to do something.

"Someday I'll kill Cumberland for this." He yelled out loud with his head tilted full face towards the rain that was now falling to earth in larger amounts. Of course he knew in his heart it would never be, for the English were much too strong a nation.

For several weeks the Scotsman hid his family well in the small cave he had played in as a child. This was the place that he often hid trying to avoid punishment from his father; mostly for acts of disobedience.

He had never once been discovered in his secret hiding place and felt comfortable making a camp in this hidden cave. Now it had become their make do home; at least until the English decided to withdraw.

Carefully he checked the hollow in the mountain making sure wild animals hadn't decided to also make it their home. He then proceeded to try and change the cave into a comfortable make shift home for Marionette and the boys. Marionette entered the cave and what she saw made her heart sink to rock bottom. It was a damp, cold hole with several large stones placed around an open fire pit.

Of course she was down hearted at what she saw but she had no intention of making her husband feel her pain.

Immediately she went about trying to help make this hole their home and at the same time reassure him that all was well.

"Oh Augus." She said. "It's not going to be so bad. We have to do what we have to do."

Even the weather seemed to work against them as it turned more brutal with the passage of time. Augus had become well familiar with the brutal points of living outdoors and had learned how to survive in the cave. During his childhood days he would play in the damp enclosure and teach himself the art of survival in such surroundings. He knew to gather moss for bedding, twigs for firewood and branches for covering the small entrance to make it undetectable.

He had become a master of disguise in the mountainous woods and these talents would certainly come in handy now. He would see to it that his family live off those that were taking everything away from the ones he loved. Every time the opportunity presented itself, he stole from the English, bringing food and blankets to his new home carved out of the mountain. Time and again, the highlander took advantage of foul weather and darkness to relieve the English soldiers of anything that would be of use in his family's surviving.

Week after week passed as Augus marked time waiting for news of the English withdrawal from their tiny kingdom but no such message came. The only word he received over and over was pretty much bad.

Day after day captured Highlanders were being put to death; women and children were without food and homes, and many others were left to wander the hills and die. He could do little but take care of his own loved ones and pray that the English would leave and never return.

One afternoon, a friend and neighbor approached the cave and brought word to McPhail that Cumberland had ordered his army to kill villagers every time supplies were stolen from his troops.

Complaints about the thefts from his officers and foot soldiers had reached Cumberland and he was now taking action. Indirectly McPhail had caused some of his friends to be killed and he certainly hadn't meant to do so.

The English General was now in complete control of the Scottish countryside, but was beginning to tire of living with the rebellious Highlanders. He ordered a sign posted in town and the word was sent far and wide that the king would grant a pardon to all highland rebels, providing they took an oath of allegiance and immigrated to America by the coming spring. Further, a blood oath was to be taken that they would bear no arms and that the clansmen would sail to the new Americas far from the graves of their forefathers.

The oath continued: "That I would be cursed in my undertakings, family and property; may I be killed in battle as a coward and die without Christian burial in a strange land never to see my wife, children, father, mother, or relations. May all this come upon me if I break my oath."

Although this was a terrible oath to take, many clansmen swore to it and prepared for the trip to America as a haven of refuge. The valuables that were hidden from the English soldiers were shared among the Scotsmen who were to make the long voyage.

McPhail heard of the blood oath, and made the decision that he would secretly take Marionetta and the two boys on the next boat, providing he could find a way of getting aboard undetected.

There was no way he would allow his family to come out into the open and trust the English. He packed everything that he could snuff into a small cart and with Marionetta and the boys began the long march to the coast. The boys helped their father pull the cart like mules while his wife walked slowly behind. They traveled mostly under cover of darkness, shunning anyone they met on the road to avoid detection.

It was not the common English soldier that was in distrust, it was their leader, the butcher of Cumberland. For he gave the evil orders that brought misery and death to so many.

McPhail knew that Cumberland was not to be trusted; he had seen first hand the bloody outcome occurring to people that had believed the Englishman's word; not once but many times. He had heard that ships sailed for the new world from a port near a town called Whitehaven and that was where his family had decided to go. There he felt he was sure to meet up with some of his friends that were probably doing the same thing he was.

Surely others were attempting to reach one of the ports to try and get passage to a new life somewhere in the world, even if it were not the new world.

When he reached the docks, he would be able to sell some of his silver given to him years earlier by his father. The fine family silver would make it possible for him to obtain passage to the New World and still have some valuables left over to start a new life.

The Scottish farmer pulled hard on the cart to move it over the rocks and each time he looked back his wife would smile a hurt smile trying to let him know all was well. The more he watched the struggle his family was up against, the more his heart sank lower as each day passed. Yet, he pulled the little cart over the rocky terrain from one hill side to another even though his hands were full of cuts and bruises and the physical pain was almost unbearable.

The flesh on his hands and legs began to look like raw meat because of the many falls he had endured from stepping on wet slick rocks. Every muscle in his body ached from sharp pains inflicted from the rough, hilly terrain; still he did not complain. His back felt like it was nearly at the breaking point, but somehow it made him stronger and more determined than ever to take his family to a new life in America.

Sleeping mostly in tall grass off the main road, they huddled together for warmth, building only a very small fire with stones around it so that it might not be seen. This way they hoped that they would not to be discovered by any English soldiers that might be passing by.

Marionetta's frustration at losing her home only came through at night when she softly sobbed herself to sleep trying not to let McPhail and the children hear her agony.

McPhail could only guess what the New World would be like. He had no idea what part of the new colonies he and Marionetta would land in. His best guess was that it would be decided by which ship he could get them safely aboard. His impatience grew daily as they traveled towards the port area and it took everything he had in him to keep his composer.

The fact that they could never look back was now hitting home in his mind. Each time he looked at Marionetta, he knew she was about the bravest thing he had ever seen; for she was giving up everything and still held strong for him.

When they reached the docks, the whole area was almost entirely invisible because of a heavy fog. It was a blessing for the Scotsman and his family when they entered the small port town undetected. Here, Augus thought he would be able to stay with old friends until the departure of the next vessel, but he would soon find that the family he had intended to stay with had been carried off by the English and most likely killed.

McPhail began nosing around the pubs looking for information about the departure of the ships that were still tied up at docks. It took very little effort to learn that the next boat would be leaving in about a month and that for a few pounds an old storage barn could be had to use for sleeping quarters. All through it was somewhat dangerous he thought it better he take the barn rather than place any other friends in danger.

The family quietly set up camp inside the building and with its straw covered floor, it was actually quite nice. As a matter of fact, compared to the wet ground in the hills, it was downright wonderful. Now they waited for word of the next ship that would be leaving and time seemed to pass slowly in the old storage barn.

The McPhail family stayed put, unable to venture outside for fear of being discovered. Then on a cold and windy day, word reached the McPhail family that several ships were leaving with the outgoing tide. Augus wasted no time in silently slipping through the door into the street to try and work his magic to get them aboard the outgoing vessel. He hid in the shadows of the waterfront walkway for more than an hour until finally an English naval officer filled to the top with fine wine came his way.

The Scotsman carefully fell in behind the sea going officer and followed him into a pub. He watched the sailor slide his body onto a stool at the bar, then he took the seat right next to him. Within moments he was making friends with the English sailor. It wasn't hard when he was the one buying the beer.

McPhail's silver would now be used to bribe the officer into the simple act of including his family's name on the list of travelers. The Scotsman assured him that his fine ship, the Bonne May, could certainly handle four more. On top of this the captain would be none the wiser, but they would have to work quickly.

Little else was necessary to be said when the silver was shown. The shiny coins changed hands with no one in the bar being the wiser. The officer was more than willing to return to the barn with McPhail to pick up his family and gear.

Under the cover of darkness the small group made their way to the officer's ship conveniently tied up at a location that was ideal for stowaways. Hidden behind large bails of corn, the gang plank was hard to watch by the officers on duty.

The small group stood for a long moment looking up at the wooden freighter that looked awesome in the worse way. The whole family couldn't believe what this so called sea going vessel looked like. They were almost ready to stay ashore and take their chances of being caught by the English soldiers. Hell, it would probably be a blessing if they were caught rather than boarding this God awful raggedy looking freighter.

This thing had seen all of it's glorious days many years before and the wooden hunk of junk should have gone to Davy Jones locker a very long time ago. Even so, to McPhail it looked like the Queen Mary and the final bargain between the naval officer and the farmer was struck. Soon they would be aboard and leave the danger behind...or so they thought as they quietly slipped up the gangplank before daybreak with the bribed officer pushing from behind.

"Move faster, move faster," The English officer kept whispering over and over to the small group. "The captain might catch us. Hurry I tell you! Hurry!"

Chapter 2

By now it was Spring of 1765, and the ships Bonne May and Excursion set sail from the mouth of the river Dee. These old freighters certainly weren't large enough or built big enough for a large amount of passengers, but their captains were being paid handsomely for each person aboard. So these little ships were loaded down with two hundred and fifty passengers each making the trip very dangerous.

Even though Augus had bribed the officer to get their names on the passenger list, he was still charged three guineas extra for each member of the family for the trip to America. It was outrageous at the time but the officer liked it. He simply said that he had to account for the number of bodies aboard and turn in the payments for each to the captain. If the payments didn't meet up with the number of bodies it would be hell to pay for the crew.

At lease the McPhail family was now on their way to a new life in the colonies and would be far away from the British Isles. Perhaps the new life they were about to start would be fantastic and exciting and their old could at lease be lost to memories.

Now that they were on board, there was no doubt that both ships were old and rotten to a point that it was very doubtful that the freighters could make the long trip across the Atlantic, but no other option was available. For the McPhail family it had to be here and now. Word was spreading around the ship that a stopover in Dublin for repairs was needed and here they would remain for about three days. On top of that, any Scotsmen that looked fit enough would be required to help rebuild parts of the ship and load provisions. Rebuilding parts of the ship meant patching leaky holes as best they could to try and keep the ship afloat.

The captain was a hefty man who loved to eat and he was determined to make sure there was enough foodstuffs for the two-month passage to New York. Mostly for himself and his officers. So his time was spent buying quantities of food stuff which was stored in a private section of the ship and placed under lock and key.

More often than not, the free labor that was at hand in the form of the "guests on board" was put to laboring in the loading and repairing duties. The job of watching their every move fell to the crew of the freighter as per the executive officer's instructions.

The sailors on board were told to constantly look over the workers shoulders; probably in hopes of dropping some of the guests off the list and putting them ashore. If any of the "guest" became ill or too old to continue the upcoming long voyage it was the only excuse they needed to get rid of some of the excess baggage. The Executive officer knew that his captain preferred this; hoping to lose many of his "guests" before the lengthy voyage had truly begun.

This captain was a fierce looking Englishman with a reputation of demanding absolute obedience from his crew and passengers. Every crew member was well aware of his brutality in the use of the lashing whips if his orders were questioned or not carried out promptly enough to suit him.

Captain Henry Biles had been a high-ranking naval officer with the British Navy and had fallen into disfavor with the king. Thrown out of the service in disgrace, his only recourse was the Bonne May, a lowly freighter traveling the world with cargo to sell for it's owners and anything else that might make money. Its owners weren't particularly picky about how they made their money or even who might die in the process; only the end results mattered.

As the final day of loading was complete, the sails were hoisted and they slowly began their voyage. Torrential rain had suddenly moved into the area bringing with it lightning and thunder that was a certain threat to the little boat, but Captain Biles was determined to leave his troubles behind.

Nothing was going to stop him from going to sea, for it gave him fantasies of being an admiral once again. He had no intention of letting anything stop him from having his dreams of glory, fame and riches.

The fat leader of the ship pranced himself out onto the quarter deck that over looked the whole of the ship. He was going to make sure that everyone saw how impressive he looked. Unfortunately impressive was not the correct word for this captain. He was laughingly dressed in a full English Admiral's uniform to play out his fantasy as he had done so many times before.

His second in command walked closely behind holding an umbrella above his head and the sight was absolutely comical. The ten-year-old uniform hardly fit an old fat sailor that was trying to wear it like a badge of honor.

Nevertheless the captain stood in the pouring rain and watched the ship clear the dock heading for the open sea. This was his moment of glory and nothing was going to take that away from him.

With his arms planted firmly behind his back he smiled while watching the dock slowly disappear from view. It made no difference to him that the old freighter leaked water from its wooden top deck to the compartments below causing the walls to reek with the odor of rotting wood. It really didn't bother him at all that the green slime was covering everything in sight in the sleeping quarters of the "guests."

It wasn't anything new, the sticky substance had been seeping through the cracks into the sleeping quarters for as long as the freighter had existed and since the officers quarters were on the other side of the ship it was really of no concern to the leaders.

The passengers were quartered in the cargo hole where the green slime ended up and there were wooden bunks set up for their sleeping area. With only three feet between them they were not exactly designed for comfort. Barrels that were filled with drinking water were placed at one end of the compartment for the captain's "guests" and salted dried meat was hung from the rafters with cones over the rope. The meat would swing as the ship rolled back and forth and the cones would keep the rats from getting to them.

McPhail worked his way to one corner of the room and used their traveling blankets to hang from ropes to give them more privacy. With the hatch leading to the top deck constantly locked, the captains "guests" were down right prisoners. All were packed together in the dark hole barely able to recognize one another. To fight off the darkness, they had little more than one or two lit candles and a small amount of moonlight that sometimes filtered through holes above them.

Even daylight was not much better for the group of highlanders; darkness controlled a great deal of the area because the sun could not reach its rays down to their sleeping quarters. If it were not for a little more warmth coming from the sunlight, McPhail could hardly tell the difference between day and night.

Day after day the crew obeyed orders and pretended that their guests were not aboard for fear of reprimand from the officers. The captain simply made up his mind to refuse to acknowledge that he was carrying dirty Scotsmen bound for the New World.

"By God, I'm supposed to be carrying freight." He said to his men. "Not laden my ship down with flea infested Scotsmen. I despise even the rotten idea of having such a group aboard."

The days passed slowly with the little ship rocking back and forth trying to cross the vast ocean. The smell of salt water was constantly in the air and it gave the highlanders the strong impression that perhaps there was no America. Maybe it was only a story that had been told by old men to their grand kids about a land of dreams in a mythical place across this sea.

Never mind, there would be no turning back now; the cold sea air and the constant motion of the ship moving forward was helping fuel the many dreams aboard. The stories about a new and exciting land had to be true and they were about to set foot on it.

In the second month, Marionette fell ill with the fever and chills and despite everything that McPhail could do, she died an agonizing death as he held her in his arms.

Augus felt her slip away as she drew her last breath and strangely at the moment of her passing an instant wind and rain begin to pound the ship as never before. Lighting struck across the sky from port to starboard and back again as the strange violent storm came out of nowhere. It blew the small boat across the sea like a cork bobbing in a bathtub.

For three days McPhail sat by the body of his wife weeping from the hurt deep inside him. He held her in his arms not able to let go and could not bring his emotions under control enough to understand the dangers to his boys and himself. The dangers that come with diseases that accompany dead flesh.

Several other Scotsmen tried to talk him into letting go of the body but could not make him understand the dangers of diseases that was fast approaching.

With all hope gone of bringing him around, the ship's crew was called into play and they soon discovered the husband agonizing over his wife's body. They, more that anyone, knew what could happen with a dead body aboard and in a very short length of time.

The seaman immediately reported the incident to the deck officer and within minutes four large deck hands made their way along the hallways of the ship headed for the storage hole. The men climbed down the stairs deeper into the ship as the storm tossed them again and again from one bulkhead to another.

When they reached the Scotsman holding his wife the sight was horrible and grotesque. McPhail was in a stunned state and was so anguished over the death of his wife he looked like a wild animal ready to fight over his kill.

He hadn't eaten or slept in days and the death grip he had on his wife's body would be no easy task to break. It was obvious that he was not in control of his senses in any way.

The sailors looked sadly at one another and knew what they had to do. They moved to either side of him trying to get a foot hold so that they might break him lose from his wife.

McPhail's eyes switched from one side to another watching the men get into position. Then suddenly he turned his body to one side and picked up an iron bar that was used to open barrels of salt pork. He lunged at the men in a threatening manner swinging the bar wildly. He was nearly out of his mind with grief and his only thoughts were to do anything to stop these men from taking his wife.

The four seamen had been through this type of thing before and within minutes they had over powered McPhail keeping him from doing much damage to them or the ship. Pale and exhausted, he finally lost all fight that was in him. Cradling his wife's body tightly in his arms for days had take every bit of strength he had had.

Two of the men sat on the Scotsman while the others carried his wife's body topside wrapped tightly in a blanket.

The English sailors violently threw McPhail across his bunk and poured a full bucket of cold water straight into his face.

With no fight left in him, he simply passed out from exhaustion, cold water and all. In his mind there was nothing left, he had lost almost everything of any value in his life...

Although the Bonne May was no warship, it was carrying ten cannons to be sold in America by the captain for his own gain.

One of the cannon balls that had been stored in the hole was placed in a sling that was sewn together quickly with cloth. This was tied to the legs of Marionette's body to be used as a weight. As the storm raged pitching the small ship back and forth, her body was placed on the top deck by the crew and allowed to be washed overboard by the high winds and water.

The only service held for the dead woman was Augus's soft prayers that he gave in his small portion of the hold after regaining his composer several days later.

The two sons, Samuel, twelve and Byron, ten, swore on the McPhail name that they would be brave and have the strength of all the past stalwart McPhail's, but this didn't stop the tears in their eyes. The boy's pain would last a lifetime with the lost of their mother and they weren't about to forget their high seas adventure.

Augus and the boys would continue to endure tremendous suffering in the cramped quarters for the rest of the voyage, along with a couple hundred other Scotsmen that had also been forced to travel to the New World.

None of this family of McPhail's had ever been aboard ship, much less crossed the Atlantic Ocean in a rotten, leaky, old wooden boat hardly 200 feet long.   After all, these McPhail's were farmers, not sea going sailors who made their living tending to ships.

Now with Marionette gone, Augus fell into a deep depression unable to function as a human being. He looked for other forms of relief from his pain but the stench and darkness caused the highlander to lose his mind in ways he didn't understand.

He began tearing into boxes of cargo not really knowing why he was doing these things, only knowing that his anguish was pushing him into doing something. Pulling one box after another over he came upon a neatly lined up row of barrels that contained whiskey. There was no question that the captain was going to sell them for a nice profit in the New World and pocket the proceeds.

With a vengeance he broke into them and began downing the alcohol. He told himself he would drown out the hurt deep within, but quickly found that there was no way he could drink with a ship tossing and rolling continuously. About all he ended up doing was throwing up again and again in the dark corners of the room, trying not to let the others hear his anguish.

If it were not for his two boys, the thought seriously crossed his mind of suicide but he knew he still had the responsibilities of his sons and now he was trying hard to get control of himself.

Of the two boys, Byron was the weaker one, continuously being ill from the dampness and poor food. In the sixth week at sea, Byron came down with heavy chills and fever just like his mother and it was clear to McPhail that the boy could no longer be kept confined in the hole with the cold and filth constantly on him.

His anger grew daily until he could stand the savage treatment no longer. With rage the Scotsman picked up a large board and climbed to the hatch leading to the upper deck. Again and again he rammed the oak door with little success, for his drinking had taken its toll. Almost overcome by exhaustion, he sat on the deck in a kind of stupor as other highlanders quietly looked on.

Finally, several of the men arose and helped McPhail to stand upright. "On your feet my lad." Said one of the Scotsman, "We'll not be locked in any more this day."

The brute of a man joined three others in picking up a larger 4x4 piece of wood and rammed the door making it fly off its hinge. Suddenly bright light poured through the opening and the men quickly cover their eyes to cut out the glare. Now the way was clear to the top deck and nothing was going to stop the captain's "Guests" from leaving the cargo hole this day.

Augus wrapped Byron in a blanket and scooped him up in his arms. He held his boy tight and climbed the stairs until he reached the open top deck. Samuel was following close behind his father as he cleared the hatch to the main deck.

The sunshine and soft breeze blew against their faces and filled their nostrils with relief from the many weeks of stench they had endured in the hole. McPhail looked back at the shocked sailors that were staring at the men climbing out of the hole and then he set the boy down and propped him against the rail.

Byron couldn't help but smile with approval of being on the sunlit deck for the first time since the voyage had begun. He could hear the gentle waves slashing against the side of the ship and feel the breeze against his face that was being warmed by the sun. The sound of the wooden hull slowly moving over the calm sea brought him peace as never before.

Almost defying any of the crew to interfere, Augus slid into a sitting position on the rough boards next to Byron and Samuel. Not one sailor attempted to move towards them. It seemed that they had began to admire their bravery.

The warm sun made Byron feel better immediately as he stretched out his legs and made himself comfortable. Within an instant the boy felt a pecking at his pants leg and there at his feet stood a farm hen trying to make a dinner of the cloth in the boy's pants. With one motion he scooped up the fowl in his arms and hugged it as if it were a pet dog he had owned for a lifetime.

The chicken was one of the live animals carried on board for food, but today he was Byron's new found friend. The bird gave him a great deal of joy; here was his very own special pet and he would be keeping it for the rest of the trip.

Just about then a deck hand passed by carrying a load of the captains clothes to be washed out. He stopped at the boy's feet and looked down at the skinny little chicken in Byron's arms and smiled. Now with a funny laugh he turned his attention to the boy.

"Me name's Truitt, me boy." He said. "You best not let the cook see the bird cause that's the one the captain picked out for his dinner pot tonight. See right there, that's why it's got the yellow ribbon around its neck. He's been picked to attend the officers mess he has, and that little fellow is going to be the guest of honor."

Listening nearby, a second deck hand smiled at the boy and immediately piped up.

"Don't worry none, young lad. I'll pluck another and the cap't will never know the difference." He said, making sure the boy knew he was on his side.

By now, most of the deck crew was watching the young lad and somehow Byron holding on to that scrubby chicken seemed to perk up the spirits of the ship's Company. Here was a group of dirty, drunken, outcast English sailors that would think nothing of slitting your throat for a pound, six pence that now felt it necessary to protect and cover for this young Scottish lad.

Almost to a man they began working close to the boy and covering him from view of the officers.

"You'll cross safe this voyage." Said one of the crewmen while placing his seaman's hat on the boy's head. Byron responded with a grateful look, as he continued petting the thin bird. Even some of the officers that knew what was going on, simply strolled aft turning their backs to the group and pretended to observe the horizon.

By this time, the crew was gaining courage and began to relax, but kept on pretending to be doing their daily work.

With his usual contemptuous look on his face, Captain Biles suddenly emerged from his cabin onto the quarter deck. He stood surveying the top deck until his eyes fell upon Augus and the boys, despite the deck hands attempt to block his view.

When he saw the open door and the boy petting the chicken, the captain blew his stack. He knew that the door leading to the hole was only opened for an hour once a week to let in some fresh air and that was at nightfall only.

Captain Biles turned to his first officer and spoke as though he were giving a strong military command.

"Mr. Andrew, kindly remove those people and send them below." He said, "I'll not have Scotsmen topside at their desire aboard my ship and you will see to it!"

Even as he finished the sentence, the hatch leading to the hole became filled with the other "guests" passing through it. One after another they climbed the latter into the sunshine having no intentions of being stopped. Even the disgraced captain began to realize that a change had to be made or there could be some dreadful consequences. The commander could now see for himself the change in the crew's attitude because of the chicken cradled in the boy's arms.

He took a hard long look into the faces of one crew member after another and begin to realize from the way they were looking back, that he best not take action against the lad.

The fact that his passengers were pouring onto the deck with none of the crew even trying to prevent the migration top side, made him turn to the first officer and bellow a second command to belay the order to remove them.

The captain then placed his hands behind his back to look statelier and returned to his cabin. He was bound for yet another liquor bottle and his dreams of past glory when he was an important naval officer. Someday he would be commanding a powerful warship again he would tell himself.

No sooner than the captain had vanished below, the deck hands went wild, whooping out loud with joy and breaking out barrels of rum stored for trade in the New World.

Now it would be a party day for the men, for the officers cared not, or dared not, try to stop the English sailors. As night fell, the sounds of bagpipes rolled across the calm waves and the stars twinkled brightly with silhouettes of dozens of Scotsmen dancing on the top deck.

For the first time since the voyage began, McPhail felt really at ease. He placed his arms around the boys and watched their countrymen kick up their heels to the Scottish music. What a difference the cruise had now turned into.

Chapter 3

The Atlantic seemed to be forever throwing storms in the path of the two ships causing the seaman to constantly run the sails up to the wind or down out of the threatening weather. Nearing the end of their voyage, yet another storm seemed to come out of nowhere separating the two vessels and damaging the sails and riggings of the Bonne May.

Now she was blown off course and the Excursion was nowhere in sight. The combination of Captain Bile's poor seamanship and liquor bottle led to the failure of correcting their heading and the ship landed in North Carolina at Wilmington instead of the trading port of New York.

Not wishing to give the Scotsmen and crew any indication that he had fowled up, the announcement was made that he had put into the nearest port for repairs. In reality, the English naval officer had every intention of relieving himself of these aggravating freeloaders.

Most of the highlanders began to explode into a rage causing chaos on board stretching captain Biles's patience to the limit. This was his chance; with fervor, he ordered all of the "guests" off the boat forbidding any of them to come back aboard.

When they went ashore wearing their peculiar costumes and speaking an outlandish language with their heavy brogue, they so frightened the people that the High Sheriff attempted to make the strangers give bond to keep the peace.

Having none of it, McPhail took his sons and quickly joined with two other families in slipping out of the crowd, making their way through the docks to the other side of the town where a stable of horses were kept.

The mares were fine animals, but the man selling them was somewhat of a questionable character. His ownership of the horses was very much in doubt. He was a funny little man that haggled for an hour with McPhail until the Scotsman decided he had had enough of his foolishness. Pouring two gold pieces from his purse onto an overturned barrel, he challenged the horsemen, John Rick's, to the tossing of the caber (log throwing) winner takes gold and horses.

"Are you daft man?" Rick's said, showing contempt. "Look at ya, with you're muscles and size. I'd stand not a chance with ya at all; but if ya a mind to, we could shoot for it. Three shots at one hundred feet is more my game, providing ya put one more of them there gold coins on the barrel against my mares."

McPhail quickly agreed and three barrels were stacked on one another in a triangle with a large X painted on the end of the top one. The shooting was about to begin but the heavens were showing their own games.

Clouds had rolled in and turned black, and thunder was now rumbling across the sky and lighting lit up the heavens like never before.

Rick's took careful aim and fired his first shot and the ball hit the barrel on the right causing the little fellow to curse and motioned for Augus to take his turn.

McPhail's shot was no better, hitting high to the right but a little lower than his opponent. Rick's smiled with contempt at the Scotsman and stepped up for his next shot. Several times he braced himself but kept shifting positions.

It seemed as if he were going to take forever, raising and lowering his rifle over an over again while spitting nasty looking stuff on the ground. He looked at the target and then back at McPhail who was now sitting on a three-legged stool watching the little man intensely. He almost couldn't prime his weapon for his next shot because the little man was causing him to go into hysterics. Again the man raised and then lowered his rifle without firing the shot.

The huge sound of thunder rolled across the sky and with it McPhail had had enough. He shouted at the little fellow in a very loud voice to make sure he could be heard over the intense roar of the thunder.

"Can you not make the shot, mate?" He said.

At the same time Rick's gun exploded missing the X by inches causing him to yell in delight. He had made a very good shot and the little man knew it.

Augus jumped to his feet with his rifle in position and took a stance on the firing line. Almost immediately he squeezed the trigger of his heavy rifle as soon as it was level with the barrel.

Rick strained his eyes at the X on the end of the barrel and his heart sank when he saw that the ball had hit right next to his own mark. Now the shooting game was a tie.

While the horseman prepared for his third and final shot, it began to rain as though the sky had simply opened up and poured a huge bucket of water down from the clouds.

Rick's took another look at the stalemate and turned to McPhail to shout his desire to call off the match but was answered with a definite no.

McPhail had no intention of having the match canceled and he once again yelled loudly over the storm that was now fast approaching.

"We'll shoot the match, rain or no." He said at the top of his lungs. "Squeeze the shot, will ya man, before your gunpowder gets wet!"

Completely drenched, the two fired their last round and now had to run through the heavy rain to see where the musket balls had hit.

Wet, Cold and totally worn out the Scotsman led his new horses off to begin their journey. He had won the last round without a question.

The dirty face little man was mad as a hornet as he stood in the heavy down pour watching his horses disappear in the distance. He could do nothing but keep shouting obscenities towards McPhail knowing that his loud calls were being ignored by the Scotsman.

The three families wasted no time in packing their belongings into several old wagons they had acquired from an old timer that did not have use for them any longer.

Since none of the small band of immigrants had ever been to the colonies before they had decided to travel as a group for safety. Hardly any good maps were available so they began following the Cape Fear River in search of good farm land. Their travels would be simple. The group made sure that they never loss sight of the overgrown muddy creek. That way water, game and fish would be close by.

It was weeks before they reached the outskirts of the town now known as Fayetteville. Here they were quite taken back at the lovely sight.

There was plenty of green grass and beautiful trees coupled with an abundance of wild life near a fine river full of fish. Everything that a farmer would need to start his own place. It made no difference that they would have to live under the wagons until cabins could be built. The trees would help shade the wagons while the families helped each other with the building of their cabins.

The youngsters of each family joined together in the hunting and fishing so that they might share the food at each meal. A kindred spirit grew strongly between the families and a peace they had never known settled on their campsite. Soon other kinsmen joined the small group and a town was laid out called Cross Creek, which still remains today. (years later the name would be changed to Fayetteville).

Here the boys Samuel and Byron grew up working with their father on the small farm outside of the city with slavery starting all around them. Oftentimes the boys would see slave owners passing by with a wagon full of blacks, some in chains and others simply walking behind with heads lowered.

They could never understand this, and would listen intently whenever the elders would talk among themselves about the buying and selling of human beings. Augus owned none, but when it was necessary, he did rent a few of the Africans from their owners from time to time.

Never once did he have a desire for slavery because he had seen a form of it called lender's slave. If a debtor were ordered to pay up and was unable to do so, even after selling all their possessions, the king's men would set the length of time to be served as a slave until the debt would be paid. Oftentimes this amounted to years, and sometimes a lifetime for the Scots.

McPhail would often furnish extra food and slip small amounts of money to the slaves when they came to work on his farm. Upon his passing in 1784 from a flu epidemic, many of the blacks cried and the senior elders gave their own special prayers that night for the kind man whose spirit had escaped to Allah.

Shortly after his father's death, Samuel met the widow Green who owned a fine plantation that had been a grant from King George III. The British favored Mary because her husband had been a captain in the English army and totally dedicated to the crown. A real beauty this Miss Green, with her dark hair and light skin and ladylike ways.

Mary didn't want for companionship as every single man in the territory was trying to call on her. She grew attracted to

Samuel and the relationship quickly led from candlelight dinners to marriage.

As owner of over one hundred slaves, and a five hundred-acre plantation, she was quite a catch for the young McPhail, instantly giving him a life of luxury. He soon moved into the beautiful lady's southern mansion with a new life-style as lord and master of a cotton plantation.

How easy it was for a young man to get use to being a slave owner. The power and status temptation couldn't help but overcome any man be he young or old. He couldn't resist such a temptation; it consumed him like an addiction and he played the part well. His desire was not to harm anyone but only to elevate himself to a much higher position in life.

His youth blinded him to the true facts surrounding the plantation; mainly that no one should own another. History had shown time and again it would not work regardless of what race was the owner and what race the slave.

Unknown to Samuel, the head overseer of the slaves by the name of Willow Trash, and Samuel's wife Mary had been seeing one another for a short time after her husband's death and Mary was with child. She had turned to the closest person in her grief, and it had gotten out of hand one night when the wine flowed freely.

The marriage between Samuel and Mary caused Trash to become meaner than he already was and he began taking it out on the field slaves more readily than ever before. Trash had had his eyes on Mary and her wealth but he had lost out to the young Scotsman. Now he was taking out his vengeance on the field workers.

Time and again Trash and McPhail fought over the brutality that Trash inflicted on the blacks, until Samuel finally ordered him off the land.

"No!" Trash yelled, in a loud voice. "You'll not order me off the property unless I'm paid a handsome lot."

McPhail's urge to physically throw Trash off the land grew stronger, but he fought to control himself. The statement that Willow was to make next would send Samuel over the edge.

"Your wife's going to have a child and his name won't be McPhail. He shouted with a cat eating the canary look.

"How'd ya like that spread around town?" He added, pointing his finger in the young man's face.

Samuel completely lost it and flew into a mad rage. It was as if a crazy madness totally engulfed his very being. Before he knew it, the Scotsman had picked up an ax that was embedded in the stump of a tree and began swinging it wildly at the overseer.

The first blow was enough; the ax was embedded deep in Trash's stomach almost cutting him into. The overseer had never expected such an action from McPhail. His face had a look of absolute shock and fear as he fell to his knees and slowly rolled over on his back; his blood pouring out of the gaping wound.

His hands held tight to the protruding ax handle as if he were trying to keep the huge flow of blood from pouring down the side of his body. He turned towards McPhail and opened his mouth to speak but it was useless. There was no sound coming out of him and within minutes he had died a painful death.

Coonie, the head Negro slave, was stacking wood nearby and ran to Samuel when he saw the blow being struck. He immediately realized who had been killed and his expression turned from horror to somewhat of a smile.

"You done killed a powerful mean man." He told McPhail almost doing a happy dance with his tired old legs.

"Best we bury him so nobody find out." He said looking all about to make sure nobody important was watching.

"I'll get me some help and we'll dig a grave out by the south fence cause nobody goes out there. It's a far piece from the house and I know's that he'll not be found."

Then almost in a happy mood he called to several of the field hands and prepared to start his own cemetery. This was not going to be a task of hard labor, rather a somewhat enjoyable endeavor for Coonie and his helpers.

Still, digging the grave was undeniably a gruesome task even if it was for the mean overseer, but it wasn't like they hadn't dug one before and besides the thought of planting a very cruel overseer in the ground made it just a bit easier. How much easier you ask? So much easier, that they were humming tunes as they performed the grave digging duty.

They dug and dug, making sure that the hole was going to be deeper than normal for the evil man. The three black men were trying to make sure no one would find this site.

When the digging job was complete, Coonie and Washington stripped the body of anything that was worth while, including the black whip hanging from a strap attached to his wrist that the two had known about so well.

Once more they looked at the body before laying him in the ground and then wrapped him in cloth. Then they rolled the corpse into the hole and almost bit their tongue when they said a very short prayer for such a man.

With that, one of the diggers said his piece out loud.

"Willow Trash was one cruel man and got what he deserved. Can't wait to tell Mary Bell; she got beat by Willow all the time cause he just like to hurt women."

Then he turned and began to walk away but the head slave grabbed hold of his arm and stopped him cold.

"Can't tell nobody." Said Coonie. "Got to protect master McPhail; besides, he done us a favor getting rid of a bastard like that. Now you ain't quite finished up here yet so you help the others and then go about your business and **keep your mouth shut!**"

Coonie turned back towards the diggers that were finishing up and bent over to help one of the men pull up a large root. Then he looked down at the newly dug grave and said something softly to himself.

The small man looked up at the tall slave and wiped his face. "What's that, Coonie?" He said.

"I said that I'll just bet old Willow is weeping in front of the almighty right now because he's coming face to face at the evil things he's done. See those small trees over there? Dig up one of them little trees and plant it on the grave. The way them branches are hanging down like their crying that'll be his weeping tree...his Weeping Willow tree."

All finished with the digging, the men carried leaves to the grave and covered the fresh pile of dirt, while the tree was being carefully planted on top. Soon there would be no telltale signs at the south end of the plantation and no one would ever know that the tree with the low hanging limbs was a hidden grave.

"Master McPhail's secret will be hidden forever." Connie told the Scotsman. "I's would see to that, you just don't worry none sir." He said.

The head slave kept his word to the young Scotsman, making all the blacks come to his hut that night and swear that they would keep silent for fear of having their tongues cut out.

Slave row was quieter than usual that evening; almost nothing could be heard except for the night critters making their mating calls. It was an eerie night because of the exceptional quiet that had fallen over the entire plantation.

Samuel apparently was extremely nervous. Hour after hour he peered out the window not knowing what he expected to find. He simply told himself over and over that he was justified in his actions; still he had a frightful night. He had killed a man only because the heat of rage had made him lose control. Each time he would add something to his memory that really wasn't there. Anything to justify his violent action for it was not like him to do harm to anyone…

Still, there comes a time in a man's life when he has to do something drastic and far away from his normal temperament and McPhail hoped that this was his one and only time…

Chapter 4

After the killing of the overseer, McPhail was never quite the same. He drank to wake up in the morning, carried a bottle with him all day and drank in the evening until he would pass out before bedtime at night. He became a mere shell of the man he once was as the bottle became his constant companion.

Samuel told everyone that Willow Trash was fired and had moved on, but somehow Mary knew that there was more to it. His certain tone of voice and the way he treated her changed, not only from the drinking, but his lack of interest in even having a conversation with her, much less anything physical. His stubborn backlash continued for months until a girl was born to Mary and suddenly all things began to change in side of him.

For some reason little voices that seemed to come from inside him were now causing his memory to flash back to the grandfather he often listen to and loved.

Josiah McPhail was closer to Samuel than any of his other grandchildren and now the man his grandson had become could actually see the wise old man setting beside him telling stories of times gone by.

Of course the old man had been dead for many years but here he was setting beside him on the banks of their favorite old river with their fishing lines in the water. The old man took the young boy fishing many times and although few fish were ever caught, the tales he would tell the youngster were intriguing to say the lease.

One of the most significant things the boy would remember all his life was a simple sentence that his grandfather had told him as they sat on the edge of that old creek.

"Nothing stays the same me lad, everything changes in time and you only have one chance at forgiveness; be it your giving or your taking of the forgiveness."

The mysterious flashback immediately gave him a feeling of calm and well being, and from that moment on he saw the child as his own. He not only accepted the newborn as his own, but he never again said one word about the fact that the child was not his. As far as he was concerned now, this baby was his and his love for her grew daily.

The girl was named Elizabeth after Mary's mother and became the center of the family. As years passed two more children were born to Samuel and Mary; a boy named William Eric and a girl christened Vickie Lynn. Time seemed to fly by and the children grew into young adults and so did the weeping willow.

Although Samuel did not know, or want to know, exactly where Trash was buried, he was somehow drawn to the now beautiful tree in the south corner of the cotton fields. He would ride past the beautiful tree and pause looking strangely at the willow as though it held a spell over him.

Never again was a whip allowed on the McPhail Plantation and Coonie was now elevated to the status of plantation foreman and he was looked upon as almost being a king.

The old slave took his new position in stride and bought a top hat on one of his trips to town to make himself stand out from the other blacks. The dark stovepipe hat, with feather sticking out the top, became his mark of authority. He rode high in the saddle barking orders to the other slaves as they worked in the fields; to the girls he was no longer an old man, he was now somebody; somebody mighty important.

On a number of occasions Coonie saw McPhail ride by the willow tree. He knew the master was troubled, but for the life of him, didn't know what to do to help. A strong bond grew between owner and slave as the years passed and before his death in the spring of 1818, Samuel gave Coonie and his wife their freedom, along with a small plot of land to farm.

McPhail was found slumped over the kitchen table still holding pen and paper in his hand. He had written a simple sentence. One that must have lay heavily on his mind. "Be it giving or accepting forgiveness."

After his father's death, William Eric was not content to live on the farm. After all it was now the year 1826, and there was a big young country out there to explore. He desperately wanted to travel; to see the exciting things happening in other states and the new frontier of Texas.

His mother had been quite ill since the first of the year and he knew he couldn't leave her alone. Someone would have to tend to the slaves and the farm and keep things together. After all, both of his sisters had married and moved off to start their own families.

Now William was the only one left to see to the farm. Still his strong itch to begin exploring ate away at him with each passing day. He felt deep down that he would be trapped for years but wasn't about to let his mother know it. He knew that sooner or later things would change but he didn't know that they were about to turn very, very soon.

Fate was about to intervene in a drastic way in his life. Mary's life suddenly came to a close. She died in early August leaving everything to William except a diary of cash for the girls.

The young man rode for two days to deliver the money to his sisters and bid them farewell. He hugged them and told the story of his dreams of Texas and the wild country out west that he would be moving to. He made it clear that in all probability he would not be returning but would write from time to time.

Then he returned to his plantation for one last time and spread the word that the house, land and all else was for sale.

William Eric promptly sold all that his parents had build. He kept one black, several horses and a wagon to begin his long trip to a new frontier. He knew that the huge open spaces would be beaming with opportunities and he was going to be part of it.

He had heard exciting and colorful tales about the land just north of Mexico. The land that was one of the biggest in all the world and it was appropriately called Texas.

After signing all the right bill of sale instruments, William stood looking at the plantation knowing that his life was making major changes. He mounted his horse and turned facing the family graveyard quietly showing respect for the McPhail elders that had passed on.

Now it was his time to live the life he had dreamed of. He turned his mare southwest and began riding down the dirt road with high excitement. He patted his pockets with his hand as if to assure himself that they were still filled full of gold coins from the sale of the farm.

He rode like a man on a new mission; one of changing the McPhail legacy.

"No longer will I be a cotton farmer." William thought to himself.

"I will live an exciting life of exploring and searching for new horizons."

His youth deprived him of the logic of considering the future. All he could think about now was how exciting his new adventure would be in the great state of Texas. Better that he be on the road to adventure than locked in a sea of never ending daily labor of repetition. So let the cards fall as they may...

His black slave rode beside him only when the ground was hard and level, otherwise he led the horses through the rough countryside coaching the animals to cross the rivers and tough roads that sometimes was almost impassable.

Salmon had been promised his freedom by McPhail as soon as they reached the lone star state and he was making the most out of every day's travel. When the Scotsman wanted to camp for the night, Salmon would talk him into traveling just one more mile.

The pair had gone as far as Marshall County, Mississippi, when McPhail stopped at a small trading post for supplies. Behind a makeshift counter was a beautiful girl of sixteen by the name of Barbara Ann Allen, daughter of Joseph Allen, owner of the store.

Eric could not take his eyes off the beautiful girl and day after day he made excuses to stay in Marshall County. All the while Salmon kept trying to get William to move on towards Texas but the young man was caught up in a sea of love. He camped at the edge of the small town and without fail he would drop by the store every day, helping with her chores, or pretend that he was there to see Joseph.

Day after day Barbara's father would watch as Eric would continue to do free chores for his daughter and stay next to her side constantly, which she seemed to adore. After a month of constantly hanging around the young girl, her father finally spoke his mind to the lovesick McPhail.

"For god's sake." He said. "Marry my daughter before planting time and we can sell your crops in the store."

With delight, Eric took a deep breath, and bellowed out the only thing he could think of at the moment…

"Yes sir!" He said, beaming with joy and at the same time almost stumbling over a pickle barrel. Between the barrel and the front door he came dangerously close to breaking his neck.

However, he managed to clear the door and reach the street in one piece and immediately after clearing the store's front door, his excitement showed.

"Ye Ho." He yelled out at the top of his voice not caring who was hearing him.

Then he realized a great many of the town folk were watching him show his excitement, but he really didn't care. He was sure they didn't know what he was yelling about, but he was wrong. They weren't stupid, they knew that somewhere there was a pretty girl involved.

Within the week, the announcement of their engagement was made to almost everyone in town and they were married almost immediately. Now most of the time in those days, a preacher was only available about once a year because the men of cloth would travel throughout a large area; so the town folk would gather together and have the bride and groom say their vows and jump a broom.

This was accepted as being married until a preacher came by and performed the ceremony. And so it came to be, that Eric would settle down, but Texas weighed heavily on his mind. To him the great state would be his Garden of Eden and he knew that he would not be happy until he continued on.

For now he would settle just being with Barbara, for nothing else pleased him more. Eric and Barbara moved into a house owned by the High Sheriff, which he had taken in payment "for services." Usually this meant he had taken a bribe which was common in those days.

It was a fine little house with a white picket fence, green grass and a small storage hut that Salmon could convert for living quarters. Eric fit in nicely as a trader of goods and he often traveled to Memphis for stock to sell in Holly Springs.

He would take orders from the folks in the area before his journey and make a profit on the items when he returned.

After his fourth child was born, he spent a great deal of time working with his new found friend Elkanah Sullivan, an Irish immigrant who later became the sheriff of Pontotoc County.

The last child born to Eric and Barbara was a hardy boy whom they named John, taken from his friend's middle name. Eric didn't like and couldn't bring himself to name his son Elkanah, for he barely could pronounce it and surely couldn't spell the funny name.

Soon after John's birth, Eric's overpowering desire to see Texas got the better of him. He scrawled out a bill of sale freeing Salmon and handed it to the black man along with two fifty-dollar gold pieces. After the transaction was completed he shook hands with the man and made him an offer that he thought the black couldn't refuse.

"Care to travel to Texas with us? Eric asked the black man. "As a friend to start your own life"

The now former slave looked at McPhail with a funny smile, rolling his big eyes and shaking his head no; indicating to the Scotsman that he was staying.

Salmon had already found himself an African woman on a farm not far from town and had been told he could buy her for a hundred dollars gold. He had planned, for sometime, on just how to make the money and now he would buy the lovely lady with soft hands and have a fine wife to cook for him, so he had decided to stay.

He looked at the two fifty dollar gold pieces in his hand and slowly turned back to McPhail with a large pleasant smile covering almost his entire face and without a word he climbed on the back of his mule. He urged the mule on and began to sing a song he had made up about Christie. The decision to call her Christie came when he remembered a part of his young childhood. A girl called Christie Ann had helped him through some difficult times in his life. She was a bit older and wiser and had taken care of the young Salmon when he had lived in the slaves quarters.

Being a black herself, she had taken terrible risks for the young boy. She had stolen food from the kitchen of the master to give the young black extra rations and shared the food only with him. This would be a high honor, naming his new wife after her, because she had died of the fever when she was barely nineteen and he had loved everything about her.

Later, Salmon would decide to become a fisherman on the Mississippi River and he was seen almost every day selling his fresh fish from a small cart that he pulled from one house to the next.

He raise six kids to become fine God fearing adults which was a credit to his memory, before being found dead on the banks of the muddy in-ways, still holding a fishing pole. Without a doubt he was probably still trying for the big one that got away.

Packing everything that the wagon could hold, the Scotsmen loaded his family and begun the long trip to Texas. The things they were unable to load on the wagon were sold to friends or given to people who were down on their luck.

The McPhail's made the trip with excitement in their hearts; at least it was so with Eric. Barbara would hold back judgment until she saw just where he intended to settle. For two months the family traveled along winding trails leading into east Texas before the wagon pulled into Houston County. When they arrived in the beautiful rolling hill country between Lovelady and Crockett, Barbara adored the place they finally picked for the farmhouse.

Land was theirs for the taking and they decided their house would be built on top of a large hill overlooking a valley with good soil to grow their vegetables.

The Houston County courthouse was located in Crockett, with its downtown stores and shops surrounding the county building in a square. On Saturdays the farmers would set up booths all around the courthouse to sell their wares and hear the latest gossip from travelers passing through the county.

Stories were told from person to person as there was not yet a newspaper, and some great tales came out of the get-to-gathers. Even if most of the stories were far fetched and stretched the truth to the limit, it was still a grand time for all who came. The beautiful rolling hills would come alive with wagons loaded to the brim as farmers brought their families and products to line the square for the weekly swap meet.

The sun would have barely clear the tops of the trees before their goods would already be displayed on tables lining completely around the courthouse filling the entire square.

Young mothers would be nursing their babies as they have for thousands of years, but with dignity and privacy by placing a light blanket over the child and her shoulder at the same time.

The father's would tend to the horses and wagons and set up the tables to show their goods. It seemed as if the only problem of the time was the red clay and dust of the County. The red dirt got all over everything during the auctions that were held for livestock around the livery stable. The cookies, candy, and cakes brought by the ladies to sell had to be completely wrapped or covered all the time, or the iron ore dust would simply ruin them.

Time and again the beautiful dresses worn by the women of the county would be stained so badly, the red clay would never come out, even when washed extra hard in lye soap. The ladies of Houston County almost started a new trend in female clothing because they were cutting the bottom of the long dresses off trying to get rid of the red clay and still save their lovely garments.

As bad as the red mud was, it was equally as good at growing fine watermelons, vegetables, and cotton. No one would dispute the great crops that grew on the farms, year after year.

Only one thing however, if one of the residents traveled out of the east Texas area, the red clay was a dead giveaway to where he had come from; even today a car traveling through the county comes out with red mud all over it's tires and on the side of it's doors indicating it was from east Texas.

By the age of ten, John was working hard on the farm, as all young fellows did in those days. There were no excuses, he would milk cows, carry firewood, feed chickens and hogs and tend to the crops, from sun up to sun down. It wasn't so hard on the boy that he dreaded getting up every morning, on the contrary, he really loved the farm and it's many animals.

Little John would look forward to the weekend, for he knew that on Saturday the family would travel to town for the auctions and sidewalk sales.

Every Saturday would become a new adventure for the young boy because immigrants moving in would bring their Old World ways with them and new products and customs were forever being shown at the bazaar.

One such immigrant was a happy-go-lucky Englishman who had moved into Houston County about six months before, stealing the hearts of the town folks with his childlike behavior and his sad smile.

Eli Hart and his wife, Paula Marie, were quite a colorful sight as they rode into the square on their crazy looking two-wheeled cart with a very rough English coat of arms displayed on the side.

Obviously painted by an amateur, the people none the less liked the little man's style. He wore English style aristocratic boots with tight pants carefully shoved into them trying to look like a noble head of state.

Calling himself the "Earl of Hart" as from a royal family, he was in reality a man crushed by a disease that had left him with the mentality of a happy-go-lucky ten year old boy. He thought of himself as a true Earl and the townspeople oftentimes gave the little man head of the line privileges for he and his wife and played the charade by bowing as they passed by.

Eli would acknowledge the bows of his subjects by slowly waving his hand with palms up, back and forth. His attention span was limited to about two sentences and his memory even worse, but when it came to flowers, none grew them better. The back of his cart would always be full of beautiful roses and chrysanthemums and he and his lady would wear their finest clothes making the cheerful cart brighten up the day for all the town folk.

Whenever Eli came to town, John ran alongside his cart knowing that the little man of imaginary royalty would let him carry flowers to sell around the square. For each bunch he sold, the little Englishman gave the boy a penny and would tell him, "Be Quick As A Bunny and you'll make Some Money"

The trips to town were a fun time for young John, and he looked forward to making the journey after working hard all week. He never seemed to tire or grow bored with making the long trip, for the boy always knew that something different awaited his arrival each time.

When Eli died, the whole town turned out for the funeral, and a rose was engraved on his tombstone with these words; "He's gone to grow better roses for the king."

Chapter 5

By the time John was twenty the fear of war between north and south was very real. The men of Houston County appropriated fifteen thousand dollars to arm and equip one hundred well-mounted soldiers. When the decision was made to travel to Richmond, Virginia, the group's wait was over and they joined up with other volunteers to fight for the confederacy.

Wearing new uniforms sewed by the ladies of Houston County, the 100 confederate soldiers mounted their new horses an hour before dawn and were given a rousing sendoff by almost all of the people in the area. With little or no training as soldiers, the men began their trip into history, unaware that their glory would turn into disaster and death for hundreds of thousands of both northern and southern warriors.

William Armstreet was appointed captain of the now southern company of Confederates, and it was his job to lead the men into battle.

The proud southern officer mounted his horse and kissed his wife good by not knowing how long he would be gone. He turned to the formation of young men that were quietly setting atop their horses and yelled out the command to move forward. The proud looking men turned their horses in columns of twos and headed northeast to Virginia with all the Pomp and grandeur of the Knights of the Round table. They looked magnificent and knew it, but not one of them had any idea how far Virginia really was or what they would be soon facing.

Armstreet was a graduate of West Point and knew of war, for he had fought on the Mexican border with honor but now was dedicated to fight for the Confederate states. He had stepped up and resigned his commission like a gentleman to keep his honor and then joined the Confederacy. At the time no one was stopping officers from choosing the side they intended to stand with and many that wore the union blue was turning to the confederate gray.

The new company of rebels intention was to join other units along the way and they rode proudly waving their new Texas battle flag with it's Stars and Bars made out of silk. They felt like true soldiers in their new gray uniforms; their swords glistened in the sun as they set tall and proud in the saddle riding in formation.

All the little towns the soldiers passed through were giving them a great send off when they rode through. The fine company now was crossing into northern Louisiana and soon they would meet up with several hundred other southerners wearing the same gray uniforms and flying their new battle flags proudly.

They were becoming an army when the soldiers joined together and rode on heading to Shreveport growing in strength each step of the way. The columns turned towards Jackson, Mississippi picking up more battle flags with each major town they entered.

Training every step of the way, orders and commands were yelled to the men as they moved their horses into Vicksburg and joined up with even more southerners, turning the company into a well-armed battalion.

Captain Armstreet was serving under Lieutenant Colonel Jonathan Ross of the First Alabama Rangers by the time the army bedded down for the night at Birmingham, near the Alabama River. The captain was happy to have such a distinguished Colonel leading them for he had even more experience in the art of war.

Late that night, five wagons of gunpowder, shot, food and blankets rolled into the camp with even more young southerners joining the battalion. Volunteers from all over the region joined the army of unprepared fighters headed to Richmond.

A dozen different battle flags waved in the breeze when they mounted the next morning. Now young McPhail would get a taste of being a true warrior. He was about to eat his first hardtack; army bread so hard it often had to be boiled or fried before it could be eaten. The bread would last practically forever fixed this way, but was downright awful.

Another volunteer from Texarkana, Texas, had recently joined the gray coats and he too learned a lesson about hardtack when he almost broke a tooth on the rock like substance. Benjamin Davis Brown would become close friends with the Scotsman from Crockett,...not yet knowing that he would ride beside him into history.

Unknown to the two southern soldiers at the time, their lives would be forever changed. They had no idea of the devastation, brutality, and sheer terror that the coming months were to hold in store for the young southerners.

Ben Brown pulled the rains to one side trying to keep his horse in formation with the other rebels.

"Damn" He said. Trying to bite into the hard bread. "What is this stuff?"

McPhail laughed out loud and spit out his hardtack when he saw Brown's expression. The look on Ben's face was funny enough to cause John to almost fall off his horse with laughter.

"This crazy rebel had better become a good fighter." McPhail thought to himself. "or we're both in a lot of trouble."

The excitement within the young men grew each day until they passed through Georgia into North Carolina. They were as boy scouts on an outing not realizing that this was about to become a real war. Not until the battalion reached Durham where the training would become intense did it begin to soak in just what they might be up against.

Long lines of the gray coats were formed to fire at dummies and attack with bayonets held high. They pierced the imitation Yankee soldiers right through the belly and yelled the rebel yells at the top of their lungs.

No longer would the young men play at being soldiers; it now begun to really sink in that facing an enemy out to kill you was becoming a reality.

Soon they would be called on for a bloody battle God only knows where and there was no turning back.

Still, the thought of any of them being killed was out of the question. Youth tends to remove common sense and replace it with outright imagination of your magnificent army being total winners with little or no casualties among your group.

Here were very young men and boys about to show their bravery. There would be no going back; they were at the point of no return. So it was with the rebels that had band together and thought themselves invincible.

After one week of training daily, orders came down that the battalion would leave the much-needed horses in Durham and march to Richmond.

It never occurred to McPhail that they would not be riding into glory on the back of their horses. Now he would be a simple foot soldier and leave his magnificent animal behind?

He couldn't for the life of him understand why, but orders were orders and he would obey the southern commanders. Little time was given for complaints about the abandonment of their horses, for the high command wasted no time in marching the men north. The battalion marched proudly into Richmond but was unable to see much of the city because they were quickly joined by hundreds of other volunteers and ordered further north.

The defense of their southern homeland against an invasion by the despised Yankees that in his mind was unprovoked, was soon to become a reality. On top of that the fact that he no longer had a horse was down right discouraging to McPhail and it made him feel inferior. He needed a mount to keep up his pride and courage but now he was on foot, marching with hundreds of others becoming just one among the huge army to fight the tyranny coming out of Washington.

The farmer turned soldier began to question why he volunteered for a war he really didn't understand. They had him marching in the hot sun wearing a wool uniform, and to the Scotsman, this just didn't make sense.

After leaving Richmond, he became totally lost in an unfamiliar world. The map that his captain was given had ended on the outskirts of the city and half the time they didn't know if they were moving north or south.

The tall trees blocked their view and made it hard to tell which way was north. Still he followed along with the others hoping for the best.

"Surely they know where we are going." He thought to himself. "Some of these Virginia boys must know the territory."

Even the officers seemed to be play acting, almost like it was their first attempt to give orders and be leaders of men. They kept yelling out commands again and again; as if trying to impress everyone in the battalion. Still, looking around and seeing so many other southern men marching in formation with rifles slung on their shoulders, made him feel ten foot tall and proud. A lot scared, but proud.

On July 21, 1861, the small town of Manassas, Virginia, twenty-six miles south of Washington, was lying in rolling hill country with streams and heavily wooded areas of little importance to anyone except the farmers living in the area.

On this morning, however, the battle of Manassas (Termed Bull Run by the union army) was to begin.   John McPhail found himself lined up with thousands of other Confederate soldiers for the battle.   The Scotsman had never seen so many men in his life.   He was dumb struck from drums playing, officers yelling commands and all the noisy activity that goes with a large army about to go into combat.

"Straighten your lines and look lively." The noncom's yelled over the sea of flashing bayonets glistening in the sunshine. "Your about to go down in history me boys, so look your best!"

McPhail had no idea what was coming until he saw a multitude of blue coming over the hills headed right towards them.

"My God!" John thought to himself. "Didn't they look fine dressed in their fancy blue uniforms and carrying brand new rifles. Just like a huge sea of fish swimming in unison but how many are there? Twenty thousand, Thirty thousand?

The sweat that poured from his head and neck came from fear and excitement rather than the summer sun and wool uniform. He knew that very soon the order would come down to begin the attack and his fear grew.

Then the unthinkable came in the form a loud voice behind him. It was simply one word that he wasn't ready to hear. A very loud one word that came bellowing out of the officer commanding the cannons.

"**Fire**." He yelled.

Immediately smoke from the rebel guns began mixing with the smoke from the union cannons and sixty-five thousand rifles began exchanging gunfire at the same time. The air was full of flying bullets that were now striking down soldiers all around Brown and McPhail. Like rain the blood flew into the air coming down all around the two Texans and within minutes there was bodies from north and south covering the entire field.

John fired in unison with the other rebels as he stood shoulder to shoulder in their almost perfect straight line. The sound from the guns was so loud his body shook from the vibration and his ear drums were almost bursting at the seams.

Each row would fire and then kneel to reload, allowing the row behind to move in front for their turn to shoot at the Yankee soldiers that were now almost directly in front of them.

This madness continued until the enemies were close enough to throw rocks at one another. The battle had begun in earnest and would rage on for hours. Screams came from the wounded that were in agony and it mixed with the loud rebel yells that the young men were using to try and cover their fears. The hills now echoed the sounds of battle as hand to hand combat was the bloodiest that had ever been seen in wartime.

Still the armies kept coming at each other, stepping over bodies to continue their march towards their opponent. The long lines of both north and south were crashing into each other with disastrous consequences. The shiny bayonets were no longer being used in military marches to impress the public. Now they were being rammed through the bodies of soldiers on both sides and some of the warriors weren't even able to retrieve the hunk of iron from the flesh they had shoved it through.

Now these boys from both sides had become men and they were beginning to shield themselves from the bloody sight of the battle field. There was so many soldiers falling all around them it was becoming common place and God help them, they were becoming use to it.

As darkness began to take hold, the union line started to break and the Yankees gave up the fight. They ran toward the stone bridge some four miles away knowing it was the only escape route from the battle. Once the word had spread through the ranks about the bridge there was no stopping the chaos. Panic swept the soldiers like the plague and the fleeing had begun.

The small stone bridge became so crowded with blue uniforms that the union men were literally fighting one another to cross first. Still the gunfire didn't stop; bullets and cannon shells rained down on the Yankees that were trying to escape. There was now no military command, only fear running through the entire army and it was every man for himself.

McPhail and Ben Brown's bravery had now enhanced and both began chasing four of the Federals onto the bank of Bull Creek.

At the top of their lungs they kept yelling rebel cries hoping it would scare the hell out of the blue coats, but in fact they probably were trying to build up their own courage.

Within minutes the two Confederates had closed the gap and now the Yankees were but a short distance in front of them.

"Ha, now we have them!" John said to Ben.

Truth was, the blue coats probably just wanted to get away from the major engagement rather than running from the two southerners.

Even so, the loud rebel yells that John and Ben were making didn't do much for their own morale. Mainly because the two Texans were just as frightened of the large battle as the northern soldiers were that was fleeing in front of them.

Now their mouths were getting very dry from breathing hard as they ran and they were beginning to wonder just what they would do if they did caught the four. Both were hoping that their adversaries' guns were empty so they could capture the union soldiers and bring them back like heroes.

Surely they had won and now they were going to return with prisoners to receive a "well done" from their superiors.

They had become seasoned warriors in one battle, but had no thought that the tide could turn on them as they chased the Yankees. They were soon to find that events could change as rapidly as it had occurred, with the hunted becoming the hunter.

The Yankees ran into a large patch of bushes and quickly began reloading their rifles so that they might ambush the pursuing men. In record time the blue coats had reloaded and now were waiting in ambush for the two rebels. They took careful aim at the two pursuing gray coats and began to squeeze off their shot, but before the weapon was discharged fate was about to take hold of the situation. The Union men were finding out first hand that they were not alone.

Wasps seemed to come from everywhere, stinging the soldiers head to toe causing the blue coats to dance around like Indians on the warpath. Some had their weapons go off harmlessly in the air and others threw their rifles away as they danced around trying to evade the flying insects.

McPhail and Brown ran headlong into the federals and they too, were covered immediately by the stinging wasps. Now all six of the soldiers began swinging their arms around wildly, throwing away pistols and rifles.

Finally with no place else to go, the whole group threw themselves into the muddy water of the creek to allude the winged pests.

The Yankees were first to emerge out of the creek and pull themselves onto the far bank. Exhausted and in full frustration they stood there soaking wet and covered with painful sting marks with no fight left in any of them.

Brown was out of the creek before his buddy and he reached back to help McPhail but was keeping his eye on the blue coats. Just as he grabbed John's hand to help him out, he suddenly screamed and drew back in horror from the pain inflicted on his leg.

A skunk that was foaming at the mouth had bitten him on the calf, below his knee. From the looks of the animal there was no question that it was mad. The skunk's body was embedded deep in the mud right next to Brown and no more than half of the creatures body was above ground. Teeth marks on the log next to the skunk showed positive signs that he was dying a slow agonizing death.

One of the Yankees saw the vicious attack and pulled a bayonet from his backpack and then moved towards Brown in a threatening manner. The blue coat passed right by the southerner and attacked the mad skunk, killing it with one thrust. Ben had seen the man coming and closed his eyes trying to say a little prayer, but when nothing happened he carefully look up just in time to see the man pull the long knife out of the skunk's body and back off.

For a long moment the Yankees stood on the bank staring at Brown and his dreadful predicament. There was no question, they knew that this rebel was a dead man and useless as a soldier now.

McPhail pulled himself from the creek keeping his eye on the Yankee that was holding the bayonet in his hand. He stood up in the shallow part of the water afraid that the fight would continue, but the union soldier just shook his head in pity as he stared at Brown. Then he turned to face McPhail.

"You rebs got you're problems now." He said. "Help your buddy if you can and we'll leave you be, cause that skunk done more to hurt you than we could have."

With that the union soldier motioned to the others and all four began walking in the direction of the stone bridge, but kept looking back at the rebels with a sense of pity.

McPhail fell back into a setting position in the mud almost in a daze. He was soaked to the skin and still trying to catch his breath. He had never been so scared in his life and felt grateful to the blue coat for not running that mean looking bayonet through him.

Benjamin held on tight to the leg that had been bit and came dangerously close to crying because of the pain.

"Damn skunk was rabid." He said. "I had to jump into the water right where that stinking animal was trapped. I'll be foaming at the mouth fore' long and ain't got a chance in hell. Say good by to me John, I'm as good as a dead man."

McPhail seemed to be ignoring his buddy. He was busy looking around, obviously searching for something he had lost.

"Where'd I drop my knapsack?" He said while trying his best to get some of the mud off his uniform.

"Its got my Madstone, I had it when the wasps got us."

At that moment his eyes fell upon the knapsack on the far bank lying where he had entered the water. Without hesitation he slid back into the creek and swam across retrieving the worn bag, being very careful not to disturb the not-so-happy insects.

The battle seemed to be over but the sound of firing from different areas of the hills could still be heard by the two Confederates. All the shots were coming a fair distance off so the boys were mostly ignoring them.

By now McPhail was totally exhausted and threw himself onto the creek bed next to Brown.

"I've got to go back to the old Henry Hill farm for some milk." John said. "I need it to make my Madstone work. I'll try and find a couple of dry blankets and something to eat while I'm there. You get some those twigs over there and strike a fire, so I can warm the milk when I get back and make it easier for me to find you in the darkness."

Once again John found the strength to swim the muddy creek and move off towards the farmhouse in the distance. Soon he had vanished into the night and Brown was left alone.

Ben began picking up twigs for a fire but was muttering under his breath the whole time.

"More'd likely it'll be them Yankees that find me in the darkness." He said with his eyes staring into the night. "I'll probably be shot in my sleep or ran over by some blue coat's horse, or something worse.

"Make a fire, Ben,...I'll find you in the darkness Ben." He continued whispering in a synthetic voice.

"Make a fire and I'll be back shortly." He kept whispering again and again to himself mimicking John.

Even so, he still continued preparing a fire but stared constantly in one direction and then the other hoping that no Yankee troops would stumble onto his location. Each time he made one of his silly comments he would lower his voice just a bit more, afraid that someone would overhear him. After all, this was a very scary place to be.

By now the sun had set completely and McPhail was stumbling in the darkness trying to make sure no one took a shot at him. He was hoping to see the silhouette of the farmhouse against the pale light of the sky so that he might get his bearings.

Working his way to the barn had been no easy matter, but the ragged and dirty soldier finally made it to the entrance. He took a moment to check out the area but saw and heard no one. Then he pushed the large barn door out of his way but still used caution to ensure he was alone. He strained his eyes trying to adjust for the darkness until he could tell just what was in the barn.

Out of the darkness of the barn he heard a noise and knew something was moving around on the floor. He trained his eyes on the spot where the noise was coming from, then he saw it. Lying on the straw covered ground were dozens of animals that were dead or dying.

There was no question that the gunfire and cannon balls had done their job well during the battle. The southerner took one more quick look around and then began checking each of the cows to see if there was hope of finding one alive.

He went from one animal to another until he saw movement once again coming from one of the stalls. There lying on her side was a wounded cow that had taken a musket ball but was still alive. Without wasting time, he began milking her just as she lay, catching the milk in his canteen and talking to her in a soft voice, hoping she would not die.

He had no idea if you could milk a dead cow, and on top of that he had never milked a cow while the animal lay on its side. The rebel tried to shake off any more thoughts of what could be, but his mind was racing almost out of control.

"There'd always a first time for everything." He said to himself. "Here I am in the middle of a bloody war milking a dying cow. What in the hell will I be doing next?"

When he had finished, the veteran of one major battle stood up and looked into the canteen to see how much he had gotten from the cow.

"I didn't get much milk." McPhail thought as he finished. "Only half the canteen, but it'll have to do."

John slipped out of the barn and began working his way through the darkness to Brown. He stopped every few minutes to hide behind one object or another. Then he came to an overturned union wagon and hunched down behind it to see if the coast was still clear. Before he could move on something made a noise inside the covered wagon. He could barely make out anything in the darkness inside that shot up wagon.

Then his hand touched something that moved and that's when he saw the two chickens tied to the rib that held the cover over the wagon. They immediately moved away from him towards the back of the wagon but their legs were tied with a small rope and they could go no further.

What a break! McPhail thought. They would make a fine meal and he wasn't about to pass that up. He couldn't wait to crawl all the way inside the dark wagon and head straight for the chickens.

Again he strained his eyes for any movement that could be hostile. He placed one hand after the other feeling his way through the darkness until he suddenly touched the body of a dead soldier and drew back in horror.

He slid himself a few feet away only to get another shock when he found himself touching a second body.

Now he looked down to see two dead union soldiers staring out into space and he was right on top of them.

He screamed out loud like a little boy having a nightmare and it took him a full minute to calm his nerves and get himself under control.

Then his eyes began to reveal much more in the darkness. The wagon was full of supplies and goods that he could use. There were uniform pants, shirts, blankets, tobacco, and yes even two live chickens that were still tied to one of the rails. He had found a bonanza of food and clothes and would make the most out of it.

With arms as full as he could make them, he backed out of the vehicle and again headed toward the fire he could barely make out in the distance.

The young rebel moved faster now and in the process tripped over bodies and fell into potholes that had been made by the canon fire. The field was a nightmare of battle scars and it was like he was finding all of them.

Finally he could really make out the creek and Ben's fire in the darkness but by now he was so tired even the chickens felt heavy.

He stopped for a moment and tied a strip of cloth around their legs and hung the birds on either side of his neck so that he might carry them with less stress. So tired was he now the rebel was whispering strange things to the two fowl hanging around his neck.

"Ain't got no dumplings, but that's all right, roasted chicken be tasty tonight." He chanted to himself.

The fire had helped McPhail find his buddy in the darkness, but he knew it would also help any enemy that might be in the area find them. He had no idea where the battle lines where now and couldn't help but look over his shoulder time and again. Once again he crossed the creek and stood by Ben's fire.

He dropped the chickens on the ground right next to Ben and grabbed a blanket to pull over his shoulders. The night wind made him shiver and the cold water of the creek didn't help any either. He picked out two sticks with a "V" branch and slid closer to the fire and stuck them in the ground on either side of the flames. By now he had decided it was better to keep the fire and take a chance of being seen rather than freezing through the cold night.

He pulled out his gun ram from his rifle and tied it between the two sticks and hung his canteen from it so that it would hang directly over the fire. He then poured the small amount of milk into the canteen and laid himself against a tree to wait for it to warm up.

The rebel picked up his knapsack and took something from it that was carefully wrapped in paper. He unwrapped the object and dropped it into a pan he had placed on the ground next to the fire. He was about to use his Madstone on Brown but first he had to prepare the agate so that it might do it's job. He carefully poured the hot milk over the healing stone and waited.

Seemingly like magic the stone began turning white, giving off a shining phosphorescence light in the darkness as Ben watched in amazement.

His face lit up with a pale green glow from the reflection of the stone causing a strange eerie look to cover his hair and eyes like never before. Ben tried to question McPhail about the stone but he simply was ignored by his tired buddy.

Now John's face took on a crooked smile as he removed the hot stone from the pan and placed it on Brown's leg over the bite marks. It clung tight to the wound even before he tied the rag around the injury. The rag would help keep the agate in place as it did its job but probably wasn't necessary.

Brown screamed out loud from the pain when the hot stone touched his skin and quickly John covered his buddys' mouth with his hand.

"Quiet you idiot." McPhail said. "There may be Yankee's close by!"

"Damn, that's hot!" Ben yelled out. "What the hell is it anyway?"

"Wait a bit" John replied, as he lay his head on the knapsack shaking from the cold wet clothes. "You'll see. It's a Madstone," McPhail wrapped the blanket tighter around his shoulders trying to better warm himself and at the same time made a temporary bed.

"It'll take some time to work, but will save you from that skunk." He told his buddy.

Now completely exhausted, John fell dead asleep in the blink of an eye. He was so tired, the rebel private had given no thought of the danger that the fire presented in the darkness. It could be easily seen from quite a distance and he had meant to go ahead and put it out but the cold and his exhaustion had flawed his caution.

An hour passed and the phosphorescent light got brighter turning to a darker green. Brown sat there staring at the stone intently as John slept. For the life of him he couldn't figure out what the hell he was doing with a rock tied to his leg.

Finally the rebel could feel the stone let go of the flesh where the bite marks were and fall gently into the rag surrounding the injury. He touched it with his fingers and it began to make him feel even more uncomfortable.

"John, you awake?" he said, "What do I do now?"

McPhail awoke feeling half drugged from being so tired. He pushed his rebel hat to the back of his head and bend over to untie the rag. The stone fell off Ben's leg into McPhail's hand when he pulled the knot free and the warm agate touched John's hand feeling almost as if it were alive.

The stone throbbed against his flesh and he was sure it had done its job. Again he turned to place the stone back into the milk knowing that any poison would flow out of the rock into the white liquid. He knew that the agate would be ready to be used again shortly.

John watched the rock fall through the air and it was almost like slow motion as it fell towards the liquid. Time for him seemed to slow down to a standstill.

In his eyes the beautiful stone was moving at a very slow pace as it fell towards the milk. He was so transfixed on the Madstone falling towards the bucket that it seemed to be floating down through the air towards the milk like a slow motion picture movie playing out a scene.

His eyes may have been transfixed on the falling agate, but his mind was flashing back to a happier time in his young life.

His thoughts were of a part of his life from long ago. A part that had happened in Marshall County, Mississippi when he was a very young boy. A fun part when he had no cares but to fish the river and hunt deer with his father. His memory brought back the day of his first kill of a large albino deer that had a rack of eight points.

In his dream of those happy days, the soldier now wished he was a young teenager again. He could clearly see himself gutting the buck, and finding a large piece of sinew in the animal's stomach. He Cut the sinew open, and discovered a stone the size of a small hen's egg and marveled over his discovery.

His father had no idea whether the stone was a Madstone or not, so John kept the odd looking rock until he could show it to several of his neighbors by their farm. Sure enough, one of the farmers recognized it as a real Madstone and told him of its value and how to use it to suck the poison from bites of rabid dogs and venomous snakes.

The farmer told young McPhail that very few were ever found and that he was lucky to find the valuable stone. Although it would be years before he knew it, the stone would change his life and he would carry it with him always.

John carried the stone around his neck in a leather pouch, very proud of his magic agate. His wait for a time that he could use it in an emergency was short-lived. A cow on old man Roberts' farm about a mile from their place was bitten by a rabid coyote.

The young boy wasted no time in riding to the farmer's place to let the old man use his stone. He had been told how the stone worked and the two of them treated the cow. It was not long before the milk cow had recovered nicely. For his help, the man paid John ten dollars and gave his thanks.

Word quickly spread across the County and the Scotsman's services were called for by the farm people on many occasions.

McPhail treated a great deal of injuries for the people of Houston County, ranging from farmers with snakebites to goats having infections. It seemed that using the marvelous stone always made it better either in reality or just the mental thought that it had done some good. Every time he took the stone from his leather pouch it made him feel important. It was almost like the stone carried a great deal of magic.

The young boy felt in awe when he would look at the grayish stone, which was quite porous and had veins running across the surface. Nothing else gave him a thrill like this. He was on top of the world being the only one, for God knows how far, that had a real Madstone.

When John would handle it, small beads of moisture appeared because it would absorb perspiration from his hands. He would demonstrate this remarkable feat at the Saturday swap meet in the square. Without exception the stone always caused perspiration to appear whenever he held it.

Before the development of the Pasteur treatment in 1885, the Madstone was widely accepted, not only in America, but also throughout the world as the only hope of survival from the dreaded rabies bite.

Madstones were very rare and when John moved from Mississippi back to Texas several years later, the people begged him to sell the Madstone and not carry it from Marshall. The whole town made up a purse of several thousand dollars to purchase the agate but the young Scotsman refused to sell. His answer was that the stone should never leave the possession of the McPhail family.

In route back to Texas, John met an Englishman by the name of Joseph White, traveling north from New Orleans. In those days, people in the Louisiana Territory built small hunting cabins along the trails so that travelers would have a place to rest. McPhail and White had ridden up to one of the cabins almost at the same time.

They looked at one another waiting to see what the other would do until finally McPhail slung his leg across his saddle horn to better face the stranger.

"The sign on the door says it's opened to all." said John "Want to share it for the night"?

"Better than sleeping on the ground," was the Englishman's reply, as he too threw his leg over the saddle horn and slid to the ground.

John dismounted and retrieved his rifle from the saddle making sure the weapon was pointed towards the ground to show he was not hostile. He had carefully checked out the gentleman while the two talked and hadn't seen any sign at all of a weapon.

"I'm John McPhail, headed for Texas, and you've got to be an Englishman from the looks of your clothes." he replied.

"Quite right," said the Englishman as he dusted his clothes with a pair of gloves he had just removed from his hands.

"But you wouldn't be Madstone McPhail by chance, would you? I've heard a bit about you down in New Orleans. There's talk you saved a child from a cottonmouth last spring."

Before John could reply, the excited Englishman continued.

"I'm from London and we know about Madstones; about the only people that can afford them are the very rich. Mostly members of the royal family or such. Even in the paintings of the kings and queens from the olden days that are hanging in Buckingham Palace, a chap can see a small leather pouch hanging around the neck of the royal person in the picture. Most people don't know that the leather pouch contained a Madstone that they carried for protection against bites from wild animals. This was very common for hundreds of years in my country. However we find the stones only in the heads of certain toads and in England it's like finding a very large unusual diamond.

Even Shakespeare was referring to a Madstone when he wrote the play "As You Like IT," He said. "I think it went like this; sweet are the uses of adversity, which like the toad, ugly and venomous, wears yet a precious jewel in it's head."

"Yep" said John, as he pulled the stone from it's leather pouch with pride. "It's a jewel, all right."

The Englishman's eye's goggled at the beautiful agate.

"That's worth a lot of money!" He said. "Want to sell it? I'll pay a handsome price in gold."

White reached for the stone with a greedy look in his eyes, but McPhail would have none of it and quickly closed his hand around the valuable agate.

Looking into the Englishman's eyes was enough to tell John not to trust this fancy dressed traveler any more than you would a sleeping rattler.

After John had refused to sell the magic stone, little else was said between the men as they prepared their beds for the night. Both tried not to make the other aware that he was watching his every move.

McPhail was dog tired and fell asleep almost immediately, unaware that the Briton planned to get up in the middle of the night and quietly steal his knapsack containing the stone. He had seen John put the stone in the sack and decided to relieve him of the burden of protecting it. After stealing it, his plan was to walk his horse a safe distance before riding off, thus he would keep from awakening the Scotsman.

The next morning McPhail began cooking his coffee, unnerved at the fact the bag was missing. He knew the Englishmen would try for the Madstone and while the man was not looking he had tied the leather pouch onto his boot during the night. The knapsack contained no more than some hardtack and a bag of dried rice.

"Hope he chokes on the jerky," thought McPhail when he realized the knapsack and Englishman was missing.

Now John's daydreaming of the Madstone find was coming to a close.

He wasn't quite sure what it was that suddenly interrupted his daydreaming of the Madstone, but he sure felt a snap that brought him out of his trance and back to the real world of the battle of Manassas.

He set upright with a feeling in his gut that something was wrong. It was damn hard for him to put his finger on it, but he knew danger was near.

Suddenly a harsh cry rang out from the darkness and it certainly wasn't good news. It was the last thing that the two men wanted to hear.

"Surrender or die, Rebs!" The enemy sergeant yelled out.

Neither of the rebels were able to see very good past the glow of the campfire that had surely gave their position away. "What would a brave hero do in such a situation?" John asked himself.

For a second he thought about it and then he knew. "Hey, he would surrender rather than take a bullet." He told himself.

Trying not to make any sudden moves for fear of panicking their enemies, the confederates slowly raise their hands and remained in a setting position on the ground.

It was well that they did just that for a full company of federal soldiers had stumbled onto the two in the darkness while trying to find their own lines. The first blue coat to enter the camp was a burly sergeant who looked like an escapee from a gorilla cage.

"Take their weapons," the non-com ordered as he trained his rifle on the southerners at a very close range. The sergeant had barely gotten the order said before the entire company of Yankees made their way through the undergrowth and approached the warm fire. The union men searched the camp for the rebels' guns but found nothing.

John and Ben had been too busy trying to treat the skunk bite to worry about the lost rifles. They hadn't retrieved their weapons after crossing the creek, besides both were dead tired and simply didn't really care.

The big sergeant moved towards the fire still pointing his rifle at John's head. He was so intent on watching the two gray coats he hadn't seen the chickens being roasted over the fire. Now he turned his attention to the smell coming from the chickens cooking over the fire and he couldn't help but move towards the foul. He didn't brother to even offer his own men a part of the bounty.

The Yankee sergeant simply helped himself to the birds but quickly had to drop them to keep from burning his hands further. The non-com had been so hungry that reason had been taken over by his empty stomach and his reward turn out to be burned fingers.

Brown couldn't help himself, he laughed with delight until the rest of the company joined the sergeant. Now the two Confederates was completely surrounded by their enemies.

Ben didn't laugh for long; A Yankee soldier hit the rebel with the butt of his rifle slamming him face down in the dirt. For a change he was lucky, the blow hit his shoulder taking the blunt of the attack and it saved Brown from being seriously hurt. The sergeants' men seemed to get a kick out of him burning his hands, not to mention what it did to his pride.

"You Yankees need to learn a bit more manners." Brown said as he tried to keep his hands high in the air which wasn't easy when his face is almost buried in the dirt. He knew he best keep his hands out where they could be seen or they sure enough might shoot both of them.

Now it was McPhails' turn; there was no way he was going to resist making a comment to the union soldier. By this time he was so tired that fear was flat eluding him and he just had to say something about losing those little old stinking chickens. With a hungry look on his face and a really pissed off attitude at the birds being taken, he turned his body more towards the sergeant and straightened his back in defiance.

Without moving his eyes off the birds he was determined now to say something about his dinner that was about to disappear.

"Try not to make a pig out of yourself," He said.

"Lease you could do is share our stolen birds with us."

Again picking up the food, this time with rag in his hand, the sergeant snorted a few dirty words while motioning for his men to move out with their new prisoners. He just smiled a crooked smile at the two rebels and began to bite into the cooked birds.

Just a few hours before, the two rebels had been let go by some Yankee soldiers. Now they were being grabbed up and this time carried off to God only knows where. The union men didn't give the pair of southern boys a chance to say another word. The tough old Yankee sergeant ordered the men's hands tied behind them and their mouths covered to prevent them from crying out in case they ran across more rebel soldiers. He warned them what would happen if they tried to escape or make any noise.

Of course, he was trying to talk with a mouth full of roasted chicken which made it a bit more difficult; not to mention somewhat silly since hardly anyone knew what he was saying.

The blue coats shoved and pushed the two rebels with the butts of their rifles trying to make them move faster. They feared that the southern army just might be near at hand and in this darkness who could tell where the enemy was? Besides the fire was stupid and a dead giveaway on a black night like this, not far from a major battle site.

Hours passed as the group made their way through the thick underbrush, with John and Benjamin trying to find a way to break free without success. There seemed to be nowhere to run without catching a bullet in the back and the pair was being too closely watched for them to break free. Their bound hands were too well tied to free themselves so they had no choice but to move on following the union men.

The group came to the stone bridge that the union army had passed over earlier and one at a time they crossed with no difficulty. They ran in a crouched position to make sure that they were not being observed but with their hands tied, Ben and John had a hard time bending over far enough to do much good. Luckily they passed over the arc of the stone bridge without becoming targets.

The small group of Yankees and their prisoners headed in the direction of Washington and walked throughout the night following the dusty road trying to catch up with their outfit but were having little success. Tired and dirty the Scotsmen were continuously pushed before the union men.

As daybreak came, the rebels did indeed find that the Yankees had finally caught up with the union army. They were now among what looked like the whole United States Infantry.

Herded together with a few other southern prisoners, the order was given to immediately line up the rebels and march them north. Now the small batch of captives would learn that they were to be taken to a prisoner of war camp outside of Washington where they would be held for the duration of the war.

The Yankee guards kept the prisoners moving as much as possible, only allowing a couple of hours sleep beside the road. Mainly because the commander felt that they might be pursued by another battalion of rebels out of Virginia.

After the first break, McPhail awoke to the sounds of more union army men arriving to take charge of the prisoners. The new Yankee lieutenant in charge of the southerner's march north was Robert McWilliams; a Scotsman from Pennsylvania.

When he saw that Brown and McPhail had their hands tied behind them and their mouths covered with gags; he wasted no time in relieving them of their bonds. He had their hands untied and the gags removed but made sure they understood that any attempt to escape would result in their deaths. Then he quickly began to move the prisoners north again.

This union Scotsman was known as a very colorful officer because he sometimes wore a kilt with his blue army field jacket. Later he was almost court-martialed for refusing to remove it, but was granted special permission by General George B. McClelland, the overall commander of the union armies.

When the general was questioned about the extraordinary order permitting the break of protocol, his comment made it clear what he expected from his men.

"The day you fight like that Scotsman did at Bull Run, all of you can damn well dress like your mother for all I care."

Even though McWilliams and McPhail were from hostile armies, they immediately became friends during the trip to the Washington area. When the troops camped for the night, the two talked about Scotland and her beautiful countryside, with lasses that were known the world over for their beauty.

Although neither McPhail nor McWilliams had ever seen the Scottish countryside, their fathers had instilled a love for their homeland and both men were longing to see the birthplace of their ancestors. Before the night was over, it would create a bond between the two men.

On the night before arriving at the prisoner camp, the lieutenant came close to helping McPhail escape in the darkness. He had hinted at turning his back while McPhail slipped away, but John would not put the kind union man in jeopardy. He knew that the penalty for aiding the enemy could mean death to the Yankee Lieutenant and he could not live with the thought that this might happen.

"If you'll not take your freedom, then may I give you a shamrock from Ireland I've carried for good luck all these years?" McWilliams said quietly for fear the other guards might hear.

McWilliam's felt sorry for McPhail knowing he would not see him again after the prisoners were dropped off at the P.O.W. camp.

John too felt sad, as he placed the shamrock in the small leather pouch with his Madstone. In his mind, he was rating it almost as valuable as his magic stone.

The young lieutenant had given another Scotsman something that he cherished highly; to him it was almost more important than gold.

John felt more at ease with these guards as they continued on towards Washington, but couldn't help feeling bitter at the fact he had been captured during his first battle. It was downright humiliating and would be downgrading if it were not for the fact that another Scotsman was guarding him. Somehow in his mind, it made him feel better.

Years after the war, John would receive word that the kind Yankee officer had been killed at the battle of Antietam in the very first attack. He couldn't help but wonder about the lucky shamrock the Yankee had given him. What if the lieutenant had still been carrying his good luck charm that he had given to

McPhail. Could it be that he just might have survived that awful battle?

John would show his sons the Shamrock and tell them the story of the kind Yankee lieutenant when the boys were still in their teens. As the years passed the story grew to the point that McWilliams almost became a Saint.

Chapter 6

The Harper's Weekly on August 18, 1861, hit the streets of Washington with sketches of the capital made by S.C. Lowe from a balloon high in the air. Professor Lowe's pictures showed the unfinished capital dome, the long bridge across the Potomac and the incomplete shaft of the Washington Monument but downplayed stories of the war.

Little was printed about the two contending forces fighting in the hills of Virginia. The government quietly pressured anyone into silence that thought of the war as being a major confrontation. The bureaucrats would make sure that the disaster at Manassas was treated as if it were a minor affair. Knowing that the north had all of the manufacturing plants, and capable of producing far more weapons because of having the larger population, the northern leaders felt they could easily put down the rebels quickly and keep the publicity to a minimum.

They had no idea what really was coming. No idea that history would let the whole world see that this would become one of the most terrible wars ever fought.

President Lincoln was now faced with a situation that he could neither reverse nor stop. No other president of the U.S. before or since has faced such a terrible and complex problem as the one thrown on Lincoln.

He had no other choice, the war between the states had begun, so the chief executive ordered his top generals to the White house to gear up to a full wartime mode after the terrible losses at Bull Run. The President knew now that it was necessary to begin full production of war materials to win this war. The first battle had shown him that the war was far more than just a border skirmish as he had been told by his commanders.

He had been informed that it would be a short war and was assured that the rebellion could easily be put down quickly with the troops already at his disposal. Now the supreme commander knew different after the battle of Bull Run had been lost and he intended to make sure that it didn't happen again. At lease, he thought so.

Lincoln was conferring with his generals around the table in the east wing of the White house. He and his commanders were trying to sort out the mystifying and complex problems that they now faced.

Suddenly he was interrupted by the in-house maid bursting through the door without being announced. Her expression told him that something terrible had happened and it was all he could do to calm her down so that she might tell him what happen.

Obediently she walked towards him, with her hands on her stomach and half bent over as if she were bowing.

"Oh sir, "Master Tad" has been bitten by a dog and I think it's mad, I just didn't know what to do! No sir, I didn't know what to do!" She said in anguish.

Lincoln jumped to his feet with the generals following closely behind. They ran to the west wing door leading to the stables where a second maid stood pointing out at a small figure lying on the ground. Not fifty feet away was a horrific sight facing the president. His young son lay near a two-seat buggy with an angry growling dog brandishing his teeth at the boy. The animal's mouth was slobbering heavily and it was obvious he had just bitten the presidents son.

Several of the yard hands had been trying to reach the boy but had to end up hiding behind the buggy because they were afraid to come any closer to the young Lincoln. The dog was fierce looking and tried to attack anyone that approached.

General McDowell, following closely behind the President, drew his revolver and with one carefully aimed shot, killed the wild looking animal.

Two army privates patrolling the grounds arrived at the ready because of the gunfire but lowered their weapons at the sight of the general holstering his pistol.

They were ordered to immediately throw a blanket over the carcass and carefully tie a rope around the body of the dog so that it could be dragged away and buried deep with dispatch. Extreme caution was to the used, the soldiers were told, not to touch the animal in any way.

Lincoln felt as if a sickness had befallen him. He was filled with fear for the boy; for he knew well that there was no cure for rabies. He grabbed his son up into his arms not knowing exactly what to do. For the first time the President of the United States was on the verge of all out panic.

"Mr. President," said General McDowell. "While I was at the battle of Bull Run, my men captured two rebels on a muddy creek bank. One of the men had been bitten by a rabid skunk, but I heard he was healed by a stone the other gray coat had with him. Some of my officers were talking about it over dinner one night shortly after and I believe these men are in a prisoner of war camp not far from Washington. I don't know their names, only that one was called Madstone, a name for the agate he carried."

Lincoln stood holding the boy in his arms and looked at his top army commander with excitement. With possible hope now in his eyes, he gave the only command a father would give.

"Please send riders to the camp and find the man as quickly as you can general." The chief executive said. "My son's life may depend on it and I've no other place to turn too." With that said, he carried the boy into the mansion followed by his aides.

The president laid his son on a sofa in the conference room while the commander summed the captain of the guard to begin the search for the southern soldier.

The general's orders were quite strong and clear when he addressed them to the captain.

"Day or night, I don't care, bring the rebel called Madstone and do it as quickly as possible." He commanded in a voice that the captain had never heard before.

The officer gave a snappy salute to the general and moved so fast he was almost out the door before he acknowledge the order.

"Yes sir, I'll find him right away." He said.

The captain was almost in a dead run when he cleared the door and turned towards the corporal that was holding the horses. He knew that he best find this man called Madstone or his career would need a ton of rebuilding. When he reached the horses he stopped and turned back for moment to take a second look at the entrance of the executive mansion. A bolt of fear ran up his spine and he knew he had better be successful in finding the prisoner.

"Damn," he said out loud as he looked back. "We had better find that reb at the P.O.W. camp corporal, or we'll both be digging latrines tonight."

He quickly mounted his horse and pulled the reins hard right turning the animal around and began galloping off. He turned in the saddle and looked back at the gate to make sure that the two guards stayed put.

"You two stay here." he yelled out.

With that, he motioned his horse to move even faster making it hard for the corporal to keep up with him. Only twice did the pair slow down on the way to the prisoner of war camp and that was to ask directions. Still it took them over an

hour before they were dismounting at the main office of the
P.O.W. camp.

The union sergeant in charge of the prisoner of war camp
nearly fell on his face trying to come to attention as the captain
from Washington entered his office. He had never seen a
Captain with all the fancy do-dads on his uniform as this one
had.

"Sergeant!" The Captain commanded. "I come straight
from the general staff, with orders to find a rebel prisoner by
the name of Madstone. He's supposed to be here after being
captured at Bull Run. Do you know of him?"

"Madstone, sir?" asked the non-com in a heavy Boston
accent. "what kind of a stupid name is that?" He said still
trying to straighten his uniform.

The captain removed his hat and wiped sweat from the
brim before answering.

"All I know about this rebel is that we are to take him to the
Provost Marshals office in town and notify the White House as
soon as possible." He said, looking more serious now at the
sergeant.

The sergeant moved to the back of the room and pushed
open a rear door of the office leading to the confines, exposing
quite a group of southern prisoners to the captain's view.

"Been git'n more rebels alm'st every day since ta big battle
of Bull Run, cap't," said the sergeant. "better take a good look,
it's going to take a bit of doing."

"Get your butt started," was the captain's stiff reply, "and
find Madstone are you'll be peeling potatoes as a private, come
morning!"

Using good sense, by not replying to the order, the sergeant
commandeered four privates and a corporal yelling obscenities
and watching their every move as the five Yankees walked row

after row of the southerners, asking the same question again and again.

"You Madstone?" He bellowed out, with most of the rebels looking at him as though he were crazy. "Which of you rebs, called Madstone?" He finally yelled at the top of his voice.

Ben Brown shoved his hat to the back of his head and shook McPhail to wake him. They were setting on the ground with a long row of other prisoners trying to catch up on some of the sleep that they had lost in the forced march to the prison camp.

"John," he whispered, "I think that stupid Yankee sergeant is talking about you and he certainly doesn't look very happy!"

Without a word, McPhail arose to his feet and stared at the sergeant walking towards him. He caused the Yankee to respond angrily because now he was the only one standing but saying nothing.

"You the one they call Madstone, reb?" Said the blue coat trying not to let on that he had no idea what a Madstone was.

"I've been called that a couple of times before." Answered John, but to a Yankee like you, that's Mr. Madstone."

Now the sergeant begin to get mad and meaner as he shoved his face into McPhail's. He pulled his pistol out of the holster and shoved it into John's neck pulling the hammer back to the firing position.

"Move your butt reb." He ordered the southerner. "You're coming with me."

Benjamin jumped to his feet and shoved himself between the men looking the enemy non-com straight in the eye almost so close he could have kissed him.

"John don't go nowhere without me unless you take him by force." He said, meaning every word but scared right down to his toes.

The sergeant moved back and to the side a couple feet getting madder by the minute. He was about to retaliate against this arrogant rebel when he turned the gun towards Brown's face until he happened to look over Brown's shoulder. There behind them was the fancy dressed captain staring at him from the doorway impatiently waiting for his quarry.

For a moment he really didn't know what to do. Then the sergeant leaned over and whispered into Ben's ear.

"You'll be back and I'll be waiting to give you a good taste of my Yankee hospitality. Count on it."

He then pulled back the pistol and carefully let the hammer down and at the same time began yelling and shoving the prisoners towards his captain. He was now trying to make it look like he was doing his job quickly.

"This one's called Madstone Captain. The sergeant said. "He say's he would only go if his buddy goes with him. You want me to help you take them back?"

"No sergeant, I need to get back to the General. Take a couple of your men and walk the two to the Provost Marshals office right away and we'll meet you there." The captain responded.

"Yes Sir" The sergeant replied, watching the captain ride off on his fine mount.

The Yankee non-com said a few choice words while he tied both prisoners hands and moved them out on foot in the direction of the provost marshals office.

The lieutenant rode like the wind towards the White house to inform the general of his discovery and he was almost sure there would be a commendation in it for him.

The southerners were unaware of where they were going or why, but anything was preferable to the prisoner of war camp. Marching across the compound towards the provost marshal's office under heavy guard, John noticed a statue being erected with a large plain cement plate at the base.

He could see that it was to be a statue of a Yankee soldier with gun in hand. His curiousity was not to be ignored and it got the better of him.

"What ya putting up?" He asked as they walked past the structure.

The union sergeant looked at the confederate with contempt and gave his reply sticking his chest out a little farther at the fact that it was a statue of a Yankee soldier.

"That's going to honor our dead from the war." He said "All their names are being written on that plate at the bottom and it makes us damn proud. Since the war will be over shortly probably won't be many names to be put on there."

McPhail couldn't help it, he smiled with a little pride when he answered the union sergeant. He wasn't looking at the sergeant but rather at Ben Brown as he made the statement.

"Seems to me, Yankee, it's a tribute to southern marksmanship." The Scotsman said, exchanging smiles with Ben.

A dirty look was the sergeant's only reply. He reached over and took a rifle from one of the guards and hit John in the back with the butt of it trying to move him faster. It was not long after that the small group reached army headquarters.

There the two rebels were led to the provost marshal's office and thrown bodily into one corner of the room by the guards. Now it had become the sergeant's second chance; he kicked McPhail hard as he fell to the floor. At the same time the guards took positions on either side of the prisoners making sure they stayed put and caused no trouble.

McPhail felt severe pain when the non-com's boot hit his side, but he was determined to make no sound. He would not give the Yankee any pleasure from his act but wasn't sure what would be next.

The sergeant slid himself into a chair near the front door and pulled out a whiskey bottle hidden beneath his uniform coat. He took a gulp of the liquor just as he hear the sound of people arriving. The non-com jumped to his feet and quickly hid the bottle as best he could.

He turned his head to one side as if to hide his face and pulled an onion from his pocket. As fast as he could he took a bite hoping to cover the smell of the whiskey for fear of losing his stripes once again.

Unknown to the Yankee sergeant at the time, it would most likely be more than his stripes that would be in jeopardy. He hadn't a clue as to who was about to walk into the room, or why.

When Lincoln stepped through the door, Brown and McPhail could not believe their eyes. Without hesitation, both men jumped to their feet and came to attention, giving somewhat of a sloppy salute to show respect.

Closely behind Lincoln, General McDowell held the door as two privates carried the boy on a stretcher into the room. The president explained what had happened as young Tad was placed carefully on a table and John could see that he was burning up with fever. Enemy or not, McPhail wasted no time in ordering the sergeant to get some milk, while he began making a fire in the pot bellied stove centered in the middle of the room.

John quickly started getting ready to treat the young Lincoln and his sudden moves alarmed the guards. They charged towards him with their rifles at the ready, but the general waved his hand as a gesture to stop. Then he turned to the sergeant to show that he was backing McPhail in his quest to treat the boy.

"Bring the milk"! He commanded without an explanation for the unusual order.

The sergeant saluted the general and answered the order.

"Yes sir." He said.

When he opened his mouth the smell of onion reached the general's nostrils and it was obvious to the Yankee sergeant that he was never going to make lieutenant. Now he moved even faster to get out of the room and hopefully out of the mind of the General.

"I'll have it brought right away sir." The sergeant said, trying to turn his face away from the general as he ran out the door.

Again the healing stone was soaked in warm milk, but this time it was placed on the bite of the young Lincoln as McPhail gave his full attention to caring for the boy.

Benjamin watched with fascination recalling his own encounter with the rabid skunk at Manassas. He could only observe in amazement as Lincoln stood near the boy watching the now green stone fall off the wound to the floor.

McPhail carefully picked up the Madstone and returned it to the warm milk as he faced Lincoln to reassure him that the agate would surely work and that he had nothing to fear.

"It's green, Mr. President." John said, showing the stone to Lincoln. "That means your son should be as good as new in a few days."

Then John turned to step back from the boy but couldn't help but muttered to himself out loud.

"Probably better than I will in this place."

"Thank you, Mr. Madstone." The chief executive said with a sigh of relief. "I'd like to repay you in some way, but I could hardly give a medal to a confederate. Can you imagine what my men would do to me if they found out I had decorated a rebel soldier? However, I do have other privileges as president and can exercise them as I please. What's you're full name, soldier?" he asked McPhail.

John could hardly control his emotions as he replied with his full name wondering what the leader was about to do. He was actually talking with Lincoln and he couldn't decide whether he liked it or not. He had mixed emotions, after all he really was the enemy. None of the boys back home would ever believe him, not a one.

"Well, Mr. McPhail," The President said. "I can give you your freedom and I will do so provided I have your word you'll not fight against the union again from this day forward. While your at it, you just might give some serious thought to using that stone a lot more in the future. There's probably a great many people who could use your help, on both sides." Lincoln paused for a moment and scratched his ear while he waited for a reply.

McDowell had stood silently by throughout the treatment of the boy and seemed to have a wave of compassion after seeing what the southerners had done for the chief executive. He turned and walked over to a desk, pulling paper and pen from the top drawer and handed it to the president.

"He'll need a pardon to cross our lines," The general said. "I've ordered heavy pickets guarding the roads in and out of Washington and we've covered the area for miles."

Lincoln pulled the chair up to the desk and prepared to write, as McPhail looked on. The Scotsman was giving down home thought's to his situation and trying to decide just what to say. He was almost totally at loss for words until Brown nudged him on the shoulder reminding him he was not alone.

McPhail had to fight back his enormous emotions at the thought of being set free and he took a deep breath before answering. He was about to take a risk that could possibly make him lose his freedom that he was just now obtaining.

"I can't hardly pass up a chance to get out of this place, sir." John said pointing to Brown. "But only if my buddy can go with me"

The president turned from McPhail, and looked at Brown with a frown that slowly turned into a smile.

"Agreed." He said. Then the chief executive turned once more to finish writing the document and add another name to the paper.

The president completed the pardon and arose placing his hand on McPhail's shoulder looking straight at the union captain.

"See that these men are given five days rations and a fine horse each." He said. "Then have them escorted safely as far south as possible."

The captain turned to McPhail, making sure the southerner saw him staring into his eyes with contempt and disapproval. Speaking somewhat over his shoulder because he hadn't taken his eyes off of John, he responded with a question: "Weapons, too, Mr. President?"

Lincoln shot his answer back at the captain in a much stronger voice, making sure the officer understood the command.

"Return their weapons, captain. It's a very hostile world out there right now and I believe they should have a chance of survival."

"But Mr. President, these men are the...

The general interrupts the captain before he can complete his sentence.

"You have your orders captain." Said the general.

Knowing that he'd best not push it any further, the blue coat officer snapped to attention as he answered in a friendlier voice, "Yes Sir."

As the commander and chief left, McPhail stood there with his pardon in hand, knowing that he would long remember this day with a great deal of pride even if this president was considered the enemy.

Thomas Lincoln (called "Tad") was born on April 4,1853. When Abraham Lincoln saw that the tiny baby boy had an unusually large head he stated he looked like a tadpole and promptly gave his son the nickname of "Tad" which stuck with him for the rest of his life. In 1861 when the boy was eight the Lincoln family moved into the White House. There he and his brother would play pranks on the servants and anyone else that would be in the Executive Mansion at the time. Thomas was permitted to be outfitted with a Union officers uniform because of the times. He played the role well marching around the mansion having a good time upsetting the servants and staff. After the death of his father, Mary Lincoln and Tad sailed to Europe where they stayed for more than two years. Upon their return Tad fell ill and died on July 15,1871. He was buried with the remains of president Lincoln and his two brothers Eddie and Willie.

John and Ben rode quietly in front of their union escorts trying not to cause any trouble. The thought of being released gave them an exuberance beyond anything they had had in their lives before and they didn't want anything to go wrong with their soon to be freedom.

The two young rebels cleared the top of a small hill and rode right into an almost unbelievable sight smack dab in front of them. Coming straight at them was wagon load after wagon load of supplies that the Union Army had taken to the battle of Bull Run; the same battle where the two rebels had been captured. Both of the confederates stared at the huge amounts of foodstuffs piled high on the wagons and just couldn't believe their eyes.

They passed the mile long train of wagons and turned again and again in their saddles to look first one way and then the other at the union caravan. This continued until the train of wagons moved off in the distance behind them.

They looked at one another and then back at the last disappearing wagon and were at awe with the sight. Their thoughts were the same; the Southern Army couldn't provide anywhere near the huge amount of supplies that the union Army could.

Brown turned back in his saddle and again was looking south, the way they were headed. His eyes got bigger at yet another sight coming towards them. He almost couldn't get the words out that he was trying to say to McPhail.

He pointed at a sight that neither of the men was willing to believe.

"John, would you look at this? There's more supply wagons coming right at us. How many did these Yankees have anyway?" He said. There must be another hundred Yankee supply wagons headed back to Washington.

Brown, McPhail and the two former enemies began to slowly pass the wagons and almost immediately could see that they were not full of supplies. The sight of the wagons passing close by literally took the breath out of the four men.

"The wagons are bringing the dead back for burial." John said softly. "It must have taken all this time to clear the battlefield of the bodies."

Both men watched the covered wagons pass by one by one and again turned their own bodies in the saddle looking up and down the long line that stretched for god only knows how far. They certainly hadn't realized how many men had died at that battle until now.

The officers guarding John and Ben took a long look at the dead bodies passing by. It was a heart breaking sight; seeing wagon load after wagon load move slowly by the ex-prisoners.

Suddenly a union captain came riding out from between the wagons right in front of McPhails small group.

He pulled back on the reins causing the animal to walk slowly by.

Obviously this captain was in charge of all this sadness.

The Union Officer escorting McPhail recognizes the smart looking captain leading the wagons of the dead.

Hey John! Long time no see. Where in the world are you taking all those bodies?

Captain leading the bizarre caravan of bodies sits up tall in the saddle before he responds.

Robert, how you been? What you doing with those prisoners? You're headed the wrong way! P.O.W. camp is right outside Washington.

Robert: President cut these fellows loose from the prison camp. Gave them a full pardon because one of them helped his son. Where you going with those bodies?

We're heading straight to General Robert E. Lee's house the captain replied. And get this! That was the maddest Yankee General I ever saw. He ordered us to bury all these bodies in General Lees' front yard! All of them! He lost the battle of Bull Run and he lost his mind. I've never seen him so mad!

General Lee?.. of the Confederate Army? Replied the captain leading McPhail.
Union men in the front yard of a Southern General? I'll be damned. You're really going to make the South mad. You're kidding right?

Nope! He ordered us to bury them all and he meant it! Not only that, he is going to rename the place. From now on it's going to be (ARLINGTON NATIONAL CEMETERY)!

Arlington Cemetery became the United States national cemetery from that day forward.

General Robert E. Lee never returned to the home he had lived in for so long. Today it stands as a museum.

The home of the Commander of the Army of Northern Virginia
became Arlington National Cemetery.

General Robert E. Lee's home will forever be the resting place
of America's Honored dead.

The two union soldiers also were watching when they respectfully removed their caps and held them over their hearts in tribute to the passing dead.

When John saw this, he motioned to Brown to join him in doing the same. Slowly the four men rode by the wagon train with their caps held over their hearts quietly taking in the gruesome sight of all the union dead.

It was almost like moving in slow motion and the Yankee soldiers driving the horse drawn vehicles couldn't help but stare back at the two rebels being escorted. The sight of the two southern warriors probably made them wonder why the four were headed south. Finally as one of the drivers slowly passed by, he spoke up addressing the two union guards.

"Hay there, Capt'n, your going the wrong way. The P.O.W. camp is the other way!" He yelled out as his wagon went by.

The last wagon of the dead passed by and as it did McPhail looked back one more time watching the wagon train disappear in the distance.

"It's pretty late." He said to the Yankee captain. "Think they will try and bury them tonight?"

The captain answered John's question almost exactly the way he thought he would. Now John had a brilliant idea and he was pumping the guard for information.

"No Reb, they'll camp by the river back there tonight and carry the bodies on into town tomorrow for burial."

John looked at Ben with one of his strange smiles and immediately his buddy knew that the Scotsman had something up his sleeve. Ben knew he best not say anything while the blue coats were riding close behind so he would wait, until the proper time.

That time came only a couple of hours later. Without any warning, the two Yankee soldiers suddenly pulled their horses to a complete stop. They turned to the two rebels and said a few words of thanks for the help given to their commander and chief and then turned their horses north.

McPhail and Brown watched their escorts disappear in the distance without any further fanfare.

The union soldiers had returned their rifles as ordered but smiled strangely at them when they poured the powder and shot on the ground. They were going to make sure that the rifles could not be used quickly. The two rebels didn't bother to try retrieving the powder and shot immediately. They were too busy trying to believe what had happened to them in the last few days.

John understood the strange look Brown gave him; for he too was at a lost for words and it was totally unlike either to remain silent.

No matter what, no one would believe their crazy chain of events. It really wasn't important now, whether anyone did or not. They probably were listed as dead, or worse, as deserters.

Now McPhail revealed to his buddy just what it was he had up his sleeve. After explaining exactly the fool hardly plan he had in mind, Ben knew for sure that John had gone crazy. They would never get away with such a loco scheme, but in the end it was getting dark and they had only that night to pull it off.

After complaining bitterly Ben gave in to the nutty plan that McPhail had come with even though it was against his better judgment.

The two rebels turned their horses around and rode north once again. It only took a few hours before they caught up with the Yankee wagons train. Just as the union captain had said the first group with the supply wagons had camped near the river and the second group with the bodies some distance away. Neither group felt that it would be necessary to have anything but light security guards on picket duty for the night.

This made it simple for the two rebel soldiers to get close to the wagons that were full of union bodies. The darkness covered their movements as they tied their animals to a bush and quietly began removing uniforms from two of the bodies. It was fairly easy to go undetected inside a wagon filled with dead bodies.

The guards had no desire to be watching over cadavers and were very relaxed in their duties. After all, what idiot would want to steal a dead man?

Within a few moments the two Confederate's were wearing union uniforms and since they had been given union horses by the president for their trip, their saddles and blankets were also US issue. Never mind that the clothing had damage and blood on them. It was almost impossible anyway for the guards to see because of the dark, moon less night.

The men rode up to the second campground where the wagons of supplies were parked and approached the guard. The fires that the troops slept by gave some light but the night was so dark hardly anyone could make out anything other than the other mans uniform.

"Halt, who goes there?" Said the guard as the two approached.

"It's OK private." Said McPhail. "We've been sent to take two wagons to the hospital and they need the supplies tonight. That damn old Colonel Sanders ordered us to bring them back and he meant tonight or he would have our heads. Hope your C.O. treats you guys better than ours does"

Tired and fed up with guard duty the private showed that he could have cared less.

"Take those two over there, underneath that tree." He said pointing to several wagons parked under a tree with the horses nearby. "You probably won't disturb any of the guys that way and there's almost everything loaded in those."

Wasting no time, they waved an acknowledgment at the guard and rode over to the wagons to began hitching the horses up. Ben Brown was very nervous and sweating hard from fear as they hooked up the horses to the wagons.

Hell, there was a hundred Yankees sleeping all around them and they were foolish enough to be stealing wagon loads of supplies and the horses to go with them.

"Good God!" Brown thought to himself as he tried working faster to hooked up the animals. "I just know we'll be discovered and shot as spies."

"McPhail" He whispered to his buddy. "Do they hang a spy before giving him a last meal, cause I'm sure hungry.

The two rebels got the horses hooked up and ready to go in record time and tied their mounts to the rear of the wagons. Quietly as possible they climbed aboard the wagons and began moving out of the camp making sure they would pass the same guard.

"Thanks private." McPhail said riding right pass the guard. "Our wounded boys will sure remember you for this. By the way, what's your name?. You know,…so I can tell them who to write home about later."

The private walked slowly along with the wagons for a few minutes just knowing that he might become famous. Everybody would be talking about the soldier that saved a lot of his army buddies by sending much needed supplies when they needed them so badly. He couldn't help but answer McPhail who was driving the first supply wagon.

"Arnold Tomlin from Ohio." He said. "That's T.O.M.L.I.N.

The last of the spelling had McPhail waving good by with his hand out the side of the wagon as he moved off into the darkness. John couldn't help but answer softly to himself. "Thanks Arnold T.O.M.L.I.N...the Confederate Army sure appreciate your efforts."

By morning the two thieves and their wagons had made it to territory held by the southern army. They had ditched their union clothing and returned to Confederate gray just in time, for shortly ahead was a large camp of rebel troops that had pitched their tents beside the road. Without giving it a second thought the two pulled the wagons up to the officers' quarters and reported to an officer standing near a chuck wagon.

"McPhail and Brown bringing in supplies sir." John said. "We kind of found them by the side of the road and we figured that you might need them."

The officer took a long look at the Yankee wagon with the USA printed on the side and smiled at the two rebels. He then turned to a sergeant standing nearby.

"Sergeant, get these men some food. I think they have earned a good meal." He said.

John and Ben ate a full meal of beans and cornbread and then thanked the sergeant. They explained that they had to get back to their own outfit as quickly as possible and mounted the horses that the union men had given them. Although they were given a lot of hard looks by members of the camped regiment, the two had no trouble leaving.

Now they were riding through the Virginia hills that were turning to beautiful colors of orange, gold and red as autumn approached. The two southerners rode in silence until Brown couldn't contain it any longer. He threw one leg over his saddle in an attempt to get more comfortable and almost yelled it out.

"You going to do it, John? Really keep you're word to Lincoln about not fighting?"

"Yep," responded McPhail, "But we can still help the south. I promised not to fight, but I didn't say nothing about using the Madstone to take the poison out of infections. As a matter of fact President Lincoln himself suggested that I do just that. Use it to help more people. All we got to do is go from battle to battle and take the Madstone with us, but if we had a whole bunch of Madstones we could treat even more soldiers." He said.

"Hell, we'd be able to help a lot of guys all at once."

Brown acted puzzled at his statement of having many Madstones. "How you gon'a get a whole bunch of them stones?" He said. "You told me that only one comes along in a lifetime and as it worked out, we almost didn't even have that one lifetime."

John looked like a man struck with a brilliant idea as he sat upright in the saddle and buzzed with excitement at the thought that had just come to him. He could hardly wait to answer the question about the stones.

"Awhile back I heard of a Madstone found in the heads of frogs." McPhail replied. "It's called the Lee Penny; an Englishman told me about it. This'n different in size and shape but works almost the same. It's red and triangular and he said it cures all diseases for man or beast and particularly in cases of rabies. This stone's not used the same way, cause you don't need no milk.

Just dip it in warm water for an hour, and get them to drink some, then use a cloth soaked in it to rub over their body. Hell, even the Church of Scotland in the old days didn't condemn this cure or brand it as sorcery, like they did with a lot of them. Don't you see? All we got to do is go frog hunting."

"Damn" said Benjamin under his breath. "Now this crazy Scotsman gon'a have me frog'ng in the middle of the night. If

I had any sense, I'd ride plum out of here and take myself west, where there ain't no war and no Scotsman with nutty ideas."

The pair rode for hours with Brown mumbling to himself about being a fool to stay with John. Still he remained with his buddy even though he thought it was a bad idea. He tried to imagine what his companion would do to his reputation if he were to go along with his wild ideas. Yet, there was something telling him to stick with this crazy highlander no matter what. It probably was because he was lucky and Benjamin sure could use some of that luck, especially in a world gone mad.

Again and again his eyes shifted to John riding beside him and he looked at the newly released prisoner somewhat in awe and amazement. He couldn't imagine whether this guy was just lucky or blessed? At any rate, he had decided that he would stick close to his buddy for the time being...

Benjamin Davis Brown (left) and R. W. Hatch, an old friend and fellow veteran (right) at a reunion of Confederate Veterans in Mobile, Alabama. Benjamin Davis Brown lost his left arm during the Battle of Antietam in the "War Between the States."

Marriage License dated November, 1863 between Ben Brown and Mary
McPhail

Thomas poses for a child portrait.
Picture from the Lloyd Ostendorf Collection.

Thomas "Tad" Lincoln as a very young union soldier.
Picture from the Chicago Historical Society.

Thomas as a young teen.
Picture from the Lloyd Ostendorf Collection.

Thomas Lincoln (called Tad") was born on April 4, 1853. He was born with an unusually large head which President Lincoln thought made the tiny baby boy look like a tadpole. Abraham Lincoln gave his son the nickname of tad which stuck with him for the rest of his life.

In 1861 the boy was eight when the Lincoln family moved into the White House. There he and his brother would played pranks on the servants and anyone else that would be in the Executive Mansion at the time. Because of the Civil War he was permitted to be outfitted with a Union uniform of an army officer and he played the role well marching around the mansion having a good time upsetting the presidents servants and staff. After the death of his father, Mary Lincoln and Tad sailed to Europe where they stayed for more than two years. Upon their return Tad fell ill and died on July 15, 1871. The young Tad was just 18 years old. He was buried with the remains of President Lincoln and his two brothers Eddie and Willie.

Chapter 7

A small squad of rebel troops, dog tired, dragging their rifles, and looking a bit like the remains of the aftershock of an earthquake, were stopped dead in their tracks when they stumbled across the scene in front of them.

Here in the middle of the Virginia woods, sat McPhail and Brown on either side of a tree stump, up to their shins in dead frogs. The scene was so bizarre even the southern farmers turned fighters were amazed. Two of the southerners began gagging while a third threw up all over his blanket roll tied across his chest.

All of the gray coats wasted no time in making a fast retreat from the two crazies and the vision of these men cutting the heads of frogs open. Surely these two had to be completely mad, cutting into the brains of reptiles to examine them. They must have totally lost their minds because of the war and they wanted no part of a couple of sicko's.

McPhail, with frog in hand stood up and threw the green reptile over his shoulder while trying to wake up a leg that had fallen a sleep.

"That's it." He told Brown, "Not one had a Madstone! Must be a special frog in a special place that carries the agate."

Brown too threw a frog to the ground as he responded to the crazy highlander, "Or a smart frog in a smart place." He said, "What do we do now, check snakes to see if they have the stones in their guts?"

McPhail tried to wipe off the smell of frog using his shirttail, but had little success. He smelled of his shirt and made a face, wondering how long it would be before the stink wore off.

"Boy, that's bad" he said, "won't do that ever again. Well anyway, we still got my stone, so we'll see how we can help General Lee treat our wounded boys."

John tried washing his hands in a small puddle of water next to the tree stump but had little success.

"We best leave now, while we still got plenty of daylight." He said.

Brown looked down at the huge pile of dead frogs as he pulled the reins and motioned his horse forward.

"Damn, at least we could have picked the kind to have frog legs for dinner tonight" He snapped.

Brown and McPhail rode across the Virginia countryside in search of sick and wounded southern soldiers after they had decided this would be their new calling. It never occurred to either one that they should return to their regiment, for technically they could now be considered deserters.

After all, in their minds they were still helping the south and were now looking to help the casualties after a battle and this meant that their personal honor would remain in tact. They had no idea that they were to become just about the first full time medics in the history of the United States.

In October of 1861, they reached Balls Bluff, a Potomac landmark near Leesburg, but neither John nor Ben really knew exactly where they were. The pair had more or less been wandering around just trying to find a battle so that they might begin practicing their new vocational skills.

As night begin to fall McPhail found a fine camping site next to a running stream with an old stone fence nearby. It was a particularly dark night but John felt his way along the fence until he found a level place to lay his blanket.

The wind was blowing pretty hard so the new medic placed the top of his head right next to the fence so that it would block the cool air. Brown slept with his face towards the stones of the fence, burrowing his entire body under the blanket like a mole. The pair had heard and seen nothing but a few coyotes howling to their mates off in the distance.

As daylight broke, Benjamin was the first to wake, raising his body up by grabbing the top of what was left of the stone fence. As he did so his vision cleared the top of the wall revealing hundreds of confederate soldiers hiding in the grass, obviously waiting in ambush.

The southerners had no idea that they had bedded down near an entire regiment of rebels because they had seen no campfires and heard no noise the night before. They had been so totally exhausted that the only thing that was crossing their mind was sleep. The two confederates had rolled up into their blankets early on and slept like babies right through the night.

So tired were they, the whole rebel army could have walked right over the top of them and they probably wouldn't have even noticed.

Ben Brown peered over the stone wall marveled at how quiet the hidden soldiers were until he sensed a movement on the other side of the stones. It suddenly dawned on him that others were hiding right behind the other side of the fence that he was now leaning on. They were so close he could reach out and touch them, …a lot of them!

He didn't know exactly why his voice seemed to crack with fear when the called to his buddy, but it did.

"McPhail, uh, McPhail, I think we've got a problem." Said Brown just as the barrel of a 44-40 musket stuck through a hole in the fence punching him in the crotch.

"You'd better wake up right now and I do mean now!" He said kicking his traveling partner in the butt.

McPhail set up with a jerk at Ben's boot hitting him in the butt. "Hay, what the hell you think your doing? He yelled out.

"Quiet down!" A voice whispered out of nowhere.

Still half a sleep John rolled over and sat upright looking straight ahead.

With his back still towards Brown he was looking in the opposite direction of the confederates but thought that was the direction Brown was observing and so excited about. Then he saw what he thought Ben was looking at.

About 1,000 yards out, was a column of union soldiers moving directly across his path.

"Hot damn!" McPhail said. "Sure wish old Stonewall was here right now; he would give them what for."

Brown heard the sound of a bolt being cocked back to the firing position causing him to look down at the barrel pointing directly between his legs.

"Better worry about this stone wall." He said. "We're about to get our own…What For." Just then another rebel peered over the fence holding a very large caliber pistol.

McPhail's attention turned to the sounds behind him. He certainly knew what the sound of a pistol being cocked to the firing position was.

Without turning around he reached slowly for his musket lying next to his side, but the cocking sound of a second pistol closed the door on any more of his movements. John could only think of one thing to do as his eyes fell upon the gray uniform and the pistol aimed directly at his head. In a weak voice he began singing.

"Oh, I wish I was in the land of cotton."

At that very moment explosions from southern cannons firing interrupted his song. Waves of confederate soldiers began jumping the stone wall making with their rebel yells and charging towards the union troops sensing an immediate and decisive victory.

Cannonballs began to explode all around them causing so much havoc that the rebels no longer paid any heed to Brown and McPhail, but instead joined the attack on the blue coats.

This was their chance; McPhail and Brown bolted to their feet and begin running in a crouched position trying to hide behind the stone fence. The same fence that had holes large enough to drive a wagon through and certainly wasn't hiding these men from the bullets that were now flying from the battle.

Now enormous amount of bullets were striking all around them and the little mini balls were flying through the air almost to the point of cutting down anything that was more than four feet tall.

"Move feet, move!" John yelled out. "Mama didn't give me two of you for nothing!

Ben beat McPhail to the top of a large hill only by seconds and dropped his body down into the tall grass. McPhail was right behind and wasted no time letting his body slide into the same grass.

Now out of breath both men rolled over and looked down at the battle overwhelmed with emotion when they saw the killing that was going on.

"Damn," Ben said. "Look at the slaughter. Would you look at that slaughter"

The tremendous roar, black smoke, and flashes from the discharge of so many rifles, was sending hundreds of warriors into eternity; some wouldn't even have a body to leave behind because of the huge explosions tearing their torsos into small pieces.

Then something suddenly came to McPhail. He realized that they were in such a hurry to get out of there, they had left their horses behind.

Confusion was all around them as he yelled out about retrieving their lost animals. He Strained his eyes to see through the heavy smoke flowing across the battlefield and even shook his head trying to focus in on his horse.

"When the fighting lets up, we'll go back after them." John said.

"I don't think so John." Brown said pointing in the direction that they had just come from. "Look over there beside those trees, there's your horse."

McPhail turned just in time to see his mare catch a stray bullet and fall on her front legs in a kneeling position. Then she slowly rolled over on her side and played dead.

"Oh hell!" He said. "I've started off a lot of days that were much better than this one! This has got to be one of my worst!"

"Well," said Brown, "you wanted to find wounded, take a look, you've found it. Boy, did you find it."

The battle raged on throughout the day, with the two southerners looking on from a safe distance. Fear raced through their bodies as they watched men being cut to pieces before their eyes. The two rebels tried not to show that they were like scared animals as they lay in the grass and watched from either side of a large tree at the sight of the bloody confrontation.

The Army of the Potomac had been completely surprised by the devastating fire coming from the advancing rebs and took precious time responding to the attack. The ambush had been successful for the south but also costly in the end for they had more casualties than had been expected in the surprise attack.

(The "Balls Bluff Disaster" as it was later called was to be the final action in Virginia in 1861. The ambush cost the Federals dearly with the loss of over nine hundred men, including an Oregon senator named Edward Baker, a close friend of Lincoln's. Baker had obtained a commission as colonel in the union army, but he was no soldier and had led his men into a situation that offered no retreat should things go wrong. The Virginians and Mississippians were concealed in the woods on higher ground and created a disaster for the Union Army.

As it began to get dark the battle had come to an end. The Yankees moved their regiment off into a wooded area to lick their wounds. The blue coats had suffered such casualties that it would be impossible to organize into a fighting force for sometime.

Brown and McPhail tried to rest under the tree in the soft grass, but throughout the night occasional gunfire could be heard. This coupled with the crying sounds of the wounded made sleeping almost impossible.

Fear more than anything else made them stay put; men were getting shot in the darkness and chances are it could be one of them. It was almost impossible to recognize anyone in the pitch black of the overcast night.

The Yankees and rebels both had posted snipers behind as they withdrew to protect their rear from sudden attack, and anything that moved was fair game.

The two shivering rebels lay side by side in the grass wishing for their blankets that had been left behind. Hours passed before the men built up enough courage to light a small fire, but they made sure it was encircled with stones so it would be difficult to see from a distance.

Soon after they heard a noise coming towards them; Benjamin grabbed a rifle that had been left behind by a dead Yankee. Checking the weapon to make sure it was ready to fire, he quietly rolled over on his belly and prepared to fire at whatever came out of the woods.

John hoped it wouldn't be a Yankee who would be hell bent on starting a fight; he hadn't forgot his promise to the president that he would fight no more but what would he do if the shooting came their way?

Both of the southerners bent their ears towards the noise that was heading their way. Louder and louder it grew indicating it was getting closer and closer causing a wave of anxiety to roll over the two men.

Brown cocked the hammer back on the musket, then used the sleeve on his arm to wiped sweat from his forehead. He stared into the night trying to see what they were about to face but wasn't having much luck.

McPhail had lost his weapon along the fence when they were running and really didn't want to find another, so he slid his body into a patch of high grass that was behind a tree.

His emotions were so mixed up he really wasn't sure that he could or would fight anyway.

Brown waited until the sound was very close before he challenged with an order to come out or be shot.

"HALT, WHO GOES THERE? SPEAK UP OR BE SHOT!" He said. Again he strained his eyes to try and see what was making the noise but it was just too dark.

Now his nerves were getting the best of him, but he was determined to stop this intruder. Again he gave the order to step forward while trying to cock a hammer back on the musket which had already been placed in the firing position.

For a very long moment the two watched in silence at the darkness but still no response came from the direction of the noise. Then all of a sudden a very weary cavalry officer's horse broke out of the bushes and wandered up to warm herself by the fire.

Both of the men fell back on the ground and sighed with relief at the sight of the animal. Then they jumped up to check the saddlebags hoping they would find some food, any food.

Unfortunately the weary men found nothing to eat but were able to share the rolled up blanket on the back of the saddle.

The wool blanket felt great but was hardly large enough to cover both men and the rest of the night was spent with each trying to get more than their share.

Somehow during the night the horse managed to slip away from the bush Ben had tied him to and vanish into the woods, so once again they had no horse between them.

With dawn breaking, the two men made their way back to the battle area, surveying the terrain and jumping behind rocks, dead horses, and trees to make sure neither would become a target.

By now the major battle was over, but left behind was a desperate scene and of course a few snipers who were playing deadly games with any stragglers.

They found some rations to eat as they made their way through the battlefield but had a difficult time eating it because of the horrible sight of torn bodies every where. There was no getting away from all the madness that lay around the two men. The horrible sights caused them to stop and stare almost like they were in a state of a terrible dream, but they were awake and this was no dream. It seemed that the whole world was dead, dying or injured.

Again and again they looked but still the same picture lay before the two men. Hundreds of bodies lay everywhere, with some of the corpses still holding onto their opponent as if they were continuing to fight hand to hand.

Then they saw something that they hoped wasn't a mirage. At one end of the huge battlefield they could see personnel erecting tents and placing blankets on the ground for the wounded that was being brought in.

A makeshift hospital were being set up under some trees and out in the open because there were not nearly enough tents for so many fallen soldiers.

Some of the soldiers were helping carry the wounded to the location and laying them on the ground side by side while a doctor moved from one to the other treating each as fast as he could.

It took only one look for each to acknowledged that this was where they belonged. Not a word had been spoken between the two men but they knew that it was time to move down the hill towards the holy mess. They would join up the few nurses that had arrived and the surgeon to do what they could to help.

Now they were right in the middle of their new calling, tending the fallen personally as they lay on the ground. They would try and help as many and as best as they possibly could.

The two new medics worked their way through the battlefield blood and guts to reach the hospital area that was being set up. They were not sure just how to start being of help, but they were going to give it a try.

McPhail was in awe as he walked among the wounded trying to take stock of what in the hell to do next. He began by checking several men that had fallen together when a canon ball exploded close to them.

When he saw that there was little he could do, he arose to his feet and turned towards more wounded but wasn't expecting what was coming next. Suddenly, without warning, a bucket of water was shoved into his gut catching him completely off guard.

"What the hell." He said, looking up to see just who dared to interrupt him.

Behind the bucket was a pretty little blonde with not so pretty blood on her dress and hands. She wasn't exactly smiling as she once again pushed against the bucket almost shoving the Scotsman down.

"Give us a hand, will ya?" She said. "Take these rags and wash them up so we can put clean dressings on their wounds."

Then she hurriedly began following a doctor that was almost overwhelmed by the huge number of wounded. They moved down the rows of the hurt soldiers mostly picking out the ones that possibly could survive.

John stood there with his arms wrapped around the bucket, not quite sure of what to do and almost unable to cope with the bloody mess all around him. His Madstone was of little use here, because there had not been time for infections to set in. Besides, these were men that had holes blown through their bodies, some of which were so large the stone would be lost in them.

At that instant, Brown bent over one of the soldiers to wrap his wounds, and looked back at John frozen in place.

"McPhail, get your butt in gear and bring the bucket of water!" He yelled out.

John had a sudden impulse to dash off and escape this madness, but restrained the feeling for fear of letting the pretty blonde see him as a coward. He took one more look at the pretty nurse working on the injured and moved over to help Brown.

The pair now had gotten caught up into being medics and were doing everything they could to help the angels of mercy as they worked on each of the men in pain, but still many died while waiting for help.

A grave detail was assembled and started burying the dead soldiers in ditches dug out in long rows. There was no other way to accommodate so vast an amount of bodies and time was not on their side.

McPhail and Brown stayed sick at their stomachs, throwing up so often they seemed to feel nothing but numbness now.

On one such occasion the blonde angel, as McPhail described her, came to him right after he had turned green and thrown up for the twentieth time. She sat down beside him and washed his face with warm water. One look into his eyes told her that he was utterly devastated by the sight of the dead and dying soldiers and had never seen anything like this before.

The pretty nurse felt sorry for him but she knew he had to snap out of it if he was to be of use. There just wasn't time to feel sorry for him long and yet she felt a strong feeling for this man. Something that wasn't going to pass by quickly for she had never felt like this before.

Totally embarrassed and trying not to show it in front of this lovely little goddess, John asked. "How can a petite gal like you stand so tall amid all this horror?"

Waiting for an answer, but hardly expecting one, John let his body slide into a sitting position on the ground because his legs had turned to jelly and he felt weak all over.

He had not returned to the main battle site at Manassas to see the aftermath before his capture and didn't realize the devastation of the conflict; that it had been so horrible and so huge.

With the cloth rag still in her hand she set down beside him and began explaining that the doctor was her father and that she had grown up with every conceivable injury and sickness known to man laid out right in front of her.

She had learned to handle it—never to get use to it, only to handle it.

John took the rag from her hand and in doing so, they briefly touched causing him some embarrassment. He already knew that a strong attachment was growing inside him for this girl and it really wasn't the time or place for such feelings.

He had a face that was almost expressionless when he wiped his nose and chin with the damp rag. He really wanted to look good for this pretty lady but it's kind of hard when your up to your ears in blood and guts.

He looked at her face and felt a true feeling down deep and it was something he had never felt before. Then he asked the next question.

"What's your name?"

The blonde was using a piece of torn cloth to tie her hair back hoping to keep the tress from her face. The old piece of bed sheet was all she had but it looked awful good on her he thought.

"Elizabeth Malloy," She said, now peering over the rows of wounded to see if she had missed treating any. Then she dipped her head in the direction of a doctor working on one of the wounded. It was kind of like using it as if pointing with her finger.

"My dad's the surgeon over there." She said.

Never missing a beat she continued tying the knot tight around her hair causing her blouse to be pulled tight across her bosom and the nipples could be seen through the thin cloth.

Now John wasn't looking at her lovely face, he was staring at another lovely sight and his hormones suddenly were becoming very active. Only once before had his feelings been so highly pitched with excitement.

The first time he sang to keep from wetting his pants with fear when he almost got shot by a rebel. This time his genitals also played a part, but in quite a different way. Only one thing to do, the same thing he did when he had been taken back with fear,…sing.

"Oh, I wish I was in the land of cotton, old time sake, not..."

Curiously, she looked back at this interesting young man and asked him a question right in the middle of his song.

"You're John McPhail aren't you. Your friend over there told me about you when he was helping me patch up a young fellows leg. He was telling me about a marvelous Madstone that works wonders. Does that thing really work? Can it stop snake bites and rabies?" She asked.

John's throat suddenly contained a lump while he was staring at the beautiful girl and it was causing him to almost whisper. He caught himself totally staring and he promptly moved his eyes down at the ground hoping she hadn't noticed his actions. Then, in a weak voice he answered her question.

"Can't stop them, but will take the poison out." He said so softly he wasn't sure she heard him. Still looking towards the ground and not knowing what else to say, he took his canteen and poured the cool water over the top of his head.

Elizabeth just smiled and stood up to continue her duties but now couldn't hardly take her eyes off him. There was something about this funny young man and when there was time she just might try to find out what it was that made him tick.

Once again she looked back over her shoulder at the rows of wounded and turned to make her way to them.

"Gota get back to helping these boys." She yelled. "I'll see you in a bit."

By now, the southern army had begun to regroup just west of the hospital area and they were preparing to move out. Stragglers were pasting by the rows of the wounded trying to rejoin their company but few of the officers were left because so many had been killed in the first volley of shots.

Because so many of the officers had been killed in the battle the whole regiment was now being led by a stiff back captain on horseback. Who wasn't quite sure he knew what he was doing.

He turned his horse one way and then the other as if he was looking for something but more than likely was still feeling the shock of the battle.

Then the frustrated officer saw John and thought he looked like he could be a possible warrior for his next battle, but why wasn't he falling in with the others? He pointed his mean saber towards McPhail and ordered him to be brought forward.

Two of his aids quickly grabbed the Scotsman and led him to the captain's horse and even made him remove his· hat. As excited as they all were its a wonder they didn't make him get on his knees.

"You able to fight boy!" The captain growled to an exhausted McPhail.

John stood in front of the arrogant officer, wearing a blood soaked apron and holding a canteen of water. He was looking like anything but a fighting man. Now, he was having about as much as he could take and his face was showing it.

He turned and pointed straight down at a totally blood soaked soldier lying on the ground right at his feet and answered with a very hard stare.

"Yes sir." He said in a quiet but firm voice while looking the officer straight in the eye.

"But tell me capt'n, just who in the hell is going to patch you up when you're brought back looking like that?"

The company commander squirmed in the saddle and looked out over the rows of wounded. Then he replied;

"Sorry doc, this damn war is not going as well as I thought it would. We need every man we can get, but you're needed here more.

Release him men!" He yelled as his attention begin to focus on the marching column. He pulled the horse's reins to one side and rode off never looking back.

John once again turned his attention to helping with the wounded, but he begin to smile as the thought occurred to him of what the commander had said. "He called me doc, and with my Madstone I could be a doctor. I surely could be"...

Chapter 8

The battle left a great many riderless horses roaming the hills with their saddles still on. While a lot of the mares were taken by deserters and the army troops withdrawing, Brown and McPhail managed to capture a couple for themselves to replace the ones they had lost, but not before the search for the animals had taken three full days, miles of traveling on foot and a lot of anger. The frustrating search for the horses made them eager to get back to the hospital camp hoping they would find a hot meal waiting.

To John, The thought of that blonde angel being back at the hospital area made him move his new horse at a faster pace. The fact that both horses had belonged to union officers and were wearing clearly visible U.S. saddles made no never mind to them. Only one thing was on their minds now, getting back to a friendly camp and hopefully some hot food.

When the boys cleared the last hill and reached the clearing, there was a large shock waiting for them. They sat atop their horses staring at a vacant field where once there were wagons, tents, wounded and hospital personnel.

Now the tents, wagons, and personnel had moved out with the last of the wounded because the threat of new battles was imminent.

This was a major blow to McPhail, an unhappy one, for his heart sank to an all-time low.

He stretched himself up a bit in the saddle trying to see over the next hill but it didn't do anything to help. They were gone and he wasn't even sure where they were headed?

"I'm such an ass," he thought, "I didn't even think to ask where she and her father were going, or where they were from."

All he could see now was the wagon tracks leading southwest and he wondered how much of a head start the group had gotten. It was obvious that the wagons had made a hasty retreat because litter lay all over the ground.

Brown had dismounted and was standing next to John's horse with an equally frustrated look. "There would be no hot meal this day." He thought to himself.

"I'll have to eat hardtack again and on top of that, what in the hell was this crazy Scotsman going to do now?"

He watched John stare at the wagon tracks leading off into the distance and had only one thing to say.

"All right, let's go." He said mounting his animal. "Your going to follow the wagons until you catch up, no matter what aren't you? Don't bother to answer...Let's just get moving."

By now the cold winds had the smell of snow and the winters in Virginia could turn brutal within a fortnight. John knew if he was to catch up with the hospital wagons, he would have to move quickly to beat the snow from covering the ground.

Brown made it known that although he had come along, he for one, wanted to head homeward and get out of the business of war but for the time being he would stay with his buddy.

By now the sun was going down and it would soon be dark and riding blind wasn't a safe thing to do nowadays so they decided to pitch camp. Tomorrow they would keep heading south as soon as the sun came up and they fell sure that it would be no time before they would catch up with the wagons.

The no time turned out to be days and nights of riding and the sun came and went as the southerners traveled southward trying to catch up with the wagons.

Brown could detect no change in McPhail's determination to find Elizabeth Malloy, but as long as they were still southbound heading in the direction of Texas, he would not part company with his lovesick friend.

A number of times the pair of travelers ran into battles being fought but they would skirt around them as much as possible. Even if they couldn't see the fighting but could hear cannons shelling a hill, or rifle fire off in the distance, they would turn away from the fighting and try to go around it.

Now another problem arose, winter had come early to this part of Virginia and snow began falling at a heavy rate. It turned out that it was one of the worst that the state of Virginia had seen in years.

The two travelers could only see a few feet in front of their horses causing them to move at a very slow pace. The early winter snow would make it more difficult for the men to overtake the wagons but at least they had managed to find some new wool uniforms and blankets while looking for the replacement horses. John had already pulled his new coat out of his saddle bags and covered himself with it which was helping, but still it was cold.

They had ridden through that snow all day before Brown finally spoke his thoughts out loud. He wasn't one to complain much but the cold wind was a lot tougher than he was, and now he was feeling it.

"We're going to have to find a town to hold up in till the weather gets better, John." Brown said blowing his warm breath into his hands.

"Sides, I can't eat no more hardtack, got to get me some steak and potatoes. You don't happen to have any hot steaks put back in your knapsack, do you?"

John just looked back through snow covered eyelids at Ben's remarks and knew his buddy was flipping out at all this cold.

Both men wrapped their scarves a little tighter around their faces to ward off the cold as they moved south towards North Carolina.

The ride was a hard one all right but it was becoming even harder because of the brutal weather.

They knew that the town of Chantilly, Virginia couldn't be far off now, where a warm bed and hot meal could be attained and that's were they were headed. Perhaps the wagons might have stopped there also and they could catch up with them.

The wind was getting worse and it was about to blow them out of the saddle to the point it was an all out blizzard. The two travelers dismounted and lead their horses by the reins trying to fight off the bitter cold but they seemed to be losing the battle.

Benjamin was the first to see the Sully farm through the heavy snow but he had to wipe the snow flakes from his eyes twice before he could be sure that it was really a farmhouse he was seeing.

The beautiful house set on a hill puffing smoke from her chimney for all to see through the snowstorm. Only the womenfolk remained to tend the crops, house and animals; that is, if there was anything left after the armies came and when through the territory. This was the case now with most farms as almost all of the men were off to war.

Because it was at least a couple days ride to Chantilly, the ladies would often put up travelers for the night in a room locked off from the main section of the house. Although Mrs. Sully sided with the union, she none the less fed the rebel troops when they came, trying to stay neutral in a war torn area.

McPhail and Brown made their way through the heavy snow and pulled their mounts to a stop right in front of the door. The fact that the Sully dogs were barking like mad didn't seem to bother either of the cold men. They would prefer being attacked by a couple of dogs rather than stay freezing in the snow.

John and Ben were preparing to dismount when suddenly the front door swung open and a pretty but elderly lady carrying a lantern in one hand and a shotgun draped across her chest in the other, stepped out.

Both men couldn't help but notice that the hammers of the shotgun were cocked back in the firing position and that wasn't good.

The two Texans obviously were thinking the same question as they stared down at the gun toting grandma.

"How on earth could this small lady juggle a double barrel shotgun with one hand and a lantern in the other and still show that she meant business?"

Somehow she had known even before the dogs started barking that they were coming and had been waiting patiently right inside the door.

"Evening." She said, holding the bright lantern high trying to get a better look at the faces of the strangers.

"Don't get down, you best stay on your horses. You boys need a place to spend the night?"

John brushed off the snow from the cloth rag slung across his face. Then he noticed a second woman standing behind the front door holding a very large pistol. He didn't have to be a genius for him to know he best answer the very determined looking lady as politely as he knew how.

"Yes'um, got a place we can get out of the cold?" He said. "We won't be no trouble and will be on our way at daybreak. I'm McPhail and this here's Ben Brown."

The two removed their hats to show respect (mostly for that shotgun) and hoped it would get them a room out of the cold for the night.

Mrs. Sully lowered her gun, smiling and pointed to the west side of the house, letting the two men know that everything was all right.

"Put your horses in the stables and go in the side door." She said, "There's a room around there; it's small but warm. Don't have much food, but maybe we can come up with some biscuits for breakfast in the morning."

A woman of few words and with nothing more to say, she tighten her housecoat firmly around herself and walked back into the house out of the cold. She did however peer back over her shoulder keeping a watchful eye on the strangers.

McPhail and Brown spent the night in front of a small but warm fireplace trying to think of something to give the kind lady, but only had one dollar in silver between them. Suddenly Benjamin came upon an idea. "Why not see if we can bag a deer or a couple of rabbits for the lady's kindness?" He said, just knowing it was a great idea.

Shortly after daybreak the two hunters had done just that, returning with a large buck, they prepared the meat for cooking and had it hanging on the front porch when Mrs. Sully brought biscuits for them.

When she saw the buck hanging on her porch she was so taken back that she hardly knew what to say. The kind lady handed each man a cup and began pouring hot coffee for them.

"Can't thank you enough gentlemen. I hope this damn war will be over soon so things will get back to normal, nobody wins when there's killing going on. If your a mind to, stay a few days and I'll cook us up some venison, unless your business is urgent."

McPhail liked the thought of a hot meal, but he really wanted to move on hoping to catch up with the wagon train that was carrying that special someone. He would however cut a slice of deer meat from the animal and cook it later. There was no way the meat would go bad in this cold weather so he tied it to his saddle horn. The pair of southerners would cook it over an open fire when they pitched camp tonight and in this weather that would be soon.

Ben and John packed their things and thanked the lady for her hospitality. Then they moved on towards North Carolina in their quest to find Dr. Malloy and his beautiful daughter Elizabeth; the young goddess that John now was determined to marry if he could ever find her...

The Sully farm was built in 1794 and still stands today on highway 50, outside Chantilly, Virginia.

Tours are given daily at the beautiful farm located in this hill country. In one bedroom used for children long ago, a crudely made glass window still has the date 1803 scratched on it that was put there by a small child. The tiny name of C. Sully is also scratched directly under the date. This was one of the original residents of the stone house, so long ago.

The Sully farm is now owned and maintained by the County of Fairfax, Virginia and open to the public, showing the hard life that the people had in the 19th century. People in those days even made their own writing paper and thought nothing of it.

The tour guide showed our small group how the paper was made out of rags and linen scraps soaked in water until it was pulp and then rolled onto a screen to dry making a very crude sheet of writing paper. There was a small hut next to the house that they used for producing such things.

Much of the furniture, beds and personal items are still in place left over from the civil war, but the feeling that one gets when they tour the land is something to remember.

The two travelers continued south, this time with a little more luck; the snow had stopped and the wind died down making it somewhat easier for them and the horses. Soon they would reach the North Carolina line, but still they had no idea where the Malloy's were going. Unfortunately the two big time trackers had lost the trail in the storm and hadn't been able to pick it up again.

John figured that if he followed the main road and inquired at each town they came to, they were bound to pick up the trail again. On the other hand this was a big country and his odds weren't very good. That is, until they had gotten within several miles of the state line and received their first break.

There the two men ran across a wagon that had broken a wheel in the snow. It held a family of four that was trying to move out of the war zone but had ran into some bad luck. McPhail questioned the father about any wagons they may have seen and was surprised at the man's answer.

"Crossed their path about two days ago," the man said, "Sure was a lot of them heading south. Mind helping me change the wheel on my wagon?"

John and Ben helped the man change the wheel by throwing ropes over a large limb of a tree and pulling one end of the wagon off the ground. When they had finished replacing the wheel, John's excitement mounted now that he knew Elizabeth had passed closely by this area and it wasn't that long ago.

"Do you know what the next town is heading south?" McPhail asked. "Why, that'll be Rocky Mount" the man answered, "Rocky Mount, North Carolina."

Without knowing it, the two southerners had crossed over the state line already and had traveled some distance into North Carolina. They turned their horses onto the road heading south and never noticed the dark blue union uniform partially sticking out of some boxes in the back of the wagon.

Again the pair headed south with John dreaming of the pretty lady that had spunk all the way to her toes. He could just hear her in his mind and Elizabeth's voice was oh so real that he could almost reach and touch her.

They continued south heading for Rocky Mount hoping to overtake the wagons soon, but again the weather turned against the pair of rebels.

The snow and wind became fierce to a point that for a while they though it was going to blow their horses over and them with it. For several days the heavy snow and bitter cold almost took the life out the two men and their horses.

McPhail and Brown both were dog-tired and about to starve in this cold windy weather when they suddenly began to hear noise ahead. Both exploded upright in their saddle and listened intently. Over the noise of the wind blowing and the snow falling came the sound of laughing from a large group of people. At first they thought they might have died and gone to heaven, but the cheers and laughter they were hearing was from this world.

"Hear that," McPhail yelled pulling his horse to a dead stop to listen a bit more. Both men cocked their heads towards the noise and once again they heard the sound of a crowd shouting. It sounded just like a party but who would be having a party in this snowstorm?

They moved their animals forward and within a few minutes a town suddenly begin appearing through the falling snow. They followed the noise of the happy people and it led them straight to the town Hall where some kind of meeting was obviously going on.

The cold and tired Confederates dismounted just as the crowd's shouting rose to a wild pitch when the speaker told them about the victory of the southern army at Balls Bluff. Everyone at the meeting felt sure the war was at an end, for the Yankees surely had lost the will to fight again.

The half-frozen travelers had no sooner cleared the front door than the smell of food caused the weary men to turn immediately to the large table filled with cakes, pies, hams and breads the ladies of the town had brought to the meeting.

Brown and McPhail passed right through the throng of people never giving it a second thought about an invitation. They were just too hungry for formal manners and when they reached the tables, both began their dinner. Several of the wives were helping serve and they simply helped the boys get a nice plate full.

Trying to look dignified as he stuffed himself, John surveyed the room hoping to see someone he knew. A group of elders were standing together talking as they drank hot rum, but McPhail's eyes fixed on a smaller group talking in a corner.

"There's Dr. Malloy!" He yelled out loud, without realizing how loud he had been. Silence filled the room as everyone looked his way, but John was hardly aware that he was the center of attention.

He practically ran all out to the doctor, plate in hand and all.

"Good to see you son." Said the doctor with a smile.

"John was of great assistance to me at the battle site." Dr. Malloy tried to explain, but was abruptly interrupted in mid sentence.

"How's your daughter, sir?" McPhail said, as he rubbed something gently between his fingers of his free hand.

The doctor's eyes caught the movement and looked with a questioning stare at the Scotsman's fingers rubbing something.

Catching his stare, McPhail answered before the doctor could ask the question.

"It's a Shamrock, sir. Brings me good luck. A new friend gave it to me, just want to see if it'll work. Elizabeth, sir?" he said again.

Still smiling the doctor responded pointing to a far corner of the room.

"Ask her yourself boy, she's standing over there with the other ladies."

He really tried to be courteous to the doctor but lost it when he saw Elizabeth across the room.

"UH…UH…thank you sir." He said quietly over his shoulder.

It was a heartwarming sight to see as John almost flew across the room once again; this time towards the girl.

The rebel moved so fast he slid up to Elizabeth almost knocking her over.

At the same time he was fighting down the impulse to grab her in his arms which right now he didn't have the right to do.

Delighted to see the Scotsman, she beamed at his approach.

"It's good to see you again, John." She said with her bright blue eyes fixed on him.

Then for a long moment the two stood there almost toe to toe, gazing at one another as the snow outside the window continued to fall in record amounts. Finally she kind of turned her head back to look at her father and at the same time tell John of their circumstances.

She explained that in all likelihood they would be iced in for the winter and that the widow Johnson had given her father and her a cabin at the end of town to use until spring. That is, if they had to have it that long.

The structure that they had been given to use was quite small but had a fireplace in one of the two rooms that did an ample job of keeping it warm. The roads were impassable and dangerous for large wagons, so they would wait it out until it was safe to travel.

Her eyes had now fixed back on John's and the whole time she was explaining the situation, she was looking deep into John's eyes.

The two stood toe to toe totally fascinated with one another and even though the room was full of people, as far as they were concerned they're alone.

Nothing else she could have said would have been nicer as far as McPhail was concerned, for he had no intention of letting her get away this time. He stood there staring at the beautiful nurse, listening intently while she spoke but really didn't hear a word. His thoughts were to grab her in his arms and hold on forever and he found it was tough to fight the desire to do so.

Finally she just stopped speaking and simply stared back as she slowly reached out and took his hand in hers. So occupied were they with each other, neither heard Elizabeth's father call out to her.

"Time to go, Elizabeth." He said several times, but received no response.

Seeing the two stare at one another caused him to shrug his shoulders and pour himself another hot rum. He took a seat on a bench to give them a bit more time and you know what, another hot rum wasn't all that bad.

Just then, a confederate captain burst through the door and with an excited look let everyone in the room know what he had discovered.

"There's a horse outside with a Yankee saddle." He said just knowing he was on to something. "Must be a federal in here!" He said.

The young confederate officer was out to conquer the world and maybe he would start by finding a union spy. He hadn't stopped to think that a spy would hardly place a marked saddle on his horse if he were trying to hide his identity.

Ben Brown stood in the middle of the room wearing a rebel hat that he had picked up at the battle site, but was still wearing civilian clothes when he observed the officer's entrance.

He quickly responded to the allegations of the young confederate.

"Ain't no blue belly in here." He said, "Just McPhail and me riding horses we got from some Yankees that won't be going home no more." Taking the mug of hot rum that Brown held in his hand, the southern officer eyed him and took a large gulp.

"How'd you boys kill them Yankees, 'fore you took their animals?" He said, waiting to see if he got the right response.

Brown retrieved the mug of rum from the rebel's hand and answered with an air of authority and superiority.

"Found them in the hills with no riders." He said, "We couldn't fight cause McPhail promised Lincoln."

Ben Brown had no sooner gotten the words out of his mouth, than he realized the mistake he had made. The whole room went to complete silence once again, as if it were now the order of the day. Now everyone wanted to know just what he was talking about.

"You know Lincoln?" the captain asked, as if he had caught an enemy in their midst.

Brown knew they were in for it now if he didn't explain and fast. The look in the captain's eyes told him he best get on with it. Without hesitation, he told the story of Lincoln's son as if he had rehearsed it time and again.

As he finished, the crowd was astonished with the facts and wanted to see this rare magic stone.

John was still standing with Elizabeth and couldn't believe what Ben had gotten them into.

It was the last thing that he wanted to do right now but he seemed to have no choice; he was suddenly surrounded by all most everyone in the room.

He turned to Brown and smiled a smile that screamed out for revenge. The kind of smile that most people would make if they were in agony and wanting to get back at someone.

He was trapped and knew it. John pulled out the leather pouch from inside his shirt and held the stone flat in his hand to show one person after another. Now it was a mob scene trying to see the magic stone and even Elizabeth was pushed away as one after another tried to get closer to see the marvelous healing stone.

It was sometime until the agate had been inspected by everyone and things calmed down.

Finally John was free to turn his attention back to Dr. Malloy. He so wanted to get up the nerve to ask for Elizabeth's hand but was having a hard time doing so. Each time he tried to approach the subject, he was interrupted by some of the town folks coming back to ask another question about the Madstone. The fury of discussion about the magic stone subsided only when the meeting was called to an end by the elders.

By now it was getting late and the town folks were beginning to trudge towards their homes in the deep snow, but Brown and the confederate captain were still toe to toe. They had started a drinking match for the swapping of the beer mug. Each time the captain took a drink, so would Brown. First the captain, then Brown, on and on.

The captain was determined not to be outdone. Neither of the men gave a foot of ground, they just stood and stared at each other.

Making sure he never took his eyes off Ben the captain grabbed a mug of his own and pulled a cigar from his coat never once failing to match each of Brown's drinks.

Ben in turn copied his opponent and he too reached over and slid a cigar out of the captain's coat and stuck it in his mouth. Again large gulps were taken by both parties. By this time many of the townspeople had stayed to see the match.

"Five dollars gold," said Brown.

"Put you're money on the table," replied the captain.

Mug after mug was downed by each as the staring went on. Still the two held the cigar tightly in one hand and the mug in the other.

Everyone in the room was watching the two rebels sway from one side to the other and bets were being made as to when they would hit the floor face down.

One of the ladies enjoying the activity brought a lit twig from the fireplace and held it out offering to light the men's cigars.

The two contestants turned their cigars towards the burning twig but never made it to her offer. It was simply not in the cards for them to have a fine smoke at this time. Both began to feel the room sway beneath their feet and within a micro second the floor jumped up to meet the heroes. Their bodies fell to the hard wood floor and hit with the weight of two dead men. Of course, by now neither felt any pain whatsoever because their mind consciousness was in La La land.

The two battle tested southerners were now laid out cold with no chance of returning to the land of active people; at least for the rest of this night or perhaps a couple more.

With a disappointed look the young woman blew out the flame as she stepped over the unconscious men and moved back to her mothers side.

"Can I take that one home?" She said to her mother, pointing at Brown as if she just might get the right answer.

The mother had a stern look when she grabbed her daughter by the arm and began pulling her towards the front door trying her best to keep her looking like a lady.

Now the meeting was really over, and everyone began to leave the hall moving out into the falling snow. Nobody seemed to care much for the two soldiers lying on the floor; they just figured the men would sleep it off right where they were.

John walked with Elizabeth and her father to their cabin, but never got a chance to discuss marrying the girl. Not much was said between the three because of the snow, cold and wind. The weather was just a bit too much for an intelligent conversation of any kind.

When they reached the front door of the cabin the doctor brushed the snow off his coat and slipped through the door giving his daughter and John a little time to be alone in the falling snow.

McPhail stumbled through a few words but wasn't showing any signs of being a smooth companion to the ladies, but it didn't matter. They both knew that they were absolutely meant for each other and words weren't necessary at a time like this. They simply pressed their fur coats together and hugged tightly to make the kiss very smooth, then he said goodnight with a reassurance that he would certainly be back in the morning.

McPhail walked backwards watching her disappear through the doorway until he suddenly realized that he had no place to go. He and Brown hadn't looked for a room and now if he didn't act fast he might end up in the stables.

As luck would have it he found that the only boarding house in town had one small room left, which he managed to acquire. The old lady that owned the rooming house was very outgoing and wasted no time in letting the young have the room.

"Beats sleeping with the horses." He thought as he paid his two dollars to the old widow that owned the boarding house.

Now it suddenly occurred to McPhail that Brown was no where to be found until a couple walked by talking about the two drunks that were still lying on the floor at the town hall.

Knowing full well that one of the men was probably Benjamin, John made his way back to the hall where Brown was still lying on the cold wood floor unaware of anything that might be going on in this world.

With great difficulty John managed to hoist his friend onto his right shoulder and move off to the small room at the boarding house he had just rented. The task became even more troubling because of the slick snow and ice but he was determined to share his room with Brown even though it was actually too small for two people.

McPhail passed through the door of the cabin wearing a great big smile as a funny thought crossed his mind. He dumped his passed out buddy onto a blanket he had thrown to the floor and then said out loud what he had been thinking.

"This was really a mark of a true friend." He told himself in a laughing manner.

He looked down one more time at his friend lying on the hard cold floor then turned to the nice soft bed against the wall.

"On the other hand, I best not over do my kindness." He said softly.

John delighted in the soft, warm feather bed that was giving him a good nights sleep. He was convinced that Benjamin would do nicely on the floor. After all his buddy was far too gone to even know the difference.

Early morning found John trying to clean up with a pan of water he had heated on the pot belly stove. He wiped his face dry and looked back at the dead body called Brown that was still lying limp on the floor.

It seemed that Benjamin had scarcely moved his body at all during the night, but alas he was still alive.

John stared down at his friend trying to figure out what to do and in a flash it seemed to come to him.

"Perhaps Browns pay back for loose lips about Lincoln and the Madstone could be a little bit of honey poured down his pants or he could wake up in four feet of cold snow. After all, his buddy had caused him so much trouble at a time he was trying to get to know Elizabeth." He thought to himself. "No, he just couldn't do it after all the two had been through together. On the other hand…

McPhail moved over to his buddy and carefully sat him in an upright position and then to a half-standing stance where he could shove his friend onto the bed. He removed the sleeping beauty's shoes and covered him with a blanket making it look like his traveling companion had slept in the bed all night. Then with another smile he threw his heavy coat on and headed out into the snow.

It was very obvious that he was going to the little cabin at the edge of town where the beautiful girl was. This time he was not going to let anything stop him from showing his love and devotion towards Elizabeth. Even the whole union army couldn't stop him from marrying the girl now. Not with the kind of determination he had at this moment. At lease that was what he kept telling himself over and over.

His confidence grew stronger as he approached the front door and prepared to knock strongly as a man on an important mission.

"I can do it." He said softly, "Ask to marry the girl and get the right answer. There's no way the doctor will say no to a great guy like me."

His knock against the frozen door made a soft sound because of his heavy gloves and suddenly McPhail no longer felt ten foot tall as he did five minutes ago.

Again he repeated his statement out loud once more to himself.

"I can do it." He said, trying to keep his dwindling confidence high. "At least I think I can." He whispered to himself as the door opened.

The doctor's face appeared with a smile as he addressed McPhail.

"Somehow I knew it'd be you young fellow." The doctor said stepping to one side to let John in.

Hot coffee had already been prepared and McPhail received a cup from a happy looking Elizabeth, but he was at a point of no return. This veteran of one battle could contain it no longer, he was bursting at the seams to ask his question and nothing was going to stop him.

He tried his best to show dignity but lost it entirely when he blurted out his request to her father.

"I wish to marry your daughter." He said a **lot** louder than he should. "I do love her you know!"

Before Dr. Malloy could answer, Elizabeth hugged her daddy from behind and showed how she felt about it all.

"Oh yes, father, I love him too!" She said in an excited voice.

With hardly any way of objecting, the doctor stood up and took a heavy fur coat from the rack on the back of the front door. Then he pulled the oak door open and turned back facing the pair.

"We'd be happy to have you in the family, son." He said with a great big smile. "Walk with me to the edge of town. Some of our wounded boys are camped there and I need to see about them."

John and Elizabeth beamed a large smile at one another as he and the doctor went through the door into the snow.

While tending to the small group of gray coats bedded down in the stable, the doctor explained that he had volunteered for only three month's duty and was headed back to Robeson County, North Carolina to resume his regular practice.

At first the doctor just made small talk while he moved from one wounded soldier to the other, but then he caught McPhail by surprise with his next statement. He looked up from the straw covered floor and invited his soon to be son-in-law to settle down in Robeson County. There he was a man of some means, and he could help him start a farm on some extra acreage he owned near Lumberbridge township.

"Perhaps you could even put the war far behind you." He said not really believing his own statement.

McPhail loved the idea of settling down on a small farm with Elizabeth, but was still troubled at the thought of not being able to fight. He knew in his heart that the battle of "Balls Bluff" was hardly the beginning of the conflict between the states. It certainly was not the end by any means. There would be a lot more blood shed in the months to come and somehow he was going to be a part of it even if he couldn't fight.

It certainly looked like he was trapped into being a medic but there didn't seem to be an alternative. Still, he couldn't shake the strong urge to get back into the fighting. Again and again he told himself that he wasn't a coward, just a man that was keeping his honor by keeping his word.

This was sure a confusing time for a simple farmer.

The Scotsman was determined to put these bad visions far back in his mind. He wanted his thoughts now to be only on a beautiful blonde nurse that was soon to become his bride. He would dismiss the bad things. as best he could...for now.

The Reverend Merriam was in town for a few days, and was delighted to accommodate the couple when he was asked to marry them. John and the doctor agreed that the marriage could take place right away which made a lot of sense to McPhail...mainly because he didn't want to wait to make this beautiful lady his bride.

The milestone of their marriage took place at the town hall with the doctor and Brown looking on and using the doctor's wedding ring for Elizabeth. She was delighted to be using her father's wedding ring even if she did have to wrap a piece of cloth around it so that it would fit.

A beaming McPhail moved into the little cabin, while Dr. Malloy put up at the boarding house with Benjamin. Brown really didn't mind sharing with the doctor; after all, his good friend John had allowed him to sleep on the feather bed the night he had drank so much and poor McPhail must have slept on the cold hard floor. Besides it would be only until the weather broke.

(Had he known that it would be March before the weather calmed down, he just might not have done it.)

Indeed it was March before the weather cleared enough for the new Mr. and Mrs. McPhail, Benjamin and the doctor to begin their travels once again through North Carolina. Brown figured that he would leave the group at that point; just as soon as they reached Robeson County. He would head out to the far west; maybe Arizona or California, where he had heard no fighting was going on.

Well there was word floating around about a few scrimmages between the white man and Indians, but nothing to really worry about.

The wagon rumbled along the narrow road with the doctor holding the horses to a slow pace as the ground had ice and snow yet to melt and the animals were anything but sure footed.

McPhail rode alongside the wagon on horseback discussing plans of settling down and raising children.

"The first boy we'll name after you, sir." He said to the doctor. "And the second after me and the third..."

Elizabeth had heard enough.

"Wow." She said while shifting her weight on the hard wooden boards of the wagon seat. "Oh yea, how many you personally planning to have, John?"

McPhail's expression became a bit more serious when he tried to answer Elizabeth's question.

"Only about six or seven." He said. "We really should keep it down to a small family."

Elizabeth could only smile as she wrapped the blanket a little tighter around her shoulders and whispered under her breath half hoping he heard her.

"No McPhail, I mean you personally. How many YOU gonna have?"

The doctor too shifted himself on the hard board seat as he addressed John.

"How you going to avoid the fighting if the war starts up again?" He said, "If we get into it with the Yankees again, they'll be calling almost everyone to fight and you're sure to have to go."

"Don't know." Answered John. "Just know I can't fight cause I promised Lincoln. To tell the truth, I really don't want to fight no more anyhow." He said.

"That's another thing, John." Replied the doctor with a worried look. "You best not be talking too much about knowing Lincoln in these parts; people might take it the wrong way. On the other hand it might not make any difference anyway. I think that the war might be truly over."

"I certainly hope so." Said Elizabeth. "We all have seen enough of this foolishness to last a lifetime."

Unknown to the travelers, the union even then was amassing a large army of one hundred thousand men and would soon be marching on the south to put down these rebels once and for all.

The north had the industrial might and manpower to crush the south and force them into submission, but also had no idea of the will power and fighting ability of the southern forces. They were soon to find that the war would also cost them dearly. Such names as Antietam, Chancellorsville, Shiloh, Fredericksburg, Gettysburg and many, many more would forever go down in American history as the war that pitted brother against brother with extreme pain for both sides.

In all of history few armies endured so long, fought so ferociously and achieved so much with so little as would the Confederate army during those dark days of the war between the states.

Chapter 9

Spring of 1862 burst forth with all its natural beauty in the North Carolina countryside as the news traveled like a whirlwind that the federal troops were assailing Virginia from almost every approach and were as close as nine miles to Richmond.

At the same time Brigadier General Ambrose Burnside's union forces had already taken Roanoke Island and New Bern on the coast of North Carolina itself securing a vital base on the southern coast for the Federals.

The arrogance of the Yankees overlooked the marked superiority of the southern generals at this stage of the war. They would however get a taste of it in the coming months, shaking the very foundation of Washington.

Benjamin was preparing to move on to Texas, when the word reached Robeson County that the north had indeed invaded southern territory in force causing the Scotsman to delay his plans of leaving. He would stay awhile and help John with chores as the newlyweds settled in. He wanted to see how much further this foolish war would go and besides he could always pack up his things and head out west any time he so desired, or so he thought.

McPhail knew that the war jeopardized his new marriage, and this was of great concern to him until Elizabeth assured the Highlander that wherever he went, she would go. After all, she was a nurse and was dedicated to the south. They may be in the midst of a great war but nothing would separate them now short of one or the other getting killed. She knew that John would help in any way that he could, even after promising Lincoln not to fight.

They discussed following the southern army to help with the wounded after each battle but John was really not a doctor. He did however have one thing in his favor, his Madstone and he was learning a great deal about medicine from Elizabeth and her father. The newly weds finally decided that they could use the doctor's wagon and round up all the supplies that could be carried, and then join the boys in gray headed north.

McPhail and Elizabeth's plan was short lived however; the doctor was now in his 60's and his energy was fading daily causing the pair to reconsider. In view of his age, Dr. Malloy had decided that the strain of traveling was getting to be too much for him to handle. It could end up with him being a burden rather than a asset and at a time like this, he didn't want that to happen. He had made up his mind to stay and practice medicine in the area hoping to be of use to the confederacy at the same time.

With her father deciding to stay put; Elizabeth and John talked it over and made the decision to do likewise. They would help as much as they could with the wounded that was returning and as it turned out it was a wise decision.

Confederate forces were now passing the township in large numbers headed north to their destiny. Word was filtering back about the battles being waged in eastern Tennessee and northern Virginia causing a huge shortage of fighting men.

By now Brown had become more restless than ever and when the next regiment came marching through he grabbed his gear and fell in step with southern soldiers that were headed north to fight. He just couldn't stand watching the southern troops passing through town day after day and not being able to go with them.

Having never given his word personally to Lincoln, he felt no longer obliged to stay out of the conflict. Although he vowed he was "Getting out of the business of war" the gray uniforms passing him by were just too much of a temptation for Benjamin to resist any longer.

September, 1862 found Benjamin Davis Brown at the battle of Antietam Creek, Virginia. He would have never dreamed that this day would turn out to be known as "The bloodiest single day of the war."

Unknown to Brown, he was about to pick one of the worst of all the killer battles of the entire Civil War.

The southern army camped next to the Rappahannock River outside Fredericksburg waiting to be joined by the Alabama and Georgia regiments, before marching northwest to Antietam.

Across the river the union soldiers were also massing for the battle and both armies were well aware that their enemies were close at hand just the other side of the river.

The ill-supplied confederates were short of coffee, sugar, overcoats, and shoes, but had plenty of tobacco. This gave one of the innovative southerners an idea. He crouched behind a tree to shout his message across the river.

"Hey, fed, ya'll want to swap some coffee for tobacco?" He yelled out.

Hardly a full minute went by before the return reply came back.

"One bag tobacco for one bag coffee, Reb. How ya going to get it over?"

"No Problem," was the rebel comeback, "I'll be ready in a minute. Don't do no shooting, ya hear?"

Several of the southerners built a small raft with large sticks and tied them together with strips of leather. They Launched the craft upstream so that it would float to the Federals spot on the other side of the river. The raft missed the mark and passed the union men by until one of the blue coats jumped in and pulled the tied logs to shore.

A rope was then attached to the logs and the wet Yankee held tight to the small raft as he slid back into the cold water. Frighten clear down to his toes but with a lot of guts in his heart, he began swimming towards the opposite shore.

The Yankee corporal fought the current all the way, pulling the raft across the river until he was close enough to push it onto the rebel shore.

Now the two enemy armies had a line that stretched across the water so that the raft could be pulled back and forth. The next time the raft reached the Yankees, there were two bags of tobacco and a sign on board.

C.S.A. ship Virginia, two bags of tobacco, send two bags of coffee. A short time later the small raft floated along the rope back to the rebels with the sign: U.S.S. Monitor, and two bags of coffee.

Afterwards the determined and innovative traders rigged another wire and rope across the river downstream at an old burned out bridge. Now they had two locations that they were able to pull items back and forth. It was on a kind of trolley device but even this seemed not to be enough.

No one had fired a shot and now the fourth Georgia and eighth Alabama men waded, swam and rode boats to exchange face to face with the fourth New York men. Each time holding both hands above their heads to show that they were not armed. To each of the soldiers on both sides it would have been unthinkable for either to break their word. This would be devastating to the fighting men's pride.

Although the officers from both sides knew of the "Horse trading", they chose to overlook the men's illicit commerce crossing the river. The leaders simply ignored the fact since no fighting was going on at the moment, and it was a good diversion from the stress of the upcoming battles. After all, didn't Hannibal allow his troops to trade with his enemies from the backs of his elephants?

One evening, a federal band set up close to the river and began playing to the troops. A number of songs were played as both sides listened. The Yankee band played "Hail Columbia" and the "Star Spangled Banner" until one of the rebels yelled to the blue coats. "Play Dixie, Fed."

Pausing, the musicians looked at each other and then at the southern shore. Shrugging their shoulders, the men in blue struck up "Dixie."

Suddenly all the troops on both sides looked up to see what the commanders would do, but no response came from the leaders. Laughter and cheers began to come from both sides as the music played on.

Now the men of both the blue and gray yelled back and forth, exposing themselves without fear to the far bank.

Hardly anyone had noticed that one of the rebels that had been watching the goings on had quietly laid his body down on the ground beside a tree in a prone position. He shifted his belly to one side trying to keep from laying on the pebbles and at the same time carefully took sight with his rifle on a Yankee clowning around on the far side of the river.

Brown had been standing nearby with his newly acquired hot cup of coffee when he saw the man preparing himself into the firing position. He quickly stepped behind the soldier and with an act of brotherhood, poured the hot liquid on the confederate's head.

The soldier screamed from the pain of the hot coffee as Benjamin pulled his revolver from its holster and pointed it straight at the man's head, making sure he would start no further trouble.

"Not now, Reb." He said. "Be plenty of that soon enough. Let it be tonight".

The illegal bartering by the troops was only halted when the order went out to begin the march to Antietam. Sporadic firing had already started and could be heard the next day, even though both armies were traveling separate paths. The armies were moving away from each other because to do otherwise would mean crossing the river, which certainly would be a blood bath and a disaster for either side.

For the north, the war department had failed to furnish pontoons making it almost impossible to cross the river with their large army and expose themselves to what would certainly be 60% to 70% casualties.

For the south, building a makeshift bridge atop wooden barrels would have put a great part of their army at jeopardy from the snipers on the far bank. Besides they couldn't come up with that many barrels quickly.

Neither of the commanders on either side knew where the battle would take place but they surely knew it would be soon and within the general area.

Even before the laughter died away, the troops were getting ready for the upcoming battle.

Captains began giving the order to strike tents and backpacks were prepared for travel, while horses were hitched to the wagons and a host of men threw their rifles into the marching mode on their shoulders. There would be no frying of bacon or boiling of coffee this morning, for indeed the move was on.

General Lee send Stonewall Jackson and twenty-five thousand men to capture Harper's ferry while the remainder of the army of Northern Virginia met the forces of McClellan head on at Antietam Creek a few miles northwest.

Here was to be the battle that Benjamin thought of when he had nightmares and the fear of combat that comes to every young man facing a foe. Brown had serious doubts about his bravery and even though his hands were sweating and he shook inside from fear, he showed none of it to the others. He was determined to make an appearance of strong will and show strength when the attack began. After the battle no one would say that this Scotsman had not shown bravery at the height of the fight, but when he looked at the long blue line of Federals, there was but one thing he could think of.

"Oh God! what have I gotten myself into?"

His mind raced thoughts of terror and blood shed as if a vision were appearing before him as he looked at the thousands of blue coats preparing their attack. Sweat rolled down his forehead into his eyes and his vision blurred as the salty water from his body almost covered his face.

The sea of blue he was seeing was rows of Federals making a long straight line across the rocky field. They were marching through the cornfield now and only two hundred yards away the southerners where doing the same. Rifles at the ready they faced each other marching and firing at the same time with unmanageable death and horror striking both armies. As one row fired, the next row stepped forward and continued while the first row reloaded changing places again and again. Bodies fell and men screamed but still the advance continued even though the troops had to step over many dead.

Only a moment ago these dead where their friends and now they are but a number that would be listed in the nearest graveyard. Benjamin stood tall in the ranks but he was feeling the worst fear of his life as he faced the approaching union men. The noise of the shot and shell exploding all around him shook him to the core.

To his left another Scotsman marched next to him that had already been in several major battles. He was playing the bagpipes and marching straight into the fierce fighting. His name was Donald Malcolm and he was trying to make sure that his pipes could be heard over the gunfire. He tried to drown out the yells and cries of the battle with his music but was having little success. The piper did know however that it helped the soldiers morale and it certainly help Benjamin's even more, as he fired again and again.

The two armies had gotten so close that they were now hand to hand clashing in bitter combat. Malcolm fell to his knees still playing the pipes until the breath went out of him and his body lay still in death. His bagpipes stumped onto the ground by the onslaught of the fierce fighting.

Benjamin suddenly realized that the music had stopped and he turned to look back just as his friend fell to the ground. The bagpiper's body had been lifted up and torn apart by a musket ball and there was no doubt that he would not be playing any more music today.

For a moment Brown's eyes were fixed on the pipers body. He stood staring at the bloody mess until a sudden noise brought him back to reality. He quickly turned back to the battle and there, a few yards out was a Yankee soldier coming straight at him with a fierce determination to kill the next enemy rebel.

Ben lifted his heavy rifle to fire at the running soldier but was too late to make a difference. The Scotsman was knocked back and reeled totally around from a deep pain that was inflicted in his left arm. He too had received a Yankee musket ball that had tore completely through bone and all. As he fell hard to the ground his rifle went off downing the federal that was coming for him. He had managed to fire the heavy weapon with his one good hand and it had hit it's mark.

The musket ball had caused a very large hole in his shoulder and it was a good thing that he had fainted as he hit the ground, for he had no idea how badly he had been wounded.

Ben was not sure just how long he had been out when he began to wake up. He was only sure that his body was being bounced around and it felt like a wooden board he was laying on. He soon realized that he was on a wooden board that was being used as a make do stretcher. He was being carried to a small building set up as a receiving area for the wounded. He had started the battle pretty early that morning and now he could see that daylight was diminishing into dusk. The Texan had never had anything like this happen to him before. "I can't move!" He yelled out. "Why can't I move?" One of the men carrying the litter motioned to his buddy to stop.

"you'll be all right Texas." He said to Ben. Your body has had a shock, it'll come back before you know it. Lay back and try and take it easy, you'll be well cared for shortly."

The pain he felt was indescribable with just words. He wished for death to quiet his cries of anguish but it wasn't to be. His eyes were starting to clear but what he was about to see was a horror he could not have possibly imagined. He had to ram his fist into his mouth to stop his screaming and fears. The salt water was keeping his eyes from focusing and it was a good ten minutes before they cleared enough for him to see. Slowly his eyes adjusted and the doctor's image came into focus. He and a young nurse were examining what was left of Brown's arm.

They were working by the soft light of a lantern trying to determine his injuries and what was to be done. The doctor finished examining Brown's arm and moved on quickly to the next patient because so many others were waiting. It was very obvious that the tired doctor needed the help of the young nurse that was standing by his side. She would get Ben ready for surgery while the physician tended to others.

Carrie Moore was not really a nurse, but volunteers were sorely needed and she had come to help. The young lady might as well have been a nurse for all intents and purposes for surely she was just as capable as any fully trained registered nurse.

Benjamin was only half awake when he opened his eyes to see the beautiful young girl cleaning his wound. Her eyes met his and she knew he had come back into the land of the living.

"Welcome back to battle field row." She said softly with a smile. Here, take some whiskey, it'll help with the pain."

A slightly injured soldier lying on the bulk next to Brown happened to overhear her speak of whiskey and his ears perked up.

"Got any more of that there whiskey?" He asked.

Once again Carrie spoke softly when she turned to the man and answered.

"We only give liquor to the more injured soldiers because we have nothing else available."

Then she turned back to Benjamin and took one more look at his mangled arm. It didn't take a experienced surgeon to see what had to be done to the remains of the arm.

Ms Moore didn't need to be told what decision the doctor had made about the arm. Her heart went out to the southern soldier for there was no question that the physician was about to take off what was left.

As with so many other wounded men during the war between the states, the doctor could do nothing else but remove Brown's arm.

The surgeon moved back over to Benjamin and quickly began working on the arm with bare hands. Ben screamed with pain until he passed out even with Carrie dipping a rag into the whiskey and pressing it to his lips.

Now three men were holding Ben down while the doctor proceeded to cut the bloody stump off. The ungodly pain caused Brown to try and move off the table or pull back from the surgeons knife but it always ended with the southerner falling back into unconsciousness.

Again and again Benjamin awoke to see three huge men keeping him in place and each time within seconds he would pass out.

The confederate doctor sutured his wounds with hair from the tail of a horse because nothing else was available. Supplies were in such demand it was the only thing that could be had quickly for battlefield medicine.

For two days Brown went in and out of consciousness with high fever while Carrie washed his body with cool water and stood by him.

On the third day he regained consciousness and looked up to see a pretty girl once again tending to him.

"You been here all this time?" He said with a mouth that felt like it was full of cotton. For the first time he really got a good look at the young nurse and it sunk in that she was even more lovely than he had imagined.

Each night Ben would go in and out of sleep and often he would awake to see the pretty young girl setting beside his bed. She had been drawn to him from the moment he was brought in and was spending more time by his side than any other.

Being a very exceptional young lady, she responded to his every move by placing her hand tenderly on what still remained of his left arm. She tried to think of things to say to make him feel better or at least take his mind off his problems for awhile. When she spoke to him she tried to make every sentence she said as cheerful as possible even if it meant she had to bite the bullet.

"Yep, they're still bringing in more wounded so I guess I'll be here a while." She said with a great big smile. "You rest now cause you got to get well. We're going to need the bed pretty soon, so you've got to get better and get out."

In Brown's torment he still tried to laugh but it hurt too much. Still, he was instantly and deeply attracted to this lovely girl and she with him. It was obvious that she was spending more time with Benjamin than any other.

Around the hospital camp the battles continued but were less frequent now because both armies had huge casualties and were pulling back to lick their wounds. It seemed as if the conflict would go on forever at this battle site, but every time brown would open his eyes, Carrie was by his side.

On the forth day the Scotsman realized it had been hours since he had seen the pretty girl. When the doctor walked past his cot, he raised himself enough to ask the question in a weak voice.

"Doc, you seen Miss Moore?" he asked, hoping she would walk up any moment. The doctor looked at the floor as if he didn't want to answer.

"She's dead son. She…she went over to the next camp and on the way back a cannon-ball fell right next to her. Never knew what hit her, she died instantly, I'm sure sorry."

Brown's eyes searched the room scanning the cots of wounded as if hoping that the doctor was wrong, but he knew that this was not to be. Now he would face the long journey home without the only sunshine that had come into his life; surely God was not with him this day.

Benjamin had lost his left arm during the heavy fighting and was out of the war, but would survive to marry Mary Margaret McPhail in Pontotoc County, Mississippi on November 8, 1863, still wearing the confederate gray.

Brown would have four boys and two girls by this pretty McPhail girl, a distant relative of John's. His son William H. Brown became a doctor and his great grandson, William Perry Brown Jr. would become a medic and be killed on a battlefield in Korea in 1952.

Benjamin Davis Brown would never cross paths with John again, nor would either know what happened to the other after the battle of Antietam.

Later on in his life he would write to a friend telling about the pretty girl at Antietam and that she had been buried along with hundreds of soldiers that would never return.

Not even a headstone with her name could be found because she had simply been lost in the crowd of bodies during burials.

He realized that she had never told him where she was from or much else about her short life. Only that she was having her nineteenth birthday the following month. The letter ended with a simple note, "but surely this Scotsman would remember her always".

Chapter 10

John and Elizabeth almost daily heard the stories of the battles, as the wounded passed over the North Carolina line headed south to their homes.

McPhail wanted to join the columns of southern troops marching north to reinforce the south's fighting men, but he'd given his word and could not for the life of him break it. He became restless and as days passed by he could hardly sleep and thought little of eating food. This was a very deep hurt within him that he found he could not shake.

One morning McPhail watched as two thousand men marched north through the town. The gray coats were moving slowly as morale seemed low and even he felt pretty bad. He stood there watching, trying to think of some way to perk up the southern troops and even waved smartly to them, but only one young private waved back.

Suddenly he stood at attention and began to sing loudly; "Oh, I wish I was in the land of cotton, old times there are not forgotten, look away, look away, look away, Dixie land."

It took a minute, but the southerners began to join in, first one, then another, until the entire company marched off singing with a little quicker stride.

"That'll do it, he said to himself proudly, sporting a funny little smile on his face."

McPhail stood watching the soldiers until they had marched totally out of sight. He now felt he had to do something with himself because helping the doctor just didn't seem to be enough anymore.

When time would allow he would play the bagpipes on the front porch of the house for hours. Otherwise he would help with meetings to gather money, food, or clothes for the war.

A great deal of the wounded was being diverted to other locations that were closer to the battles, giving him a little more time on his hands.

The ladies of the area would sew uniforms, make bandages and knit for their gallant men in gray, but John found that he had less and less to do.

Late one evening McPhail sat playing his pipes on the porch when the sound of a fast moving buggy drew his attention to the north end of town.

There, driving at breakneck speed was Donald Ross, a neighbor with a small farm about five miles out.

The dust storm had no time to settle as Ross jumped from the buckboard before it even had time to stop. He summoned John to come quick, as he took the young girl from the back of the wagon and began carrying her into the house.

"Damn rattler bit her!" He shouted in an excited voice. "Where's the doc?" The farmer carried the little girl straight to the kitchen table and laid her down shoving plates and utensils onto the floor with John and Elizabeth following close behind.

By now several friends had run to the house after seeing the commotion, and a volunteer quickly went to fetch the doctor.

As everyone watched, McPhail took the Madstone from a glass jar over the stove and placed it in some warming milk. He stood there for a moment whispering to the milk as if it could hear him.

"Get warm in a hurry, you bastard" He said turning to the little girl to examine the bite.

"How long it been since she was bit." McPhail asked the father.

"Found her out back of the house." Ross replied, "Lying in some grass; Don't know how long she'd been there, but I killed the snake less than ten feet away."

153

John's voice had a hint of fear when he saw the bite marks on the little girl. "She's been bit four times!" He said. "I've got to work fast."

McPhail retrieved the stone from the hot milk and applied it to the bite mark closest to the trunk of the little girl's body, practically at the same time that Dr. Malloy rushed through the door.

It took only a moment for the doctor to look the young girl over before his expression turned to sadness.

"She's gone, son." He said. "Just too many bites and too long a wait. We probably couldn't have helped even if we had of gotten to her sooner."

The doctor placed a blanket over the small body but he couldn't help it; he kept looking a second and third time as if he were hoping she would jump up and run off to play.

Ross cried with pain at the covering of his small daughter and McPhail felt sick in his gut and could take it no longer. He held his hand over his mouth trying to stop the event that was about to take place while he ran towards the back door.

He didn't quite make it. The Scotsman threw up all over the back porch, making quite a mess. Across the room Elizabeth moved back and forth slowly in a rocking chair and quietly wept. She had seen this many times before, but kids were always the worst.

Rattlesnakes were a real problem in the area; they seemed to grow in numbers every year and there were hundreds of snakebites each spring.

Years after the war, people from all over the area would join together to have what they called a Becky hunt. A substantial reward was paid to the one capturing the most snakes in three days. They were then used to make antivenin and their skins made into belts, wallets, and even hats; not to mention that the reptiles were good eating to many.

Becky Ross was quietly buried with the entire town looking on and even the war seemed to take second place while the young girl was taken to her final resting.

That night passed slowly because John's emotions were carried to new highs of hurt. It couldn't have been worse if he had been bitten by the rattler himself. The sound of his bagpipes could be heard in the darkness that night as McPhail lost himself in the Scottish songs for the dead.

Only one lit lantern was hanging on the front porch but it was enough to let everyone in town know where the music was coming from. Sadly, it was to continue throughout the night.

The shrill train whistle filled the air interrupting the Scotsman's pipes as the sun began to rise over the treetops. Dr. Malloy had received a wire from the confederate army that many wounded would be arriving shortly but wasn't expecting them quite so soon.

As was his custom, McPhail arose from the rocker to join the doctor at the station to treat the incoming wounded. Nothing else came first when that train whistle blew; everyone responded knowing that the wounded were arriving.

Elizabeth too heard the whistle blowing in the crisp morning air as she was making morning coffee. She knew of John's deep hurt at the little girl's passing, and appeared on the front porch with hot coffee in hand for her Scotsman. She too felt as if she had been in some kind of a trance at all that had happened. It was almost unreal and she found that she was unable to disengage herself completely from the sadness buried deep in her heart.

After a moment of silence with the couple staring in the direction of the train whistles, she squeezed his arm in a loving fashion.

"I'll get my things and join the ladies at the hospital." She said while McPhail nervously drank several gulps of the coffee.

John arose and retrieved a heavy coat just inside the front door to ward off the cool morning air, then he downed the rest of his coffee.

He had feelings of anxiety towards facing the horror that he knew was waiting for him at the train station, but began moving toward the train station anyway.

Many of the local residents flocked to the incoming cars almost at a dead run; but John's movements seemed to be in slow motion. Time had slowed down for this health giver…almost to the point of a dead stop.

When the large group of locals reached the train, they could not believe their eyes. The locomotive was pulling more boxcars than ever before. Surely all of these cars couldn't be totally full of wounded and sick soldiers?

A large man with authority in his voice began yelling to the people of the town to break up in-groups.

"Each group take a boxcar to help unload the wounded." He yelled out loudly.

One quick look told them all the cars were indeed full of soldiers in dire need. The amount of wounded and sick overloaded the compartments and staggered the imagination. Without a doubt the temporary hospital setup would be inundated with this hoard of fallen men.

A few surgeons on the train were still treating the multitude as John climbed aboard. He began helping the injured army personnel that could still walk to disembark from the railroad cars.

After the last of the walking wounded had been helped from the cars, John and several others climbed back on the train and began to make their way from one boxcar to the next. It was not easy working their way through the blood soaked straw that covered the floors but they had to make sure no one was left behind.

What the group didn't know was that all of the wounded hadn't been taken off the train. A loud scream penetrated the cars sending a cold chill down the men's back. It was the scream of pain and it made them run even faster towards the sound swinging open the car door with a very large bang.

They had slammed the door into the wall with such force it nearly scared the two surgeons out of their wits that was now standing before them.

The small group had stumbled onto the car that the surgeons had set up for their operations and what they saw before them was nothing short of horrible.

To say that McPhail was stunned at the sight would be an understatement of major proportions. His brain could not believe the sight his eyes were seeing.

Set up in one corner of the doctors car was a door placed on two barrels being used as a cutting table. The surgeons were probing with bare fingers in search of musket balls in the soldiers wounds while on another makeshift table an amputation was being performed crudely on a young man still awake and screaming.

Dead bodies of the ones that didn't make it were piled into one corner. Another corner contained piles of arms and legs that had been tossed by the surgeons after being cut off in haste. Because time and pressure was great, the doctors had cut, slashed, and sewed as quickly as possible, moving on to the next patient being given chloroform in the event the decision was made to amputate.

John's mind was almost unable to receive the scenes unfolding before him; he all but totally snapped. It was just too painful of a scene for a man who had just gone through the trauma of a young girl's death. How could any civilized man go through such horror?

He turned and burst out the side door of the rail car jumping to the ground and ran past the nurses and their helpers. Like a mad man he ran right by the crowd of sick and wounded being laid out on stretchers everywhere. He had never run so fast in his life and had no idea, nor cared where he was going.

All his mind would allow him to think of now was a quiet setting under an old oak tree high atop a hill north of town.

The sickness in him was overwhelming with a feeling of all the ills and pains plaguing the troops rolled into one ball and placed in his stomach. He fell like it contained typhoid fever, malaria, dysentery, and a host of gastroenteric problems that many of the soldiers carried with them.

Panting like a large over weight dog he ran straight up the hill where the old oak was, until finally he became subdued and exhausted to the point he could go no more. The old tree was just a hundred feet away now and surely he could make it there he told himself.

Again and again he spoke words of encouragement to himself trying to convince his body that he could reach that old oak until finally McPhail dropped himself down on the ground underneath the branches of that old tree.

His body fell onto the grass and as he hit the ground a sharp pain penetrated his right side. It was the pain coming from a hard object in his coat pocket that he had landed on. He raised his rear up enough to slide his hand into the coat and retrieve the item. It was the Madstone; the only thing giving him a little peace in his mad world.

He stared at the stone that saved lives and took a deep breath knowing that he was one in a million to own the jewel of jewels.

As if to keep anyone from taking it from him, he locked his hand around the stone in a dead man's grip and laid his body back on the ground and a restless sleep fell upon him but his hand still held tightly to the stone. John was not sure how long he had slept when something awoke him.

It wasn't the sound of footsteps that arouse him, but rather a sense of someone being nearby. The last thing he expected to see when he opened his eyes was a very young girl standing over him trying to smile with a mouth full of sugar cookie. "You sick?" she said still holding the cookie to her mouth.

John looked at the dirty face girl with tears in his eyes and tried to explain in terms she would understand. He placed his hand flat on his chest indicating that he had sickness inside so that she might understand better.

"You know how it feels to lose your puppy?" He said. "Well, the town's full of lost puppies and I'm sad inside."

The nine-year old pulled on her dress to look more ladylike as she knelt beside him and offered him part of her cookie. McPhail smiled weakly as he took a small part of the treat and nibbled on it.

"When I'm sad inside," she said, "my mom sings to me and I feel better. She's down at the train station and told me not to come or I'd get her to sing to you."

John thought for a moment before answering the button nose young girl with curly blonde hair.

"Ya know honey, you're right; maybe a little bright music might help. Yep, it just might help at that and I think I know who could do it."

He jumped up and hugged her with one quick move, never noticing the cookie crumbs pressed firmly against his coat as he headed for his cabin. He would do the only thing that he knew he could handle right now. He knew it would help him and maybe, just maybe, a lot of the incoming wounded.

The colorful plaid kilts and cap gave the look of a true Scotsman as McPhail carried the pipes and returned to the hospital area. No sooner had he stepped into the building than he began playing "Scotch on the Rocks," a Highlanders' cheerful song. For a brief moment everyone looked up in surprise at this crazy Scotsman playing songs in the middle of all this chaos.

Then several of the helpers wasted no time in joining with John as he played. One retrieved a trumpet and several more came up with bagpipes as if they were waiting for someone to ask them. Heaven only knows how they came up with them so fast. One of the men even brought a set of drums that he had retrieved from his home. Now they were very close to having a full band and it did indeed seem to brighten the day for the wounded warriors and local residents in the camp.

The beautiful marching music seemed to act like a strong tranquilizer to the wounded southerners. Even though most were in severe pain they still responded to the happy music. What a welcome change seeing this crazy highlander playing and dancing up and down the rows of the injured men. Even the nurses hummed to the tunes and felt better as they began trying to smile and cheer the soldiers even though they, themselves were hurting inside.

When Confederate Major General John B. Hood heard of this, he ordered that bands be set up to play for the wounded as much as possible. After many battles the federal troops would hear music coming from areas they knew were hospitals and were puzzled at what the rebs were doing. Even though the southerners were short of men, the musicians would fight during the day and play their instruments at night.

This went on almost throughout the entire war. Sometimes the gray coats would confuse their enemy even more by playing songs that they knew would get the goat of the Yankees because the tunes were popular northern songs. Occasionally a federal soldier would wander into a southern camp because he heard the Yankee music and thought he was returning to a federal encampment.

Embarrassing to the union officers, an order was put out to pay no attention to the nightly playing. Soon after, the Federal's too began playing to their wounded and it was not long before it became routine; fight during the day, play at night. It was the first time in the history of warfare that music became a part of the weaponry used against the enemy.

Chapter 11

Dr. Samuel Preston Moore directed the Confederate medical department in September 1862 when the Confederate Congress organized a system of "Way Hospitals" along routes of major railroads. Quarters and rations for troops on their way home were to be provided to care for the sick and wounded. The Robeson County, North Carolina train station was one such line that fell among the first ordered to improve the situation and the McPhail's were one of the first to volunteer.

John and Elizabeth helped organize the new hospital built in an old armory; the only structure large enough and easy enough to convert. Elizabeth was nearing her time to give birth but she was still determined to make herself useful. There was no way she could do all the nurse duties normally assigned to her but she could help with the light work of making bandages, changing bed sheets and preparing foodstuffs. And without a complaint she did so with enthusiasm.

The old armory was transformed into a hospital by the locals with McPhail helping rebuild the interior, patching the roof and cutting holes through the brick walls for windows and fresh air. They then set up an ambulance service to shuttle the injured men from the train to the armory where the doctors would be waiting.

New wells were dug for fresh water and provisions stored for the upcoming disabled in need of help. Now they would be ready and could handle many more than ever before. They had no idea just how many more was about to be sent to them and just how bad the horror would be.

By year's end the Federals were fighting within fifty miles of Richmond but the battles of Second Manassas, Harper's

Ferry, Antietam and Fredericksburg were sending thousands more wounded south by rail.

The union medical corps under newly appointed Dr. William A. Hammond was so deluged with sick and wounded it took a full week to clear the field of the dead and injured soldiers at the second battle of Manassas alone.

The Federals too, were unprepared for such a mound of returning personnel in desperate need of medical treatment. The sick and wounded were flowing back to the Washington area by the thousands. Quite often the high command of the military would not allow trains to enter Washington except late at night for fear that the public would really discover how dangerous and brutal this war had become. Government propaganda had continuously informed the public that the war with the south was going well and would soon be over.

Daily they downplayed the battles and oftentimes reported very little of the conflict. Had they unloaded huge amounts of wounded men at the station with everyone watching it could have been disastrous, so the officers were ordered to have their men meet the train outside the downtown area and unload the returning soldiers into wagons where they were taken to different areas for treatment. This gave the impression of less wounded and allowed the army to boast of winning big battles with fewer casualties.

Later however, people of the northern states would find out the truth and a great deal of rioting in New York and Washington took place in protest of the draft.

Several generals were given a court martial and thrown out of the service for covering up the truth about mountains of wounded returning from the front but still a great deal of the truth was covered up. The war was to get more brutal as engagement after engagement occurred in every part of the country. Still it would be years before the true facts of the civil war would be known.

John and Elizabeth had a new son by March 1863 and the war had new battles centered around Colonel John Mosby, known as the "Gray Ghost." Operating in Northern Virginia with cavalry charges that went down in history as some of the most spectacular on the face of the earth, John Mosby caused absolute frustration among the union generals trying to capture him. His hit and run tactics made his unit one of the first guerrilla warfare armies in the world.

McPhail had heard stories of the exploits of Mosby and much admired his daring. He didn't realize how close he would come to getting his dreams granted of being one of the colonel's Mosby's colorful and dashing men until something happened one day right after the birth of his son.

As if by fate, word reached John that the gray ghost had camped several miles outside of town and was seeking volunteers as replacements for soldiers killed in his company. Without giving a second thought, McPhail bolted onto his wagon and headed for the southern hero's campsite. He arrived filled with excitement at the thought of meeting the colonel, but instantly encountered a hostile reaction. A few of the Colonel's young rebels grabbed the reins with what seemed to be fire in their eyes and ordered him off the wagon seat. John was completely dumfounded at their actions. His voice became louder as more of the cavalrymen moved around the horse drawn ambulance. Now he was beginning to get shook.

"Colonel, Colonel Mosby." He called out.

He had simply come to meet the one man he admired most and now he was about to be attacked? He stood straight up on top of the seat of the wagon and once again yelled out.

"Colonel, Colonel Mosby, which one is Colonel Mosby?" He said.

A short distance away, leaning against a tree next to an open fire was a bearded soldier wearing a very dirty gray uniform. He was a colonel but McPhail hadn't caught sight of the man's uniform in time. Before he could say anything more, several of the gray coats pulled him from the wagon causing the Scotsman to hit the ground hard. The impact with the hard ground was severe enough to knock the breath out of him causing the southerner to roll about in the dirt trying to regain his normal breathing.

Finally he recovered enough to get back on his feet but he had to push himself up butt first in order to stand. He bent his back and tried to push himself up but suddenly felt something shove against the seat of his pants causing him to once again go sprawling flat down on his face.

Colonel Mosby ordered the men to back away, but a corporal had already placed his booth square in the middle of McPhail's back and saw to it he remained face down in the dirt. The commander became irritated at the actions of his men and raised his voice making sure his order was quite clear this time.

"Pick that man up and bring him by the fire." He said.

John couldn't understand what had happened but had an immense sense of relief that at least the senior officer had stopped it. Two of Mosby's men picked up the bruised McPhail off the ground and carried him with feet dangling to their commander. At that moment John caught sight of his wagon and suddenly the reason for their actions stood out boldly in front of him. Painted on the side of the wagon in great big letters was "U.S. Army." It was one of the ones taken at the battle of Manassas and brought back for use at the hospital. Clearly they had forgotten to paint over the lettering! "What a fool he had been; from now on he would make sure it didn't happen again." He thought to himself.

McPail placed his hands over his face and bent his head over facing the ground. Then he turned to Mosby with a hurt expression and begin to explain how he had come to be driving a Yankee wagon.

"Furthermore." He said. "If they should care to inspect the contents of the wagon, they would also find some blue coat's medical supplies that he had been using for wounded confederates."

Finally he regained his composer, but was now hell-bent on kicking the ass of the cavalryman that had left his boot mark on his back. In one quick move, John lunged at the corporal with his head hitting squarely in the soldier's stomach knocking him to the ground with such force, it clearly took the wind from him.

"I feel better now." John said, "Next time make sure it's a Yankee when you decide to beat the hell out of somebody!"

With his pride more intact, McPhail extended his hand to help the rebel up but the noise of a fast approaching rider caused him to glance in that direction dropping the soldier once again to the ground. By now, the entire company of men turned their attention to the messenger jumping from his horse before the animal had even stopped running.

"Message from Lee's Staff, Colonel" he said. "I was ordered to get it to you as quickly as possible."

It took but a moment for the Colonel to read the letter and rise to his feet. He addressed his men slightly holding the message up high for them to see.

"We've been ordered north again men; the Army of the Potomac has a new general by the name of Joseph Hooker. He's about to face Lee's men at Fredericksburg and they want us to disrupt any supplies on the way to reinforce the Yankees. Mount up your gear, we're moving out immediately!"

John could only stand there holding the reins to his horses trying to keep them from moving around in the excitement while the company of men grabbed everything in sight and mounted without any hesitation at his orders.

These men had been through this very same situation many times and knew the drill. They had not slowed down even though their animals had already begun following the colonel north to glory. The rebels swung their bodies into the saddle as the horses moved out of camp. All but one was disappearing down the narrow road.

The man that McPhail had butted in the gut hesitated before joining the rest of the group. He turned his horse towards the healer wearing a great big smile that seemed to tell John he was sorry for knocking him to the ground. Then he once again turned his horse and began riding fast to catch up with the group.

"Good luck." He yelled back over his shoulder to John. "I'll be more careful about jumping someone next time; until I'm sure!"

The Scotsman stood there dreaming that he had joined with the group and was about to ride into history.

It wasn't until the last man faded out of sight did his body jerk to reality. Now he was left standing alone by the fire with a sinking feeling.

There was nothing left to do now but climb aboard the wagon and go back to the hospital area. The Scotsman shoved his bagpipes a little further over on the seat to keep from setting on them. Then he turned the horses slowly towards town still looking back in the direction the riders had gone.

Oh, how he wished he was riding into history with those men in gray! McPhail told himself. He hadn't even had a chance to talk to Mosby, but at least he almost met the great man.

He had desperately wanted to join the fast moving group of heroes and found it hard to keep from looking back to what was now an empty horizon. John still wasn't sure of just how brave he really was and now he probably would never find out. His heart sank as he moved the horses at a slow pace not really wanting to return to his job of treating the wounded. He so wanted to be a great warrior like Mosby or Stonewall Jackson, but his dreams of glory was not in the cards. He would have to live out the hand that fate had deal him and await the final outcome.

John Singleton Mosby became a lieutenant colonel while serving as a partisan ranger in the Confederate Army. "The gray ghost" had been commissioned into the Virginia state forces but had begun his career as a private, serving with the First Virginia Cavalry in early 1861. He had fought at the battle of first Bull Run and scouted for J.E.B. Stuart making a famous name for himself by guiding the confederates around McClellans' forces. Soon after, he was given permission to organize his partisan rangers and engage in guerrilla warfare starting in Loudoun Valley of northern Virginia. His most famous act happened in March of 1863, when he captured B.G. Stoughton from his bed in the middle of the night. He uncovered the sleeping union general and slapped him on the rear taking him prisoner at 2 am on a dark and rainy night. It was downright embarrassing for the union general especially because thousands of his Yankee troops were camped very close by.

After that the union army went all out to try and find the Confederate ghost but their huge army was unable to track Mosby down. It was said that the life of the Confederacy was prolonged by the gray ghost diverting much of Grant's strength to combat the partisan rangers.

Rather than surrender at the end of the war, Mosby disbanded his rangers totaling 200 on April 20th, 1865. He would later become involved in reconstruction politics and live a long full life traveling to Hong Kong and California before settling back down in Virginia. He died in his bed peacefully in 1916 and was most known for wearing an ostrich plume decorating his rebel hat that waved in the breeze as he rode into combat. It was often said that the union officers gave orders to look for the ostrich plume so they might recognize and strike down the gray ghost. When President Abraham Lincoln heard of the union general's capture he had only one thing to say.

"I can make brigadier generals, but I can't make horses." He was more concerned about the loss of the horses than the capture of the general.

John's ride back to the "armory turned hospital" was really not what he had in mind and he dreaded returning to treating the wounded. He felt that now he would never have a chance to show his true worth in this great war.

He had dreamed of being able to have fascinating stories to tell his children and grandchildren. Stories about heroic deeds he had done in the great battles and the many lives he had saved from his sheer brilliance of fighting large engagements. Instead he had become no more than a nurse treating the aftermath of conflicts and that's about as far from being a hero as you can get. Hell, he might as well be wearing a dress as far as he was concerned.

The truth of the matter was that McPhail hadn't seen the whole picture. He failed to recognize the fact that he and many others like him had indeed saved a lot of lives by helping the doctors and nurses treat their wounds. He could not have given more of himself to help than the treatment and care of the sick and wounded.

The horses pulled the wagon up to the front of the hospital just as Dr. Malloy emerged with a cigar in one hand and a hot cup of coffee in the other. The tired doctor shifted the cigar to the hand holding the coffee and began digging for something in his apron pocket. Then he pulled out a telegraph cable to hand to John and promptly switched the cigar back into the empty hand.

John could see that the doctor was more than tired, he was exhausted. Elizabeth's father was at the point of being overwhelmed with both emotion and sheer exhaustion. He was well aware that their little hospital was already short handed and that the telegraph was not good news.

"Richmond's asking that we send all the men and wagons we can spare towards Fredericksburg." He said. "They're expecting a large battle in that area, and will really need help, but I don't know who we can spare. We've got too much for our people to handle now and their still asking for more."

John couldn't help but beam with delight when he responded to the news.

"Can't spare nobody, but me and old man Adams. John said. "We'll pack as much as the wagon will hold and leave at sunrise."

The doctor attempted to object but John interrupted him several times not wanting to hear any logic that might convince him otherwise. He managed to crawl back aboard the wagon and leave ending the conversation. It was McPhail's way of giving the doctor no further chance for debate. He intended to pick up Adams and load the wagon full of supplies so that they could leave early next morning.

John was a changed man as daylight began the next day, he felt that somehow he was back in the battles. It became uppermost in his mind that if only he could once again pick up a rifle and join his comrades from the south to help stop the

Washington dictators. At least he would be close to the battles coming up and be of some help rather than watch an army of torn bodies returning. He didn't know it at the time, but he would soon be literally screaming to get out and stay out of the coming conflicts.

Although Elizabeth had not wanted him to go, she knew that it was the best thing in the world for his morale. He was returning to the battlegrounds and she realized somehow that it was in him; he must go and it would be futile for her to try and prevent the Scotsman from doing so.

The baby was much too young to travel and it prevented her from joining him on the trip. Anyway she knew that her place now was with the children and she could best be of help to her father as he treated the almost daily incoming wounded. How was she to know that this southern girl would soon go down in history. She and a lot of other ladies in the area started a movement that was to make North Carolina known as the Waiting Ladies State.

The sanitary conditions of the troops and wounded were worst than poor; they were downright pitiful and getting worse after John left.

Elizabeth had seen enough of the unbelievable lack of even the slightest attempt to have sanitary reforms.

As everyone knows, the force of the women's movement was powerful even in the 1860's, long before the time of voting rights for ladies.

Hundreds of the women were anxious to emulate the work of Florence Nightingale, as they began their work to pressure the southern army to build latrines, improve food rations, provide more blankets and distribute tobacco and letters.

Descending on the confederacy with a fierce vengeance, the women forced pamphlets to be printed stressing sanitary measures; brought to bear the female persuasion that only they could achieve against the preoccupied military commanders, and kept the troops from falling back into a state of apathy. As more and more rallied to their support, they began performing wonders in educating the troops in the basic sanitary procedures. Although few had any nursing experience, they provided a morale boost for the first time by cleaning up wards, improving the preparation of food, and in general giving tender loving care.

Each day fresh meat, fruits, and vegetables as could be gathered up were carried to the troops, along with clean towels and soap.

Elizabeth looked like an Indian squaw with papoose, when she carried her newborn strapped to her back while making her errands of mercy with the other not so ladylike angels. Often the ladies carried pots of hot beans and rice and anything else they could find. Rows of the ladies would march into the camps loaded with foodstuffs, blankets, and hot coffee.

It was an ominous sight to see, as the flood of self trained nurses jumped into the middle of a war never before or after seen by this great country. They showed great courage facing these men with arms and legs blown off, or hideous wounds that had been inflicted at some god-awful battle.

Only a few months before they were southern ladies knowing little of life's tragedies and sheltered from life's heartaches. They were the cream of southern society and their only problem was likely to be what to wear to the next dance. Now things had changed and these same ladies had changed with it, showing the real stock they were made of.

In the midst of the desperate situation, corruption and inefficiency were considerable, but the new association of homemakers took action that was effective and finally beneficial in correcting the lack of care needed for the fighting men.

Heartwarming care was given by the women to their men folk, while at the same time corruption was handed a firm blow to the chin. The women became bold and aggressive, showing the world that they no longer would sit quietly by while the soldiers suffered because of corrupt politicians.

On several occasions the ladies broke into stores of supplies intended for the black market and passed the goods to the sick and wounded. The demand for huge quantities of medical supplies caused the price to rise at alarming rates for alcohol, castor oil, turpentine, and a variety of other medicines. In one move the wives turned their attention to the sellers of opium and quinine, forcing them to supply the drugs fairly, with a minimum of profit.

North Carolina became known as the waiting lady's state because of their aggressive actions against the evil corruption. They were always waiting for the dealer selling products unfairly, particularly if it had to do with their men in gray. After the word had spread about the ladies being on the warpath; the black market trade in North Carolina dropped to an all time low causing a number of stories to be written about the ladies. Even after the war, stories were still being written about the waiting ladies state and the marvelous work they had done.

The months to follow exploded with battles across Virginia costing fifty thousand casualties. The southern wounded were poured into rail cars and ambulance wagons to be moved south while the northerners spread their injured among the towns around the Washington area. The battle statistics were grim, but both sides had a greater threat because of sickness. Outbreaks of measles, mumps, chicken pox, whooping cough, scarlet fever, and diphtheria spread like wildfire causing the towns and cities resources to be taxed to the limit.

Still the flow kept coming and coming. No one could have anticipated the amount of sickness that would come to both armies because of inadequate diets and downright dirty field conditions.

The Army Medical Corp. was actually forced on both the Federal Government and the Confederacy by the wives and daughters of the fighting men on both sides. For the first time in American History, notoriety was given to the fact that there had to be sanitary conditions available to the fighting men. So much so, that the head generals on both sides set up and took notice because of the publicity the women had caused...There was about to be hell to pay for both the northern and southern leaders.

Chapter 12

McPhail and old man Adams had traveled for days before reaching the outskirts of Fredericksburg, only grabbing a few hours of sleep a night to make better time. Since John had almost been forced into the fighting once, he had decided to paint the word "Doctor" in large letters on both sides of the canvas covering the top of the wagon. He was sure it helped, but it still didn't stop snipers from shooting at the wagon on occasions. Half of the time he couldn't tell if it was northern or southern bullets flying through the canvas. He was just grateful that the bullets didn't fly through him or the old man.

The ride had been tedious and by now the wooden seat of the wagon was as hard as a brick on John and the old man's butt. Several times they turned and looked back at the supplies because the load was shifting back and forth in the bed of the wagon as it bumped along slowly climbing the steep hill just outside Fredericksburg.

They had tied strips of cloth over their faces because the dust from the horses hooves and the wagon wheels was pretty bad the whole time they had been trying to reach the top of the mountain. Now at last the one wagon caravan had reached the top the two men could see the valley below.

John pulled back on the reins to bring the animals to a stop and peered out over an awesome sight that lay in a large field below him.

There stretched out almost as far as the eye could see was row after row of rebel soldiers camped in the field below him. It was pretty obvious that they were resting from their forced march to join up with Lee. There was no doubt that there was soon going to be a very large battle. It didn't take many brains to know that tomorrow they would unite with the main Army of Northern Virginia for a fight with the Yankees and that the conflict was going to be in Fredericksburg that was close by.

The two southerners move the wagon on down the hill and approached several rebels on picket duty. John pulled the cloth off his face and stopped the wagon a few feet from the guards to identify themselves. The Confederate soldiers on picket duty wasted no time in carefully searching the boxes to confirm that it was indeed medical supplies. When they were satisfied that John and the old man were what they said they were, a mean looking sergeant was called over. The non-com was having stomach trouble and the guards thought that the doctor on board the wagon could be of service.

Now John was wishing he hadn't written doctor on the side of the canvas. Never the less he gave the sergeant a white powder that doctor Malloy had told him was good for the pain of stomach trouble. Perhaps this would help to get him and the old man able to be moving on their way. Problem was, when the sergeant realized that the vehicle was full of medicines and a doctor was on board he had other ideas. McPhail was politely but firmly invited to treat a few of the men in the group when they saw "doctor" printed on the side of the covered wagon. His few turned out to be five hours worth of work and 16 were treated with the Madstone for infections and other ills. The two medics were escorted from one campfire to another with the rough looking sergeant leading the way. The sergeant was feeling better by now and telling everybody about the great doctor here to look them over…if they needed anything. There was no stopping the non-com now, he was determined to check out almost all his men. John, Adam and the sergeant moved from one tent to another doing their best to be of help, but by now the travelers were worn out. Still John noticed that the troops looked in worse shape then they were. Most had clothes that were worn and dirty and their body was likewise. An uneasy calm had settled over the entire group probably because of the long distance most of the men had come.

They were about to go into another fight for their southern homeland and even though the ferocity of the battles had taken it out of them, the confederate soldiers became men with a mission. Even knowing they were vastly outnumbered and outgunned, the rebels were more determined than ever to fight on.

John had looked into the faces of a hundred men that stared back with blank expressions when he turned to the sergeant to ask a question he really was afraid to put to the noncom.

"Just how far away are the Yankee troops now?" He questioned.

"Not far enough" the noncom answered pulling his wide belt back over a potbelly and then pointing off into the distance.

"If you were to fire in that direction, it just might hit a blue coat in the butt."

"Well, glad I'm not going in that direction." McPhail sighed happily pointing 40 degrees to the west. "We'll be heading a bit more over that way, to the west."

McPhail had no idea that he was pointing directly to where both armies would clash in bloody combat in a few short days.

After the sergeant had finally decided that they had treated their last patient John and Adam arose to their feet and stretched their bones before walking towards their wagon.

Suddenly the air was filled with the smell of something delicious being cooked and it did not go unnoticed by the pair. They had stumbled upon a young soldier cooking something in a pot of water and boy, the aroma was delightful. The young private setting on a rock stirring the hot liquid looked barely fifteen years old. He was sipping at a spoon full of the soup when his eyes caught the two men approaching.

He smiled and greeted them as if he were happy to have someone stop by. "Hi Doc!" He said to McPhail. "Saw your wagon come into camp. Sure glad to have you with us."

McPhail was busy eyeing the food because he and old man Adams hadn't eaten for quite a awhile.

"It smells pretty good" Said John, as he and the old man bent over to get a better look into the black kettle hanging over the fire. The two men almost burn themselves getting so close to the pot. They were so hungry they stared hard at the liquid but the darkness of the night kept the men from telling exactly what was being cooked. They bent over and smelled the aroma again and again trying to figure out just what it was and of course hoping to be invited to supper.

"What is it? rabbit?" A tired John asked the young soldier. The rebel didn't bother to answer; he just smiled and filled a tin plate with the food using a large wooden spoon, then handed it to McPhail.

Then he pointed to a log that was close to the fire and invited John to join him. "Have a seat." He finally said.

When Adam saw this, he stood a little closer to John with a hungry look on his face causing the private to again dish up a plate and this time offer it to the old man. "Want some?" he said, "It's pretty tasty".

Now McPhail was not about to pass up a hot meal of rabbit, so he ate two plates full. His belly was full now and as was his custom he pulled his pipe and tobacco from his coat pocket and lit up with a burning stick from the fire. Trying to get more comfortable he turned his body a little more towards the fire and as he did so something under the young private's wagon caught his eye.

The underside of the wagon had seven small cages attached to it, hanging down between the wheels. Each one was marked for a day of the week, with the first three being empty and the remaining four containing a thin ground hog, two rattlesnakes, one opossum, and something unknown to John. He quietly stared at the cages trying to figure out why anyone would have animals under their wagon. He took several more puffs from his pipe and then it dawned on him; it was Wednesday, the same day marked on the third empty cage. These creatures were for food! Tomorrow would be Thursday, which would mean a ground hog day meal and Friday would be rattle snakes.

McPhail pushed himself up into a better setting position and tried to act nonchalant about the question he was about to ask. He turned to the soldier and put his trigger finger on one side of the bridge of his nose and his thumb on the other side as if to ward off a headache. Then he closed his eyes and in a soft voice asked the question he really didn't want to know the answer to.

"What kind of stew did you say that was private?"

The young soldier was very busy trying to ward off biting insects when he gave his reply.

"Don't rightly know sir, but it ran on four legs…at lease I think it did…cause it slid on its belly part of the time. On the other hand it was so fast it must have had legs. Anyway I sure had a hell of a time catching it, fastest critter I ever did see! I didn't bother to check it, just threw it into the cage and you know something, it fit just right in my cooking pot. Almost as if the little critter was raised for it."

Old man Adam bit down on his chewing tobacco smiling at the look on John's face and couldn't keep himself from saying it.

"Y, That there must have been a yankee rat. Was it wearing a little blue coat?" he said, trying not to laugh out loud. John spent the rest of the night worrying about just what that animal was that was on his plate.

179

McPhail was anxious now to reach the main body of troops at Fredericksburg and hand over the wagon full of supplies. He had already become tired of the trip and perhaps he could begin his ride back just as soon as he unloaded. He really wanted to move out of the area before the huge battle started, not to mention that he missed Elizabeth terribly.

By now John and the old man decided the best way to spend the night was to roll up in a wool blanket underneath their wagon. Of course, it wasn't anything special, they often did that especially if it looked like rain.

The next night John lay between the wheels of the wagon trying to deny any thought to himself of being a coward. Every time he had decided that he wanted to join the fighting once more, a little clock in his brain began ticking off fear signals when he reached the scene of upcoming battles and this was certainly one of those times. He was unnerved at the thought of seeing a huge blue coat army with bayonet clad rifles held straight out in front of their bodies coming right at him. The rest of the night he spent tossing and turning trying to ward off his fears.

At first light the pair of medics hooked up the animals and climbed aboard. John had made the decision that he was only there to deliver the supplies and not try to become a doctor again. If he were to get caught up in the battle trying to help all these men, god only knows when he would be able to get out of there.

John was moving the wagon so slowly all the soldiers were scurrying around him, mostly heading in the same direction. By the hundreds they were moving straight towards a stone wall that was to be used for cover. When he reached the edge of town there was so many rebels perched behind the stone wall he couldn't count them and they were certainly getting their rifles at the ready.

John couldn't understand it, there were no Yankees that he could see in the immediate vicinity. The streets were empty and there was no shooting or fighting of any kind anywhere. There was however, an impressive looking officer that seemed to be in charge standing with a group of others just down the road. Mcphail decided to ask the Colonel where he might unload the supplies. After all, since he had seen nothing going on he was still confident he could get the medical supplies off the wagon and be out of there before the Yankees could attack. This was a big mistake. Even before he could ask the Colonel anything, all hell begin breaking out in every direction.

At that very moment the Yankee army began shelling the town with heavy guns from across the Rappahannock River, trapping the two men before they could withdraw. Hundreds of falling shells from very big guns came raining down from the sky. Explosions and chaos were everywhere.

John dove for protection behind a large tree landing hard on the rocky ground. In the confusion of so many explosions the Scotsman suddenly noticed that the leather pouch containing the Madstone had fallen from around his neck. His hand no longer could feel the bag hanging inside his shirt and he began to panic, trying to figure out where he had lost it. Now his panic doubled. He was desperate to begin looking for the precious stone, but couldn't move with so much firepower being used against the southern army.

Now he was trapped right in the middle of it. He placed his hands on top of his head as if he could protect himself against cannonballs, and could do nothing but watch as the shells rain down from the sky. Cannon after cannon fired in sequence from long rows across the river. Again and again with a vengeance the explosions covered the area for what seemed to be an eternity. Some of the confederates were immediately blasted to kingdom come while others flatten their bodies against the ground just hoping to stay alive. Again and again the shells rained down in fierce fashion on the large southern army and McPhail just knew he was a dead man. He pulled off his hat and said a quick prayer.

"Lord either make me bullet proof or make the blue coats very bad shots cause no one could live through this".

The shells were bursting dangerously close now to the point of throwing dirt, dust and rocks all over his body. He hugged the tree so close it was as if he were making love to it.

Then suddenly the shelling stopped and there was almost complete silence. With a sigh of relief, he stood up and looked around to see how many others were as scared as he was. Then once again his panic button activated when he remembered that his Madstone was missing. The scared Scotsman turned back to retrace his steps trying to find the one thing that made sense in this mad world. He hadn't gone far when a large rain barrel began to slowly move right in front of him. Within seconds old man Adams' had turned the barrel over and fell out on the ground. He looked straight at John and then turned and ran. It was obvious that he was trying to put some space between him and the cannons across the river. As much space as was possible before it started again.

"Let's get the hell out of here, before it starts again!" The old man yelled out. John thought that was a hell of a good idea but he couldn't leave without his Madstone.

For a moment he watched the old man run but hesitated when he felt something stuck in his trousers. It was his leather pouch containing the Madstone! What a sigh of relief came over him when he realized that the strap had broken and the pouch had fallen into his pants. He stuck his hand inside his trousers and carefully retrieved the stone. You might know it, out came a loud voice from behind the stone fence where all the rebels were still hiding.

"Won't protect it from the cannon-balls laddie! The voice said in a bold laughter. "You might as well let go of your pride and joy."

John shoved the leather pouch in his coat pocket and turned to follow the old man. At that moment a large cracking sound came from directly above him.

What now, he thought to himself as he stepped back and looked up. With a loud roar, a large limb came falling down at his feet carrying a small squirrel that was desperately clinging to the wooden branch. So scared was the little animal that he held on with a death grip to that big old branch, refusing to let go. The squirrel's big eyes met John's and they strangely stared at each other for what seemed a long moment. Finally McPhail spoke to the little rodent.

"What ya complaining about?" He yelled at the four legged tree climber. "You made it through the battle; Go about your business of collecting nuts for the winter little fellow, but don't wear a blue coat, one of the boys might shoot you."

With that he jumped up and ran towards the stone fence where hundreds of rebel soldiers now prepared once again for their deadly defense.

Somehow McPhail had gotten between the combatants, and when he looked back over his shoulder the whole gall darn union army was coming across the river and up the rocky hill straight for the southerners; not to mention also straight at John. He suddenly realized that the southern boys would begin shooting at any moment and he swung around just in time to see hundreds of rifles one after another being braced on top of the stone fence.

Rifle barrel after rifle barrel was being swung over the top of the stone wall at such a fast rate he was unable to even guess how many there were. There was no question that they were preparing to greet the oncoming Yankees with a hot welcome and John was smack in the middle of the welcome mat. All he could do now was run like hell and dive over the stone fence to take cover. John never ran so fast in his life, but he knew he better. It was his life that depended on it.

He Screamed at the top of his lungs to make sure that the southern troops behind the wall would know who he was. As he ran by the little squirrel that was now halfway up the tree he was not being shy about his screaming. Especially when he turned and looked back towards the river at thousands of Yankees coming straight at him. One more quick turn of the head to look back at the rebels behind the stone fence told him he had better do something...fast!

"Gray uniform coming in...Don't shoot, don't shoot...young southern boy coming. Look back there, the Yankees are coming behind me, see right over there...behind me!"

With a lot of sweat on his troubled forehead, he literally dove headfirst over the fence right into a rebels' lap.

He was not about to let a slight fall over a fence slow him down, not this southern boy. Back on his feet within seconds, John began running in a crouched position as fast as his legs would go. The only thought now that was running through the young Texan's mind was to get out of range of the Yankee rifles.

Now if he could just work his way back to his wagon on the other side of the hill and move farther back to the rear, then he was a cinch to unload the supplies and be able to head south out of there. John was never so scared in his life and he was the first to admit it. Well, not really out loud.

Mistakenly the union cannons began firing once again causing the shells to land on their own advancing troops. Within seconds a sea of bullets was being fired by the Union troops because the Yankees thought the shelling was coming from the rebels and they opened fire on the rebels.

Of course the rebels responded with like fire and it made it difficult to even see through so many bullets flying through the air. Shells and bullets were being exchanged at such a heavy rate hundreds of bodies were being blown to bits between the river and the stone fence. The Smoke, dust, and flying debris was nothing compared to the screams, blood and body parts that were sailing across the battle ground.

No one was expecting the first fire fight to cause so many wounded and it took the breath out of both sides. The southern boys were first to host a white flag and begin yelling at the Yankees to do the same. Again and again the cry went out to hold fast the firing.

Then to every one's surprise a sudden calm fell across the battle field. Even the generals were astonished at such a thing happening. There was no order given from the leaders of either side to stop the battle, but here it was; the bloody fight on the entire battlefield had stopped in its' tracks.

Both armies had suddenly showed respect to the white flag, and not one shot was being fired. Even the cannons had ceased as soon as the commanders saw what was happening.

Now Union and rebel alike were running out into the open field within a few feet of each other to remove the wounded and dying warriors. Most of the seriously wounded were Union troops because they were the ones that were caught out in the open.

Even before the white flags went up a young southern sergeant by the name of Richard Kirkland of the Second South Carolina infantry made history because of his compassion. He was so moved by the cries of the wounded Yankees in the field, he went past the line of southern soldiers that were still firing and made his way into the northern side of the field to give the hurt Yankees water. Bravely the sergeant moved from one blue coat to another helping the fallen men to be removed from the crossfire area before returning to his own lines.

Word spread through the union army about the rebel that gave help to the hurt Yankees and later he would be dubbed the "Angel of Fredericksburg" by the northerners.

A large statue now stands at the battle site in Fredericksburg of sergeant Kirkland giving water to a downed federal. Kirkland would be killed at the battle of Chickamauga in September,1863, holding a canteen in his left hand when he was shot. He was only twenty years old…

After the brief pause to remove the wounded, the field once again became a roaring battleground. The slaughter raged on for hours with the Yankees taking a major beating of such proportions that they began to retreat trying to carry their heavy losses with them.

John had been unable to get far enough away before the battle had gotten into high gear. He had found himself a nice little stone house with a big hole blown in side to hide in. Once the firing ceased, McPhail helped with the wounded and had gotten so involved with the fallen soldiers, it was an hour before he realized that old man Adams was nowhere to be seen.

He finished wrapping a rebels' arm and peered out across the bloody field of bodies hoping to spot the old man. If he didn't find old man Adams soon, the firing might resume and they could get caught up in it again and then it would be too late for them to get out of there.

He couldn't imagine where the old man could had gone to this time, or why he hadn't come out to meet him when the fighting stopped. The tough old bird just couldn't have been killed in the barrage, he was too much of a survivor to be killed so easily.

John begin to run towards the last place he had seen Adam fearing that he had been killed. He hesitated at every dead body lying on the ground long enough to see if it might be the old man. After all, he just might be wrong about the old fellow being a survivor.

The Scotsman worked his way down the stone road as fast as he could. He ran between the houses and up alleys almost totally overwhelmed at the enormous amount of bodies everywhere.

Fear raced through him when he realized that the sound he was hearing was cries of wounded men. Cries that were coming from across a thousand yards of battlefield and John knew there was not much time before the action would fire up again.

Exhaustion was about to overcome him but still he moved as fast as he could trying to find the old man.

"I've got to find him." He told himself out loud running from building to building. "Can't just leave the old jerk."

McPhail was beginning to lose patience with the hard headed old man and his antics. He was a buffoon but still in all he was a good man.

For a moment John stopped beside a brick building to catch his breath and take a second look around. He bend over and took deep breaths and then slowly stepped around the corner and that's went he saw the small saloon that had one wall completely blown out. For some reason unknown to him he took a long look inside the beer tavern.

Sure enough, under a table drinking whiskey was Adam shaking and sweating heavily. It was obvious that he was desperately afraid that the Yankees were almost upon him and couldn't seem to get enough of the hard liquor.

The old man looked up at McPhail only after his friend had grabbed him by the shoulders and almost pulled him out of his trousers. Now the man with the white beard was being hauled off through the hole in the wall and literally sliding across the ground as McPhail pulled him towards the supply wagon.

Adam however was not about to let go of the whiskey bottle even though John pulled, shoved, and prodded him up the stone road, away from the battle site.

John finally got him to the wagon but he still did not know if the old man had been hurt in the exchange of gunfire. He was too busy trying to get him out of there.

"You hurt?' McPhail said looking him over for any blood or damage. By now Adam was breathing heavily, but he wasn't letting go of the whiskey bottle. He was beginning to feel too damn good from the effects of the alcohol and it was just what he needed; or so he thought.

The only problem was, he had to hold on to the wagon to steady himself in order to reply to the question. He was however determined to answer the question in style. With an air of distinction the drunk old man stiffened his back and tried to look like an aristocrat when he answered.

"Only my pride so far, but I think my dignity is also in trouble." He said looking back at the river.

"But I suggest that we don't waste time, let's move on out of here, 'fore them Yankees start coming again."

Deciding that he was absolutely right, McPhail pulled him aboard the wagon and whipped the horses into a dead run never looking back. It was only a few miles outside town before the two medics began to hear the dreadful sound of yet another battle beginning.

John began to grit his teeth in anguish as he looked back to see smoke rising in the sky. Once again the heavy union guns were raining destruction on the town and the dark smoke rising was showing the terrible results.

Just the thought of it sent cold shivers down his spine and he felt it in his bones that the regiment was catching hell from a well-equipped army that vastly outnumbered them.

Now he ran the horses wide open until he was sure there was enough distance between them and the battle. When he could no longer heard the sounds of the fighting that was going on or see skies filled with black smoke, he pulled back on the reins to slow the horses down.

John knew now that he was safe, but still his body began to shake in an uncontrollable manner. He was not sure if it was from fear or from something he was not aware of.

"Maybe it was an unconscious something." He thought to himself. "Like seeing so many die and not being able to do anything about it. Like having it build up in side of him until the dam broke. Surely it will pass shortly." He whispered to himself.

At any rate he was not going to let the old man see his fears, or anxieties, or whatever was happening to him.

Now his impatience grew to get back to North Carolina and Elizabeth and it was getting the better of him. He made up his mind he wasn't going to stop the horses that was pulling his wagon until he got home.

"Pulling his wagon?" He suddenly said out loud. "Pulling this full wagon." He said one more time.

Now the Scotsman realized that he had ridden the wagon right out of town and it had never been unloaded. It was completely full of supplies and he knew it!

Pulling back hard on the reins, he brought the animals to a halt and angrily cussed out loud almost staring the old man out of his wits.

"We damn well got to go back," He said. "We still got the medicines and those boys back there are going to need them."

At that moment the sound of singing reached McPhail's ears and he recognized the Confederate song that was coming from directly in front of them. He had heard it before and knew that it was the sound of troops marching to war.

There, about a half mile out was a large group of southern soldiers coming straight at them headed for the battle he had just run from.

He had to think fast and think fast he did. In thirty seconds John had come up with a plan for getting the supplies back to the battle site. With a little bit of luck he would get the commanding officer to trade him a couple of horses and saddles for the wagon full of supplies.

Remarkably upon reaching the regiment, he found that the Major General in charge was quick to make the exchange. The General wasted no time in ordering several soldiers to attend the wagon and relinquish their horses to the men.

Adam and John mounted the animals that were turned over to them and saluted the commander as they turned towards home. They knew they could make far better time on horseback than riding in the wagon, but their hometown would now be short one wagon.

Oh well, to them losing the wagon was a small price to pay seeing how they were heading back home. The two medic's kept right on riding south but now at a slower pace.

McPhail rode atop the saddle horse trying to make himself feel that he had not run out on a fight. He really felt it in his heart that he was not a coward, but only keeping his word to Lincoln. He refused to admit that he had the very living hell scared out of him at that battle he just left behind.

Over and over he kept telling himself that he would fight.

If only he could somehow get back into a battle without breaking his word. At any rate, he was trying to convince himself that he truly belonged in the fighting part of the army, but it was not in the cards.

After the battle of Fredericksburg, collections were taken up in Lee's army for the civilian population of the town. The people were without food and had been left homeless from the artillery fire and looting by the Federals.

A.P. Hill's division donated about ten thousand dollars and Stonewall Jackson's Headquarters about one thousand dollars. All told, the army of Northern Virginia raised quite a sum for the besieged town folk and helped move supplies to the area giving much relief when it was badly needed.

Adam and McPhail traveled the roads south almost without incident. They were moving steadily away from the Rappahannock River and Burnsides one hundred and twenty thousand man union army. The on going battle that the Union troops were having with Lee's ninety thousand men made it plain to McPhail that shortly train loads of wounded would be heading towards North Carolina.

The rare jewel hanging around his neck seemed small compared to this holocaust. Even so, the Madstone somehow still made him feel important...

So far, John had managed to keep from breaking his word to Lincoln not to fight, but Adam was unaware of his promise. The pair had been riding side by side almost in complete silence until suddenly the old man pulled up the reins and completely stopped his horse.

McPhail was taken back by his sudden actions and stopped his mount so that he might turn his horse around to face the old man. For a moment he wasn't quite sure what to say to Adam. Then, with a question look on his face he spoke first.

"What's up?" John said.

Old man Adam pulled his chew tobacco from his pouch and took a nimble, but still gave John a strange look over the top of his glasses. He was about to catch his friend totally by surprise with his next statement. There was no way McPhail would have guessed what his companion was about to say.

"John." The old man said in a serious tone. "I can't help it. I've got to go back. The 26th North Carolina Regiment was there. Hundreds was right there…lined up behind that wall and I belong with them. I got to help those boys fight. I just can't tend to the wounded no more. It's just not in me; that fight is where I belong. I might be a bit old, but I can still fire a rifle straight into a yankee's belly and these young fellows need a hand, and they need it now."

John sat in the saddle almost dumbfounded as he gave some thought at the old man returning to help fight. He shifted his position on the saddle and listened to Adam talk of fighting in that huge battle. McPhail knew he was too old to be involved in the fighting but admired his guts.

The only thing he could think of was that maybe the old man had suddenly gotten some bravery. Then another thought flashed straight through his mind causing him to smile a bit.

"yea, right, firing from under a saloon table I suppose?"

For a minute McPhail didn't know what to say, then answered his friend with the only reply that didn't come as a surprise to the old man.

"The boys coming back need me more." John said. "I'll go back home and help the wounded that comes in as best I can, but you take care those blue bellies don't over run ya, you hear?"

McPhail smiled and shook hands with old man Adam's in such a way that he knew John really meant it.

Sadly he watched as Adam turned his horse towards the direction of the battle and rode off. He wasn't quite sure how he knew it, but he was sure that this was the last time he would ever see the old man again.

Unknown to Adam, he would survive the battle of Fredericksburg but would find himself in a hell-of-a-fight at Gettysburg just four months later. There, he would be captured and eventually die in a prisoner of war camp after just eight months of confinement.

As John watched, Adam disappeared over a hill leaving the Scotsman alone. He turned his horse back towards the direction of North Carolina moving the animal at a little faster pace. He knew that he best be getting home as soon as possible because he would be needed there when the wounded started pouring in.

The thought of it was still hard on McPhail. Here an old man goes back to fight and what does he do but put his tail between his legs and head for home. It just didn't add up, somehow it just wasn't right.

Even John had no idea just how badly he would be needed. In the coming months the wounded did come back in droves. Just from the three-day battle of Gettysburg alone, seventeen miles of wagons full of wounded returned.

A great many of these died before they could even reach their homes. The ones that made it, badly needed people like McPhail in the worst way. The shortages of medical personnel were enormous and were relieved only partially when town after town began putting their own hospital areas and personnel together. This was started mostly by the ladies of North Carolina during the war between the states.

Chapter 13

After returning from Fredericksburg, things were fairly quiet for John, Elizabeth and the baby. Wounded was still returning, but help had been sent by the confederate command to better handle the large number of injured soldiers. McPhail had been back a little over a month when a friend came to him with a daring plan.

Frank Kennedy wanted the Scotsman to join a group that was about to relieve the Yankees of a bit of their supplies. They would travel to New Bern on the coast and steal supplies from the federal naval base that had been set up after the recent takeover by the union.

Kennedy was extremely excited about his bold plan and couldn't wait to explain how it was to be done.

"The plan was simple." He said. "They would sneak in at night, hitch up horses to the wagons and quietly ride out."

There seemed to be only one small problem; there were a few hundred union troops stationed there who just might not like the idea, so they would steal union uniforms and blend in with the other Yankees.

Somehow John had heard this plan before and it worked then so why wouldn't it work now?

He knew the odds of pulling it off were pretty bad, but they sure needed all the supplies they could get, so that made the adventure more appealing. For the most part John was a young man and as everybody knows the young are unaware of the consequences of such actions. He didn't even stop to think that if they were discovered, he just might have to fight his way out of a bad situation.

All he could think about now was that he had promised not to fight against the north; again nothing was said about stealing supplies. The more John thought about the crazy idea the more excited he got. This was as close to fighting as he was going to get. It would give him another chance to show bravery, mostly to himself, and still do something great for the Confederacy. At lease this was what he kept telling himself.

"Sure I'll do it" He said, "When do we leave?"

McPhail had hardly said the words when it suddenly dawned on him, "How do I tell Elizabeth that I'm leaving again? He thought to himself. She surely would insist on going, so I must be tactical when I tell her and break it gently."

He would be very smart in the way he would approach the subject he told himself as he dismounted in front of the cabin. He even practiced his speech before going in, but how do you tell your wife that you're off to steal from an enemy that surely would kill you if you were caught?

Elizabeth was busy tending her pots on the stove when her husband entered the kitchen.

"Now." he though to himself. "How would the smartest man in the world approach the subject of telling his wife he was about to do something stupid once again.

John took a deep breath and almost bit his tongue as he slid into a chair at the kitchen table.

"Boy," He said. "Something sure smells good; must be your famous chicken and dumplings. Oh and by the way, I'll be going to New Bern for a few days." He blurted out.

Right then and there McPhail's mind began to race wildly. He knew he had handled the situation just about as bad as it could have been handled. He quickly changed tactics and started trying to make light of it. He began looking the food over that was on the stove but his thoughts seemed to be almost jumping out of his head.

"You call that breaking the news gently, you stupid idiot." He told himself. "Now you've done it, you jerk."

"Ain't chicken John." Elizabeth answered with a smile. "It's cornbread and beans tonight honey and I already know why you're going.

She turned and pointed her spoon to a neighbor that was quietly setting in one corner of the room that McPhail hadn't even noticed.

"Mary Ann told me." she said. Most of the town knows by now.

"Mary Ann had already heard through the grape vine that a group of men were going to try and steal wagons from the Federals at the old navy base. I knew you couldn't stay out of it, that you would surely be among them. Wouldn't do any good to try and stop you when your mind's made up. I just want you to come back in one piece." She said. "Now sit and eat your dinner and we'll hear no more about it tonight."

McPhail's anxiety had him up before dawn waiting for the group of men to assemble at the railroad station. Fourteen men wandered in and would make up the party that intended to liberate supplies from the Yankees at New Bern.

All fourteen had packed their horses with extra rations to the point of all most overloading the animals. They were ready to go and it took only a few handshakes and pats on the back to encourage the adventures to move out towards their quest.

The small group would travel off the main roads to avoid detection even though the thick woods meant longer traveling time and much tougher going. It did however make for safer conditions in the long run.

On the third day they came upon the remains of a skirmish between two patrols in thick underbrush and several bodies both northern and southern were lying where they fell. It looked as if two squads had stumbled upon each other in the thick woods and shot it out at close range. It was impossible to tell just who had won the battle or how many may have survived.

When they examined the bodies John and the others suddenly realized that this battle had happened very recently and the fighting was almost hand to hand.

Now, without even being told, all fourteen men brought their weapons to a fighting stance and began looking in every direction to make sure that they were alone.

"We had better get out of here and fast!" John said almost in a panic. "There may be others coming back to check on these men and it might not be rebel soldiers."

Cautiously John and the others remounted their horses and moved on towards their objective. After they had inspected the bodies, the thought of compassion in burying the fallen soldiers was put behind them. Without even speaking of it every man in the group decided that it was best they got the hell out of there.

Shallow graves for those poor devils would have to wait along with the thought of looking for more bodies. They couldn't take the chance that they might run into soldiers coming back to see about their men. Soldiers that just might be wearing the wrong uniform.

Who knows what patrols might still be in the vicinity and they sure didn't want to attract any more attention than was necessary.

The group of would be thieves moved as fast as they could through the dense underbrush fearing that more union men might be in the area. To a man the idea had suddenly sunk in that this trip just might not be the fun adventure they expected.

They began to take more caution in their movements to the point of talking in whispers and even padding the hooves of their horses. They hoped that if they did run into a union patrol they would spot them first and avoid the encounter.

The closer the men got to New Bern, the more cautious they became. They moved their animals more slowly now in a single file across the rough terrain. Constantly the rebels were on the lookout for the blue coats and it cost them precious extra time they didn't have.

As a matter of fact they moved so slowly it was four more days before they reached the naval base at New Bern and their frustration was sorely showing, but now they were even more determined than ever.

The squad of Confederates checked out the surroundings and picked out a high hill that overlooked the town. As they climbed, the group kept to the tall grass as much as possible to conceal themselves. When they reached the top it turned out to be a perfect vantage point for them to look down on the base. Now the rebel soldiers would get a better idea as to what they were facing.

Quietly they hid themselves in the grass and peered down at the union soldiers moving around the base camp.

"God Almighty." John said softly. "There's got to be a thousand men down there. Our spies told us there was only a few hundred…but I guess that was quite a while back. They must have brought in a lot more since then."

There was about five times as many blue coats encircling the town than they had anticipated. So taken back with the sight of such a strong force it was several hours before the small group of rebels made the decision to carry on with the plan.

The old plan of attack was now thrown out and a new idea was about to take shape. With so many union troops surrounding the town, their original idea of attack would not have worked; so it called for a very large bond fire to be added to their plans. Patiently they quietly rested in the grass and waited for nightfall.

When darkness came the raiding party began to make their way down the hill circling through some nearby heavy woods to avoid detection. This route however turned out to be a complex of affairs starting with Kennedy cutting his leg above the knee when he brushed against some farm equipment. Soon after, Robert Baker became ill from some food he had eaten and started throwing up violently.

Kennedy was still bandaging his wound from the farm equipment when Baker began heaving his guts out. Never giving it a second thought he gave him an order to return to the staging area where the horses were being held and stay with the animals until they returned.

Baker managed to obey the order even though he was having a lot of difficulty keeping things down. He slipped away from the others and slowly made his way back to the location where the horses were supposed to be but he find nothing.

The horses and their keeper were gone from the area and that meant only one thing. A group of Yankees must have passed nearby forcing the man caring for the horses to move them to a second location. Obviously he must have quietly slipped away unable to alert the others.

There was nothing else the sick private could do but found himself some deep grass to lay in and hide his body until the man and the horses returned. Besides he was just too worn out to continue.

Even with these bad events happening, the group decided to carry on. It was amazing how quietly and patiently they hid in that grass until full darkness could cover their moves. While they lay in the grass and had the daylight, the rebels were smart enough to draw a map showing the locations of the army barracks.

They first drew the barracks that housed the union soldiers and then the warehouses containing supplies. Finally they added the wagons that were lined up neatly in a row next to the loading docks. The only thing that they forgot was that the night would be very dark and they wouldn't be able to see the map because they were unable to light a fire for fear of giving themselves away.

When night did fall it had really, really had gotten dark. Never mind, they told themselves. They still knew exactly where everything was located. Hell, it wouldn't be that hard to find their way around in the dark.

McPhail now was beginning to feel a sense of panic. He had felt his stomach tighten when he saw the force left behind to guard the supplies. The closer they had gotten to the union troops, the larger the enemy army looked. These blue coat guys seemed to be everywhere and Lincoln wouldn't be around waving another pardon this time.

Kennedy's bold and exciting idea suddenly didn't seem so great to John anymore and now it was like his bravery had begun to elude him. He wasn't real sure he could continue on without showing the others his fear.

His stomach churned upside down and he felt that if he could chew on something it would help him control his tension, but he had nothing to chew. Then he saw some rags hanging from one of the wagons and he quietly made his way to the pieces of cloth with his knife in hand. He cut off a piece and stuffed it into his mouth and frowned because it was not so clean.

Clean or not he had something to bite down on and with a mouth full it would surely take away any chance of him screaming from fear. Now…he could be brave.

The next thing was the plan of action, which was very simple for a lot of old country boys.

They would set a couple of the buildings on fire that surely would distract the guards nearby. Then one by one they would steal into the barracks and grab a union uniform and quickly change into the Yankee blue. All without being caught. It certainly sounded fairly simple.

Surprisingly enough this really was done with some ease even though there was a lot of fear being carried in the guts of these rebels. A few drops of coal oil here and a pile of paper and clothes there was all it took to make a roaring fire. The Confederate soldiers had now started a full fledge chaos in the camp and fear ran through the Yankee soldiers. This was all they needed, it give them the break and time to change uniforms.

Suddenly loud gunfire started going off all around the group. Each man jumped for cover but was quick to see that they weren't being fired upon. It was ammunition exploding in the fire!

A moment later large explosions were blowing the buildings sky high and the blasts were causing the clouds above to reflect the light back to the ground giving the fire an awesome sight.

The rebels dressed in Yankee blue stood froze like statutes with their mouths wide open. They were shocked and surprised even more so than the union guards were.

How would they know that the first building they picked to set on fire contained gun power? Now the fires had jumped to other buildings and the explosions were getting out of hand. All hell was breaking loose everywhere and the group realized they had made a big mistake. Nothing to do now but take full advantage of the huge chaos.

The second part of the plan was to walk boldly out in northern uniforms and hitch up the horses to the wagons.

Things were going so well that this probably would be a cake walk.

It wasn't, one of the blue coats on guard duty challenged the men as they opened the gates to the horse's pens. He happened to be a very young ambitious soldier that believed in doing his Duty.

With blasts from the igniting gunpowder shaking the ground like an earthquake and the sky lighting up the debris that was flying pass their heads, McPhail stood tall in front of the young guard. He did the only thing that he could think of.

"Rebel troops are about two miles out." He yelled in a powerful voice. "Get the horses hooked up to the wagons and move em out and be quick about it! General's orders private!"

John was sure glad the soldier didn't ask what general he was referring to. Instead the guard yelled out to a group of Yankees running by that was trying to get away from the blasts.

"Rebels are coming. You men give us a hand to get the wagons hooked to the horses. Without giving it a second thought, a dozen union soldiers came to their aid and began attaching the horses to the wagons.

McPhail knew he had to make it look good so that the charade would keep going at a fast pace. To let it slow down was to give them time to think and that would be dangerous.

"Move it!" He shouted at the top of his lungs still trying to cause strong authority in his voice. "Let's go! Get those wagons ready to move!"

Now more blue coats showed up until there was rows of the army men helping the group readying the wagons for travel.

They pulled the horses into position to attach the yokes as fast as they could. They certainly were trying to do their duty and John was glad they were so conscientious about their loyalty and duty.

Again more explosions were still going off causing the surroundings to shine almost as bright as daylight.

McPhail ran up and down the row of wagons acting like a Colonel trying to push them into moving faster. They hitched one wagon after another to the mares and pulled them into the street ready to travel.

John had gotten the shock of his life when he found the freight wagons were still full of supplies and ready to go. In short order there was twenty wagons full of goods lined up with drivers at the ready. All of this was almost unbelievable but totally acceptable to McPhail.

With a really big smile he climbed aboard the lead wagon just as a union captain ran out of his quarters yelling crazy orders while trying to get his uniform pants on. The chaos had obviously awoke the captain from a sound sleep.

"What's going on soldier?" He yelled over all the loud confusion.

The guard snapped to attention almost scared to death that the captain was going to blame him for all of the goings on. He answered his commander and tried to clear his throat from nervousness at the same time.

"Word is rebels are coming, sir." he yelled back. "We're ordered to move the supplies to safer ground by the general."

The young soldier held his salute waiting for the commander to return the courtesy but none was given. The captain's brain had come alive from the excitement and possible opportunity that had dropped into his lap.

His eyes lit up in the glow of the burning buildings.

Surely this was the opportunity he had been waiting for! His men had not been paid in months as the payroll had not been getting through on time and duty at the docks left much to be desired. All of this was causing the troops to desert at an alarming rate. Desertion had become a major problem and now the captain saw his chance to break the bad chain of events and it would make him look good in the colonel's eyes.

"Hell, it might even mean a promotion." He thought to himself. His mouth seemed to spit out what he was thinking without him even realizing it.

"Sound recall!" He yelled out. "By God, we're going to meet the damn rebels head on. You there…you non-coms. Get those men moving, we're going Rebel hunting!"

The captain could now picture the lovely major bars on his uniform and began speaking with more authority while giving his commands.

"Kick it in gear, let's move it." he screamed at the bugler. "Get the horses saddled; the damn rebs are gonna have a hell of a fight before this night's over!"

Forming all the troops that were in sight, the captain paid little attention to the wagons now as John and the others began to drive them out. This captain now was having an almost complete transformation into what he saw was a heroic fighting commander. He was blinded to everything else around him except for his obsession to become the officer that saved the day. Several times he helped hold the horses that were attached to the wagons to keep them from being startled. He keep right on yelling orders while he would grasp the reins to calm the animals in all the excitement and noise.

Unknown to the Captain, he was helping rebel soldiers that were dressed in blue climb aboard wagons laden with supplies. He ordered the regimental colors brought to the front of the column and screamed commands one after another. When he saw his company of men mounted and ready to go, the union captain pulled his revolver and pointed it at the sky.

So worked up was he, it went off accidentally making a loud bang and for a moment it caught him by surprise.

Immediately he tried to make it look like he had done it on purpose. He yelled a little louder at the troops.

"Load your weapons, men, get ready!

He mounted his horse that was being held by a corporal and turned to his men to give them what he thought was a speech of bravely, but with all the noise and commotion the soldiers couldn't heard him anyway. They just acted like they understood every word and cheered when he had finished.

By now, about half the wagons in McPhail's column were manned by union soldiers, while the remainder was being driven by southern drivers.

They moved the wagons pass the burning buildings and now almost the whole town was at a point of being on fire. The noise and confusion had only gotten worse with every passing moment that went by.

McPhail lead the wagon train out of the coastal town just as more barrels of gun power exploded throwing huge fire balls into the sky. Debris filled the sky and much of it flew over the top of John's wagon like cannon balls.

Kennedy was the first to see the flying scrap coming and ducked so fast and hard that he almost knocked John off the seat. He turned and jumped into the back of the wagon to get a better look at the fire ball rising high in to the sky. Then he took a good look at the wagon train following close behind. For a long time he stared at the other drivers, both northern and southern behind them. Then he turned back to McPhail with a face that was sheer white from fear. The sight of all the real union soldiers driving wagons behind them was beginning to take it's toll. They had their rifles leaning against the wagon seats beside them and he knew they were loaded and ready.

Trying not to show that his nerves were cracking, he pointed his thumb over his shoulder at the wagons behind them and tried to speak in a normal voice.

"What...ah. we gonna do with the union men back there?" He said. "Half those wagons are being operated by Yankee drivers that are going to find out where we are going sooner or later. Exactly what are we gotta tell them? Hey blue belly, we're going to a rebel town with these here supplies. Wanta go?"

John really didn't have time to answer his friend. He was too busy watching a whole company of union soldiers riding past the wagons at top speed. They were being led by the hero of a captain on his way to make history and a big name for himself.

McPhail simply turned to Kennedy and smiled a great big smile as his eyes lit up with delight. At the same time he turned the wagon in another direction, leading away from the galloping horsemen.

John was now heading in the direction of home, and he wondered how long it would be before the federal soldiers at the end of the wagon train would question where they were going. Also the fact that he was wearing a union uniform was of some concern cause it just might cause him to be shot by a southern soldier they were sure to run across.

He knew it would take about three hard days of travel to get the supply wagons back to his hometown. This time they had to stay on the road because the wagons were to heavy to cut through the woods. But how was he to do it with the enemy driving half the wagons?

Only one thing to do, find a confederate camp and turn the whole thing over to them. But what would happen if the Yankee drivers decided to fight once they discovered they were headed for a rebel camp?

John didn't want to break his word to Lincoln about fighting and have to get into a fire fight with the Yankee drivers. He hadn't figured on a situation like this one where half of the wagons being driven by Yankees. On the other hand, if he's not careful he just might be the one to get killed.

Hours passed with McPhail holding his head down whispering small prayers and trying to figure out exactly what to do. Then like a slap in the face he was struck with a new plan. In his thoughts it sounded like a great idea, mainly because it was his only idea.

He turned to Kennedy and told him of his brilliant plan. Kennedy would ride ahead of the wagons to search for rebels that he could tell their situation to. He was to find a southern company of soldiers and have them ambush the wagon train capturing the Yankees.

Meanwhile, McPhail would keep the union drivers moving in order to conceal their true destination. Only trouble was that the rebels had to capture the wagon train without firing any shots. They might shoot some of their own men since they wouldn't know who was union and who was southern.

Somehow Frank knew he would be given an impossible task and boy this was it.

"I'm on the way." He called out. "Try to slow down them wagons behind us a bit so that I'll have time to put some distance between me and them."

He climbed onto the side of the wagon and worked his way to the rear where the extra horses where tied. He slipped his body into the saddle of one of the mounts and rode off in front of John's wagon as fast as the animal would go.

After he was a mile or so ahead of the wagon train, he stopped to take off the federal uniform. He changed clothes, throwing the blue Yankee uniform into the weeds. The rebel slipped his foot into the stirrup and climbed up to remount when the sound of gunfire reached him. Clearly it was coming from the wagon train where he had just been.

"Damn." He yelled out finishing his mount. "Now what's going on?" He turned his horse back in the direction of the wagons and rode full out. He wasn't sure what was happening, nor how bad the situation was, but he did know that he had to go back.

When the wagons once again came into view, he could see that a southern company of soldiers had attacked what they thought was a Yankee wagon train. The wooded area was so heavily laden with trees and underbrush on both sides of the road he had ridden right pass the rebels hiding in the weeds.

The first round of shots fired by the gray coats killed two and wounded one, catching the drivers completely off guard. McPhail jumped from the wagon throwing his Yankee hat and coat to the ground and raised his hands in surrender before the aggressors could reload.

Kennedy rode hard straight for the shooters, shouting at the top of his voice. He was trying hard to make them understand the situation.

"Stop firing, stop firing, they're not Federals!" He yelled at the top of his lungs.

At the same time the drivers stood upright in their wagons with their arms held high in surrender.

Frank slid from his horse and limped towards the southern troops, making sure he held his hands as high in the air as they would go. He had managed to get his gray pants on but was still wearing a union coat when he once again yelled at the rebels.

"We're confederates, we're confederates; don't shoot no more." He yelled over and over again as loud as he could hoping they would believe him.

Finally a confederate sergeant rode up to Kennedy pointing his revolver straight at his head. He bend over in the saddle and took a long look at his new prisoner's gray pants and blue coat.

"What are you boy?" He said. "Half rebel or half Yankee?"

Kennedy couldn't help but bend down and hold his leg; the cut that he had sustained from the farm machinery was causing severe pain and he was trying to rub the hurt away. The infection was setting in and really beginning to take its toll.

"I'm all rebel, sergeant." He said still trying to rub some of the pain away from his injured leg.

The southern drivers now were all beginning to talk at the same time. They still held their hands high in the air, but were desperately trying to explain why they were wearing the Yankee blue.

From the expression on the their Confederate captures faces it looked like the situation was turning worse by the minute. It certainly didn't look like the guards were beginning to believe that they were not union soldiers.

One after another began tearing at their union uniforms to get them off and change back into the Confederate gray. Even some of the federal soldiers threw their coats to the ground hoping to confuse their rebel guards into believing that they were not the enemy.

The southern sergeant leading the attacking force set on his horse watching the chaos until finally he had had enough. He spoke out in a commanding voice to make sure his men still trained their rifles on the prisoners; whoever they were.

"Hold it" He said, "Which of you is really blue coats and how in the hell am I suppose to know for sure?"

McPhail stepped forward to confirm their identity. He was taking a wild gamble that he could to keep everyone else from getting shot and really wondered if he could make the southern sergeant believe him.

"It's pretty simple sergeant." He said. "Help us drive the wagons to Lumberbridge Township, and you'll see the supplies used for the rebel wounded being shipped in. We can drop these real Yankees at the first regimental headquarters we find.

The mean looking sergeant was still not totally convinced but He would go along with the plan…after disarming all the captured men.

"Make sure no one has a weapon and load them up on the wagons!" He yelled to his men. He was going to get the wagons moving but carefully watch all his new prisoners, trusting none of them.

With the sergeant's men helping put even more distance between the group and the union soldiers in New Bern; this plan was quite acceptable to McPhail. He was even breathing a little easier as he sat on the seat of the bumpy wagon.

By now McPhail's enthusiasm had began to drain but he had to smile a bit at the thought of that crazy union captain riding off to meet an imaginary southern army. He wondered how far the union commander had lead his men in the search before returning.

He could just see that captain trying to explain where the wagons were and just how in the world half the town had been burnt to the ground while he was in charge. Boy, the trouble that captain would face upon his return to New Bern would be no less than incredible. It had to be out of this world when his superiors found out about the missing wagons and how he had been outfoxed by a bunch of dumb old southern boys…

The whole group traveled through the rest of the next day and on into nightfall with the rebel guards watching them closely. By now they were all dog tired and ready to pitch camp as always, off the road in a place that was heavy wooded for security.

The night guards were posted around the wagons to ensure that their guest truly were not Yankees and to picket the area for any unwanted incoming guest.

Rocks were piled in circles and small camp fires were lit so that the men could begin cooking beans and salt bacon. Next came the coffee that was a welcome part of their meal and the whole camp settled back while the guards carefully watched their captors.

Frank slid himself up against a tree by John's fire and moaned from the pain in his leg. McPhail took one look at Frank walking like a hen with a broken wing and addressed the problem head on by moving his buddy even closer to the fire so that he might inspect his leg.

McPhail took one look and began cutting Kennnedy's pants leg open with the large knife he used to gut deer.

"Good God, look at this nasty thing! John said. "How come you didn't tell me about this earlier? You've got enough infection built up in this leg to kill my horse."

By now, the southerner could hardly stand and sweat pored from his forehead, making it obvious that he had fever coming from the infected limb. The wound had festered and red streaks were beginning to run down the side of his leg causing extreme pain.

After seeing Frank's leg, John knew that something had better be done and it had better be now. He had seen this before and knew of the consequences if the injury wasn't treated right away.

McPhail shoved his knife into the coffee pot that was still setting on the fire. He was hoping the hot metal would help in cutting the wound open and force out the pus. He carefully picked the side of the infected cut with his knife and forced out the pus until no more would come out. Then he washed the leg area with water from his canteen and dried it as best he could with a somewhat dirty handkerchief.

Next he placed the Madstone on top of the wound to suck out any other poisons and carefully wrapped the injured leg tightly when he had finished.

Frank set quite still with a funny grin on his face and just as John was finishing up he through his buddy a kiss.

"You really do care, you lovely man, you!" Frank said.

McPhail slid back up against the tree and answered Frank's statement.

"Shut up and relax dummy! You've got a lot of traveling to do tomorrow."

Now both men started to relax around the fire and for a moment they just sat looking at one another. Slowly a smile came across their faces. The more they looked at each other, the more the smile turned into laughter; until the laughter was almost to the point of being hysterical.

It had suddenly dawned on both men that they had done it and in McPhail's case it was his second time.

Their little group had stolen twenty wagons of much needed supplies from under the nose of the Federals. Nothing could have tasted sweeter to the two young men.

Kennedy pulled two cigars from his knapsack and threw one to John. Then he lit the other with a small stick from the fire and passed the burning wood to his buddy.

The smell of the cigars caused one of the rebel guards to watch as they smoked the fine tobacco.

"Got another one of those?" The guard said motioning towards the smokes.

Without giving it another thought, Kennedy once again dug into his coat and came up with another. Then he threw it to the rebel guard and picked up another piece of burning wood to give him a light.

"Here you go." He said handing him the stick.

Then moaning once again he laid back on a blanket that McPhail had thrown to him. He placed one hand beneath his head in order to be more comfortable and enjoy his cigar.

John slapped at mosquitoes and blew smoke into the air trying to ward off the insects as he too spread out his blanket.

Now both men were looking straight up at the night sky. They couldn't help but see millions of stars shining out from the black space above them. It was cool and clear and there was so many small dots of lights up there no one could count them.

"You know, Frank," John said. "Some day we'll be able to fly, and talk to one another over a machine and see things that's going on around the other side of the world and we'll be able to do it in a blink of the eye."

Kennedy drew a puff from his cigar and tried to blow a smoke ring, but the wind blew it away. Then he answered the young Scotsman as if he were crazy.

"Your daft man, that's a mystery that will never be solved. People won't ever be able to talk over a box and see things as they happen on the other side of the world." He said, also taking in the blinking lights above.

Unknown to either of the men, a young Scotsman by the name of James Clerk Maxwell had already made enormous contributions to astronomy and physics.

His discovery that electricity and magnetism join together to become light became a now conventional understanding of the electromagnetic spectrum, running in wavelengths from gamma rays to X-rays to ultraviolet light to visible light to infrared light to radio waves, and the discovery of radio, television and radar.

All of this was done in England in the 1860's; a time of great tragedies for America. (This paragraph reprinted with permission from Parade, copyright c. 1995 and author Carl Sagan.)

McPhail and Kennedy could only wonder what tomorrow might bring, but as for tonight, they felt great and would sleep soundly even if the ground was hard.

After all, they now had their very own guards protecting them. Well, even if it was because they were prisoners, they didn't mind. At lease they didn't have to do guard duty.

The next day the train of wagons rumbled into town with "U.S. Army" plainly visible on the sides escorted by a proud company of rebels. Amid all the cheering crowds, Frank and John rode with their heads held high like heroes, leading the loads of blankets, food, and medical supplies right down main street.

Once the Confederate sergeant realized that not all of the men were union soldiers even though they had been wearing the uniform, it became a simple task to sort out the real prisoners and release the southern men.

It even became a pleasure for he and his men to help the whole town unload the crates into the stables. There, Elizabeth and the other ladies began counting and stacking the new bounty for the war effort.

It had been a long time since this much supplies had reached them. Everyone including the mayor was totally excited when wagon load after wagon load pulled into town. It would not only be a marvelous help in treating the incoming wounded it was one hell of a morale booster. It was almost like a huge party for everyone.

McPhail was even whistling as he unloaded the eighth wagon because he was happy to see so much come in. Suddenly he pulled on a crate to remove it from the back of the wagon and wouldn't you know it, there before his very eyes was five cases of whiskey. Now these were obviously supposed to go to the union officers at New Bern, but McPhail had no way of returning it could he? So, the Scotsman would see to it that the alcohol would go to the small group that liberated it. You know, for services rendered.

"Those little devils" said John, as he eyed the fine looking liquor bottles. "We'll just have to drink a toast to our boys in blue."

And drink they did; all night long and half the next day until the wives decided that the men had had enough. The end of the party came swiftly when the ladies showed up, bringing their heroes back down to earth.

Within a few days the wagons had been reprinted and new signs appeared on the sides.

C.S.A. with a sign underneath: "Carried supplies away."

Chapter 14

The Fourth and Thirteen North Carolina regiments were ordered to march north towards Fredericksburg, with Frank Kennedy making the decision to go with them. With a rolled up blanket slung over his shoulder and pulled across his chest, brand new Yankee boots taken from the raid and a burning determination to win the war for the south, he marched off with the southern soldiers seemingly into the history books.

Serving with valor unsurpassed in any war, the Fourth North Carolina regiment engaged the One Hundred and Twenty-Fourth New Yorkers in thick wooded areas west of Fredericksburg.

Entangled in the dense undergrowth, the foot soldiers on both sides were rained down on by exploding shells as the armies fired at almost point blank range. Without even realizing it both armies were about to get a full taste of the worst of mother nature. Flames began to spread in the trees and underbrush from the canon fire and the wounded from both sides became trapped.

There was no brave battle going on now, only a horrible forest fire that was trapping hundreds of men from both armies and sending them to an early death.

Frank lay beside other Carolina soldiers behind fallen trees, scrubs or rocks firing their muskets into the thick underbrush. The gunfire was so extremely heavy they had hardly noticed that the woods were beginning to burn out of control. The only thing on their minds at the moment was all the bullets that were flying through the air by the hundreds and the fact that they were keeping their heads down.

Then a few began to notice the heavy smoke but scrubbed it off as coming from their gun power being fired in the rifles.

Within minutes however it became apparent that there was entirely too much smoke just to be gunfire.

One after another the men in Kennedy's platoon ceased firing when they realized the Yankees were also lowering their weapons because of the huge smoke and flames approaching.

Suddenly the scene that the men from both armies were seeing was almost unbelievable. The whole forest was on fire and burning at an alarming rate straight towards them. It would do no good for either to continue the fight for no one was going to win this battle.

The terrible fire was at a dead run and was showing no signs of slowing down. It had a life of it's own now and it was cutting through these woods as the killer of men. There was no sign of a battle now from either side.

Yankee and Rebel alike turned their attention to rescuing the wounded trapped in its path. There were no enemies now, only men working together to save lives.

Most of the trapped men were Federals and not all could be saved because the intense heat grew by the second.

The worse part was that many of the dead and dying could be seen but not reached. They were engulfed in a wall of flames from all sides and the men from both armies just threw down their weapons and raced to help the fallen warriors.

The screams of the soldiers sounded the same whether they were blue are gray, it made no difference. For the first time, the horrible screams caused the soldiers from both sides to be enemies no more; at least during the ferocity of the battle they were now raging to save the men from the fires.

Kennedy was one of the combatants to race back into the burning woods time and again pulling the wounded to safety. Showing true heroism, the southerner placed his life on the line dragging both rebels and Yankees from the fire.

The trees, bushes, and grass had turned into a inferno and flames shot hundreds of feet into the air and raked the entire area until both armies retreated from the disaster they had committed.

The last time Frank was seen, he was carrying a severely wounded federal on his shoulders as the firestorm completely engulfed the two, reaching to the very point of cremation.

Both the north and south showed fortitude and courage as 90,000 men took part in the battles around Spotsylvania, Chancellorsville, and Fredericksburg. These warriors in determination charged headlong at each other with guts and glory, but ending up with nothing more than dead and wounded.

After the battles, a classification was given of whether they won or loss strictly by which had the most casualties. The battle of Chancellorsville was a victory for the south inflicting seventeen thousand casualties on the north, while the south suffered thirteen thousand itself, but still straining the Confederacy beyond repair.

The north simply had more of everything and this included fresh troops by the thousands to replace their fallen soldiers, while the south fought mostly with the same troops at each conflict.

Thousands of Confederates silently trudged back with their wounded after each battle, but now John, Elizabeth and the surrounding residents were better prepared with their newly acquired supplies.

When word spread through the town that the southerners were coming in, the whole population would run to meet the returning warriors by helping then with hot food and blankets for the night.

A list was made of the dead and missing by one of the elderly town folk and would be posted at the county building for all to see. More often than not names were spelled wrong or incomplete because the people making the list had little or no education.

At the end of each day John lit lamps and candles around the wounded to better see in the dark. He and the others of the town worked to prepare beds for the soldiers to make them comfortable.

It had become a daily routine, looking after the worn out warriors when they entered the town with heads bowed low and dragging their rifles after a battle. Each time became a little sadder than the one before and it was beginning to show on McPhail.

Often only half returned with a great deal of these so badly injured, they would never fight again.

On one particular dark evening, McPhail was carrying a candle to one of the bedsides, when the bottom of his right foot suddenly exploded with pain. A nail had penetrated his boot and punched a large hole almost completely through the ball of his instep. He fell to the ground yelling out a painful cry to Elizabeth.

"Pull it out!" He screamed to his wife as he fell to the floor in agony.

The sound of the painful cry coming from her husband caused Elizabeth to run towards him still holding the alcohol bottle and rag she had been cleaning with.

She had never before seen her man roll around on the floor flopping up and down like a fish out of water. He held his leg screaming from the pain and at the same time was trying his best to get the nail out.

At first she thought he had been bitten by something, until she grabbed his side and rolled him over.

The foot he was holding popped up exposing the bloody boot and the heavy nail sticking out of one side of it. She could see it was a bad one and that the nail had caused heavy damage. Now she had to calm him and try to remove it.

"Hold still" She said. "I'll get it out." But there would be no easy way to remove the invader. Still she kept trying to pull out the nail without success. She positioned herself to get more leverage, but again she was unable to remove the nail. It was now coming to a point that she was fearful of hurting McPhail further. She set back on the floor beside him trying to figure out the best way to remove this hulk of iron.

Her agony increased when she wrapped a rag around the nail and prepared to try once again. She had hoped to stop the bleeding and at the same time was trying to build up her nerve to try yanking out the damaging nail one more time.

"It's stuck solid!" She exclaimed, as she examined the damage. Her attention was now squarely on John as she was trying to decide what to do. Then it came to her; an old saying her daddy had always said when he needed to get something done. "kick it in the butt and it will move."

Elizabeth quietly sat on the ground beside him and braced her foot against his, and in one quick kick yanked out the painful hunk of iron.

Screaming in agony as the nail came out, McPhail looked at the amount of blood pouring from the hole and almost fainted. He rocked back and fourth holding his leg from the intense pain and was almost swimming in blood.

He fought off dizzy spells and found that he could no longer set up. Again and again he caught himself weaving back and forth and had to fight to keep from falling face down.

Elizabeth gently cradled John in her arms and slowly laid him flat on the floor. Trying not to panic, she raised his leg up to help stop the flow of blood and called for hot water and rags to clean and bandage the damage. She knew this nail had done a job on his foot and it was serious.

The lady of mercy sent for Dr. Malloy and then concentrated on stopping the flow of blood. She had propped his leg up all right but it still wasn't stopping his essence of life from flowing out onto the ground.

The scene was a bad one; blood covered her, the floor and her husband to a point that she couldn't see how he had any of the life giving fluid still running through his veins. Hopefully she would be able to ease his pain, but as of yet, she was having little success.

"Damn it all", said McPhail. "I had to get it from a hunk of iron and the damn thing probably was a Yankee nail made in New York."

After doing all that they could, Dr. Malloy and Elizabeth managed to get John home to his own bed sure that he would feel much better knowing he would be looked after there.

Every couple of hours Elizabeth poured salt in a pan of water and heated it to soak his foot in, hoping to keep the swelling down.

All that night, the rebel lay drifting in and out of sleep from the extreme pain. There was little or no break to his torment. He became delirious, covered with sweat and would speak like a crazy man. The puncture wound was fast becoming infected; fever and nausea was following close behind.

Again and again Elizabeth cleaned and dressed the wound and hardly ever left his side. She made chicken soup and tried to get it down him but food simply turned his stomach. He would sleep in a restless state all during the day, and at night the pain was almost unbearable from the terrible throbbing that ran up his leg and side.

Nothing she was doing seemed to turn the tide of McPhail's injury.

Each passing day the throbbing grew more intense. On the fifth day Elizabeth and her father once again removed the bandage and gasped from the sight they were seeing. The infection had grown worst and she knew that it would be almost impossible now to save him if the damage wasn't reversed.

"The infection's getting worse." She said to her father with downright fear in her voice. "I don't think I can stop it."

John seemed to become even more delirious; it was as if nothing was stopping the infection from advancing. Even the Madstone's magic had failed to stop the spread and Elizabeth feared that she was about to lose her highlander.

"Sometimes even doctors can only do so much." Elizabeth's Father said. "I can't see anything else to do. We'll have to remove the leg. Help me get him ready."

For a moment he just stood there and looked at Elizabeth with sadness in his eyes. He knew how badly she was hurting but had no idea what else to say.

The doctor raised the blanket covering his leg and took one more long look.

"Honey, he'll die unless we take the leg; the poison's up to his knee and getting worse."

Elizabeth was frantic by now and willing to try anything except that.

"What about the old spinster Fannie Mae?" She said in desperation.

Everyone living around that area knew that the topic of Fannie Mae was hardly ever discussed in polite circles and the doctor was astonished at the mention of her name.

"The old witch doctor that hates everybody?" He said in astonishment. "Even the Indians called her (The one of mole) because she uses the fungus in her medicines."

Elizabeth responded abruptly even though she knew she was grasping at straws.

"She saved old man Kenner last year when he fell from his horse and broke his leg. The bone was sticking out and the infection had started when she snapped the broken limb into place, wrapped it with wild leaves and mold from some old bread and now he's back working on his farm.

By now, Elizabeth had made up her mind totally and was growing tired of the conversation. It made no difference, good or bad, she had made her decision.

"Henry, fetch Fannie Mae from her cabin." She said to a young neighbor boy standing nearby.

"Hurry boy!" she shouted, slapping him on the butt as he ran out the door. "You bring her back just as fast as you can!"

The young boy ran for all he was worth covering the few blocks to a barn in only minutes. He had seen the old woman working on some of the injured soldiers in the barn a short time before and knew he could find her there.

The small boy was fast but he still reached the entrance gasping for breath. He bent over to get more air in his lungs as he relayed the message to Fannie Mae of Elizabeth's request.

There was no doubt about it, if Elizabeth had sent for her, she must really need help and the old woman knew it. She paused only long enough to grab her carpetbag and fill it with odd looking medical supplies that she had been using and then she turned to the boy.

"Well boy, don't just stand there, take me to her!" She said.

The youngster took off out the door without looking back causing the old woman to literally run to keep up with the boy's young legs. Within minutes the two were at McPhail's house stumbling through the front door and feeling a bit exhausted.

Fannie Mae went right to work on McPhail as Elizabeth stood with her arms crossed rocking back and forth from being so nervous. She was much too upset to stand still as she watched the old woman examine John's leg.

She didn't really know why, but for some unknown reason she had all the faith in the world in this so called lady doctor. Still, she kept crisscrossing the room impatiently with her arms wrapped around herself almost feeling the pain coming out of McPhail. It turned her stomach to see her husband hurting so much and made it impossible for her to be still.

The old woman lifted John's foot into the air examining it from one angle to another before giving her command. With out a doubt it surely reminded Elizabeth of a veterinarian examining a horse with a broken leg just before announcing that the animal had to be shot.

"Bring me some corn husks and long strips of cloth," Fannie Mae snarled, "If you don't want him to join his ancestors before nightfall."

Pulling moldy bread from her bag, Fannie Mae mixed and mashed some special dry leaves and a sticky substance, making a paste she put inside the corn husks. Placing it over the puncture, she then made another cut on top of the foot with a very sharp knife.

"Bring the Madstone!" She said, once again scowling. "Be quick about it, I haven't got all day and neither does he."

Placing the stone over the incision, she wrapped the strips of cloth around the whole foot and tied it off as quickly and neatly as any surgeon could have done.

"Now we wait till it's done it's work." She said packing her bag. "I'll come back tomorrow but don't feed him anything until I return."

Elizabeth stopped her pacing and looked up at Fannie Mae in a very strange way. "Don't feed him?" She thought to herself.

"As if he were eating anything." Elizabeth said under her breath as she closed the door behind the old woman.

The night seemed to drag on forever as Elizabeth set by John's side trying her best to think of anything else that might help.

Sweat poured from his limp body and all she could do was wash him down with warm water over and over. She really didn't think it was helping but it made her feel better just being close to him. There was little else she could do but wait now.

Hours passed, and Elizabeth began to get hungry as the aroma of food from the kitchen told her the soup was still simmering on the stove. She pulled herself up out of the chair and made her way to the hot pot and began dishing up a plate.

Then a strange thing happened, she noticed the bag that had contained the Madstone was lying on the table. She gently began to run her fingers across the brown slick leather surface and as she did the lucky shamrock came into view. Without hesitation she rubbed it between her fingers with care as though its magic would come upon her.

She knew there was no magic in a small piece of shamrock, but on the other hand what could it hurt to look it over?

"I need your magic now, little fellow." The field nurse said. "Just one more time. That's not a lot to ask is it?"

Utter exhaustion begin to sweep over her and it became an overwhelming task to simply keep her eyes open another minute. She laid her head on the table but her hand never quit touching the shamrock. She fell dead fast into a deep sleep.

Early next morning there came sounds of people approaching the front door and Elizabeth awoke to the sound of the old woman's voice.

"Let's get on with it." Fannie Mae said. "We'll have to clean that ugly hole in his foot at least four or five times a day.

We'll need to stay on top of it to make sure it doesn't fester up any more."

Each day Elizabeth and Fannie Mae would change bandages a number of times adding more of the medicine to the wound, and trying not to make it hurt in the process.

Slowly McPhail began regaining his strength and the feeling was returning to his leg. Still, it was weeks before he was able to struggle onto his feet and pull himself upright. The throbbing in his leg was massive and showed no sign of leaving. It was almost more than he could stand.

He was like a small child trying to learn how to walk and needed to stabilize and strengthen the injured leg. He felt like somehow he had lost his manhood every time he raised himself up, but day after day he kept trying.

There was no question about it, he knew he would no longer have his distinct gate in his walk that he had been so cocky about all his life.

"Hell, why would I concern myself with a limp?" He reasoned. "I'm still alive and that should be good enough. Besides I'm not planning to join a grand parade anytime soon." He thought out loud to himself.

All the young Texan had to do was look over at his beautiful wife and he knew that now he had more immediate things to concern himself with. He had to get well quickly; he was still the man of the house and needed to protect the ones he loved.

"What a pompous ass you are." He rambled on to himself! She was the one looking after him! Still yet, he was more determined than ever to heal faster. He had to have something to look forward to and in his crazy mind he was thinking up things.

You know, like being brave and protecting his wife. Of course, on the other hand it might take forever for this stinking hole in his leg to heal.

All in all, the Scotsman was still sleeping a great deal and that was good. He would heal much faster even if he didn't know that it was good for him.

One thing that Elizabeth had not anticipated was the fact that she and Fannie Mae would become very good friends and be working together to treat the wounded gray coats with the old woman's special medicines. Even though they didn't know it at the time, their friendship would become a very special alliance.

A far cry from being society ladies of the south, she and the medicine woman would quickly become an unlikely looking pair and be a large part of the new women's movement.

Daily they would join other ladies in treating the sick and injured soldiers as they came back from the battles. Even Fannie Mae took to joining the others in their nursing duties.

Hell, she worked strictly alone to the point of even isolating herself from everybody but the ones that needed help. That is until she and Elizabeth became friends.

The year 1864 saw the union closing in on the Carolinas from all directions as the Confederacy began to lose city after city with no hope in sight.

McPhail was soon to recover and knew the collapse of the rebellion meant military occupation and political corruption for years to come. He had to find a way to insure that his family would get enough to eat and a place to sleep if the occupation were to get so bad there would be no way to make a living. He had to find a way to get out of the path of the oncoming hoards of union soldiers advancing like ants swarming over food dropped on the ground.

The southerner would do whatever it took to protect Elizabeth and the baby, regardless of his personal pride, feelings or safety. This meant even if he had to kill or steal, something that he thought he would never do outside actually being in combat.

He spent many hours sitting in the dark at night wondering if he really could take extreme action if it became necessary. It weighed heavily on his mind and he thought of the number of occasions when he had been offered as much as ten thousand dollars for the stone. If he were to sell it now, he knew he could not accept confederate currency, for it would be worthless within a few months.

The thought of selling the stone turned his stomach, but little time was left and besides he was still barely able to get around on his leg. He tried to turn what confederate money he had in for gold, but to no avail.

Word reached McPhail that the union troops were burning the homes and crops everywhere they went, leaving nothing standing behind them. Sherman was using cannons to destroy all the buildings in every city and on top of that, the rebels were also torching the fields, leaving nothing for the northern soldiers.

It seemed that the only thing left for McPhail was to work for the Yankees. The thought of it turned his stomach but he could be a doctor's assistant and help care for their wounded. He feared that even Dr. Malloy's farm probably would be burned to the ground if the blue coats passed through that area and then they would have nothing left, not even a place to stay. On the other hand they would have a better chance of being left alone there because the farm was off the beaten track and fairly hard to find.

Therefore he decided to move Elizabeth and the baby to the farm and this would also allow him to travel in search of such work. Besides, he could plant a garden come springtime and have fresh vegetables for her and the baby.

All of the stories and rumors were beginning to panic John now, and he wasted no time in loading the buggy time and again, making the six mile trip to the farm. He was stripping the cabin bare and moving as much as he could to keep their things out of the way of the union troops.

The old woman, Fannie Mae was also invited to live with John and Elizabeth, but she refused to even consider the idea of leaving her home.

"I'll not let the damn Yankees burn my home." She said. "They'll take a blast from my shotgun. My Charlie built the place with his own two hands and there'll be no one destroying his work, rest his soul."

No one would have guess it, but the old witch turned out to be quite warm and outgoing. She had made her own sinister reputation on purpose but now it was coming out. She was just the opposite of the stories that were told about her.

She even gave four one hundred dollar gold pieces to Elizabeth for the baby, and settled down to wait for the outcome of the war. Despite insistence from John that she move in with them, she still stayed behind to protect her home.

Later John and Elizabeth would find out that she had been killed by sharpshooters harassing the Federal's marching through North Carolina. The musket ball had pierced her cabin and caught her squarely between the shoulder blades.

When the news reached McPhail, he and several of the other farmers rode to her cabin only to find it burned to the ground. In silence the group dismounted to look over the remains of the farm but there was nothing left. Only burnt timbers and ashes where the house and barn used to be.

John couldn't seem to believe what he was seeing. He just stood and stared at the surroundings with a numb look.

Then one of the men called out to McPhail in a soft voice.

"Over here, John." He said pointing to a small body in one corner of the burned out cabin.

John walked over to where he was pointing and took a hard look at the remains that lay in the corner. His whole body began to shake as he stared at the remains of the old lady. Never before in his life had he been more upset then now. His first reaction is that he wants to strike out at someone or something but who? He almost looses it completely but deep down knows there's nothing he can do now.

The farmers remove their hats in reverence and looked up at McPhail with compassion. They know that he is deeply distraught at the fact that his dear friend is no longer on this earth.

For a long moment the whole group stood in complete silence. Then one of the men picked up an old bag that looked like it belonged to a doctor. The piece of leather was burnt so badly and there was not enough to even know truly what it was.

The man lets it slip out of his hand back onto the ground and then turns to McPhail hoping to make him feel better about losing his friend.

"It really was an accident." He says. "There was a battle going on and the crossfire killed her and set the house on fire."

McPhail now gets even madder at everything.

"This damn war caused it! The politicians caused it! Hell! The whole human race caused it!" He screamed.

He tries to regain his composure as he walks over to his horse and pulls out a bottle of whiskey hoping the liquor will help.

"Help me bury her proper." He says. "Over there by her favorite tree where her husband is buried."

Quietly the men dig a grave under the doctors favorite tree and bury the old witch's body, carefully placing her bag in with her as a sign of respect.

Then each of the men in their own way said a little prayer just for her.

Before leaving they stood among the ashes of the house one more time looking at the tragedy that the lady doctor had endured. There was personal sadness in their hearts for the woman called the old witch. Almost each man had had a family member treated by the lady and they knew of her kindness.

Now one by one mounted their horse and replaced their hats to travel home from the old woman's farm.

McPhail also had never in this world thought he would have such a friend, but this lady was different. She was certainly someone he felt a strong kin ship with and now she was forever gone from his and Elizabeth's life.

The last man climbed onto the back of his horse and turned to follow the others when a beautiful sight appeared in the sky above him. Excited beyond words he pointed to the clear blue sky and yelled out to the others.

"Look there, I've never in my life seen such a thing. It's like it was made just for us to see!" He said.

His finger was pointing directly up to the northeast where there was not one, but two huge beautiful rainbows stretching clear across the sky. One was on top of another with only clear sky between them. The beautiful colors of red, yellow, green and purple lit up the heavens as never before causing sheer amazement in all the men.

A wave of compassion came over McPhail as he stood staring at the beautiful rainbows that stretched from horizon to horizon.

He too could hardly believe his eyes. They were so large and so beautiful, that he doubted anyone had ever seen such a sight before.

McPhail couldn't keep his eyes off the display in the sky. He mounted his horse and began to ride slowly towards home, all the while taking in the beautiful sight.

Never taking his eyes off the phenomena in the sky, he reached back to his saddlebags and took out his bagpipes and braced them against his chest. With a funny looking smile he began playing the Black Watch Polka.

The young Scotsman's deep sad eyes now were giving away his thoughts. What else could he be thinking about but that…

"She surely did let me know, she make it all the way to heaven."

For the next few weeks McPhail did what he could at the farm to keep Elizabeth and the baby safe. He felt he should keep the Madstone as security; just in case times got even worst, if that was possible. He had considered selling it for gold, but thought better of it knowing that the Yankees were out to levy taxes. This was their way of supposedly making it legal to confiscate everything.

He knew it had to be hidden, for much like a diamond, the value of it would cause someone among the invading hordes to steal it or simply force him to turn it in with all the other loot being taken.

Only a few of the townspeople knew about the stone, and the secret would more than likely be kept, but gold was quite another story.

The best hiding place he could think of, would be under a board in the corner of the farmhouse. Unfortunately, John discovered that if he lifted the board in the corner of the room it could easily be seen by anyone coming in the house. Again he looked for a suitable site until he realized the perfect hiding place was the small tool shed connected to the side of the house.

He carefully wrapped the stone in a cloth and placed it under the floor of the tool shed next to the house. Then he nailed a board back over the beautiful stone and stepped back to make sure it was not easy to find. It was a perfect location and it made him feel good that he had found a great hiding place.

All across the countryside people were hiding their weapons too for fear that the union men would make everybody turn them in first. The idea that the entire population would be left defenseless alarmed everyone and caused the word to spread.

The commander of the Army of Tennessee, Joseph E. Johnston moved into North Carolina from Mississippi to try and contain Sherman, but his small force only numbered about 20,000. He succeeded in delaying the huge conquering union army for only a few days.

The Confederacy was beginning to totally fall apart because of the lack of everything from personnel, weapons, clothing and even food; everything the union soldiers had plenty of.

Despite even this, Lee's army hit the Federals hard again and again causing the war to spill over into 1865, before the fall of Fayetteville on March 10.

Weather, more than the Confederate army, bogged the union troops down in the winter of 1864. The bitter cold and rain stopped the hoard of union soldiers in their tracks far better than the rebels could have. Overflowing rivers and streams were impassable, and food supplies were not getting through to the troops on a regular basis, causing many desertions among the blue coats.

It was not a permanent situation however and the Yankees were soon joined by more troops and on the move again.

The main body of the union army was passing miles north of McPhail's farmhouse but stragglers were seen from time to time passing through the woods near the farm.

One day four Yankee deserters stumbled across John's farmhouse while making their way through the woods trying to avoid the main roads. This time they were coming straight towards the house and it was obvious they meant no good.

Elizabeth was completely occupied with preparing breakfast and hadn't notice the intruders coming out of the forest. McPhail had seen them first and grabbed up his rifle, running out the door towards the Yankees who by now were about two hundred yards out. The Scotsman felt that this was protecting his family, not fighting for the south as he had promised Lincoln he would not do.

It seemed as if the decision was at hand and he was being tested. It remained to be seen if he really could do anything to protect his family and yet, not break his word.

He moved directly towards them and had gotten within thirty yards of the men, when they began to spread out on either side of the southerner almost circling McPhail. The deserters knew that he only had one shot before he had to reload his musket and he couldn't stop all of them.

They became very brave and the obvious leader spoke out trying to frighten John.

"Which one you gonna take, farmer?" Said the man. "With that cannon, ya can only shoot one of us before we get you. Put down the rifle and give us what you got and we'll not harm you or yours. At least not right now." He said smiling back at the others.

John felt deep inside that he was lying and refused to drop the rifle for his instincts told him to concentrate on the loud mouth one. He took direct aim at the man's head and cocked the hammer back on the rifle. Now that the hammer was in the firing position, the big mouth soldier was not quite so brave.

Then McPhail made sure the man understood just what his statement was when he said it.

"You're the one I'll kill first." He said. "I believe my musket ball will blow your head plum off making it look like a watermelon that has been split wide open."

The man had already realized that he was the one McPhail was going to shoot first and he began to shake from fear. He quickly called to the others with a lot of panic in his voice.

"Hold it, boys; we'll let these people be." He said holding a hand up in a stop position towards the other three.

"After all we're really not interested in what they got."

Now the man turns to McPhail to see if he can make another deal.

"How about you just give us some breakfast and we'll be on our way." He said. "And we won't make no trouble."

He knew that even if one of the others shot McPhail, the Scotsman would more than likely still be able to fire his musket before dying and he would be taken down too.

John was not about to turn his back on these four. He took a better aim at the man's head and made sure his voice was even stronger.

"Get, before your head is blown all over my land!" He yelled loudly. John was now focusing his entire attention directly on the loud mouth one. He was hoping that the others were unable to see that he was shaking inside and that his hands and face were almost covered with sweat from fear.

The Yankee began to back up making sure that he still faced McPhail. "Okay, lower that hog killer down." He said, pointing his rifle back towards the ground. "We'll leave, no need to get mad when your gonna get your way."

Without interfering, the others lowered their rifles and began walking away, but still looking back over their shoulders at the serious Scotsman.

John, thinking no more about it and relieved that they were leaving, slung his rifle across his left arm and turned towards the house but kept looking over his shoulder to make sure they were still moving away.

By now the Yankee was about fifty yards out when he suddenly turned and aimed at McPhail with hate in his eyes. He was fully intending to kill the Scotsman.

Before the army deserter could pull the trigger on his intended target, gunshots rang out from the surrounding trees and all four of the men were completely knocked off their feet by musket balls tearing large holes through their bodies. Not one was left alive!

John stood looking at the downed men totally in shock. He hadn't seen the man turn to shoot him or for that matter know who was doing the shooting. At any rate he would have surely have been killed if it wasn't for the shots coming from the woods.

He was so totally shocked that all he could do was lower his rifle and wait to see what would happen next.

With guns still smoking, eight union soldiers emerged from the woods still pointing their rifles at the dead men. They were making sure none of the deserters would cause any more trouble.

McPhail put both hands on top of the barrel of his rifle showing that he would not be making any hostile moves. He knew it would do no good to try and fight off eight more of the Federals. Best he just give in hoping that these Yankees had good intentions.

"Lieutenant Summers of the Fourth New Yorkers." Said the obvious leader of the group. "You okay?"

It took a moment for John to regain himself. He just stared at the bodies with a blank expression hardly knowing what the hell to say.

"I think so." He said fearful of what these Yankees might do. "Where did you fellows come from?"

Summers busily reloaded his revolver while explaining to McPhail that he had been assigned to run down deserters and bring them back, one way or another. He had been tracking the men for days and had arrived in time to see McPhail confront the four soldiers.

"Guess we went a little deep into southern territory without realizing it." Said the lieutenant. "Least we won't have to take them back. We'll bury them out in the woods and be on our way. All I ask of you is not to warn any rebels of our presence.

John sighed with relief, very thankful for his help and promised that no one would hear from him that Yankees were in this area. He was just damn well happy to have their help.

McPhail really didn't realize how ghoulish it sounded when he turned from the bodies lying on the ground and offered the lieutenant and his men breakfast. It's not every day that a rebel would ask some Yankees to have a meal while standing over dead soldiers. He just considered it an honor and wanted to do something to thank them.

The union lieutenant looked as if it were of little concern to him that he had been asked to breakfast standing over dead men. He had seen many bodies in this war and gotten used to it and he didn't hesitate to reply.

"A hot meal sounds like a great idea. Thank you. We'll join you as soon as we have finished here."

McPhail carefully lowered the hammer down on his rifle and returned to the house. He had no sooner cleared the front door than he moaned a sigh of relief out loud and slid to the floor still holding the rifle with both hands.

He was leaning against the wall calling himself names like stupid ass, and jerk when Elizabeth entered the room.

"My god honey, what's the matter?" She said. "Glad you didn't shoot those Yankees?"

John looked up from the floor and took a deep breath before answering.

"Hell no." He said. "I forgot to load the damn gun!"

Deeply moved at the thought of the Yankees saving John, Elizabeth whipped up a large batch of eggs and biscuits with McPhail helping set the table. This would certainly be different, feeding a bunch of blue bellies at their table and being glad to do it.

By the time the eight soldiers reached the kitchen, the dinning table was prepared with piles of biscuits and eggs to fill their bellies, and a large pot of coffee standing by. It would take about all the food left in the house to feed the eight men, but she felt good about doing something to return their kindness. In her eyes now these Yankees were heroes.

Still, Elizabeth made each one of the men wash their hands at the back door before coming in.

"Wipe your feet before sitting at my table." She told the men in a joking manner but meaning every word.

John was amazed at the reaction; The Yankees only reply was to remove the caps from their heads and softly say "Yes'um" as they looked at the floor while taking a seat at the table. Their courtesy was certainly unexpected by the southerners, but highly accepted by a grateful family.

McPhail hardly noticed now that the men were wearing the blue uniforms that he so despised; rather these were friends and he was delighted to have them for breakfast. After all, they had just saved his life for whatever reason and he wasn't about to question why.

The union men dug into the eggs like a newborn babe eating his first solid food and it was obvious that a good meal had not been on their daily schedule. The captain even ate as if it were his first hot meal in months and McPhail figured it probably was.

Half way through the meal, the Yankee officer suddenly noticed a gray uniform hanging on a nail in a corner of the kitchen and instantly recognized the rebel clothing. He finished his eggs while keeping his eyes on John the whole time. Feeling somewhat at ease with the situation, he nevertheless quietly slipped his hand over the butt of his pistol but still continued eating the biscuits with his free hand.

Elizabeth had noticed that the captain's hand was resting on the revolver after he had seen the confederate uniform hanging in the corner. Slowly she arose with grace and moved to the union officers chair placing her hand softly on top of his as if to prevent the removal of the weapon.

"There will be no need for that." She said, smiling at the captain.

"Would you like some more coffee?" Elizabeth continued as she picked up the pot from the stove.

The captain removed his hand from the revolver and smiled as he answered.

"Yes um, about half a cup if you don't mind."

With bellies full, the men disappeared into the woods after thanking John and Elizabeth for the hot meal. McPhail couldn't help but think out loud as he watched the men walk away.

"They'll be back with a lot more of them Federals."

The flurry of news reports reached John and Elizabeth of the fall of Wilmington in January 1865, leaving little of North Carolina still held by the Confederacy. Even the heavy snow and ice had done little to stop the invading armies; it was now only a matter of time before the total occupation.

McPhail wanted to move to Texas as quickly as possible, but traveling through the war zone was very dangerous and he couldn't be sure of getting supplies along the way. Best thing now was to sit tight and ride it out, come what may.

The snow had stopped falling as John and Elizabeth drove the buggy towards town with John Jr. warmly wrapped in blankets on the seat beside them. Wild rumors were spreading across the countryside and panic had taken over reason. John thought it best to buy any supplies such as salt, sugar, or coffee he could find to help ride it out on the farm.

They had the gold pieces that Fannie Mae had given them and gold talked. The stables where the Confederacy was keeping the bulk of their supplies would be their first stop, but McPhail thought they would be lucky if anything was still there.

The buggy moved along the icy road and all John could think of was what they might find. Perhaps nothing would be available, but he had to try.

Hours slipped by and it was almost noon when they reached the small creek bridge leading to the main road. Allowing only one carriage at a time to cross because the bridge was so narrow, McPhail slowed the horses to a leisurely pace as he approached the ice covered bridge. The horse seemed unsure of his footing on the incline leading to the bridge causing John to stop the buggy and climb down.

"I'll lead him across." John said, grabbing the reins and trying not to excite the horses.

Instantly an odd noise caught his attention, and he stood there astonished at the sight before him. Wearing a large fur coat with coon skin hat was the biggest man McPhail had ever seen. The dog beside him barked furiously and was almost as big as the stranger. The huge man wore fur covered boots that were tied with leather straps and a pouch around his waist much like a Scotsman, but without the frills. The rifle he carried was like none John had ever seen. Four long barrels stuck out, the size for shotgun shells and two leather straps were attached, one on either side obviously so that he could carry it much like a backpack. The awesome weapon was damn scary just to look at.

The giant's face was covered completely with hair, making it impossible to tell if he were smiling or frowning. He held the gun loosely in one hand, making no aggressive moves and McPhail was thankful for that. It gave John a slightly easier feeling but still he was unsure of the big man. One look at this guy and all John could say under his breath was…"Oh boy."

With the same grunting sound John had heard a short time earlier, the monster abruptly hollered across the bridge."

You gonna move that buggy across the bridge today or tomorrow?

Or would ya like I come and carry it for ya?" The big man said.

Relinquishing first right to the bridge, McPhail yelled back trying to make light of the situation.

"Got to go slow, cause of the ice, my friend. You and your dog go first, we'll wait."

John still held on to the reins but moved slowly back to the buggy where Elizabeth could hear him whisper. He spoke in a soft voice so the giant couldn't hear.

"Be prepared with my rifle, just in case. It's lying on the floorboard. If he starts anything," he said, "use the gun." With that, John turned to the seven foot, 350-pound man and watched him cross the icy span. He was amazed as the boards of the old bridge creaked under the huge man with each step he took, The big fellow moved ever so slowly as he crossed over.

McPhail's eyes grew big and his mouth fell open as he watched this phenomena move slowly across the bridge.

He turned to his beautiful wife in the buggy and whispered a second thought. "I'd hate to shoot him you know, he just might get real mad. There's a good chance he would eat my rifle for lunch and spit out the bullets."

Each step on the ice was like walking on greased glass. It caused the giant to sling his rifle over his shoulder so that it would free both hands for the guardrail. So slick was the ice, the large flea hound looked much like an ice skater, spinning and sliding in circles across the boards. With both hands on the rails, the man pulled himself clear of the last board onto the bank in front of John, looking a great deal like a very large Goliath.

"Lost my horse a few miles back," he said reaching down to pull his dog from the bridge. "She just up and died while I was riding her."

"No wonder," thought McPhail, as he looked straight up at the large man in awe. "So would I with Paul Bunyan on my back."

Neither the giant nor the dog made any hostile moves, now putting Elizabeth a little more at ease. Nevertheless, she placed John's rifle across her lap with her thumb on the hammer.

"The name's McGee; George McGee," he said as he shook hands with McPhail. "I was hunting and trapping in the hills until damn soldiers run me out."

John glanced at Elizabeth with a frown on his face, "What soldiers?" he said, "Blue or gray?"

McGee's reply concerned John.

"Blue, whole damn countryside covered with blue." The big man exclaimed, "About three days back! Everybody's going crazy. Roads are full folks trying to get away from them

Yankees, that's why I'm not traveling on the main roads. Best you stay on these back roads and avoid the craziness too."

By now, the cold was getting to be too much for Elizabeth and the child, causing both to shake even with the warm blanket wrapped around them. She fiddled with the child's blanket trying to cover him better against the cold wind, but the blast of arctic air was getting too much for her to handle.

"I think it best we return to the farm," she said addressing John. "The baby can't take much more of this weather."

Nodding his approval, McPhail questioned McGee about his destination and where he would spend the night.

"It'll be freezing cold tonight" John said. "You're welcomed to stay at our farm until it warns, but you'll have to sleep with the chickens."

In his grumpy manner the huge man pulled on the dog's leash and replied, "Sam and I would be much obliged to ya for getting us out of the cold tonight. We sure don't mind the chickens if they don't."

Even as McGee spoke, McPhail pulled on the reins slowly turning the buggy around on the icy road. The cold wind seemed to blow even harder almost as if it were passing completely through Elizabeth and the baby, causing them to shake uncontrollably.

McGee was almost numb himself, but he hesitated only for a moment to pull a heavy buffalo skin coat off his huge frame. He then turned to the pretty lady and was able to cover her, the baby and the rifle with the one coat.

With a smile that could be seen beneath his beard now, he cautioned her to let the hammer down slowly on the rifle before something happened.

Elizabeth seemed thankful for his concern and the coat as she nodded an approval softly to this mountain of a man. John climbed back into the buggy and sat beside Elizabeth. He looked at the large coat covering her and the baby and smiled at the mountain man. Then he threw a blanket over his own legs and began to turn the horses back towards the farm.

McGee and the dog took the lead and led the way over the icy road as snow once again begin to fall.

Hardly aware of the reins in his hands because of the cold, McPhail pulled a cloth bag from the floorboard and took out some crisp bacon and a biscuit that Elizabeth had prepared for the trip. Frozen or not he took a large bite then handed the rest to her. At the same time he squeezed a little closer, putting one arm around her shoulders. It was his way of trying to reinsure her during the trip back and it was working.

She smiled and kind of hugged him as best she could while still holding the baby…

The small group would move as fast as possible to get out of this terrible weather and in front of a warm fireplace and that large buffalo coat was a great deal of help until they made it home.

Chapter 15

The Winter of 1865 was one of the worst on record, stopping almost all the war activities for months and giving the confederacy a much-needed break from the northern siege.

McGee built a makeshift fireplace in the barn and bedded down with Sam, waiting for warmer weather. He took to living with the animals in the barn, for he preferred the creatures over his fellow man. He was a mountain man and lived mostly alone the greater part of his adult life, but something had touched him about this Scotsman and his wife. They seemed to be different somehow and he felt a closeness and a sense of responsibility that caused him to respond immediately towards the McPhail's.

Elizabeth's smile and willingness to cook extra at every meal convinced the mountain man that these people were truly friends. Never before had anyone treated the huge man as an equal; they had ignored or shielded away from the hunter; for he was so menacing looking they were gripped with fear the moment they saw him. This had been true from the time he was a young boy of ten. Even then his size was overpowering to most.

As time passed it was almost a daily occurrence for the big man to knock on McPhail's door carrying a freshly killed deer or rabbit to help supply food for the family. Often he cut firewood in the snow, cared for the animals and help John make repairs to the house and barn. Returning John's kindness, McGee made trips to town picking up what supplies he could and he always brought news back about the occupation by the Yankees. For some reason he had created an image of being no threat to the union when he wandered into town, or perhaps too menacing looking to be confronted by a few blue coats.

Whatever the reason, the big man and his dog was stared at but never approached. He freely came and went with no thought of losing his weapon or anything else he might be carrying as the other southerners did. It never occurred to him that the curfew imposed on the people in the surrounding area would apply to a mountain man also. He often traveled the roads when everyone else remained in their homes from fear of the Yankee troops.

McGee was totally admired by the people seeing him boldly walk past the blue uniforms with his funny looking rifle strapped to his back. They soon began giving him whatever extra food, tobacco, or other products he might want for his show of bravery. He hardly ever came back from town without bringing something for the McPhail farm.

Union troops were often seen roaming the hills in search of any rebel stragglers, but Lee's remaining army was still causing Grant major headaches in Virginia. It seemed as if the rebels would never give up fighting for their land even though they were losing territory daily.

Winter held on even as April came around, but the days finally mellowed causing the snow to melt and give way to spring.

McGee had made one of his trips to town in search of food and returned to the farm with exciting news. The big man could hardly contain himself and he practically yelled out the news that the whole town was talking about.

"Courier just brought the word in John. Lincoln was assassinated. Somebody said an actor killed him in a theater. Shot him in the back of the head, but that's not all…

This news you're really not going to like. Lee surrendered personally to Grant, the war's all over."

John stood there like a statute; could it really be true? The war was over? He couldn't believe what he was hearing.

"Did you hear what I said?" McGee asked. "The war's over, the whole damn fighting's finished. Everyone will be going home now, the Yankees got it all."

The only thing that McPhail could think of at receiving the news was moving back to Texas and the life he knew in Houston County, but Elizabeth thought of all the people needing help in rebuilding their lives.

It was just hard for the news to soak in. Neither could hardly believe the news they were hearing. Lincoln was dead and the war was finally over?

With all they had been through, the idea of it frankly made them numb. The farm boy from Texas seemed to stare blankly into space with a shocked expression. He was out and out stunned by such dreadful news because it affected his life in a way as no other.

First, he had personally met Lincoln and the news of the great man's death gave him images of a sadness falling over the country. He may have been the enemy but never had this president lost the admiration and respect that he certainly had earned, at least in this southerner's eyes.

Second, the last thing to enter his mind was the thought of Lee surrendering to Grant and the south losing the war. It must have been a truly sad day for one of the greatest generals the world has ever seen. Tears began to roll down McPhail cheeks as he answered McGee.

"It's all over, really over." He said sadly with a sincere concern in his voice.

The Scotsman took out a handkerchief to try and keep from choking up any more. Once again his left hand squeezed the leather pouch hanging around his neck giving him comfort; it was the only sure thing now he had.

He knew he would have to trade with the Yankees now to survive and it would be sooner than he had thought. Later that night John, Elizabeth and McGee would break out a bottle of wine kept for a special occasion and drink a toast. It was not exactly the kind of special occasion they were expecting to toast to, but it seemed appropriate now. They raised their glasses out of respect for the valiant men who died fighting for the south and then to the Confederacy itself; finally, they toasted to the end of a bloody war.

McGee stayed on through June helping with the spring plowing using the only horse they had, as one had died during the cold weather. At times the giant even helped the horse pull the plow when it hit a difficult patch of ground that refused to give way.

By July the crops were in and McPhail had swallowed his pride enough to make a deal to sell his vegetables partly to the union army. The rest he would sell at a common market in town or trade for products that Elizabeth and the baby might need. It still galled John to even think about riding onto a Yankee post as something other than a conquering warrior, much less selling food to the soldiers; but times dictate your life and he had no choice if his family was to survive in a conquered land.

All of their hard work had paid off; McPhail had a great crop and was able to sell several wagons full of vegetables to the army and now was picking tomatoes, carrots, squash, and corn to sell or trade in town.

Things were certainly picking up and soon John and his family could head towards Texas, far away from the Yankee invaders. He thought that most of his troubles were behind him, but the hundred and fifty-acre farm, along with the animals was set upon by carpetbaggers coming from the north.

If they didn't get what they wanted, the newly appointed government would impose heavy taxes that were impossible to pay and use force to foreclose on the surrounding farms. Greedy northerners following the troops took everything including the southerners pride that they could get their hands on knowing that the army would enforce their will.

One day as McPhail and McGee were loading vegetables from the field, a buggy containing four men, along with two soldiers on horseback rode onto the farm. Elizabeth was washing clothes in a iron pot hung over an open fire at the back of the house.

The arrogant men rode within a few feet of her demanding to know where her man was. She stood there holding a wet pair of trousers, caught by surprise. When she didn't answer immediately, the man making the demand bounced from the carriage and grabbed her arm forcibly repeating the order.

"I said where's your man, girl?"

Elizabeth reacted automatically making sure she struck a nerve and his face at the same time, when she hit him squarely between the eyes as hard as she could with the wet pants and ran screaming towards the field where John and George were working. The army sergeant on horseback jumped down and gave chase running ten yards behind her into a cornfield that was between the group and McPhail.

Elizabeth's speed was no match for the sergeant. He grabbed the back of her dress hurling her to the ground landing squarely on top of her with his legs on either side.

"Don't run away when we're talking to you, pretty girl." He said. "You might begin to like our company."

No sooner had the sergeant said the words than he heard a noise behind him. The Yankee noncom turned toward the clamor and began pulling his revolver from its holster, but he was not fast enough to get the weapon into position.

A huge hand caught the side of his head with a strong blow that lifted the union soldier completely into the air and threw him about six feet.

He landed face up with blood flowing down his right side and his eyes were almost bulging out of their sockets from the shock of the impact.

He rolled over on his side and grabbed at the injured part of his face and now could see huge amounts of blood flowing between his fingers. As yet he had no idea what had hit him until he quit screaming and tried to calm himself down from the pain and shock.

Finally he looked up to see who had delivered the blow and his shock turned into disbelief at what his eyes were seeing.

There, standing directly over him was the giant he had always feared as a child; the monster in all his nightmares that he had hoped would never return.

Fear took over reason and he rolled himself into a fetal position hoping nothing else was about to happen, but was almost sure that more punishment was on the way.

McGee grabbed the sergeant and lifted him completely off the ground by his coat and was preparing to ram his large fist once again down the man's throat just as McPhail reached him.

"Let him be." John said. "You'll kill him."

George allowed the sergeant to fall to the ground making sure it was not an easy landing. Then he wiped his hands off on his trousers as if he had handled some disease ridden animal.

John smiled back at McGee when he made his next statement.

"You mean that would be a bad thing if he got killed?" He said.

George then turned to face the other five approaching men when he heard them coming. He picked up a large stick and assumed a fighting position causing them to think twice before getting any closer.

At the same time, McPhail helped Elizabeth to her feet and also turned towards the approaching men.

"You probably haven't heard that we're the new government around here." One man said, "and we've got the army to back it up."

Before the man had finished his statement, the second soldier pulled his revolver from his holster and pointed it at McGee, making sure he kept his distance.

"Not now," the obvious leader of the group said as he pushed the gun towards the ground. "I'll handle this.

Here's your tax papers on the farm." He continued. "You best pay by the 15th or we'll be coming for you."

The man wrote a figure on the paper and threw it at John, motioning for the group to return to the buggy. Unknown to John, the man had seen them at the fort and thought that McPhail might have some clout with the colonel in charge because he was allowed free access when delivering the vegetables.

He intended to deal with the troublemakers another day provided these people had no significant pull with any of the high brass at the army post. He was positive that he could get back at the farmers even if the Scotsman had a strong connection with the commanding officer.

Reconstruction was a joke and political corruption under President Johnson almost became impossible to live with throughout the south. After several of the carpetbaggers had been shot by irate southerners for the theft of their land, McPhail was sure life would be better in Texas. He reasoned that it would be best if they moved as soon as possible.

The sum of money written by the Yankee would be impossible for him to acquire, and they needed to leave before the 15th deadline. John knew that the Yankee sergeant would find a way to be back in force to retaliate against McGee for almost breaking his jaw.

Working through out the night with lanterns, he and George cleared all of the vegetables from the field and quickly sold them in town. Several times McGee carried the vegetables into town for waiting buyers while John worked in the field and Elizabeth prepared their personal possessions. They were moving fast to leave this land that now had become extremely hostile territory.

George too, planned to move to Texas with the McPhails, for he had killed one of the carpetbaggers during his last trip to town. When John saw that McGee was totally upset about his recent trip, he practically forced the details of the problem out of the huge man.

"The Yankee bastard was cashing in on the misery of B.J.'s farm and was about to drive him out." McGee said to John. "You really didn't think I was going to let him get away with it, did you?"

McPhail knew after hearing the story that they must begin the long trip back to Texas as quickly as possible. The man had been found on the edge of town with his neck broken and not many men in the area was able to kill a man in that way.

As soon as the union sergeant heard of the killing, he took several soldiers and wasted no time in questioning the farmer that was about to lose his farm. The soldiers used considerable force to make B.J. talk but was unable to learn anything. The farmer swore he knew nothing of the killing.

The union soldiers questioned a great many of the towns people but ended up with nothing. No one was talking.

Shortly after, McGee received two bottles of fine whiskey, compliments from a stranger with many thanks.

Selling his crop in record time, McPhail acquired a larger wagon and filled it with their belongings to begin the long journey.

With the Madstone neatly resting in a leather pouch around his neck and union money tucked away from his sales; McPhail, Elizabeth, John Jr. and McGee set out for Texas. Elizabeth was delighted to be leaving to make a new life in the great state of Texas, but sad that her father was staying behind.

Dr. Malloy had moved into a small house in town and wished to stay close to where Elizabeth's mother was buried. He would live out his life there and would be laid to rest next to his wife when his time came.

"This is where I belong." Dr. Malloy said, sadly bidding them goodbye the day the four began the trip south.

He knew at the time he would probably never see his daughter again but was happy that she and the baby was moving far away from the major occupied areas the Yankees held. He too felt his daughter and her child would have a better life far from where the main battles took place.

Although they were excited and happy to begin the trip south, Elizabeth turned in the wagon seat and looked back at her father until he was totally out of sight. She wanted to remember him staying behind waving a last farewell. She loved the thought of starting a new life for herself and John Jr. but leaving her father behind deeply disturbed her.

Doctor Malloy's farm had now become insignificant to all of them compared with their lives. They would leave it to the greedy northerners who would undoubtedly sell the place for a profit.

John could still hear the bitter sounds of the battles in his mind as the wheels of the wagon rolled over the rough road. One thing though, the thought of going home made him more determined to keep the horses moving at a steady pace.

He still couldn't believe it was over and that the south had lost after fighting so bravely against overwhelming odds. What had become of all the rebels he had fought with? Where would they go without being totally dominated by the Yankee army? He tried to wave off his negative thoughts by looking at Elizabeth and the baby, contemplating how lucky he was to have them.

On top of this, to have a good friend like McGee traveling with them clear across the country was a break for the McPhail's. He looked over at the huge man riding on the back of his horse beside the wagon and a thought suddenly hit him. What if this giant were to get sick? How could they possibly attend to such a huge man? Maybe he wasn't so lucky having his friend with him after all.

"Well, never mind." He told himself, mumbling in a low voice. "I'll just put the thought out of my mind…although, the big man had best not come down with anything. He's libel to be left beside the road."

John turned back to look down at the mountain man's dog keeping pace with the wagon a few yards in front of the horses. The huge animal was really quite tame and made a fine guard dog and pet.

O K, he again mumbled to himself. The dog is more than welcomed on this long trip too. He makes a fine guard dog and besides, if he gets sick we'll feed him to the first bear we can find.

McPhail took out his canteen and helped himself to a long drink of water. He then poured some of the liquid into his hand and washed his face mumbling once again to himself.

"I'm sure to lose my mind before this trip is over." He said softly.

All he wanted now was to make his journey back to Texas as safe as possible, for he had heard stories of hideous things happening to travelers moving through the war torn areas.

The war had left bitter evidence of the vicious fighting everywhere they traveled. They could see homes that had been burned; fields that were still left bare and the skeletons of animals that had been destroyed laying everywhere. It seemed that the union Army had made it a point to miss nothing in their quest for destroying the South. The small group kept moving their wagon through the devastated areas trying to avoid contact with any of the union troops occupying the countryside. It was bad enough to see what the blue coats had done during their march through the south but it would have been far worse to have seen them doing it.

They tried as hard as possible to discuss nothing but the new life waiting for them in Houston County but it became almost impossible as each new day brought more scenes of the Yankees' bloody march to be seen.

McGee looked forward to his new life as a Texan with his adopted family and was considering taking a wife. Almost without letup the big man began questioning John about the girls of Houston County until McPhail finally grew weary of his constant discussion of the females. John rarely used strong language, but he had totally tired of the questions put to him hour after hour about what the girls looked like, how many were there, their shape, their size, did they wear perfume and so forth that the big Scotsman would ask.

McPhail finally shouted out that all girls were alike and that the giant would have an anchor around his neck for life soon enough. He had hardly said the words when it dawned on him that Elizabeth was setting on the hard board of the wagon seat right next to his right elbow.

He looked out the corner of his eye without turning his head and quickly added a phrase that he hoped would allow him to see a happy expression on his wife's face; or at lease get him safely pass this stupid statement he had just made to his friend right in front of his wife.

"Unless of course you're lucky enough to marry the best of the crop like I did." He added.

Elizabeth simply ignored the statement and continued to do her knitting, pretending she hadn't heard a word, but smiling at the crude attempt John had made to cover his stupid outburst.

By now, John had traded or bought several fine horses from farmers along the road. He was trying to make the trip faster by keeping fresh ones pulling the wagon.

In many cases, about the only thing left for the displaced southerners to sell was some livestock that had survived the onslaught. They passed families camping beside the roads trying to rebuild their lives because the homes they knew and loved had been deliberately burned to the ground.

Although the travelers had had their share of desperate situations themselves, and certainly had their own problems, they began to see how much worse it had been for others. They felt lucky that finally the war was over for them and they would be able to live peacefully away from the hell and corruption coming out of Washington.

By July, the small group passed through Columbia, South Carolina and again Sherman's troops had left little or nothing remaining. It was a virtual ghost town, with buildings half standing and most of the people still gone. It was obvious that storehouses were ransacked and the food, supplies, and weapons had been carried off by the Federals. So it went, as they traveled from town to town, seeing the aftermath of what the union troops had done.

Their officers had not lifted one finger to prevent the troops' actions, but had actually taken part in the stealing, burning, and general raping of the land. It would take years for things to even begin getting back to normal. This was not what Lincoln had intended; rather his orders had been to the contrary but was now being totally ignored by the union generals because of the vast distance from Washington.

McPhail anguished at the sight of town after town being destroyed with only the civilian population being there when the Yankees overran their area. He couldn't help himself, his hatred of the Union Soldiers grew every time they rode through a town or passed a farm that had been burned, even though no resistance had been given the federal troops.

Sherman had done his job well. He forced women, children, and the old out of their homes and then gave the order to burn everything. The brutality was almost unlimited towards any southerners. Washington had total and utter power now and had used it to the utmost.

Soon after leaving Columbia, McPhail turned his wagon west trying to take a faster and easier route to Atlanta hoping things would get better as they moved further south. The group kept the horses moving from sunup to sundown, trying to waste as little time as possible.

On the third day out of Columbia, John had stopped the horses beside a small creek permitting the animals water and giving a much-needed break to the family. They had scarcely climbed off the wagon when a union patrol rode up to the small group.

The Yankees stopped within a few feet of the heavily loaded dray and looked the group over. The soldiers at first said nothing. They simply sat astride their horses silently staring at McGee and the others standing next to the cool stream.

George's eyes shifted towards his rifle hanging by its sling from his saddle horn and he seriously considered going for it. It was only a few feet away on back of his mare and he knew he could get to it fast but then he looked back at one particularly mean looking soldier that was watching him carefully.

His thought of trying for the weapon faded because he knew he wouldn't be fast enough to prevent at least one or two of the eight men from firing their rifle. All he could do was stand quietly by waiting for their next move, hoping if something did happen he would get a chance to fight back.

After a moment of evil looks, they seemed to be satisfied with whatever they had seen and the lieutenant in charge motioned for his men to move out. Strangely not a word had been spoken by the Yankees before or after they rode off. It was almost as if the blue coats expected the travelers to take some kind of action because they were there.

The only thing McPhail could think of that would cause their leaving was that the Federals by now had become so accustomed to seeing homeless families that they were simply ignoring the southerners unless they suspected them of being a danger to the union.

John watched the eight men ride off and was amazed that the troops hadn't searched their belongings, and perhaps taken whatever they wanted. He hoped that they would be able to avoid the rampaging union soldiers from now on but he wasn't banking on it.

When the travelers reached Atlanta, they couldn't believe their eyes. There was no Atlanta, only burned out buildings on either side of the road with chimneys sticking up from the ashes. It was all that was left behind by the Yankees handy work.

Besides Richmond, Atlanta was the most important focus point of the war, and Sherman was hell bent on its complete destruction. It was certainly obvious that his orders were carried out to the letter.

The group had passed Yankee wagons heading north that were laden with goods, and now John knew why. They were still stealing from the south and shipping the goods north.

This made John move on almost without stopping for he knew their little group could still be caught up in some kind of confrontation that might breakout at any time.

They were determined now more than ever to keep moving west hoping that Texas had not been hit as hard because of its size and distance from the main fighting. They could only dream of being on a small farm raising their crops without blue coats harassing a now peaceful family.

McPhail kept the horses moving well after sundown each day in an effort to put more miles behind them. He was hoping that each mile would give a better chance of a future without union soldiers dictating their lives.

The travelers were bone tired by the time they reached the Alabama River outside Montgomery. Here they decided to rest a few days before continuing their long trip. Fresh fish out of the stream made for a fine meal and the wild berries along the bank were being picked by other families living beside the river because of the war.

Small huts had been erected all up and down the riverbank making the area look like the California gold rush with so many people fishing the warm waters. Here was the only free food other than the wild animals that the people of the area could find.

Daily the people traded and swapped with whatever they could come up with for their needs. Flour for salt, sugar for coffee and buttons for cloth; anything that they might need.

Elizabeth traded her old shoes for baby clothes with one of the other ladies. She needed extra clothes for John Jr. and McPhail managed to acquire gunpowder and shot for his rifle in return for fish he had been lucky enough to catch. After a week of much needed rest, they moved on passing through Mississippi and on into eastern Louisiana.

The crossing of the Mississippi at Natchez scared Elizabeth to death the moment she saw it. An old man had built a large raft out of logs and used two strong boys to help with the drifting craft crossing the river.

Sometimes it took a full day to make the crossing and return, as the current often carried them downstream for miles. Because of the boats traveling the river, the raft sometimes would wash back towards the bank due to their wake causing the boys to start all over again.

For the old mans services, his charges were always five dollars in gold. He still didn't trust Yankee money; gold was more to his liking but If a customer didn't have the fare, he would trade for goods of value out of a small shack, which he called "The old store."

McPhail had some gold left but knew that he would need it for a fresh start in the lone star state. He thought that Elizabeth certainly deserved to be able to have some of the basic needs for her home when they reached Houston County. He tried to bargain with items from the wagon, but nothing suited the old man. That is, until he saw McGee's strange looking rifle.

He turned his attention from McPhail and pointed toward McGee's gun.

"I've got plenty of the kind of stuff you got." He said. "But I'll take ya across the river for the big man's gun, but he'll have to help my boys get'er through the tough currents."

McGee had been standing quietly by until the old man started pointing to his unique rifle. Now he had seen enough of the old man's foolishness.

His left hand gripped the multiple barrel gun a little tighter and with his large right hand he grabbed the old man's shoulder nearly crushing his collarbone.

"Old man," he said in a growl, "It's time for you to become one of the Samaritan's that we see so little of today. Now I'm right sure that you want to help your fellow man in his hour of need, don't you? Cause if you don't, you might fall overboard in the dark and no one would ever find you."

The old man's face turned to fright as George squeezed his shoulder even tighter causing his body to bend over closer to the ground because of the pain.

"I've never tried to cross in the dark," he started to say, but was interrupted by an even stronger pressure being put on his shoulder. Now he was at a breaking point. He either gave in or something on his body was about to break and there was no stopping it.

When McGee's dog saw his masters actions he joined in. Sam put his bad breath face right into the old man's and began growling in a fierce manner.

That did it. The old timer turned his head enough to yell out a command to his two helpers in a very painful voice.

"What ya standing there for?" He said loudly at the two boys. "We gotta get these fine people across before dark. Help move their wagon onto the raft."

Although they ended up almost five miles downstream because of the current, the group made it to the Louisiana side with George and John holding the horses steady all the way.

Unloading the wagon was difficult because no docks were in the area where they landed. This crazy old man had to fetch his horses to pull the raft back to his starting place each time he crossed and returned.

After finally getting the animals to pull the wagon completely ashore, McPhail and the others stood on the bank trying to decide which way would be the simplest and best road to travel.

The old man and the two boys pushed the log raft off for the trip back to the other side but was having difficulty controlling it. As soon as the current took hold they jumped aboard and began pushing the raft with long poles headed for the other side.

McGee had given him a few Yankee dollars for his efforts, but he was not at all happy about making the trip. As soon as the old man thought the raft was at a safe distance, he yelled at the group of rebels in defiance.

"I might not be so nice the next time. I've got friends in high places around here who'll take care of the likes of you if you ever come back you southern pig."

McGee pulled his rifle off his shoulder with one move and pointed it dead aim at the old man on the raft. He slowly cocked the hammer back making sure the old man saw his threatening movements. Then he spoke loudly so that the man knew exactly what he was saying.

"You're on your way to heaven for the good deeds you've done this day, old man." He yelled out.

Fear and panic gripped the old timer as he looked for a place to hide on the open raft. Unable to find anything to use for cover, he jumped overboard but held onto the side to keep from being washed away.

George couldn't help himself. He began laughing at the old man floating in the water holding onto the raft. However he was soon to change his attitude when he turned around and saw a stern looking Elizabeth staring at his actions. You bet she was totally upset.

"Weren't loaded," He calmly said as he pointed the rifle to the sky and pulled the trigger snapping the hammer down.

"See, it's empty, I wasn't really going to shoot the old man."

The large man now had the look of a child answering his mother as he waited for a response from her.

Elizabeth couldn't help but turn the shocked look into a big smile as she now responded to McPhail's voice behind her.

"Hand John Jr. up honey and climb onto the wagon." He said. "It's time we move on; not too much daylight left and we've got to get George to Texas so he can find himself a bride."

Chapter 16

Traveling across Louisiana was mostly uneventful except for some foul weather that caused delays in their quest to reach the Texas state line.

They felt good for days because there had been no sight of union soldiers since leaving Mississippi.

Other than the Red River Campaign started by the federal forces in March of 1864, this area of Louisiana near Natchez didn't justify heavy military ground action. Perhaps Washington was too far away to be of total domination to their lives when they settled in the lone star state.

John felt he was home when they reached the red clay hills of Houston County, but somehow things were not quite the same. Although they saw no union troops when they finally reached Crockett, they found it still controlled by the Federals out of Galveston.

The Civil authority was almost nonexistent, as many of the leaders of the Confederacy had fled to Mexico. Things were better than in most parts of the south, but a puppet government was in charge, set up by the federal authority in Galveston and doing almost what they pleased. They did walk softly however, knowing that the nearest federal troops were one hundred and fifty miles away and the nights were awfully dark around the Crockett area.

My goodness, injuries had been known to happen to quite a few of the population around Houston County, especially those people interfering with the lives of the farmers and ranchers. The motto was, mess with me you mess with us, meaning all for one because of the occupation.

McPhail quickly found that military operations were never extensive, only confined to the gulf area and the border, leaving Texas with plenty of food for her people and hard money to buy products coming into the port of Galveston along with crossing the border from Mexico.

As they passed the graveyard outside of town, John pointed out Eli Hart's grave and told the story of the flowers that he sold as a boy. Elizabeth was taken back by his stories, and she too felt that they would make a fine home here for John Jr. She felt in her heart that there wasn't a better place to be than the Texas area they called the Piney woods.

McGee eyed the girls they passed, picking one and then another as his bride to be, never considering they just might not be interested in him.

As it worked out, the tiny woman George later married was only four foot, six inches tall but handled the Scotsman with ease. Like a football coach she yelled and he jumped. Sam too, knew who was the mistress and who was the dog. The animal obeyed her every command enforced with the end of her broom.

John and Elizabeth found a boarding house within minutes of the downtown square that sat on top of a hill near the train station. The rooms were small, and only held three or four people at a time, but they were quite comfortable and convenient to the shops downtown.

The house was long and narrow with a porch and five rooms so that each person had to pass his neighbor's door in order to reach his room. It became a nuisance listening to the footsteps on the wooden floor every time a neighbor came or went, but the cost was right and the people next door were mostly friendly.

For a year John worked at the stockyards, preparing the cattle for shipment to the slaughterhouses outside of Galveston. He was quite content to live comfortably and quietly with Elizabeth and John Jr. with no thought of war or union soldiers dictating their every move. McPhail thought that he was now in total control of his life. That is until one day Elizabeth came to him with the news that she was once again with child and would be having the baby around Christmas.

This made John happy, but the addition to the family meant it would be necessary to get a larger home. He had been looking at farms around the area and one had stood out as being the ideal place for them.

As it turned out, McGee and Tiny had taken a farm not more than an hour's ride from there and they would be their neighbors.

McPhail had saved enough money to buy it if old man Kenner would except half payment now and the balance within a year. The deal was easily struck because the old man was getting on in years and his wife had died sometime back leaving him alone.

Moving into town with other people around him would make the elderly man more comfortable, so he wasted no time in accepting John's offer.

With George helping, McPhail moved the man's belongings into the boarding house while transferring his own things to the farm. Elizabeth took to the place right away and loved the hundred and nine acres that had been cleared out of the forest and plowed for crop growing.

Completely circling the farm was heavy wooded areas of pine, pecan, and oak trees which could be cut for lumber that could be sold for firewood and building materials during the off season when there were no crops.

There was a large porch with a swing allowing them to sit in the evenings and look out over the small valley while John Jr. played around the house.

Settling down fifteen miles from town was to McPhail's liking, especially the peace and quiet. He didn't want to hear anything more of Washington or the crooked politicians running the country. They were a long ways from that kind of foolishness and he wanted no more of it. John began tending to the plowing to prepare the spring planting using an old mule he had managed to buy from the farmer.

Now old man Kenner had trained this beat up mule to respond to whistle calls. Each whistle told the mule to turn right or left, stop or begin to pull the plow.

McPhail Learned the whistles well from the old man and had been plowing for about a week when John stopped one afternoon to drink some water in the hot sun. As he took a few large gulps and poured some over his head, he noticed that a mocking bird was setting on a fence nearby watching the farmer.

Since mocking birds love to eat tomatoes and lots of other vegetables, John picked up a rock and threw it trying to scare the pest off. With a loud squawk, the winged animal flew away but for days he returned to watch the southerner plow. The mocking bird often sat on the fence or in a tree watching McPhail give commands simply by whistling to Astor, the mule.

On one very hot day, John kept to his schedule by working through his lunch hour and stopped only to drink his cool water he had brought along. Sure enough the old mocking bird returned and sat on the fence once again watching the farmer plow his field. Only a few moments had passed until the feathered animal began proving that he was indeed, properly named.

The bird whistled the command for the mule to turn right and then left causing McPhail to cut across his rows. Picking up a rock, John threw it at the new command voice making it fly to safer ground. He thought that this would be the end of the mocking bird's foolishness but boy was he wrong.

For weeks the winged animal returned giving the commands again and again until John finally brought his gun to end the problem.

The only thing was that the next time the bird showed up he had eight or ten of his closest friends with him. Now the bird caper was growing and John knew that if he shot them all, Elizabeth would more than likely yell at him for killing these sweet little fellows.

Besides with a number of them parading around his field, which one of the mocking birds knew the whistling code?

The Scotsman looked at the old mule and then back to the birds trying to come up with an answer. All the while the little jerks were acting as if they knew they were teasing him.

Maybe he could just shoot the mule he reasoned in his mind.

Naw, best he try to figure out another way; he needed that old mule.

Another restless night came and went, but by the time he hit the floor for another day our hero had a plan in mind.

The sun had cleared the trees when McPhail walked out into the fields leading that old mule. But this time he had a specially treated bag of seed that was sure to have an impact on the little flying pests.

He had ground up hot peppers and carefully mixed them with the seed so that it would be hard for them to notice the combined ingredients. The peppers were so well mixed the birds had no idea they were in with the seed until it was too late.

John had solved his bird situation with the help of a few peppers. **That and the fact that McPhail had traded his mule for another.**

As for McGee, the red clay yielded fine crops of cotton, corn, tomatoes and other vegetables. Tiny too, gave him a crop of three sons and two daughters making him a proud man. He settled into a quiet routine and couldn't have been happier doing pretty much what he liked.

He did miss some of the excitement of not knowing what the next day may bring in a war zone however, and the freedom of roaming the hills with his dog, but every time he smelled Tiny's biscuits he thought better of it.

Early one morning in August, 1868, McGee was tending his cows when a lone rider approached the farmhouse.

Tiny was boiling clothes in a large black pot over an open fire close to the house with a clothes line full of shirts and pants blowing in the warm breeze. The smell of boiling clothes filled the air with a tar like odor as the stranger turned his horse towards the front porch and dismounted.

Sam stood up from his morning nap and began growling as if preparing to attack the man and his horse.

"Hush up Sam." Tiny said, wiping her hands dry on her apron as she walked towards the stranger.

"Morning Ma'am," He said removing his hat. "I'm Captain Mason Andrews of the Rangers. Would Mr. McGee be about?"

Before she could answer, McGee rounded the house in time to respond to his question still holding his hoe he had been using in the fields.

"What can I do for ya, Mr. Andrews?" He said in his usual growling voice.

The ranger held tight to the reins of his horse as he pulled a letter from his coat pocket and unfolded the piece of paper.

McGee couldn't help but notice that he was wearing captains bars on his shirt and wearing two 44 caliber pistols on his side. He wondered if the man could really use both hands at once.

"Major Barnes sent me to scout for new men for the rangers." He said. "We lost so many men in the war, we're having to build a new company of Texas Rangers that will work out of our headquarters in Waco. Folks hereabouts told me you'd make a fine lawman Mr. McGee. Pays thirty dollars a month and board when you're traveling. I got a letter here says I can swear you in right now, cause we're about the only law there is. If you ride with us, you'll come to Waco every three months and pick up your orders and pay. There'll be two of you working these three counties."

McGee couldn't believe what he was hearing and busted out all over with pride. He placed both hands on top of the hoe and then kind of leaned on the farm tool, so that he could stick out his chest to proudly show his pride.

"Me, a Texas Ranger and thirty dollars a month? He said turning to his wife. Hear that Tiny? A Texas Ranger."

George couldn't wait to stick out his large hand to shake with the captain acknowledging his acceptance to the Post.

As the captain shook hands with McGee, the large man felt something being placed in his palm at the same time. A ranger's badge had exchanged owners with the handshake making George officially a employee of the state of Texas.

McGee held tight to the badge and looked back at Tiny to see just what her reaction was going to be. He had no idea what the little lady would say about the big man traveling across the huge state after bad men. At this point, he was waiting for a thumbs up or thumbs down from the only person he would really listen to.

Tiny turned her eyes to George's large frame with a funny little smile she would come up with whenever she was about to put her stamp of approval for something.

"Guess I can get the Allen brothers to help with the farm when you're gone." She said. "You best get your things together, it's a long ride to Waco."

McGee and several others from the area joined Captain Andrews the next day headed for Waco and their new job. George had only his odd rifle slung on his back causing the captain to question whether he should have side arms.

"Don't have any pistols." George said patting his odd looking rifle. "Never had much use for them. I got along just find so far with old blower."

The captain decided he would accept that without comment, but when they reached headquarters he would offer the big man some of the extra guns that had been taken off criminals.

The tired group of new rangers dismounted in front of Headquarters in Waco and walked through the door to report in. Immediately McGee was struck with awe at the sight before him. The state had hundreds of weapons covering the walls of the ranger headquarters. From one end of the room to the other was all types and sizes of pistols that had been taken off of every kind of bad man a person could think of.

The sheer volume of the pistols so impressed George he gave in to temptation and began looking for a weapon he would like. Soon it had turned from a simple choice of a sidearm to an all out passion to have the finest weapon this side of anywhere.

McGee couldn't help but look over his shoulder thinking people might wonder if he was about to steal one of the these fine weapons.

Ranger Andrews noticed that George was kind of nervous and he simply placed his hand on the huge mans back to reassure him that it would be quite OK for the big man to take any one he wanted.

"Go ahead George." He said. "Help yourself."

George reached up to a fine looking revolver hanging in its holster and retrieved the weapon. He tried putting the belt around his waste but it was much too small for the huge man. As he tried in vain to strap the holster on, a voice from the next room called out.

"Come in Gentlemen. I've been hoping you would arrive today."

"Yes Sir." Andrews responded while motioning McGee to enter. "Hang onto the pistol." He said softly to George. "We'll get you a larger belt for the holster as soon as we finish here."

When they entered the room McGee took one look at Major Barnes and saw that he was not a tough looking ranger. Yet something told him that this man indeed had had his share of gunfights and had always come out on top.

When McGee walked into the Major's office he didn't know it but he had started his training in becoming a Texas Ranger. It would consist of one solid hour of Major Barnes informing the new men that a great deal of their assignments would put their lives in extreme jeopardy.

So, within two hours of reaching headquarters in Waco, McGee had now completed his Ranger training and had been given his first assignment.

He was to travel alone to San Antonio and meet up with a ranger by the name of Jim Randall to help escort three murderers to Waco for hanging.

It seem to be a fairly simple trip for his first assignment and McGee was pleased. He thanked Andrews for all his help and strapped on the larger gun belt that he had been handed. This one was still a bit tight but he slid his new pistol into its holster and shook hands with his new friend as Andrews mounted his horse.

"I've got to be moving out this evening." Ranger Andrews said. "My assignment calls for me to leave immediately. There's some trouble up north and the wire asked that we send some rangers right away. I'll see you in a few days, George."

McGee watched as his friend rode off without even having dinner. He knew now that this was an amazingly dedicated lawman. As for himself, the giant had decided that he would have a hot meal and a good nights sleep in the barracks before leaving early the next morning. George took one more look back at the dirt road where Andrews was a few minutes ago, but all there was to see now was an empty road. He turned and headed towards the chow hall where they were playing his tune. Dinnertime on the chimes.

Normally it was an easy round trip of six days to San Antonio, but this trip was to be anything but normal for the brand new Texas Ranger.

George's first problem came from a rotten bridge that crossed a stream of fast running water his second day out. He climbed off the animal and stomped his heavy foot onto the boards pushing his full weight down on the bridge to see if it would hold. Convinced that he could make it, George moved the animal very slowly across. He wasn't really very sure of this old bridge so he led the way holding the reins and listening carefully to the creeping sounds of the boards. He was just about half way across when one of the creeping sounds began to turn into a very large cracking sound.

McGee's face turned to one of shock as the horse started to rock back and forth. The old board directly under his animal's front leg gave way from the combined weight of the ranger and his horse.

Within seconds George and his horse went flying into the very cold water. For a while the Scotsman wasn't sure he was going to get out of that river alive, but fate endured and after a unwanted swim he turned back to help his mount limp out of the water. One look at his mare told him that there was no other option. It was obvious that he had to destroy the horse because of the damage done to the animal's leg and now it was the only humane thing to do.

With a deep breath and a very heavy heart he took careful aim and with one shot from old Blower he was without a mount.

"Damn." Was his only statement as he removed the saddle from the dead animal and patted it on the back.

He stood up and threw the heavy bulk on his back and began walking to the next town. The ranger had no idea that the town was some ten miles away, but it didn't matter, he had to find another horse.

Soaked to the skin the giant of a man began to talk to himself out loud to calm his nerves.

"Next time I'll wade the horse across or let the animal ride me to the other side!"

By the time McGee reached the town his clothes were dry but he felt like he was coming down with a cold. At least, each time he sneezed he though so.

He was watched by everybody in town as he walked down main street to the horse stables. The sleazy Blacksmith, owner of the barn, came in the back way muttering to himself. He was busy hanging rope onto a large nail on one side of the barn when he looked up and turned to see a huge gorilla of a man looking at him with unkindly eyes.

"Five Hundred Dollars for any of My Mounts and not a Penny less!" He said trying to be tough.

McGee was in no mood to hear this man run his mouth off. He simply looked the blacksmith straight in the eyes and pulled out a new ten dollar gold piece. With one move he took the man's hand and slapped the gold piece into his palm forcing his fingers over the coin. Then he turned and wrote out a simple note that said the Texas Rangers would pay him the remainder of forty dollars for his horse. With a small smile George threw his saddle onto the mare and thanked the man for his help. Once again McGee set out to keep his appointment in San Antonio.

With only a few miles behind him the San Jacinto River appeared directly in front of his path. The large menacing river with it's rapid currents carrying sticks and debris down stream at a fast pace caused George to look long and hard for a place to cross.

He was not about to get in a hurry this time. After hours had passed he hadn't found anything that even looked like a bridge. There might have been one but he was unable to find it.

Now he looked for a shallow crossing and when the Scotsman was satisfied that the one he had found was suitable, he urged his horse on. Never mind that he was forgetting the sworn oath he had taken not to ride his animal across again. Oh well, the mare seemed to be doing ok on the promising sand bank, at lease at first, but now that was about to change.

She began to slowly sink into the mud beneath the water. The huge man's weight didn't help much as the horse sunk deeper and deeper.

"Well hell, not again." He said, trying to throw one leg across the saddle horn so that he could easily slide off the animal.

Unfortunately this was not destined to be his only problem. A large log riding the fast moving current aimed itself directly at McGee's horse and on top of that the water was getting deeper.

Still hanging halfway off the animal, he gave a girlish scream as he sighted the projectile moving right for him. No amount of "giddyup" could free the stuck animal's legs from the mud. His destiny was sealed.

The Scotsman closed his eyes and looked up to heaven. "Oh lord" He said out loud. "Let that log take a turn towards the bank and push a little mud ashore instead of hitting my horse."

Then he waited for the inevitable collision, wishing he had learned to swim a bit better in case he ended up in deep water. While he was unable to dismount or force the horse to continue, the huge log slammed broadside with full force, throwing McGee for an unwanted swim and knocking the horse downstream.

The big man surfaced holding onto the log that was still riding the current. A half mile later it ended when he came close enough to the bank so that he could drag himself onto the muddy shore. His four-barrel rifle was still strapped across his chest, but his pistol given to him by the captain had gone the way of the current.

Badly bruised and limping from the pain in her side the horse wandered up to the new ranger to show him she was all right.

Acting as if it had happened many times before, George softly rubbed the forehead of the animal as he coughed and spit river water out onto the ground.

"Well, we made it didn't we?" He said to the horse. "I don't think we should try that again though."

Once again he was wet and cold when he slid his body into a setting position next to a big old tree and leaned back to rest a spell.

After his second encounter with a river, McGee decided this time he would take a couple of hours to build a fire and dry his wet clothes out. He would rub the animal as dry as he could using moss from a tree. It was the only thing he could think of that was still dry; besides it would help him start a fire.

After the couple of hours had passed he was now mostly dry and ready to move on. The new lawman was certainly not looking for another encounter with a river so he said a small prayer about not meeting another stream and pulled the mare slowly behind him.

For most of the day he moved along the dusty road with his stomach growling from pains of hunger. Finally the hunger pain was getting the best of him and he began thinking he might bag a rabbit or two for dinner.

He pulled the rifle from his shoulder and laid it across his saddle wrapping the sling around the saddle horn to prepare a camp alongside the trail. He hadn't seen anyone and the road was deserted as far as he knew but that was about to change. Two hijackers suddenly set upon him from behind some trees with their rifles in hand.

Unfortunately for them, the bandits were on the opposite side of his horse and before the two men could finish saying this is a holdup, McGee swung the four- barrel rifle to the firing position and shot both while the weapon was still draped over the saddle.

Only one of the men was able to get off a shot before falling to the ground. Of course the bullet struck McGee's horse in the side bringing the animal to her knees right in front of him. He stood there with the smoke still pouring from his rifle, as the mare slowly fell sideways onto his legs knocking him back a few feet.

"Son a of bitch." McGee said out loud; as he looked sadly at the scene of the two dead men and the one dead horse.

"What a waste of such a fine animal. It's so damn hard to fine a good mount these days." He said.

Then it dawned on him that he best reload his rifle. There just might be more of the outlaws close by and he better be ready.

He sat behind a tree to catch his breath and wait to see if anything more was about to happen, but all seemed to be o k.

Nothing left now to do but try and find out who these "gentlemen." were. Still eyeing the woods to make sure nothing else showed up, the ranger moved over to the bodies and checked them out for anything that might identify the dead men.

He rolled one over and checked out his face for any scars or markings that might identify him but there was only one thing he could think of.

"God he's ugly" he thought to himself.

When he rolled the man over a fifty-dollar gold piece fell out of his shirt that was hanging around his neck. Since he was the smaller of the two this may give a clue as to who they were later on. Someone may remember the little guy wearing the coin when he got into town.

The task of burying the two men caused McGee to be covered with dirt when he had finished; not to mention the fact that his clothes were torn from the rocks in the river. He tried several times to wipe off some of the dirt with a handkerchief, but he only spread more mud over his face.

Now he began walking towards the direction the outlaws had come from. He was hoping that he might find their horses hidden close by. Sure enough, the men had tied them a short distance away in the woods. He softly rubbed his hand across the back of each horse to calm them while he searched the saddlebags for any signs of identification. He found nothing at all except a child's toy doll.

Why would a outlaw have such a thing in his saddlebags? He thought to himself, it just doesn't make sense.

Dirty and disgusted, he continued his journey to San Antonio, leading one of the outlaw's horses and riding the other. He had ridden only a few miles before finding a campsite that had recently been used with a small wagon parked a few feet away. It looked like a home made wagon that a poor family would own but still why would they just leave it?

There was clothes and personal belongings scattered everywhere making George feel cautious. He quietly dismounted with rifle in hand and began looking the area over making sure he was alone.

His search ended when he found three bodies in the bushes a short distance away, lying in the tall grass obviously shot to death. The man, woman and child had been brutally killed for their few possessions and George was sure who had committed these atrocities.

Once again he was to be on burial detail, only this time with a heavy heart, for now he knew why the doll was in the saddlebags. The horse had belonged to the dead man and the doll was his daughter's.

He just couldn't help himself when the job was complete and the small wooden crosses had been placed. The giant of a man stood over the grave sites and cried.

Chapter 17

This time McGee would make it to the Alamo city without further mishap. He rode into town looking much like many other drifters that had come and gone. The town folks simply paid little or no attention to the huge man riding in with the exception of his size. Dusk had began falling as he dismounted in front of the sheriff's office and tied the horses to the water trough.

By now George had only one thing on his mind. He wanted to find Ranger Randall so that he could finish his business and crawl into a hot bath. Then he would dive into a large steak and finally into a large soft bed.

McGee walked through the jailhouse door and the first thing he saw was that there were no prisoners in the cells. This was pretty strange since he was there to take back three killers for hanging. Then he noticed the middle-aged sheriff setting behind an old wooden desk that looked like it should have been made into firewood long ago. It was obvious that the county wasn't shelling out much money for a first class sheriff. The old man was chewing tobacco; his feet were propped up on the desk and he had his eyes closed.

George couldn't believe that a man could chew tobacco and sleep at the same time but here he was, a lawman that was trying to do as little work as possible.

McGee made a loud sound by clearing his throat scaring the living hell out of the county lawman. He fell hard to the floor looking back up at a giant standing over him.

George reached down and helped the sheriff to his feet and at the same asked about the whereabouts of Ranger Randall.

The old timer regained wits but seemed to act as if everybody should have known what had happened to the ranger.

"Ain't you heard?" The sheriff said. "Ranger was kilt about two days ago. Prisoners broke out and shot him dead in his sleep. Posse got one in the big thicket, but the other two got away."

McGee pulled up a chair hardly believing what he was hearing. He looked the sheriff straight in eye as he asked a question he just knew he had the answer to.

"You know what the two looked like?" He said. "Was one wearing a gold piece?"

The sheriff spat into the spittoon making a mess and then replied to his question.

"Sure was, a fifty dollar gold piece; it was on the small one; he was the meanest of the three.

McGee took a bottle of whiskey he had seen from a cabinet by the sheriff's desk and downed a large gulp.

Now he knew, he had killed the men he was suppose to take back.

The sheriff looked at George with one eye closed as if he didn't believe the giant of a man was a lawman. McGee was really dirty and his clothes were down right awful but sure enough, he was wearing a Texas Ranger's badge.

"Looks like you'll have an easy trip this time ranger," He said not knowing the horrible things the Scotsman had just gone through.

McGee was now paying little attention to the tobacco chewing sheriff. He downed a couple more large gulps from the whiskey bottle and slammed it down on the desk before he walked slowly out the door. He hadn't bothered to ask where the hotel was because there was only one and it was just down the street. He stopped for a moment to consider what the sheriff had just said and then he thought to himself.

"If this was an easy one, what the hell would the rest be like?"

Next day he was headed back to Waco and he made the trip in record time. George couldn't wait to met up with Major Barnes again and deliver the dead Ranger's belongings. Sadly he placed the dead lawman's badge, gun and wallet on the major's desk and began making his report including where Ranger Randall was buried. When he had finished with his statement McGee took off his badge and laid it down on the major's desk indicating he was about to become a civilian again.

The major gave George the standard pep talk about being a Ranger, but McGee knew he was not cut out for this life; he missed Tiny and the kids too much and could smell her hot biscuits and gravy even in Waco. After a hot bath and full meal, he headed for the farmhouse and the life he really loved and wanted.

George McGee would never again put on a lawman's badge. He lived to the ripe old age of seventy-six, dying on April 8, 1901, in the farmhouse he shared with Tiny all those years. The burly Scotsman was never given credit for killing two of the most notorious outlaws ever known, that had escaped seven times from penitentiaries and jails. The Baker brothers were known to have killed at least thirty people in their criminal career not caring if they were men, women or children.

Chapter 18

By now McPhail had settled down to being a farmer and loving every minute of it. No more would his life be turned upside down by a vicious war and the dying of men around him. He would work hard in the fields during daylight hours and at sunset relax on the porch playing his pipes while Elizabeth cooked supper. The southerner felt that he was now a lucky man for at last he had it all. He just flat couldn't believe all the things that had happened in his life, good and bad.

Only on occasion did John see federal troops passing through the area, mostly coming from Galveston. Since Crockett was but a small town, little heed was paid to the population by the army officers. They mostly rode through trying to look stately, indeed like royalty on horseback. The officers would lead their troops to various forts set up around the state and only then would pass through town.

They weren't seen very often because of the extreme distance between the posts. Nevertheless the state was still under federal control but less and less attention was paid to the soldiers by the civil population. The people went about their business, setting up a government of their own with no interference from the union army because Crockett was of no importance to them.

The year of 1869 had been good to John, with a fine crop and a strong son of six growing up nicely, not to mention McPhail's small herd of cattle that would bring a better than average price at market.

The Madstone was still in demand from time to time and John would help when he could with poisonous bites and infections. The local doctor known as "Doc Anderson" called on McPhail to help in the treatment of patients when he had more than he could handle and knew that the Madstone could be valuable in some of the treatments.

Once again McPhail liked the feeling of being needed because of the magic stone. He could now freely use the agate without fear from the northern oppressors confiscating the valuable stone. Word spread about the healing powers of the Madstone and offers to buy came in from as far away as St. Louis, but John rejected all of them. The Scotsman never turned down anyone in need of the stone, but he was determined that it remain in the McPhail family.

The farmhouse sat next to a curve in the main road, about one hundred yards to the west. John and Elizabeth would often sit on the front porch in rocking chairs and watch for any neighbors passing by. It had been years since he had left to go to war, but now he felt at home once again.

It was obvious to him every time he looked at the vegetables growing in his fields that he was no longer living in a hostile land. He finally felt at peace just by looking across the rolling hills from his front porch. The sight of peaceful flowing streams, neighbor's cornfields and cattle herds grazing quietly in the distance gave him a lot of pleasure.

No more sounds of massive gunfire echoed across the hills. No cannon balls were flying overhead causing explosions that would literally shake him out of his boots. There would be no more droves of wounded men being carried in with stumps that were once legs or any of the other horrors that was called the civil war. It was ready over for him and it felt good to be home and he could only dream that John Jr. would never have to go to war as he did.

On one cool evening in May, the Scotsman relaxed alone in his chair on the front porch gently swaying back and forth. He smoked his pipe and wondered what the future might hold in store for John Jr. He envisioned his son as being a lawmaker or statesman enjoying a better life than his had been. An old mutt dog that John Jr. had brought home from the field one day lay at his feet. The dog was doing what he did best, taking an afternoon nap.

Elizabeth had been surprised and pleased to discover that her neighbor and friend, Susan Anthony, was giving birth and asked that she be brought to help with the delivery. Everyone in a fifty-mile radius knew that she was a nurse and would come in times of an emergency. Susan's son, Daniel had been sent to fetch her as quickly as possible, because Doc Anderson was traveling to Harris County and would not return for several days.

Elizabeth quickly packed a bag and followed Daniel some eight miles to their farm when she was told about Susan's water breaking. She wasted no time in kissing her Scotsman goodbye, for she knew that Susan had had difficulty with her last birth and would be needing help.

John was aware that she might be gone for a couple of days because this had happened before with other families. His wife just couldn't say no to someone in need and even though she was pregnant herself, she rushed to the buggy and began the trip. Her baby was not due for five to six months and she knew that Susan had had difficulties before, so wasted no time beginning the rough eight mile ride.

McPhail loved the thought of Elizabeth helping others and was more than willing to share her with their friends when they needed help and this was one of those times.

John was enjoying the cool air at the end of this day because shortly the long hot summer would be upon them and Houston County was well known for extremely hot summers. He thought that perhaps he would play the bagpipes as soon as the stars came out, but for now his smoking pipe would do nicely.

Windpipes suddenly jumped to his feet and began barking at something coming from the woods behind the house. The crazy dog seemed to go wild and despite John's calls, the animal ran into the cornfield leading to the woods. Since Windpipe was not known to bark unless someone was near, John retrieved his gun and followed the mutt, overwhelmed at the dog's speed.

Dusk was closing in, but McPhail could still see quite well in the thick woods except for the fact that he had lost sight of Windpipes.

The deer that ran out of the thick underbrush almost knocked McPhail to the ground as it rushed by with old Windpipes hot on its heels. John yelled at the dog to return but to no avail, the mutt was moving too fast.

"Damn dog", said John under his breath as he turned back towards the house. The rush across the cornfield was causing him to breathe extremely hard and obviously had taken its toll on the southerner. He began to feel weak with pain in his chest and a numbness in his left arm, causing him to drop to his knees. The weakness he felt frightened him as he fell all the way to the ground landing hard on his side.

He rolled over on his back and looked at the stars, which were beginning to come out. The only thing he could think about now was that this was surely the end of his life. He was convinced he was dying, as he took a deep breath and closed his eyes trying to relax while lying between the rows of corn stalks. This would be it he told himself, and Elizabeth wouldn't even know where he was when she returned.

How could he end up like this, when he had been through so much? Surely he could at least been killed while doing something heroic on a battlefield or saving a whole regiment of men,…not chasing a stupid dog.

With his eyes tightly shut, his mind couldn't help but begin reliving the days of the bloody war between the states and the part he played in it. The flash-backs John was having while lying among the corn were all too real, as if he could look down and see his body standing in the middle of a battle fighting the blue coats and do nothing about it.

He began to not only think he was at Bull Run, but could almost smell the gun power; and hear the screams of the warriors and feel the explosions rumble the ground. As much a man as he was, fear gripped the Scotsman and he felt his heart pounding wildly while wondering how long he had on this earth.

He tried to think of his youth and the happy times when he and his brother were growing up and would travel to the square downtown for the sidewalk sales, but his visions kept popping back to the god awful aftermath of the battles. The pain in his chest was almost unbearable causing him to pass in an out of consciousness even though he fought desperately to remain awake. He could only lay on his back looking at the stars, and oh how brightly they shined in the darkness now. He tried to force the fun times that had happened in his life into his mind, but each time he closed his eyes all he could remember was a field of blue and gray in bitter conflict and he was once again thrown right in the middle of it. His hand clutched the leather bag around his neck containing the Madstone and a small shamrock that he prized above almost everything else.

It gave him somewhat of a relief from the pain knowing what the articles represented in his life, even if this would be his final chapter and he were to die here. Not for a minute did he think he would survive this one, with Elizabeth gone and no one around to help him.

Hours passed as he lay there in pain with sweat pouring down his face into his eyes. The only time it had ever been worst, he thought, was when the nail had rammed through his boot, but even then he felt little pain because of being unconscious most of the time.

He clutched the leather pouch a little tighter and felt the small diary containing the four leaf clover and the magic stone hoping to somehow feel better because of it, or just maybe he feared someone was about to steal it. He wasn't quite sure himself and couldn't distinguish fact from reality. His face began to show signs of the stress he was under, and sweat continued flowing heavily into his eyes.

With his right hand he rubbed the water from his eyelids and once again, like lightning from the sky, the past flashed before him bold and colorful. As clearly as if a movie were being shown, a small lake appeared before him with hundreds of frogs in the water and around its banks.

McPhail now was remembering a time long past when as young boys, he and his brother visited his uncle in Houston County. They had decided to do a little exploring before calling on Uncle C.C. at his farmhouse and approached the lake seeing a sight that no young boy would or could pass up.

There, lining the banks of the lake were hundreds of frogs enjoying the cool water. Carefully situating themselves on a large rock with guns in hand, the boys began shooting frog after frog with new rifles their father had given for long hard hours of work put in on the farm. For several hours the two brothers fired repeatedly at the unsuspecting frogs killing several hundred.

What fun! At least for a couple of kids out to break the monotony of the day after doing chores on the farm starting from first daylight. When they had tired of the sport, the young boys moved on playing and laughing as they walked through the woods.

When they approached Uncle McPhail's well kept farm, the young men smelled cooking coming from the house and knew that Aunt Janet served fine meals, which made them move even faster. They ran through the front door like a herd of buffalo causing uncle C.C. to point at the wash basin and yell one word. "Wash", which the youngsters did in a hurry, for they knew that this uncle was one to be reckoned with.

A great meal of fried chicken and mashed potatoes was eaten as small talk passed between them, and the boys filled their stomachs. Uncle C.C. McPhail was very proud of the boys and was glad to see his favorite nephews, for they rarely made the long trip to his farm. He suddenly thought of something new he had added to the farm that the boys were not aware of.

"John", he said, "have you seen the new little lake I built in the woods? I worked all summer digging the pond in the hot sun and waited for the rains before stocking it. I'm raising bullfrogs; you know, to sell their legs in town, cause their bringing a high price right now. Want to go down after supper and take a look?" He said, smiling and very proud of his accomplishment as the boys slid down in their seats and tried to grow smaller hoping they would disappear right before his eyes.

John's Uncle Clement C. McPhail was also at the battle of first Manassas and had shown so much courage, the yankees were still talking about the fighting Scotsman years after the war. C.C. as he was called by the rebel troops, had brought the union attack to a halt when he took command of a company after the fall of the captain in charge.

Distinguished looking, with an air of command, McPhail took control of the advance even though he was only a private in the confederate army. C.C. opened a gap in the union lines while Jackson stood like a stone wall to his left. He exposed himself recklessly, yelling at the southerners to take down the row of Union cannons that was firing on the main body of southern troops only 300 yards to the west.

When the smoke cleared, the union infantry, cavalry and batteries retired from where they had come, by Sudley Ford. The whole union army dissolved in retreat causing panic to race across the congressmen and sightseers including women in carriages.

They had followed the army from Washington to watch the glorious victory that was to end quickly the rebellion of the contemptuous southerners.

Kemper's four gun southern battery wrecked a wagon on Cub Run bridge, blocking the road which thoroughly demoralized the retreating yankees and caused them to abandon 14 cannons and scores of other vehicles.

On April 18,1862, C.C. McPhail would apply for and receive a commission as artillery captain in the Southern Army. The last entry in the National Archives shows that C.C. McPhail was commander of the Columbia armory in South Carolina on January 20,1865.

Of the many McPhails that served the army of the confederacy, two deserted and joined the Union Army. In March of 1863 Rufus McPhail deserted to change sides convinced the north would win. On the same day James A. McPhail (listed in the National Archives) also left company A Third Regiment of the Confederate infantry to take the oath for the blue coats. Both were from the same town and it is believed they were brothers.

The records show that neither survived the conflict, but does not tell what caused their deaths. The two privates were laid out side by side for burial and confederate records revealed that both were privates from Arkansas, but no message was sent to their relatives of their deaths because Washington did not notify the families of confederates.

After a careful search of the archives in Washington, it was found that ninety McPhails served for the confederacy as privates and non-cons, with seven others serving as officers. Of the enlisted men, eleven died, twelve were captured, seven deserted, five were disabled and the rest were unaccounted for.

As for the officers, the only record shows one to be captured and later released with no further record as to where he settled down.

Chapter 19

McPhail's body jerked causing him to wake from his dreaming and he realized that he was still lying on his back among the corn stalks with the moon now rising and outshining the stars. He felt chilled to the bone and his chest gave him more pain than ever, but he still chuckled out loud to himself in a dreamy state.

"Adam and I got the hell out of there when the fog rolled in that night." He said out loud. His mind raced from the battle of Fredericksburg to his travels to New Bern as he once again lapsed back into dreams he would rather forget.

His vision turned to just a few months back when the year 1868 became clear in his mind and he received sad news. Word had reached McPhail of the death of Sam Houston, another Scotsman that had resigned his office as Governor of Texas because he did not want to see the union destroyed when the state joined the Confederacy. John so admired Houston because the former governor had fought and saved Texas after the fall of the Alamo.

McPhail often traveled the forty miles to Huntsville to trade and buy goods, but he had never met the great man even though the governor lived in the city. On one trip to Huntsville shortly after the governor's death, McPhail rode the bumpy wagon playing his bagpipes all the way in remembrance of the great man.

He often wondered what part of Scotland the governor's people had migrated from and how he had come to be in Texas and most of all, whether his people had also been forced out of Scotland or merely immigrated of their own free will.

John could clearly hear the sounds of a hundred bagpipes playing in his ears and he couldn't believe it was only in his mind. He tried to bring himself mentally around and even though the ground was cold, he was covered with sweat.

His lips were dry and he had trouble swallowing making him wonder if this was how it was to die. The night moved on into early morning with his eyes scanning the heavens trying not to lapse back into unconscious. He had no way of judging how long his body had been stretched out on the ground but it was getting daylight and he knew that a way had to be found to get back to the farmhouse. He couldn't imagine how he had survived this long, as the sun began to shine into his eyes.

Once again he tried to raise himself to a standing position but was overcome with exhaustion and fell back to the ground.

"Stupid damn dog." He said out loud. "Should have run him off months ago."

McPhail seemed to grow worse, unable to focus his mind on the current world but rather he drifted in and out of the past. "I found my place in this damn war." He said out loud again. "Wind to the pipes, heal to the sick.

I will see that the story of the Madstone is told from generation to generation." He muttered slowly because he was growing weaker. He tried to rolled back and forth on the ground hoping to find a way to get back onto his feet but to know avail.

John did manage to raise himself up on his elbows and it was then that he realized that he had been speaking out loud again. Still in a hallucinatory state, he gave a quick turn of the head both ways checking to see if anyone had heard his babblings. Satisfied that no one was listening, he sighed out loud and lowered himself gently to the ground falling once again into unconscious.

McPhail didn't hear the buggy pull up to the farmhouse when Elizabeth and John Junior returned, but old windpipes did. He raced to them making an awful barking noise, which was totally out of character for a mutt that slept all the time.

John Jr. approached the shaggy dog trying to calm him, but the animal would run towards the cornfield and back at a frantic pace finally causing Jr to follow after him curious to see what the dog had found. He was sure the animal had found a rabbit or squirrel that had been injured or wounded by a hunter.

The discovery of McPhail lying between the corn stalks made John Junior yell at the top of his lungs for his mother; at the same time he placed his fathers head in his lap trying to ease the pain and comfort him until help came.

Once again John chuckled out loud not really knowing what he was saying. "Kept my word to Lincoln, didn't fight no more, but damn sure wanted to; wonder if Aunt Janet will be at the sale downtown this Saturday?"

After another moment he called for Elizabeth to help with the wounded for the battleground was clearly being laid out before his eyes and it was all real to McPhail. He was reliving the battle of Frederickburg and the stone wall at Marye's Heights where the casualties soared to six thousand within hours of the attack. No one would walk away untouched by this battle where even bullets collided in mid-air falling to the ground welded to each other.

McPhail heard Elizabeth call to him in an excited way and he began to respond to the sound of her voice but fell unconscious once again as he tried to raise from John Jr's lap. She reached him in time to see his 200-pound frame fall back against her son causing the boy to stretch his arms to the ground behind him in order to keep his balance.

Elizabeth knew that the two of them would be unable to carry her husband back to the farmhouse. Thinking quickly, she took McPhail's head from the boy's lap and yelled for Jr to run to the house and fetch a blanket, knife, rope and the horse and buggy.

"We'll drag you back." She said. "You'll not die on me now Scotsman after what we've been through."

John Jr. returned at a dead run and threw the blanket to his mother. Elizabeth spread the blanket out beside McPhail and the two of them gently rolled his body onto the spread. John Jr. watched closely as his mother folded the end of the blanket and cut two holes in order to tie the rope securely.

The other end was fastened to the back of the buggy much like an Indian travois and with this they drug the unconscious Scotsman to the farmhouse.

With difficulty, they managed to pull the blanket containing John up the steps and into the house where Elizabeth removed his shirt and washed his chest with cold water hoping to revive him. It would be hours before McPhail would come around to Elizabeth's tender care. Just like the nail incident she never left his side for a moment until he seem to be responding in a good way.

She was exhausted but excited when her man awoke and recognized his wife with a smile and one sentence.

"Damn, I'm hungry." He said, rising slowly into a setting position.

Now she knew that he was going to make it and she showed it as she collapsed into the rocking chair next to fireplace.

"It's a wonder I didn't have this baby here and now." she laughed out loud. "Don't do this to me again if you can help it honey." She said with a smile. There was still a lot of love and now relief in her voice for her Scotsman.

Chapter 20

For the next few months Elizabeth saw to it that McPhail stayed in bed making sure he did as little as possible. She was really hoping that he would quickly grow strong again. After he was feeling better and able to sit up, McPhail began to grow bored and started spending his time playing his pipes for hours on end.

He was trying his best not to get underfoot of Elizabeth. He felt damn lucky that he had married a nurse that knew how to care for people and he enjoyed the labor of love.

Dr. Anderson dropped by every so often to make sure the Scotsman was doing well. It was now September and the doc called on the McPhail's with an announcement. First, it was time that John began to return to his normal duties. The doctor didn't mince words after listening to John's heart.

"You're sounding like a strong horse again." He said. "Now get out and exercise more and help John Jr. with the farm."

Second, Elizabeth was about to come to term; everything was looking good for her upcoming birth of the child but he would feel better if a midwife stayed at the farm until the baby came.

"Now." He said. "I'm going to tend people that are really sick." With that he wandered out the front door with medical bag in hand and mounted his horse and buggy riding towards the Samuel's farm some five miles north.

Next day an old woman arrived to serve as a midwife for Elizabeth, obviously sent by the doctor. Immediately she reminded Elizabeth of an old friend with her bluntness, and barking of orders to get things done.

It was as if Fannie May had come alive and returned from the North Carolina hills. She couldn't have been happier with the care that Tressie would give her, for she was known all over the east Texas hills as a tobacco chewing, heart warming, fully experienced, excellent nurse who had delivered hundreds of babies in her 65 years.

She parked her bag by the fireplace and threw a blanket on the floor, preparing her a bed for the duration of the upcoming birth. Tressie was here for Elizabeth, and stay she did, even for a full week after a little girl was born to the McPhail's.

John had hardly gotten to say a word because Tressie paid not one bit of attention to him, but rather rushed McPhail out of the way and out of the house. He was lucky to see his wife at all during the entire birth.

"This is women's work." She told John. "Best you tend your farm animals and leave us be."

All John could do was pretend he was working close to the house, when he was really listening for signs coming from his newborn. Days went by with McPhail pretending to fix the wagon, or leaning on a hoe as if he were going to strike the ground any minute to plant a vegetable, but always close to the house waiting and listening with John Jr. nearby.

On several occasions he knocked gently to ask about dinner, causing Tressie to respond by opening the door with cheese and bread in hand or some such, which was shoved into McPhail's gut immediately followed by a slamming of the door.

"I was treated better as a Yankee prisoner." John said quite loudly "I'll fix her, I won't eat the cheese."

Of course he made the statement with a mouth full of hot baked bread as he stood on the front porch trying to figure out what was happening inside the house.

John Jr. too decided to take his fathers example, and also go on a non-eating rebellion, but ate the cheese when his father was not watching.

When Elizabeth finally did have the baby, she could see that the newborn girl instantly brought joy to John and she knew that the only name for the infant had to be Joy Ann McPhail born September 11, 1869 and baptized Sunday October 5th, 1869 in the first Methodist Church, Crockett, Texas.

Congratulations and gifts were brought to the McPhail farm, along with foodstuffs from the ranchers and farmers in Houston County.

It was customary to pay your respects to the mother and newborn and the McPhail's received quite a lot of them because Elizabeth had helped most of the farmer's wives at one time or another. The gifts were mostly hand-me-down baby clothes given with a great deal of love, for not many of the donors could afford to buy new.

Even tobacco chewing Tressie showed up with hot baked bread and a large round five-pound cheese. McPhail made sure that while the grumpy old mid-wife was there, he remained inside the house checking every few minutes to see that the front door remained unlocked.

Elizabeth had few complications and regained her strength quickly enabling her to return to being a housewife but with the addition of what she loved most; being a mother.

For the next few years it would be quiet and relaxed on the farm, with John Jr. growing into quite a young man of fourteen which in the 1800's would make him ready to take on the duties of an adult. Like his father, he loved going to town on Saturdays to the sidewalk sales around the square and seeing the pretty girls that came in from all over the county.

He and the other boys often danced with the girls in and around the courthouse, to the music provided by the local townsmen. Nothing was planned as far as dancing was concerned, but everyone knew that it would come about when the music would start. John Jr. had been taught by his father to play the bagpipes and each Saturday several of the young Scotsmen would play lively songs for the crowd.

After a few weeks of this, the boys got together and wore their colorful kilts and hats making for a grand time for all. When McPhail saw the boys dancing to the music of Scotland he told Elizabeth how proud he was.

"Now we're really home."

Chapter 21

The winter of 1878 started off with a bang, dumping snow, ice and sleet on the county harder than the folks had seen in twenty years. It began early in September, but John Jr. loved the ice all over the trees and bushes and the snow on the ground, allowing him more time from the daily chores.

As a young grown man of twenty three he had discovered that beautiful girls could dominate his life and he liked it although he didn't see many, except on Saturdays at the sidewalk sales. Girls were about all he could think of now, but when he was able to get a date it usually consisted of popping popcorn in front of a fireplace with her family close by, allowing privacy about like a snowflake in a snow storm.

When a new family moved into the farm next to a small lake about three miles from their house, Elizabeth cooked mashed potatoes, corn, and ham to take to the new neighbors as a welcome gift.

She asked John Jr. to ride over to the neighbors with her so that she might deliver the food. He really didn't want to go, but his mother insisted that he ride along because of the cold weather.

The young Scotsman helped load the food into the buggy, wrapping a blanket around the baskets to keep them warm and placed another around his mother's shoulders to break the cold wind. It reminded her of the time the huge Scotsman, McGee gave her his coat at the one way bridge to warm her and John Jr. when he was just a baby in her arms.

The ride down the hillside slowed because of the snow, but they still made good time because young John had been taught well in the art of driving buggies.

McPhail Jr. pulled the horse and buggy up to the front door of the farmhouse that looked in worse shape then he had remembered. It had been abandoned for quite a long time and the wind and weather had taken its toll.

He began to climb out of the seat onto the ground and suddenly, without warning a very pretty redhead fell from the sky onto the ground right in front of the buggy. Luckily the pretty lass landed in deep snow and was not hurt.

Boy, was John Jr. excited at this unusual affair. How many of the fellows his age had a beautiful red head fall at their feet into the snow? His mind was now racing with possibilities. All he could think of was she had been dropped from heaven just for him.

"Are you hurt?" He asked looking down at a real beauty.

The girl brushed away the snow from her face and hair and looked up at the young McPhail who by now had slipped back into the buggy seat caught totally by surprise.

"I don't think so." She said. "I was just trying to close that damn storm window upstairs and slid on the icy roof."

Just then her mother came out the front door. "Laurel, watch your mouth child, a lady doesn't curse".

John Jr. jumped from the buggy and helped the girl to her feet holding onto her arm longer than was necessary. Their eyes had locked on to each other and he stood holding her arm until she became aware that they were being watched.

"I'm not hurt, you can let go of my arm now." She said with a smile. He had been staring at her the whole time and found it difficult to take his eyes off the beautiful young lady. It wasn't spring but his thoughts had certainly turned to love and all that goes with it.

After everyone had introduced themselves, the food was brought into the house and coffee was served off the hot stove.

It was obvious that the family was still unpacking because boxes and personal items were all over the room.

Mary O'Connell turned out to be seventeen and looked a great deal like her mother Kathy. The family had moved from Atlanta because most of the policies were still coming from Washington and they had decided to get as far away from the Yankee influence as possible.

Mike O'Connell had been a lieutenant in the fourth Georgia regiment fighting in Tennessee and had been totally immersed in the war when the end came. He returned home to find his house burned to the ground and all of his belongings carried off.

Mike loved the peach state but was still remembering the brutality, stealing and arrogance of the union soldiers. They took what they wanted and destroyed the rest with no decency, compassion or remorse for the families of southerners. His hatred for the blue coats ran very deep, and who could blame him after Sherman's march through the south.

The Irish blood in O'Connell was cooling over time and now he was here to forget the past; not forgive, just forget. "I'll settle my family here," he said. "T's a fine place to rebuild and begin again."

John Jr. listened intently to all of the small talk that was going on over coffee, but really heard not a word of it. His sole attention was focused on Mary who was quietly sitting beside the fireplace staring back at this handsome young Scotsman, while thumbing through a book she would probably never read. He tried to look sophisticated and worldly while racking his brain for something wise to say next.

Finally Elizabeth arose and announced that it was time for she and John Jr. to go.

The young McPhail stood up and paused long enough to say a few of the wise words he had been groping for.

"See Ya." He said, feeling down right stupid.

All through that winter, the young McPhail went by the O'Connell farm calling on Mary and ending up doing chores in the process. Over time the foot prints in the snow would meet half way between the McPhail and the O'Connell farms; one set of his and one set of hers rendezvousing in a special place next to a fence near the small lake.

J.R. (as his father had begin to call him) often brought his bagpipes and would play cheerful songs that they both enjoyed even when the wind was bitter cold. The weather was really not a bother to them for the two young people hardly felt the bitter cool winds when they were together.

By the time Christmas was close at hand, J.R. was hungry for her and was inspired to make his move. He would fulfill his fantasy that he had begun the first day he saw the beautiful slim creature.

Now he had chosen, this would be the day, while the two of them were alone in their special place. He slowly and carefully put his arm around Mary and began to unbutton her blouse but found that the gloves he was wearing were too thick. He removed them and tried again using bare hands. He was so nervous as he tried removing a button out of it's hole that he slipped on the icy ground falling towards her causing a tear down the front of her blouse and ending up with his arm stuck inside her clothes.

Now what does a gentleman do when his hand is caught in a lady's blouse? His clumsiness embarrassed the Scotsman so much that he pulled out his arm and retrieved his bagpipes lying next to him and began to play a song.

Mary recognized the tune that she had heard before as the "Dance of the Fools" but had decided to take things in her own hands by grabbing J.R. and replacing his hand inside her blouse. She would control the farce this time and control she did to a point that neither meant to go.

Their almost naked bodies was undeterred by the cold snow with John Jr.'s fantasy no longer a dream and both lost their virginity beside the frozen lake that day. It seems that Mary had been having the same fantasy and had every intention of fulfilling hers also.

Chapter 22

The holidays passed quietly as a joyful time, mostly for the children in the Crockett area; Christmas trees shined bright with lanterns and the tiny bells on sleds rang as the kids slid down the hill sides in the snow.

February of 1879 was approaching fast and J.R. would soon come to an awakening in his life. He and Mary had been seeing each other whenever it was feasible for her to sneak out of the house. On this Friday they would meet at a trading post near the square as they had done so many times before. The young Scotsman had received a note telling him that she would be there around noon, while shopping with her mother.

Sometime back they had set up a drop off spot on the fence that ran next to the lake. The messages would be stuck on a nail that J.R. had driven into the fence post to use as their mailbox.

When he arrived at the town square, it was only eleven so he bought a few items of cloth that Elizabeth had requested and paid for the merchandise at the counter. He had no idea that he would see Mary's father standing at the front door when he prepared to leave.

The former confederate soldier was standing alone, looking pretty mean, causing concern for J.R. He wasn't sure if he would get a pat on the back or a fist in the face. The young man pondered the reason for Mr. O'Connell being in town and felt ready to explode with impatience to get out of there.

He decided to walk right up to her father and wear a smile when he greeted him with a "Good Morning Sir." No sooner had he started to make his move, than the old man came at him with his face changing into a great big smile. The girl's father grabbed J.R. in a bear hug and told the boy he was extremely happy to see him.

"Damn glad to have a Scotsman in the family boy!" He said, almost crushing the young McPhail with his hug. "Come to the house tonight and we'll make plans for the wedding."

Stunned at Mr. O'Connell's statement, J.R. mounted his horse and pushed the animal to the limit riding to the neighbor's farm.

Nothing had been said about marriage, he said to himself as the farm came into view. He was going to give her a piece of his mind when suddenly something occurred to him.

"What am I doing?" he said aloud. "I'm crazy about that little redhead, why not marry her?"

The young Scotsman slowed the horse as he got closer to the house, and had decided that the whole idea of marriage had been his. Just then Mary came running to him from the fields. She wasn't sure whether he would be mad at her or not as she grabbed his foot that was still in the stirrup and looked up at him with her big blue eyes.

"I didn't know any other way to tell my folks." She said, moving back so he could dismount. "So I told them you had asked me to marry you. Is that O.K.?" She continued, hoping for the right answer. Then she dropped the block buster on him.

"We're going to have a baby." She said. "I hope the child looks just like you."

Now, there was no way John Jr. could stay mad at the perky young lass after he looked into her eyes. He grabbed her in his arms and squeezed so hard she thought her ribs would break. With one quick move, he carried her in the house to formally announce their engagement and plan the marriage.

A small cottage was built between the McPhail and O'Connell farms for the couple, and a boy was born to J.R. and

Mary in October of 1879, named Michael J. McPhail beginning a new generation of McPhails.

John and Elizabeth were delighted at becoming grandparents and hoped for many more. The McPhail's clan began to grow along with the rest of the population in Houston County over the next few years, but the city of Houston attracted more people because it was closer to the port and created many more steady jobs because of the import and export businesses.

By the year 1885, the McPhail's were hauling their vegetables and cotton to Houston for higher profits until they found that even more profit could be made delivering their products on to Galveston and its busy docks.

The trip of a hundred and sixty miles would take about a week but was certainly worth it when they returned with a great deal more money.

Often the silhouettes of John and his son could be seen riding a freight wagon over the flat planes of Harris County.

It wasn't long before Mike O'Connell and other men from the area began to roll their wagons towards the docks at Galveston. Not only did it mean more money but it also meant an excellent seafood dinner for the whole group and they certainly looked forward to eating fresh fish and oysters right out of the gulf waters.

Crossing the bay to reach the island was somewhat of a dangerous task, because the old ferries had been known to sink with freight wagons aboard. A bridge leading from the mainland to the island was planned, but it would be a few years before its completion.

On this trip the wagons were full of cotton to the point of overflowing and were tied down with canvas covering the top. All eight wagons from the Crockett area made it safely across the bay and to the warehouses that lay next to the docks.

After unloading and receiving top dollar for their goods, the group checked in at the Hotel Galveston to spend the night and eat fine seafood as they had done many times before.

With the horses taken care of and bedded down for the night at the stables, the men found a really quaint restaurant that faced the cool breezes coming from the gulf.

The tables sat on a wooden porch and looked out over the sand beach that led out to the sea. Nothing was finer than the cool salt breeze coming in from the Gulf that refreshed the travelers as they drink beer. They filled themselves full of fish, oysters, and crabs until they thought they would explode.

Tomorrow morning they would head back, but tonight the men would enjoy the town with its southern charms, which the Yankees were unable to destroy. Only a small U.S. Army base was still left to control smuggling and didn't interfere with the civilian authority any longer.

The next morning at daybreak, the entire group hooked up the wagons and headed to the ferries. Only one thing was wrong, McPhail couldn't find John Jr. or the money from the sale of cotton that he had entrusted his son to carry. The young Scotsmen had downed too many beers and wandered off from the group while his father had gone to bed.

John began searching the island for J.R., including the nightspots that were well known for their ladies of the evening.

He rode the wagon as it rumbled slowly up one street and down the other trying to find the boy and finally decided that he had better get help from the men in their group before they all crossed over to the mainland.

He arrived at the ferry in time to stop about half of the group from crossing over and they immediately joined John in his search for the boy.

They paired off in twos and each took a section to search for the boy. McPhail played the bagpipes while O'Connell drove his wagon yelling at the top of his lungs. John hoped the boy would hear the Scottish music and come running from God only knew where.

Hours passed before John Jr. was found passed out on the beach with his face in the sand and the entire proceeds from the sale missing. All of the money was in a small pouch attached to his belt and the boy had no idea where it had gone.

McPhail Sr. was furious; they had worked so hard and the entire $600. was gone; how could he tell Elizabeth that they had lost it?

McPhail and O'Connell got the boy to his feet and managed to get his hangover body onto the wagon.

"We'll head on back." John said. "Ain't much we can do here now anyway." McPhail Sr. felt that he wouldn't be playing happy songs on the bagpipes during the long trip home this time. John turned the team around and began to head across the island to the ferry, when an old man carrying a cane and obviously in his eighties called out to the group.

"Hold on a minute young fellows." He said. "I've got something for you, which I hope will teach the boy a lesson."

John pulled the horses to a stop and waited for the old man to catch up.

The man limped to the wagon and threw something at McPhail Sr., which was caught with one hand by the Scotsman and immediately recognized as John Jr.'s purse.

"Only kept ten dollars for my troubles." He said. "Saw the boy laying face down in the sand late last night and checked to see if he was dead. When I knew he was all right, I took the money and left him a note in his right pocket. Didn't want him to get rolled."

The man pointed at John Jr.'s coat with a hand that shook from side to side. Age was certainly taking it's toll on his body. "See there." He said. "Right there in his right pocket."

Everyone turned to watch J.R. pull a poorly scribbled message from his right hand pocket. It read Old lacy has your doe, lives at 1211 w 9. Get it in a.m. and was signed L.V.

John Jr.'s face turned red, and yes indeed he had learned a lesson. McPhail was delighted to let the old man keep the ten dollars, but he was going to take it out of the boy's share of the trip.

For the next three days, the eight wagons rumbled back towards Crockett with four of the occupants playing happy music on their bagpipes almost all the way. After each tune, a loud voice from one of the wagons would yell another Scottish song, and all would play the same melody, making a game of it to see how many tunes could be remembered. It definitely helped pass the time while the horses labored to pull the wagons home.

This trip had definitely turned out to be a good one and the McPhail's would rest easily this night.

By the year 1890, the farmers were hauling freight regularly from Crockett to Galveston including lumber from a new mill set up near the farms. Profits from the hauls were great and a new bridge spanning the bay lead directly to the Galveston docks, eliminating the use of the ferries.

McPhail and J.R. had purchased several more large wagons and decided to discontinue being farmers because it had become more profitable to haul freight. Most of the men in Houston County had discovered that their products would bring far more money in Galveston and was paying the Scotsman handsomely to haul it to the docks.

A new company was started by the two and the name McPhail and Son, was painted on the sides of the wagons, with regular trips to the coast and a set cost charged to each of the farmers for the haul.

The McPhails were now businessmen and making a nice profit for each delivery of goods to the Galveston ports. It seemed to be the best of times for the Scottish clan. There was no way they would know that the Houston County Court House in Crockett was about to be destroyed by fire in 1882 that would bring them misery because of the destruction of all the records...

Chapter 23

By now, McPhail was getting older with his birthday just around the corner, making him fifty and old by the standards of the day. The average life span of an American male just before the turn of the 20th century was about fifty years and with what he had been through, it was a wonder that he was still about. The Scotsman was definitely feeling his age daily and had decided that J.R. could make the trips to the coast with younger men helping.

After all, he told himself, wasn't it time for a man of his age to kick back and relax? He would raise a few crops for the family and hang around the house with Elizabeth and shop in town on Saturdays. What could be better than that for a old timer?

For a year, he did just that, until the routine became too much of a routine. He played his bagpipes on the front porch hoping someone would pass by the farm so he could at least wave at them.

His trips to town began to get monotonous and working in the field mostly alone was starting to drive him a bit nutty until one day he could stand it no longer. He would take Elizabeth to Galveston for a few days, to relax and enjoy the beach. J.R. had left four days before with six other wagons to make another haul to the docks. Perhaps they could convince Mary and the child to join them and surprise John Jr. in the gulf coast city to make a real vacation of it.

Convincing Mary was no real task, for the idea of eating fresh seafood and enjoying cool breezes on the beach was just the break she needed. Early the next morning, all five McPhail's climbed aboard Johns wagon and began the long trip to Galveston hoping to rendezvous with J.R.

John and Elizabeth sat up front tending the horses, while Mary and Michael played on blankets laid out in the bed of the wagon. They passed through Groveton and Trinity heading southwest to Huntsville following the dusty road towards coastal town.

Weaver's trading post was just a mile or so ahead, and the group had decided to buy a few things before continuing on. They had no sooner arrived at the post, when a fast moving rider approached from the same direction that they had just traveled. John was shocked to discover it was Jean Sadler, the daughter of Jim Sadler, a good friend and neighbor from Crockett. McPhail had once used the Madstone to treat him for a bite from a black widow spider and the man was in his debt.

Unlike most of the women of the day, the girl was dressed in jeans like a man, but every bit of her body said she was a woman. She rode up fast and dismounted before the horse had even stopped completely. The pretty girl pulled a scarf from around her neck and wiped the trail dust off her face.

"Mr. McPhail", she said, "Dad sent me to catch up with you folks to bring you back. There's some men saying that they own your farm and have already taken it. They even got the sheriff to bring papers showing that it's theirs and they took possession of your place right after you left. It ain't only you, but five or six of the other farmers too. You best follow me back and join the others that have lost their farms and just don't know what to do."

McPhail begin to panic at the sound of her voice. He couldn't imagine who could simply take over his home. Was it something coming out of Washington again? He loaded the family and climbed aboard the wagon and began pushing the horses as fast as he dared go following Jean back towards Crockett. Because of Elizabeth, Mary and Michael, he kept the Sadler girl from riding at all out speed on her mare.

He couldn't imagine what in the hell was happening, that someone could take his home he had bought and paid for from old man Kenner the moment he was gone. The civil war veteran kept the horses at a steady pace, holding the reins tight while he checked the rolled up blanket under the wooden seat. He felt he needed to make use that his new repeating rifle was still there. Losing his farm was not an option, he would take it back by whatever means was necessary. He had no idea of who or how many he had to contend with in his quest to retake his property, and now the sheriff was in on it?

Surely it couldn't be carpetbaggers now, with the war over for some 25 years! There has to be another answer to this crazy situation.

John's wagon cleared a large hill overlooking his farm and the first thing he saw was a group of people from town standing around their horses, buggies and wagons obviously in a rage over something. He turned his wagon towards the open field and headed directly for them. His farm was still several miles to the west, but he knew the answers to all his questions would lie with these farmers.

Most of Houston County's population had gathered at the site, including the mayor, sheriff and Doc Anderson. Several of the men were going over a map laid out on the tailgate of one of the wagons. Others rushed to greet McPhail as he arrived to join the meeting. Three or four of the citizens begin talking loudly at the same time pointing towards town and making little sense to John. Not until Doc Anderson approached and calmed the group down was McPhail able to understand what they were saying.

"What's going on, Doc?" McPhail said frustrated almost beyond repair. "Jean said that someone was trying to take our farms?"

The doctor looked at John with disbelief in his eyes.

"Climb down off the wagon", he said in a disgusted voice. "You're not going to believe this one. Six men rode in and checked into the Crockett hotel a couple of days ago and brought papers from Austin saying they could buy out any farms that might be in their way to build a new railroad through Houston County. Your place is one that lies right where the tracks are going to be laid and you have no say about it, you have to sell to them. Here's the papers from the State of Texas giving them the right to buy you out. It's called the right to dominant domain. Tracks have already been laid through Longview and are headed our way. Hell, the railroad people started before even getting permission from Austin."

McPhail held the papers handed to him by the doc, and muttered under his breath.

"Might as well have been carpet bagger from the north." Fourteen days later rows of buggies, wagons and riders on horseback set out from Houston County headed for Austin and a showdown with Governor Mike McLay. The entourage pulled in front of the state capital making a long line to deliberately block the front door. When the governor and legislators were told of the three hundred odd people in front of the capital, the lawmakers feared that an uprising was occurring and many ran out the back door concerned for their lives.

Mclay however was a strong man and decided to face the crowd head on. With five of his top assistants he walked through the front door and stood at the top of the stairs looking down on the huge crowd standing silently before him.

"What do you people want?" he said loudly. "Why are you blocking the door and causing trouble?"

By now the whole group had gathered around the steps with the doc and McPhail approaching the lawmakers as spokesman for the Houston County residents. They had hardly began to speak when city marshals and sheriff's deputies begin to arrive, but far too few to do much good.

McPhail told the governor why they were there, hoping to get a favorable response. He however knew that the Southern Pacific Railroad had a great deal of power in 1890 and pulled a lot of weight with politicians because of the money they possessed. It would be difficult to save a few farms when going against the mighty railroad.

To the groups amazement the governor was very sympathetic, giving the Texans every chance to present their grievances.

Governor McLay listened intently until John had finished. He stood wearing a brand new suit and tie with a sensitive ear towards a fellow Scotsman.

The law of dominant domain could and was totally unfair on occasions and this sounded like one of those times.

McLay began to make a speech to the crowd sounding almost as if he were trying to get elected once more. When he had finished telling the group that he was surely going to bat for them and would talk to the railroad on their behalf, McPhail felt he was sincere and would give him time to work on the problem.

The entire group returned to the wagons and left peacefully although promises were made that they would return if the railroad tracks were not placed elsewhere. A few weeks would pass before John would receive a personal letter from Southern Pacific stating that the railroad tracks were to be installed at a new location, running parallel to the roads used by the farmers wagons.

The fire at the Houston County Courthouse had left no trace of records showing ownership of these farms giving the Southern Pacific Railroad a right of way through what they thought was dominant domain. The governor's staff had gotten to the heart of the problem and it was soon corrected.

McPhail felt proud that he saved his farm and helped others at the same time. To this day the tracks in most counties runs parallel to the highways with little personal property affected.

Chapter 24

A year or so later, the Scotsman would sit on his front porch listening to the train whistles and watching the six o'clock evening train go by his farm heading south for Houston and Galveston pulling many freight cars. John could see that a way of life he knew was changing and things would never be the same again.

The turn of the century was upon him and rapidly beginning a new era that he was not sure was for the best. Trains were now bigger and better, hauling many more freight cars and many, many more loads of cargo could be shipped in a single run. It ended the freight company of McPhail and Son because they were unable to compete with the cheaper prices of hauling, much like the Pasteur treatment made the Madstone obsolete in the treating of poisonous bites.

John Jr. became a farmer once more working with his father raising crops on both farms. He was also bringing in the next generation of McPhail's to continue the bloodline.

Time passed and a new war broke out. A World War called the war to end all wars. It was World War One and all John could do was set on the front porch watching troop trains pass by. He felt sad for the young soldiers packed like sardines being shipped to the docks in Galveston to be sent to France. He knew that many would never return, giving up their lives for politicians with short memories. He really didn't understand this war any more than he had the civil conflict that he had personally endured. He had seen too many young bodies buried without tasting the real joy of life.

McPhail lived on the farm until his death in 1922, at the ripe old age of 82. His last words before he died must have been predominantly on his mind. "Wind to the pipes, heal to the sick." He said moments before dying, the leather pouch still around his neck.

Elizabeth sat beside her Scotsman at the moment of his death, and oddly visualized a grand parade of a hundred highlanders in colorful kilts with drums, fifes and bagpipes marching through the clouds with McPhail leading, playing beautiful marching music. It was oh, so real to her as she tenderly caressed his body and said goodbye for the last time.

Elizabeth would live to smile at World War Two troops boarding trains just outside her window of the nursing home in Crockett. The young men in uniform standing on the train station platform often smiled and waved back at the friendly old lady. She would pass on to her reward on January 12, 1942, at the age of 99, still talking about the crazy Scotsman she married in a snowstorm. Her legacy would live long after, with the kindness and gentle care she gave so many, asking nothing in return.

All told, John McPhail carried the Madstone for some fifty years using it to save many lives. It never left the McPhail family until the beautiful stone was given to the Sam Houston Museum in the 1970's, where it still remains today.

The war between the states was characterized by historians as our supreme national experience. During the war, official war department records show the union army suffered 359, 528 deaths. Confederate records were unavailable due to the war being fought mostly in the south, but it was estimated that at least 133,765 rebels died in battle. The union soldier went home to the sound of brass bands and received a cash bonus of $250 when he was mustered out. He had a strong voice on congress for the grand army of the republic, to argue for pensions and jobs. The confederate went home, if he had a home, as a straggler; on foot, hungry and tattered. He had no government to turn to for aid nor any hope of bonus or pension. He was completely on his own.

On Memorial Day in 1869, United States Troops guarded confederate graves in Arlington to make sure southerners wouldn't decorate them. On the same day, other union soldiers in tribute to their fellow Americans, took it upon themselves to help decorate confederate graves at nearby Alexandria, Virginia.

There was little difference between the men of the north and south. Both were Americans. They shared the same national traditions and fought with equal valor; brothers that bled the same blood. Most couldn't even answer the question. "Why are you fighting?"

The last rebel survivor of the civil war was sergeant Walter Washington Williams, A 117-year-old southerner from Houston, Texas, who died on December 19, 1959. Williams was a forager for Hood's Texas Brigade during the war. Asked once what a forager did, the old confederate replied, "I stole food, that's what". William's body lay in state in the rotunda of the Harris County Civil Court House for forty-eight hours in downtown Houston. The United States Army from Fort Hood provided an honor guard and escort with the story being carried on the front pages of major newspapers across the country. The casket was draped with the scarlet, blue, and white confederate battle flag, while the stars and stripes were placed nearby at half-mast.

The news of his death was flashed to President Eisenhower, in Paris at the time, by the White House. Eisenhower proclaimed a national day of mourning and called for the flying of United States flags at half-mast throughout the land. Lyndon Johnson, then senate majority leader, stated, "The passing of Walter Williams seals the door on a great but tragic era of our nation's history. With our sorrow at the passing of the last of the men who wore the blue or gray, comes a new national recognition."

The last union veteran, Albert Woodson of Duluth, Minnesota, died in August 1956. His distinction is commemorated in granite on the battlefield of Gettysburg. The valor and sacrifice performed by both union and confederate soldiers during the war between the states is something that all Americans can be proud of.

In this day and time, some people in our society are attempting to reduce each individual to a series of numbers stored somewhere, with someone controlling the computer that could eventually turn the American people into a socialist country.

I leave you with the quote at the bottom of the McPhail coat of arm.

"Memor Esto" ("Be Mindful")